NEVER ENDING

NEVER ENDING

ISAAC M. FLORES

authorHOUSE®

AuthorHouse™
1663 Liberty Drive
Bloomington, IN 47403
www.authorhouse.com
Phone: 1 (800) 839-8640

Published by AuthorHouse 10/16/2015

ISBN: 978-1-5049-5452-5 (sc)
ISBN: 978-1-5049-5454-9 (hc)
ISBN: 978-1-5049-5453-2 (e)

Library of Congress Control Number: 2015916386

Print information available on the last page.

For all those souls who lost
their fight for Freedom,
And for those who continue to seek it

NOTE TO READERS

The beginning chapters of this book are a straightforward account of changes in American and Cuban relations after their more than half a century of controversy and estrangement. This account includes the visit of Pope Francis to both countries. After that, the major part of the work is historical fiction depicting Cuba as seen through the eyes of those who lived there in the period from the 1960s until the present. It also updates and amplifies material in a 2005 novel written by me under the title The Plot Against Fidel.

The words in quotation marks attributed to President Barrack Obama, Fidel Castro, Raul Castro, the U.S. Secretary of State, the Cuban Foreign Minister and Pope John Paul II, Pope Benedict and Pope Francis and their hosts were spoken by them at the events cited in the text. They are part of the public record.

The activities and utterances of the fictional characters speak for themselves.

NEW PROMISES BETWEEN NEIGHBORS

Havana today is still wrapped in its centuries-old mystery.

To the visitor, be you a frequent one or a newcomer, the old city does not appear much different than it did 50 years ago. Some of its decaying buildings date back to Colonial Days, with Art Deco trim and even a midcentury overlay. The shells of 1950s American Chevies and Fords with Audi engines and European-made spare parts ply their way along poorly maintained streets lined with tenements and their overhanging balconies filled with the day's laundry.

Habana Vieja looked this way in the 1950s and 1960s and will probably exhibit few differences next year, or the next, although there is a slow-motion modernization taking place.

Santiago, Cuba's second-largest city, 650 miles away, never changes. And most of the island's interior regions and towns have remained virtually the same throughout the ages.

What is different is the pace among the residents in America's neighbor country. Cuba seems to have a renewed energy, and it's not just the younger people, who constitute most of the nation's population now. Most of the middle-aged and even many of the aging appear to have a new sense of purpose.

Why? Most of the changes are a result of two major events.

1

(1) The latest significant alteration is the transition brought on by a renewed relationship with the United States. After half a century of antagonism, there are changes slowly underway between the two neighbors.

(2) Another reason is the appearance of regime change. This is a more limited one, although greatly important. It is limited to the extent that power goes from one brother to another, you might say. What seems likely to international political specialists is that Fidel Castro has had a gradual shift in his thinking over his many years in control and is letting his brother, Raul, do the talking and revising of some of the domestic policies they have long practiced as part of their odd style of Caribbean communism. The Castro brothers are slowly diversifying the economy and even more slowly bringing politics back into the game.

Some may classify the involvement of Roman Catholic Pope Francis as a gamechanger, too, along with his visits to both Cuba and the United States.

Together, these events promise to be the most significant developments in Cuban society in more than five decades.

Whether this will all be for the better remains to be seen.

The changes between the democracy of the United States and the socialism-communism of Cuba seem to be taking place quickly, but for some time they will be more cosmetic than substantial. And, as they say, some things never change.

This is a summary of what's happened in recent months:

On December 17, 2014, President Obama surprised most of the world by announcing that he would seek an end to the embargo imposed on Cuba by the United States fifty-four years ago and restore diplomatic relations. The key phrase here is *restore diplomatic relations* because only the U.S. Congress can lift the embargo on trade and any related commercial activity.

Even so, the president's action is already having profound effects.

The president believes that allowing more diplomatic interchange would enable expanded travel and communication between the two societies. This, in turn, could empower the Cuban people to seek more of the freedoms that have been unavailable to them for most of those fifty-four years. The hope in the United States is that this may eventually lead to a more open, democratic Cuba.

On the other hand, Cuba would get a big financial boost (from American tourists, for one thing) and ensure that its side of the story isn't overlooked, not only in the United States but by the watching world. In addition, Cuba will obtain significant leverage in further talks about a long list of grievances.

"We will end an outdated approach that for decades has failed to advance our interests, and instead we will begin to normalize relations between our two countries," President Obama said. This will constitute "a new chapter among the nations of the Americas," he added, and replace a "rigid policy that is rooted in events that took place before most of us were born."

One of the president's remarks that stood out had to do with cutting loose "the shackles of the past."

The short history to that is that Fidel Castro's Cuba and the old Soviet Union of Nikita Khrushchev secretly installed intercontinental ballistics missiles on the island which threatened the United States. This brought about what came to be known as the October (1962) Missile Crisis. Castro, supported by Khrushchev's Cold War empire, said he would rain down the Soviet missiles throughout the eastern seaboard from Key West to New York unless the United States withdrew its aggressive shipping blockade and political embargo.

Castro and Khrushchev eventually backed down in a confrontation with President John F. Kennedy. The Soviets supposedly removed the missiles, although the Americans were not allowed on site to confirm this. But the American political and trade embargo remained in place, although American ships and submarines surrounding the island were withdrawn.

Along with the short-lived CIA-inspired invasion at Cuba's Bay of Pigs in April, 1961, those events are set down in detail in histories of those long-ago days. This is by no means one of those histories, but this short review of the past serves to explain the "shackles."

President Obama's announcement came after months of bargaining with Cuba's new President, Raul Castro, who succeeded brother Fidel as Presidente de la Republica de Cuba. Obama had been encouraging a change for years. Soon after taking office in 2009, the new president loosened some restrictions against travel to the island, and he declared then he wanted "a new beginning with Cuba."

3

So once again, the stars and stripes now fly over a newly restored American Embassy in Havana, and Cuba's red, blue and white-starred flag has gone back on its flagpole in Washington.

After the Obama administration removed Cuba from its list of countries that support terrorism, Cuba appointed an ambassador to Washington and the U.S. designated a high-ranking career diplomat for Havana.

The Americans are now reinstalled in the same seven-story building on the Malecon waterfront that formally served as the U.S. Embassy until 1961. It continued to function as an "interests section" after the break. The Cubans reopened their own diplomatic headquarters in an elegant neighborhood in Washington. President Obama presented the new Cuban ambassador, Jose Ramon Cabañas Rodriguez, his credentials at a White House ceremony on Sept. 17. The American ambassador to Cuba had not been formally nominated.

The Obama administration then began a series of regulatory changes.

But trust remained elusive. More than half a century of acrimonious feelings were not be easily overcome, and there remained plenty of skeptics on both sides. Many barriers remained.

According to the official communist newspaper Granma, Fidel said he did not have complete confidence in American intentions, asserting, however, that, "We will always defend cooperation and friendship with all nations on earth, among them our political adversaries."

His brother, now-President Raul Castro, welcomed the change and said the new relationship would bring about a period of further negotiations over longstanding issues, including the U.S. Naval base at Guantanamo. The base has long been a sore spot with the Cuban regime because it wants that territory returned to its sovereignty.

On the U.S. side, there remained the open question of Cuban expropriations of American property on the island that took place in the 1960s. The total amount involved has been estimated as high as $5 billion (in American currency). A lengthy list of claimants included owners of farms, sugar mills, factories, oil companies, hotels, retail businesses and electric and cable utilities, as well as palatial seaside mansions, once-occupied by wealthy families who fled into exile.

What's next?

Possibly a total relaxation of the travel ban between the two countries. Travel has been limited, with certain restrictions both ways.

Commercial trade trickled in and out, but the U.S. Congress was not expected to consider lifting the overall Cuban Trade Embargo for many months. Its fortunes depended to a great extent on the politics of the moment.

Generally, more than 70 percent of Americans supported ending the trade embargo, according to polling by the respected Pew Research Center.

A POPE'S PRIORITIES

One of the surprising facts disclosed after President Obama's announcement was that Pope Francis pushed for the renewed accord between the two countries. Support by the pontiff, who represents more than a billion Catholics, was seen as a change of attitude in Cuba toward the outside world. The pope appealed directly to Raul Castro to release an American aid worker in exchange for Cuban spies held by the United States. The prisoners were freed. And an accord was reached.

Pope Francis visited both Cuba and the United States In late September, insisting that his message was pastoral and not political, but occasionally veering into the political side on his favorite worldwide issues such as the environment, the powerless and immigration.

El Papa Francisco, as the Argentina-born Pope is known to many Latinos, received an enthusiastic, red-carpet welcome in both countries.

In Havana, He was met at the airport by President Raul Castro, who thanked the Pope for mediating in the negotiations between the two nations and agreed with his long-stated concerns about the world's economic imbalance between rich and poor and climate change.

Never mentioning his role in the negotiations, the Pope said, "For several months, we have witnessed an event that fills us with hope: the process of normalizing relations between two nations after years of estrangement. I urge political leaders to persevere on this path and to develop all its potentialities."

Raul Castro said the U.S. and Cuba had reestablished political relations as "a first step in the process . . . which will require resolving problems and correcting injustices." He called the U.S. embargo "cruel, immoral and illegal."

On the Sunday after his arrival, Pope Francis celebrated Mass before hundreds of thousands of Cubans at the Plaza de la Revolucion, which features huge portraits of revolutionary heroes Ernesto "Che" Guevara and Camilo Cienfuegos.

Later, he spent a quiet half hour with Fidel Castro in a private meeting which a Vatican spokesman described as an informal and familial chat. He disappointed dissidents who wanted a meeting with him in Havana, although his remarks always expressed hope for more open expression of competing ideas.

In his sermon at Mass, he spoke of the ideal of Christian service to mankind, saying that "we do not serve ideas, we serve people." He also celebrated Mass at a church near the Sierra Maestra mountains that is home to the shrine of the Virgen del Cobre, Cuba's patron, and held large public gatherings in Holguin and Santiago de Cuba.

In the United States, where he was received by President Obama and other dignitaries, crowds lined the streets along the pathway of his vehicle as it traveled from the suburban airport into Washington, where he began a journey of six days that took him to New York and Philadelphia, including Masses and an address to a joint meeting of Congress.

At the White House, President Obama expressed appreciation for the Pope's contribution in helping restore diplomatic relations with Cuba and for speaking out forcefully for the poor.

"You shake our conscience from slumber," the President said. "You call on us to rejoice in good news and give us confidence we can come together in humility and service and pursue a world that is more loving, more just and more free."

Obama expressed his pleasure after the Pope explicitly embraced the administration's efforts on climate change and its immigration policies.

"As the son of an immigrant family, I am happy to be in this country which was largely built by such families," the Pope told Obama. On climate change, the Pope said, "I find it encouraging that you are proposing an initiative for reducing air pollution. . ."

Latinos flocked to all of the Pope's public gatherings. They constitute a growing constituency in the U.S. and have expressed overwhelming support for his policies even though disagreeing with some of the church's established doctrines such as its stand against abortion.

Speaking to some 300 bishops at the Cathedral of St. Matthew the Apostle, Francis praised their work on behalf of immigrants. Referring to the church's sexual abuse scandals, he told the bishops, "I am also conscious of the courage with which you have faced difficult moments in the recent history of the church in this country without fear of self-criticism and at the cost of mortification and great sacrifice."

Not all American bishops agree with church teachings or some of the Pope's policies, and he acknowledged that. "Be pastors close to people" he urged. "Know that the Pope is by your side. The Pope supports you. He also puts his hand on yours, a hand wrinkled by age, but by God's grace still able to support and encourage."

He celebrated his first Mass on his trip to the United States at the Basilica of the National Shrine of the Immaculate Conception at the Catholic University of America. There, he declared Father Junípero Serra a saint, the first canonization held in the United States.

Speaking in Spanish, the Pope said he had received opinions of many church leaders and scholars and that through the the assistance of divine grace and great deliberation, "We discern and define to be a saint Junípero Serra."

Serra's elevation to sainthood was not without controversy He was a pioneer missionary in California's colonial period of the 1700s who became a leader in the establishment of Catholic missions. The controversy came over his treatment of Native Americans, who had first settled the lands. The Pope praised Serra by saying he "sought to defend the dignity of the native community, to protect it from those who had mistreated and abused it, wrongs which today still trouble us . . . because of the pain they cause in the lives of many people."

But many Indian leaders tell a different story, saying the missions resulted in the deaths of many Indians of that day and created cultural injustices still suffered today.

Many scholars acknowledge Serra's complicated legacy. "But I don't think Pope Francis wants pristine saints," the Rev. Timothy Kesicki, president of the Jesuit Conference in Washington, told CNN Television, "because then no one will aspire to sainthood."

The next day, Francis became the first pope to speak before a joint session of the U.S. Congress. In carefully worded English, he appealed to lawmakers to strive "at restoring hope, righting wrongs, maintaining commitments and thus promoting the well-being of individuals and of peoples."

The lofty words received high praise from both Democrats and Republicans, who chose to focus on different aspects of his speech. Liberals were inspired by his passionate references on immigration and his endorsement of legislation on the environment. Conservatives, mostly on the Republican side, focused on his defense of the traditional family and the church's stand on abortion, expressed by the Pope as the sanctity of life "at every stage of its development."

A great deal of his speech to Congress concerned immigration, alluding to his own circumstances and his family's move from Italy to Argentina.

"We, the people of this continent, are not fearful of foreigners because most of us were once foreigners," Francis repeated his remarks at the White House. "I say this to you as the son of immigrants, knowing that so many of you are also descended from immigrants." He urged lawmakers to view immigrants as people and "respond as best as we can to their situation."

Resolution of many of the issues brought up by the Pope were evaded in the last several sessions of a Congress of elected legislative representatives of the American people. Cast aside and awaiting answers were such pressing problems as the economic division between rich and poor, threats to the environment and immigration issues at home and abroad. Some nineteen members of the Pope's audience were otherwise busy raising millions of dollars for a try at the presidential office, most of them seeking to replace many of the policies of the current president.

Pope Francis later flew to New York City, where again he received a colorful welcome by big crowds amid great ceremony. At St. Patrick's Cathedral, the Pope delivered a homily and concentrated on the desperate struggles of the poor, later wading into a crowd of many of the homeless, the mentally ill, victims of domestic violence and others in dire circumstances. He whispered to individuals, patted heads and kissed children.

He then addressed the United Nations General Assembly in what was the largest gathering of presidents and prime ministers ever to come together in one place. He called for the elimination of nuclear weapons and praised world leaders for the agreement with Iran over its nuclear energy program.

With Nobel Peace Prize laureate Malala Yousafzai of Pakistan in attendance in the gallery, he called for quick decisions on education for all girls. He also spoke of "absolute respect for life in all its stages and dimensions" but did not dwell on details of the church's stand on the issues of abortion or providing access to reproductive health services.

Some 150 leaders from 193 nations adopted what U.N. Secretary-General Ban Ki-Moon described as a "to-do list for people and the planet" to be implemented over 15 years. It was described as a a global mission to curtail poverty, inequality and environmental degradation.

Pope Francis was quick to endorse the 17 Sustainable Development Goals.

But he warned that some of the goals needed immediate attention. The future "demands of us critical and global decisions in the face of worldwide conflicts which increase the number of the excluded and those in need. Our world demands of all government leaders a will which is effective, practical, constant, with concrete steps and immediate measures for preserving and improving the natural environment."

This, he said, will put an end "as quickly as possible to the phenomenon of social and economic exclusion, with its baneful consequences."

On his final day in the United States, Pope Francis visited Independence Hall in Philadelphia, where he stood at a lectern used by Abraham Lincoln and praised the nation's founding fathers, who proclaimed the Declaration of Independence. The following day, he celebrated a Mass marking the end of the Vatican-sponsored World Meeting of Families.

He met with three female and two male victims of sexual abuse and spoke about his own "pain and shame" for the injuries caused by clergy and church workers. "Please know that the Holy Father hears you and believes you." He promised that youth will be protected "and all responsible will be held accountable." He also met with inmates in his first visit to a prison.

Before the Sunday mass, an estimated million people, waving flags from Argentina and many other nations, cheered as the Pope wound his way around the long boulevard leading to the makeshift sanctuary in his open-sided popemobile.

He lamented how young people are delaying marriage and then departed from his text to engage in a little humor. He told about how women in Buenos Aires have often said to him, "My son is 30 or 34 years old and isn't getting married, what do I do." The Pope said his response was, "Don't iron his shirts anymore."

Vice President Joe Biden saw him off at the airport Sunday night.

The Pope's parting words were that he was returning to Rome after hectic trips to Cuba and the United States with "a heart full of gratitude and hope."

SUSPICIONS

The historic agreement for political change by Cuba and the U.S. was warmly welcomed everywhere — with the exception of Russia, which never officially said anything, and by Cuban exiles who had long been dead-set against any rapprochement between the United States and their mother country. Most residents of the island welcomed the accord. According to polls, many exiles in the United States and elsewhere, some with little knowledge of Fidel Castro's revolution and long dictatorship, also agreed with the new relations.

In other words, most Cubans, either in their country or in exile, agreed that there was no longer reason for permanent conflict between the two governments. And it was difficult to find anybody in Cuba — and for that matter, in this country — who didn't think that Cuba was receiving the immediate practical benefit of this new relationship.

But there was plenty of skepticism on both sides whether the arrangement would work.

Suspicions about U.S. intentions extend deeply in some Cuban quarters. Many Cubans are unsure what future U.S. presidents and lawmakers will bring. On the other hand, some officials in the Obama administration were also taking a "wait-and-see" attitude on the new policy.

If there was any question as to the deep issues still involved in coming negotiations, look no further than those pointedly expressed by U.S. Secretary of State John Kerry and Cuba's foreign minister, Bruno Rodriguez, following the raising of the American flag at dedication ceremonies at the U.S. Embassy in Havana in mid-August.

"There is no way Congress is going to vote to lift the embargo if they're (Cubans) not moving with respect to issues of conscience," Kerry told reporters during his 12-hour visit to Cuba. "It's a two-way street. . . We remain convinced the people of Cuba would be best served by a genuine democracy, where people are free to choose their leaders."

Showing little signs of flexibility on this issue, Rodriguez replied at the joint news conference, "We, too, have concerns about human rights in the United States. Cuba is not a place where there are acts of racial discrimination or police brutality that result in deaths; nor is it under Cuban jurisdiction or on Cuba territory that people are tortured or held in a legal limbo."

Josefina Vidal, lead negotiator for Cuba in restoring relations, told an interviewer that Cuba's internal affairs were not negotiable.

Aside from that issue, Fidel Castro's longtime description of the U.S. as "the monster of the north" has brought a, perhaps unlikely, comparison to Iran. Skeptics have noted that Iran's Ayatollah Ali Khamenei has for several years been calling the U.S. "the Great Satan" and has regarded the U.S. as the root of all evil in the world.

But since there has been agreement over Iran's possible production of an atomic bomb, that rhetoric has been toned down by Iran. And, so it may be that Fidel could soften his own stance. Analysts also make other comparisons between Iran and Cuba viz-a-viz the United States. But Khamenei makes clear that the Iran nuclear deal will not lead to mending ties with the U.S.

A steering committee of American and Cuban officials was formed to take on some of the thornier questions.

Various European countries have retained a foothold in Cuba throughout the years.

The European Union has committed to spending at least $75 million in Cuba this year to help in reconstruction projects and over the years has become one of the island's major trading partners. Countries of the EU supply most of Cuba's tourists.

The German foreign minister, Frank-WalterSteinmeir, told reporters after Obama's announcement that "we in Europe, and we in Germany, are happy that many decades of standstill and silence are coming to an end."

Things are not going to be all rosy for Cuba in the future, however. The country's old guard, along with plenty of new faces, look to step up soon. There may be a clash there. Raul, who is now 83 years old, has said he will step down in 2018. There is much to do domestically, and some of those at the top are not in total agreement with Raul's liberalization of the market economy.

There remain a myriad of economic problems to face.

Flag-raising observances in both countries were relatively quiet, simple affairs. Three retired U.S. Marines who had lowered the American flag when the embassy was closed in 1961 were in attendance in Havana. They presented the flag to be raised by a Marine honor guard. A poem was read and musicians played.

Cuba's Foreign Minister Rodriguez presided over the ceremony raising Cuba's flag in Washington just hours after diplomatic relations were restored in July.

Venezuelan president Nicolás Maduro wrote a congratulatory letter to Cuban leader Raul Castro, emphasizing that "there is still a long road to travel in order to arrive at the point that Washington recognizes we are no longer its backyard…"

"Congratulations Raul, congratulations to the people of Cuba and the United States," the Venezuelan leader later messaged. "Now on to the fight against the criminal embargo against Cuba and to overcoming interventionism in our region that so loves its independence!"

Kerry noted in his remarks in Havana that the United States also plans to improve relations with Venezuela, which has been highly critical of Washington over the years because of Chavez' close friendship with Castro. Cuba and Venezuela have enjoyed friendly commercial relations and have expressed similar feelings against the U.S.

Although Fidel, 88, is quietly slipping into Cuban history, he remains a sleeping giant to the U.S. Fidel has always been the gray eminence in the background. Many policymakers believe that without his quiet background presence, there would not have been a rapprochment. But there appear to be no discernible differences between the Castro brothers. Their views on foreign policy are similar.

Shortly after the new agreement was announced, a Miami Herald correspondent interviewed students at the University of Havana, where Fidel achieved distinction so many years before. The newspaper found what many of them perceived as a new reality: "Fidel Castro is increasingly a figure of the Cold War, to be celebrated, scrutinized, reviled — but almost never experienced," the newspaper wrote. "To many of them (the students), the relentless campaign against the ever-present enemy of the United States — Fidel's lifelong mission — seems as dated as the tanks that dot the campus and countless public spaces all over Havana."

There is a definite scent of optimism throughout the big island, however. This has always been, after all, a land of paradox.

The renewed relationship has brought about some changes in the capital: new nightspots, expensive restaurants, more music concerts, seemingly more people out on the streets enjoying life. Raul Castro's relaxation of regulations to increase business activity appeared to be bringing some improvements along those lines. Well-to-do exiles from Miami and elsewhere in the U.S. are encouraged to start up small retail shops and expand those being run by relatives on the island.

Bureaucratic regulations were holding back some eager, would-be investors, including some American businessmen, however. Trade groups from several American states have trekked to Havana to talk to government officials and their counterparts, with little to show for it in the long run.

Changes, either from improved relations or government economic policies, come more slowly in the barrios, the poorest neighborhoods, the teeming tenement sections of Habana Vieja and among the older residential areas that could be considered middle-class. They house the people who stayed throughout the course of the Cuban Revolution. If they chose to stay, their employment and manner of living hasn't much improved. Many of the young are unemployed, or under-employed. They have little to say either way.

Strong voices in the U.S. Congress urged an end to the trade embargo, but there were equally strong voices of those opposed, including several leading candidates for the Republican presidential nomination. Among the latter were Sen. Marco Rubio of Florida, the son of Cuban exiles, and former Florida Gov. Jeb Bush. Former senator and secretary of state Hillary

Rodham Clinton, a leading Democratic presidential contender, has made forceful appeals to end the embargo.

Cubans want broader contact with the United States, Hillary Clinton told a crowd in Miami, "They want to buy our goods, read our books, surf our web and learn from our people."

U.S. Rep. Tom Emmer, a Republican of Minnesota, said, "The embargo has benefited the Castro regime and hurt the Cuban people. We've given it plenty of time."

U.S. Rep. Amy Klobuchar, Democrat of Minnesota, who introduced a bill that would permit regular commerce between the two countries, thought she had summed it all up by saying that by continuing the trading ban, Americans who travel to Cuba are "going to be staying in Spanish hotels, eating German food and using Chinese computers."

But the reality is that Cuba started opening up to Spain, France, Germany, Brazil, Canada and other foreign countries when the Soviets pulled out after the breakup of the Soviet Union twenty-five years ago. Foreign companies have built hotels and started businesses, especially along Cuba's beautiful beaches. Europeans flock there on extended vacations. There are but a few restrictions on American travel to the island, and dedicated Americans tourists have always found a way around regulations.

Tourism has become big business in Cuba. In fact, it has become Cuba's biggest business. As a means of acquiring foreign exchange, tourism began surpassing sugar, tobacco, nickel and other exports in the mid-1990s.

The agreement that brought the new relationship to fruition was not merely an abstract exercise in tough diplomacy. President Obama was eager to succeed where Presidents Jimmy Carter and Bill Clinton had failed in their reconciliation efforts. Beyond that, what appeared to bring everything to a head after years of frustration were proposals for a prisoner exchange.

Cuba was holding an American government contractor, Alan P. Gross, a frail, elderly man, who had once threatened suicide in prison. Years before, the U.S. had imprisoned five Cuban intelligence agents convicted in the United States. Now, pressed by the Gross family and their lawyer, Obama agreed to try to get Gross released. Raul Castro was adamant that the U.S. had to free the Cuban Five, as they were known in their country, before releasing Gross.

After his second-term re-election, Obama had directed that a highly secret confidential channel be established with the Cubans. Two White House officials, Benjamin J. Rhodes, a top Obama aide, and Ricardo Zuniga, the National Security Council's leading official for the Western Hemisphere, were appointed to carry out the secret talks. They spent about a year in hush-hush meetings with the Cubans in Canada before the talks moved beyond a prisoner exchange and into details about restoring diplomatic relations.

When a potential agreement was finally reached, they took it to the Vatican.

"When we initiated the discussions, we didn't know exactly where it would lead," Rhodes was later quoted by the New York Times. "The talks frankly ended up leading in all kinds of directions that we couldn't have anticipated in the beginning."

Meanwhile, Secretary of State John Kerry was doing his own negotiating with Cuba's foreign minister, but few others in the State Department and Congress had knowledge of the secret talks by Rhodes and Zuniga.

At the Vatican, Pope Francis expressed enthusiasm for an accord. After that came President Obama's announcement and that of President Raul Castro.

Under this avalanche of change, what cannot be pushed too far back in memory are some of the reasons that caused a break in relations in the first place. The Castro brothers, along with Che Guevara and others, were ruthless in their takeover of government after dictator Fulgencio Batista was chased out of the country in 1959. Those opposed to Fidel's tactics who escaped the killing fields became victims of the largest network of prisons in the world.

Those who could do so fled their homeland forever. Those who couldn't stayed and endured, for decades if they lived long enough.

In short, Fidel Castro caused the greatest transformation of Cuban society in the island's history. This is not to say he didn't have some support along the way, but that support often came with a price. And the lengthy life of Castro communism has caused turbulent times in the lives of millions of people in Cuba itself, along with many of the exiles in the United States and a number of countries where they have settled.

Here's a look back in novelistic fashion at some of those historic times.

THE 1960s

THE 1960s

A MISERABLE DAY

Still groggy from disease, beatings and interrogation, Miguel could sense the far-off rumbling and hear the muffled whispering before word finally reached his rockfaced *galera* that everyone was to gather up his belongings and move out to "el patio."

This place to which they were invited was a weedy, patchy-grass courtyard about the size of a soccer field used for exercise by a select few of the Castro regime's political prisoners. These favored ones were on a "rehabilitation plan." Miguel had only heard about the sun-drenched place called el patio.

He stood up, dizzy and disoriented, and with help managed to get together his few things — shoes, shirt, pants, a windbreaker and a battered old sombrero. He wore only his undershorts and a torn filthy T-shirt. Something big was going on, he thought. Something definitely out of the daily routine was taking place at notorious La Cabaña prison, on Cuba's northern coast in old Havana.

"Attention all prisoners in galeras seven to seventeen," came a voice echoing throughout the cavernous prison over a speaker system. "Everybody in those galleries: Take all your shit and move quickly outside. Take only what belongs to you, nothing else." Not that there was much else in those damp, smelly cells.

The rumors flew. What was happening? Are we being transferred? Released? Selected for execution? *"Nos van exterminar!"*

Guards roamed the cellblocks, prodding with bayonets and clubs, rousting everybody out through the maze of narrow, drippy corridors until they reached the sun-brightened patio. Some of the healthier ones pushed ahead with their meager belongings strapped on their backs. Miguel had sores on his legs and backside and moved slowly but purposefully at the point of a bayonet.

"We're being freed. We are leaving here. I just heard it from a guard," a fellow inmate whispered excitedly in his ear.

By the time Miguel and a crippled stocky cellmate he knew only as Romero stumbled through the massive iron gate into the outdoors, many of the prisoners were abuzz with rumor and speculation. The same story was being embroidered no end.

Even some of the guards were playing the game, insinuating that the inmates were to be flown out to Miami or boarded on boats and sent into exile from the nearby Port of Matanzas. There was no more talk of mass executions. Several of the uniformed political commissars who conducted indoctrination courses added to the speculation as the shaggy, smelly prisoners shoved and shouldered their way along. The word was that there were four ships ready to take them out. Everyone would be fed and then transported to the port, the story went.

"You can't imagine the emotions," Romero would say in reflection many years later. "There was delirium, a wild excitement mixed with confusion and fear. It was crazy out there."

Romero became Miguel's self-appointed "mentor" in their early days of imprisonment. And their paths would keep crossing for years in the various prisons, camps and hospitals where they would be transferred. This, their latest stop, was La Cabaña. He was a gruff former rancher who had been interrogated and brutalized repeatedly because he refused to accept the communist regime's rehabilitation plan. In their beatings, the guards had crunched a leg so badly that Romero now had a permanent limp.

The prison system's program for what they called rehabilitation consisted of a long period of communist indoctrination and a prisoner's repentance for any crimes against the revolution. In exchange, the prisoner's sentence was reduced. But, along with many other diehards, Romero, who had refused to become part of the plan, came to be known as a *plantado*, his revolutionary ideals unchangeable.

Several weeks after his arrival at La Cabaña, prison officials demanded that Miguel accept the plan. He, too, refused, and he was now suffering the consequences of a plantado.

The one idea that sustained the plantados was that one day they would be free. They lived for the day when the regime would be overthrown. They longed to see their loved ones again, to walk around and breathe the fresh air. To sleep in a real bed again and spend their remaining years like ordinary people do.

Talk among the scores of prisoners who were now evacuating *galera siete* soon turned to what they would do in exile. Of course, they would become political pariahs, banished from their homeland. Los exilados would eventually end up in Miami, in New Jersey, Omaha, Albuquerque, Los Angeles. Or Spain! Even Mexico or Panama!

Now, after so much time in confinement, some of the prisoners began to shred hoarded letters and photos from their loved ones believing they might be confiscated and lead to further problems. Others gave away some of the candy, bandages and other personal items they'd been keeping since their infrequent visits from relatives.

But as the hours went by and nothing happened out under the blazing sun, a strange silence began to settle over the prisoners. Heavy beads of sweat ran off their heads and down their faces and arms.

"All of us wretched souls, many of us sitting there in rags, shielding our red-rimmed eyes from the bright sunlight, we began worrying about our families," a prisoner remembered many years later. "What about our relatives? Will they be left behind? Will they be told what's happening? We all had questions no one could answer."

Their elation over the dream of freedom eventually turned into gloom as the fiery hot afternoon wore on. And doubters began to speculate about other things.

"We'd learned about the Freedom Flights," said another former political prisoner soon after completing his sentence. "But we also knew there was no big enough reason for Fidel to turn us loose. We were 'the enemies of the people.' This whole idea of being freed was bullshit, I thought. We were living proof to the world of what happens to those who oppose Castro and Communism. He wasn't going to let us go anywhere!"

Romero and Miguel were quietly convinced of that, too. Their eyes reddened, their dirty sweat dripping onto the sand.

After several hours in the courtyard, many of the guards who had been rooting around in the galeras were back. The loudspeakers went back into action: "Everyone get your shit together and then strip naked."

This was a surprise. But maybe they want to give us physical checkups before we leave, one said. Maybe we're going to get some immunizations. Or showers, or they want to check for contraband.

Nothing but more waiting, sitting and standing under the pitiless sun. Finally, another loudspeaker command: "Okay, okay, we are going to start filing back to the cells. Everybody return to the same places you were in before. Nobody's going anywhere. Nobody is leaving La Cabaña, *desgraciados,*" the disembodied voice ended loudly, boisterously.

That was it. End of dream. There was to be no freedom. No exile. No nothing. Back to the reality of the dungeons.

As they started moving back, hastily pulling on some of their smelly clothes, the prisoners bitched and argued among themselves as they shoved their way along. One argument led to another and emotions finally broke loose. Some cried and screamed in rage, holding their hands to their heads as they were pushed along. Guards, poking and goading, began to threaten the use of their bayonets to subdue the more wild ones and force them along.

Only they wouldn't be subdued.

Banded together like that, some of the prisoners suddenly turned on their guards. Others joined in. Guards to the left of Miguel had their weapons stripped from them. *"Pégale, pégale a ese,"* came an encouraging shout (hit him again). It became a melee, a wild-swinging free for-all, the beginnings of a fullfledged riot.

Gunfire erupted, whether it came from guards or some of the newly armed prisoners no one knew. Security personnel and prisoners fell and were trampled by others. Ear-splitting gunshots echoed off prison stone walls. Blood began running freely.

Miguel tried to help a prisoner on the ground bleeding from a blow above the right ear. He received a well-placed kick to the head for his troubles. He saw prisoners with blood gushing from their faces and from wounds to their bodies. He looked quickly away from guards crumpled on the ground, some being incessantly pummeled by the angered prisoners.

Miguel and Romero were shoved back into the open yard from the dark hallway they had managed to reach before the fighting broke out. Blood-spattered guards came running out swinging long batons against fleeing men. Panicked prisoners and guards were everywhere as the two of them crumpled down among a small group of disheveled and bloody men who had their backs against a rockface wall in the shadowed courtyard.

Suddenly, off to their left, the wide metal gates closing off the compound were flung open and mounted troops waving rifles and glistening bayonets come trampling through the crowds using their weapons as clubs. Crushed bodies were thrown about by the whinnying horses.

The armed men on horseback eventually forced everything to a halt.

"Bring them all in — the wounded," an officer barked as the battle calmed. Prisoners and guards were dragged out of the yard, some of them never to be seen again.

To Miguel, it seemed like hours before some semblance of order was restored. But maybe the whole thing took place in minutes, he thought later. The subdued prisoners were prodded and shoved back to their galeras. Romero said he learned later that there had been five guards killed and many injured. Half a dozen prisoners lost their lives and ten were seriously wounded or pistol-whipped enough to be dragged off to hospitals.

Finally, back in their prison holes after everything quieted down and the anger and bitterness dampened, one of the prisoners with blood still slowly seeping from his skull began shaking his head, talking to himself and quietly laughing. Another saw the irony, too, and began hooting and screaming out. Others began slowly understanding and were soon joining in laughter and shouting.

The stupidity of it, they said shaking their heads to other bewildered souls. It just proves how quickly desperate men grasp at straws. What kind of counter-revolutionaries are we, they screamed in bitter jest.

The reality of the situation had set in. This was just another lesson to prove the guards' domination, to break the prisoners down. The talkative Cubans soon spun other, more intricate theories. But the truth now dawned.

"Those stupid sons of whores wanted to find and confiscate absolutely everything we had — pencil stubs, radio parts, pills in folded and refolded envelopes, cigarettes, writing paper —precious items that had been smuggled in at great peril by relatives and friends," Romero later told a writer. "They thought we might have had weapons. They overturned beds; they even dug into walls for our stuff."

Instead, what they got was a prison riot.

"They found a lot of our things," Romero said bitterly. "But they paid a price."

Some precious items were hidden so well, however, that they remain in those walls to this day. Years from now, they'll still be finding them — at La Cabaña, at Isla de Pinos, at all the other prisons and former internment camps scattered throughout the island of Cuba under the Castro dictatorship.

Another objective of the cruel deception, the story went, was to try to force down morale so much that more prisoners would be forced to "volunteer" for the rehabilitation plan, which was in reality a carefully worked out Communist indoctrination program. This was more likely.

"They would've tried anything to get us to go on the *plan*," Romero said.

The political captives didn't get anything to eat this bloody day, not from the prison slop-kitchens. Instead, they made do with the spiders they could claw off the clammy walls and the bigger ants and crawlers that had somehow made their way into their cells. They drank from the ugly, powdery puddles that formed in the lower reaches of their little kingdom.

From that infamous day on, the prisoners referred to that event as *El Dia del Engaño,* the Day of Deception. Word of it quickly traveled to other prisons, and soon all the political inmates throughout Cuba had heard about El Engaño at La Cabaña.

They would shake their heads slowly, pondering in dismay the cruelty of Cubans against Cubans.

A FATEFUL STUMBLE

It can be argued that Fidel Castro *stumbled* into power. Even after seven years of rebellion and exile, he was befuddled about his position when his ideological enemy fled the scene. But once the smoke cleared, Fidel assumed the presidency of his island homeland, and he was to become one of the most notorious dictators in the world.

He ruled absolutely, with no letdown and little mercy, for more than half a century. Here's what happened:

On New Year's Day, 1959, Fulgencio Batista abandoned the highest office in the nation by hopping on a plane and escaping with the loot. Fearing for his life, he left the door wide open for anyone who wanted to walk in and declare himself *jefe*.

Fidel and a small group of *rebeldes* had been fighting Batista Army troops in the mountains of southeastern Cuba for just such an opportunity. But several days of total confusion followed Batista's abrupt departure from the capital.

Suddenly, there was a power vacuum.

Army commanders, the Communist Party leadership, former presidents and individuals in a university student directorate and the Havana-based 26th of July Movement — all jockeyed for position for the suddenly vacant office of president-dictator.

Representatives of the United States, Cuba's next-door neighbor, were mere spectators, looking on helplessly, puzzled by it all. They had had little inkling of Batista's plans or what might be ahead for this strategically situated island — some 760 miles long, East to West, and 60 miles wide, nearly as big in area as Pennsylvania

Fidel Castro was 600 miles from Havana in Cuba's rural area near Santiago de Cuba. He was visiting at the home of a friend. When the news about the vanishing dictator finally reached the back country, the rebels found it hard to believe. Fidel exploded with anger, not knowing the full extent of the sudden events.

His first thought was that there had been a *coup d'etat* by Batista's army, usurping what he believed was his right to power.

"It's a cowardly betrayal!" The army is "trying to steal the triumph that belongs to the revolution," he was widely quoted as saying. Fidel Castro vowed not to yield to the military or any other group: He and his rebels would continue fighting. He went on to declare Santiago the capital of the Republic, awaiting developments in far away Havana.

As one confusing day followed another, Castro eventually became convinced he was the one man truly destined for power.

It seemed that the whole of the country suddenly stopped to consider the situation seriously. The bickering and posturing in Havana slowed to a trickle. It now seemed that many were agreeable to that barbudo who had been fighting Batista's army in the Sierra Maestra. He was to be the chosen one to replace Batista.

Castro's dreams, schemes and seven years of turmoil had paid off.

Everyone in Havana was now waiting for him — for some sign that Fidel would take over, and when. The wannabes in the capital city had exhausted themselves after days of talk, premature negotiation and controversy. Castro seemed the best choice. A sense of anticipation gripped the nation. The people waited for Fidel Castro to assume their proffered mantle.

And he did, trekking through the country's heartland to Havana with his scruffy bunch of warriors.

Cubans who had lived through earlier days of presidents, dictators and military strongmen cheered the revolutionary reforms that Castro promised. They installed him as leader, and then most of them suffered because of it in one way or another. They eventually discovered their dreams were not to be.

Several generations have now come and gone.

Under Fidel, the Cubans have seen an invasion of their country by their sons and brothers, a missile crisis that brought the world to the brink of nuclear war, gradual improvements in education and medical benefits. El pueblo was a large part of an exodus — ranging from the rich, to most of the well-to-do and many of the poor. Those who stayed witnessed terrorist attacks from inside and outside the country. Many endured torture, many were imprisoned and many died.

The list is long.

Fidel's disciples thought of him as God descended from the heavens. His enemies later came to compare him to Genghis Khan, Stalin and Hitler. He was there by accident, some said.

Does it really matter how Batista, Stalin, Hitler, Mussolini, Franco, Salazar and so many others assumed their positions of absolute power? Here it was, more than half a century later, and there he was.

In the end, most historians agree that Fidel Castro misjudged his people — he could not forcibly transform Cuban society from what it was — an amalgamation of its historical past and its emphatically more practical nature. There is nothing psychological or philosophical about this. Cubans had abided with dictators before, some thriving, others suffering along the way.

But they didn't put up with anything for long. They were restless and driven to change.

One of the basic mistakes by the Castro regime was in believing that the Cuban psyche would allow a transformation of an open, democratically inclined society into a Marxist one. If it were to be done, it would have to be under threat of torture, imprisonment and death. And much of it was done in that manner.

Quoting novelist Walter Mosley, "a dictator sees the truth as a matter of will. Anything he says or dreams is the absolute truth, and soon the people are forced to go along with him."

There were some who refused to go along.

REVOLUTIONARY CUBA

The 1960s and the 1990s

23.8´ NORTH 82.2´ WEST

An American in Castro's Cuba—the 1990s

The Ilyushin passenger plane banked steeply to the left, giving Ed Brophy a sudden clear view of the impossibly blue water below. He felt as if he could touch the lazy, foamy waves sparkling in the copper glow of the late afternoon sun.

As the plane dropped altitude for a landing, a crescent of snow-white sand that stretched below and out of sight, way beyond his view, constituted his first glimpse of the Pearl of the Antilles in several years.

He was coming back to Cuba for a visit. Just to play tourist, reminisce, maybe look up some friends. His bitterness toward the leaders of the revolution that forever transformed this troubled country, that destroyed the lives and dreams of so many people, were put aside. They weren't forgotten, but they weren't at the forefront of his thoughts as they had been for so many of his recent years.

"So what do you think, Eddie?" nudged his friend Pete, bringing him back to reality. "Must be a kick coming back as a *turista* ready and willing to give a lot of your American dollars to Fidel Castro and his gang," Pete teased.

Peter Stephens was a longtime friend. They'd been newspapermen together in a number of places: Lisbon, Madrid, Rio, Santiago, a few of the African countries, the Caribbean hotspots — wherever they could get to a revolution, coup or even a bloodless government overthrow. It was their business to ask and report on who, what, where, why and how.

They'd met during the days of "Papa Doc" Duvalier in Haiti, where they first learned just how little the world's crackpot dictators valued human life. In their more mature years, they had wound up in South Florida for awhile before going their separate ways.

Ed was retired from active journalism, but he still wrote magazine pieces and had lately tried writing children's stories, but found it took up more of his time than he was willing to give. Still unmarried at fifty-eight, he was a serious amateur photographer, a jazz enthusiast and an avid reader of history. He was brown-haired, a tad under 6-feet and a healthy 180 pounds. He was unattached, mainly he told himself, because of his travels and his too many and too-varied interests.

Pete, shorter and chunkier, was now happily married after years of carefree bachelorhood. He was a skilled photographer and the editor of a prosperous little newspaper in Virginia. He, too, had many varied interests.

They'd kept in touch all these years, visited each other occasionally, played some bad tennis together and still maintained a lively interest in world politics, especially cruel dictatorships such as Fidel Castro's. With little prompting from each other, they decided on a trip to Cuba.

Here they were now, violating the American embargo prohibiting visits to the Communist country for ordinary Americans.

They could have applied for official "licenses" from the American and Cuban governments to visit as journalists, but they thought they'd too easily be labeled and watched by the Cuban G2, the intelligence service. So they preferred to do as so many thousands of Americans were doing in the 1990s: Get on a plane to Nassau, catch a Cubana Airlines flight to Havana, stay a week or two and return to Nassau — without the Cubans even stamping passports. Nothing to prove you had ever been there.

Until they later started clamping down on such trips, U.S. Customs and Immigration officials didn't try hard too hard to find out where tourists had been or what you were bringing back from the islands. Unless you were obvious about it, no one knew or cared when you re-entered the U.S. that you had spent some time in exotic Cuba and come back with your pockets stuffed with strong Cuban panatelas.

Ed and Pete had carefully planned their trip and now, finally, they were about to touch down at Jose Marti International Airport in the seedy Havana suburb of Rancho Boyeros.

The travelers had joined up at the airport in Nassau and waited for hours for the flight into the Cuban capital, which was jammed with Americans. Most of them traveled with official permission from the U.S. State Department. Their groups had a special "license" which authorized them to go to Cuba and return to the United States without a problem. They were declared official members of one of three groups: a church or religious mission, bonafide academicians studying the Cuban revolution or professional journalists.

Ed and Pete had no official status or sponsorship, but they wanted it that way.

Legal and "illegal" visitors were treated alike by the Cubans, both at the Nassau airport terminal and in Havana, as long as they spent plenty of dollars. Those in the three groups never wandered far from their little circles and spent much of their time on official tours of the Cuban capital. The Cubans liked it that way for Americans.

Of course, the fact that citizens of Canada, Mexico and virtually every European and Latin American country came and went as they pleased was instrumental in the steady economic recovery of Cuba after the departure of the Soviets. To everyone's surprise, tourism again was becoming the island's top industry in the 1990s, surpassing the exports of sugar and tobacco.

The U.S. President and Congress had imposed an embargo of American goods and people to the island in the early 1960s, when the Castro government began expropriating American businesses, factories and other holdings. Before they were done with the illegal grab, the Cubans had confiscated about $2 billion worth of American commercial properties.

Previously, U.S. companies and some European enterprises had provided and produced most of the goods and services on the island since the early part of the 20th Century. But those prosperous days come to a halt in the late 1950s and early 1960s.

Castro's anti-government uprising in the mountainous southeast of the country had been largely discounted for years by Batista government bureaucrats, diplomats and even most of the common people. "Oye, otra revolucion" -- just another revolution in a land of many was the way most people thought of it. In the end, of course, it became a fullscale insurgency that forced dictator Fulgencio Batista to flee the country on New Year's Day 1959.

Fidel Castro and his gang took over with a vengeance.

Ed Brophy had spent four years as a resident news correspondent in Havana in those heady days after Fidel took over. And he had been to Cuba on several specially authorized reporting trips since being forced to leave by the Castro regime.

Years previously, his mother, Marina, had divorced her Cuban husband and emigrated to Florida. She had left behind her first-born, Miguel, who was then three years old. Miguel Hidalgo was brought up by his father and grandmother in Cuba's lush sugar and agricultural heartland around Trinidad.

Marina remarried in Palm Beach, Florida. A year later, her newborn son was christened Eduardo Joseph Brophy. Ed Brophy grew up as an American, lean and handsome. His father was a boisterous Irishman named Patrick Brophy.

Ed Brophy and his Cuban half-brother, Miguel Hidalgo, first met as youngsters on a Brophy family trip to Cuba in 1945. Ed owed his life to his older half-brother. At the age of 10, Miguel had unhesitatingly risked his own life in Trinidad by jumping into a deep lake and pulling Ed to safety after the 6-year-old fell from a canoe.

But for many years after that, they didn't see or correspond with each other. When Ed finally managed to track down Miguel in Cuba in the late 1960s, many things had changed in the intervening years.

Now, once again in Havana, Ed Brophy's thoughts went back to his last meeting with Miguel.

After his release from Cuba's prison cells, Miguel became a determined *contrarevolucionario*, an active rebel leader fighting against the Castro regime. It was now a quarter century later.

A TOURIST WELCOME

Ed Brophy had been with AP a few years before he was promoted from covering the legislature and politics in Santa Fe to a desk job in New York. He wasn't sure he wanted the desk job, although New York was the top — it was headquarters and where everything the AP represented was based.

At that time, AP was situated at 50 Rockefeller Plaza, in midtown Manhattan, just across a little square from St. Patrick's Cathedral on Fifth Avenue. He had made it from New Mexico, to midtown Manhattan in one giant leap.

Ed had been informed there was no way to become an AP correspondent in a foreign country without putting in a stint in New York, at the "foreign desk" or its Latin American desk. He eventually earned his way onto the foreign desk, which edited and rewrote all overseas copy for American newspapers and radio stations.

At that time, competition was fierce in the overall news business. Newspapers were highly competitive with each other, to say the least. The same was true among journalists of all types. AP staffers vied over coveted assignments — both domestic and foreign.

Ed's first foreign assignment was made with a photographer by the name of Eddie Adams. They hurried to Port Au Prince, Haiti, to cover a possible breakout of war between Papa Doc Duvalier's Haiti and its Hispaniola Island neighbor, the Dominican Republic. It never happened, but the two young staffers came up with a few stories and photos before they went back to New York.

Eddie Adams later won a Pulitzer Prize for photography in Saigon. This brought him fame and fortune, but that's another story.

Another short foreign assignment Ed Brophy vividly remembered was in becoming part of the AP team covering JFK's and Jackie's visit to Mexico City in June, 1962. Ed had later been assigned to other Caribbean hotspots while serving as an editor. Because he was bilingual, he also became an editor on the World Services desk. That finished product went to Latin American newspapers.

Now, twenty-five years later, coming back to Havana as a tourist, he found himself giving a lot of serious thought to his previous AP assignments in Cuba: the coveted resident -correspondent post and later short-term reporting trips.

As the Soviet airliner from Nassau descended into Havana, Ed thought back on his abrupt ouster as a resident-correspondent in the mid-1960s. Although he had encountered no serious problems on the previous short assignments since he was expelled, he was now getting the jitters as plane touched down and began disgorging its passengers at a new terminal built just for Cuba's newly burgeoning tourist traffic.

He knew his name remained on the lists of the G2 secret police and immigration officials. He didn't believe there would be any problems now, in 1997. During those shorter postings, however, he'd been restricted to covering special events and conferences and he was among other journalists given special, onetime visas. Even so, he'd managed to break away on his own several times during those short periods to do stories off the beaten path.

Two things were different now: He hadn't been back here in five years, and he'd never been here as a tourist.

After mulling it over, Ed quietly told his friend that if there should be any question involving his entry as they checked in at the airport, Pete should ignore him and just go ahead into the city. They would somehow make contact later.

But they breezed through the formalities together, with the unsmiling but courteous *milicianos* conducting little more than a cursory check of passports against airplane passenger lists and waving them through. No stamping of documents, no problems.

A taxi ride from the airport led them into the sprawl of Havana through a hodgepodge of poor residential and commercial areas, apartment buildings in need of paint and repair and, finally, right through the immense Plaza de la Revolucion, which featured a huge portrait of revolutionary leader Ernesto 'Che' Guevara and a giant statue of Cuba's Independence hero Jose Marti.

Government buildings surrounded the paved plaza, including those of the Communist Party and the offices of Fidel Castro and the Council of State. Che's outsize portrait, high on the façade of the Ministry of the Interior, bore the slogan: *Hasta La Victoria Siempre*, Onward to Victory.

The Plaza was familiar to TV viewers worldwide as the place where Castro delivered his marathon speeches before hundreds of thousands of cheering men, women and children, laboriously educating his countrymen in every aspect of his revolution, spelling out the problems of consumer rationing and of deprivation still ahead, and haranguing the "monster to the north" as the villain for all that went wrong.

After the ride into the city, Pete and Ed checked into a guesthouse that had been recommended by friends who were knowledgeable travelers. The large, private home converted into a Cuban version of a bed-and-breakfast afforded the ex-journalists close contact with ordinary Cubans. It provided most of the necessary comforts and was certainly more private than a downtown hotel. Virtually all tourists in Havana stayed in hotels and usually were escorted everywhere they went in small groups — a system which allowed close monitoring of their activities by government officials.

Their own hosts, the owners of the two-story house, were a retired professor of philosophy at the nearby University of Havana, his wife and her sister. The *turistas* were treated like part of the family, fed sumptuous breakfasts and spent a comfortable ten days at the house in a middle-class neighborhood in the Vedado section of Havana.

At the Hotel Habana Libre in the commercial section, they signed up for several tours of historic places in and around the capital and a night out at the famous Tropicana Nightclub. They did a lot of walking, shooting pictures, talking to Cubans and relaxing at bars and restaurants. They hired a car and driver to take them along the coastline east of Havana to the beautiful beaches at Santa Maria del Mar and Varadero.

Ed acted as unofficial guide to those places he had known. Both he and Pete spoke Spanish fluently, and they had long, sometimes-provocative conversations with friendly Cubans.

One of the highlights of their self-directed minitours was a Sunday afternoon spent at a newly inaugurated Book Fair of the Americas, held at the infamous La Cabaña Fortress on Havana Bay.

This rambling, Spanish-built citadel on the ramparts overlooking the city became a notorious political prison for thousands of Castro enemies following the Bay of Pigs invasion in 1961. In more modern times, most of its counterrevolutionary inmates had been moved to other institutions, and only in recent years had parts of the formidable military complex been cleaned up and opened to the public. This weekend, part of the structure was teeming with visitors from Europe and Latin America, along with Cuban families, attending the fair booths and exhibits spread throughout the compound.

They were holding a literary festival in a once-infamous prison.

"The *galeras* where they housed the political prisoners are either closed-off or of-limits," observed Ed in whispered wonder to Pete. "But these battlements, these courtyards and open fields also saw a lot of use. Raul and El Che used the stone walls as execution spots. The most-feared place in the prisoners' minds was El Muro, the wall."

This book fair was an ironic juxtaposition, an example of how the Castro regime was able to change its stripes, transform a place, an event, a fact of history into whatever it now decreed it to be to suit its purposes.

Their days as tourists seemed to fly by. As they prepared their documents and packed to return via Nassau and Miami, Ed began trying to examine the uneasy feeling he'd had all week, as if he had left something important undone. His conscience was uneasy. Something was definitely bothering him, making him feel guilty.

He tried to analyze it but could only come up with a partial answer: that his trip had brought up unpleasant memories as well as a pleasant nostalgia. He thought of his brother and —as usual on any of his Cuban visits — of Lydia, the Cuban woman he'd known and loved in the 1960s.

He decided to stay another week, if it could be arranged, and do some more wandering . . . and thinking by himself. He knew that as long as he had a return trip ticket and plenty of money to spend, an extension of his tourist card was perfectly fine with the Cubans.

Realizing his strange mood, Pete had tried to talk him out of staying on by himself. When that failed, he left him with several telephone numbers and told him to be careful.

"Call me, amigo, anytime," Pete said. "If you get into any trouble, I'll come down and help or bail you out, or whatever. But don't do anything foolish. You're getting too old for that."

Ed had packed his own bags and went along to the airport with his friend. After Pete's Cubana Airlines flight took off, Ed had the cabdriver take him to the Hotel Nacional, a rambling, eight-story landmark right in the heart of Vedado's busy commercial district.

Automotive and pedestrian traffic was thick and noisy as the taxi approached the Nacional's semicircular driveway. The Mediterranean-style resort, resembling The Breakers in Palm Beach, sat grandly aloof from the bustle in landscaped splendor atop a gentle hill. The Nacional was built in1930 and saw its heyday in the 1950s' Batista era when American mob bosses built and operated most of the luxurious casino hotels and nightclubs. The hotel was now restored to its former elegance for well-heeled international tourists.

And it quickly brought up distant memories for the former Havana correspondent.

It was here, at the then-secluded bar, that Ed had met some of his contacts and news sources in the mid-1960s. He and his Cuban friends, a few foreign embassy personnel, and his journalistic competitors from Agence France Presse and Reuters would occasionally attend a floor show at the hotel's Cabaret Parisien and flirt with the beautiful dancers.

At the rear of the hotel, guests now sat in sheltered nooks in garden-like surroundings overlooking the ocean and the Malecon seaside boulevard. Peacocks roamed freely.

Ed remembered that the famed Nacional had become rather seedy by the mid-1960s when he first arrived in Havana, but its prime location and fading grandeur kept it popular with government officials and infrequent foreign guests during the early revolutionary years. Now, it had been transformed into a modern, five-star tourist mecca while still retaining its old-world charm and much of its fine, highly polished woodwork.

But Ed hadn't chosen the Nacional for its luxury, good food and scenic views. Despite its bustle with well-heeled foreigners from Europe and elsewhere, the hotel fit in well with his heavy mood and his sense of *déjà vu.*

For one thing, he could clearly see just across busy Avenida O the apartment building where he had lived for several years, not long after the Bay of Pigs invasion and the Cuban missile crisis. His office was just around the corner from the apartment building, on Calle 23. He'd been the first resident American correspondent for The Associated Press since the Bay of Pigs era in 1961.

Sitting and smoking a cigar in the hotel's luxurious gardens, Ed gave himself over to nostalgia. His thoughts were of Cuban times gone by, of his own escapades in trying to do his job under trying circumstances.

And he remembered Lydia, his beautiful green-eyed companion through much of those trying times. How they had lived and loved until he was expelled. How Cuban bureaucratic measures had forced her to remain behind to struggle for years to leave the country. He thought of her later arrest and humiliation — and her death. Since his ouster, he was prohibited from reentry for several years afterward, and he had been helpless in that as well as in so many other things dealing with that period.

"I feel so guilty," he muttered to himself, shifting restlessly in his chair until he stood and walked slowly around the landscaped grounds.

He also thought long and fretfully about his half-brother Miguel. Where was he? What was he doing now? Surely he was no longer involved in plots to overthrow Fidel Castro. Ed had promised to help Miguel, but the few opportunities to do so had flown by.

He remembered old friends. Tomorrow, he would try to locate some of them, hopefully meet with some of them and relive the bad old times.

In the following days, as he wandered around from one end of the capital to the other, Ed was far from content. His dark mood became darker and his soul became ever-more troubled. He tried to explain it away by saying to himself that he was now an outsider, getting on in years, and poking into a world no longer his own.

But, deep down, he knew better.

He sensed he'd come here to do something other than just visit, that he was here for reasons other than just reliving history and then returning to his busy retired life in Florida. His thoughts turned, again, to his half-brother, the *contrarevolucionario*. What had happened to him? Was he still alive?

Ed was coming to believe he was back in Havana to make a little difference, to somehow help what he felt were his people in this troubled land. Any assistance he could provide, whatever it might be, could help to make up for some of the bitterness he now felt. The former correspondent was not at all sure how he could conceivably help. But in the long days and nights of introspection, he began to put some form to a passing thought, the germ of an idea.

Ed began seriously to contemplate a course of action, and its possible outcome. He now began to believe he had a sense of direction and purpose. More than anything, he wanted to find his brother, to help him somehow, even *join* him in his dangerous endeavors if Miguel was still involved in his idealistic battle against Fidel Castro.

Ed knew Miguel had spent more than seven years as a political prisoner in Cuba's worst institutions, and it would've been a much longer time if Cuban authorities hadn't believed he was on the verge of death and released him to die on his own. The correspondent and the broken-down shell of his brother had been able to spend a few days together after Ed had tracked him down in the late 1960s before he was expelled.

Ed had tried at that time to convince Miguel to leave the country for his own safety and for the sake of his wife and daughter, who had escaped from Cuba and were now living in California after a time with her relatives in Florida. But there was no turning back for Miguel. In the second of two secret meetings with Ed, he'd made it clear that he was prepared to die while fighting to free Cuba.

What was only vaguely known to Ed Brophy was Miguel's activity after his brushes with death in Castro's dark prisons.

Miguel had been forced to give up his ranch and other properties. His wife and daughter were now safe in exile in the United States, but they could rarely correspond because of government restrictions. He was prohibited from leaving the country, and his poor physical condition probably would prevent him from escaping.

With the help of good friends and expert medical attention once he was freed from prison, Miguel eventually regained his health. He would never forgive or forget his enemies. Unable to shake his rebel mentality and despite the great odds against him, he resumed his activities as an anti-Castro dissident, this time as part of a small but growing network of clandestine counterrevolutionaries who were struggling to help overthrow the regime or provoke enough attention to foment international action of some sort.

Mulling over this now, Ed was determined to keep his promise to help — a vow he'd been pushing aside for too many years. In doing this, he believed, he'd also be working to ensure that the treatment of Lydia could never be perpetrated on others.

Meanwhile, his thoughts kept drifting back to the start of his Cuban adventure in the 1960s.

1964

A Rude Reception

Ramiro del Campo was a small man with a big title. Ramirito as some called him,was director of the Departamento de Informacion, Prensa y Comunicaciones del Ministerio de Relaciones Exteriores, the Cuban Foreign Ministry's censorship czar in effect.

Ed was called to Ramiro's office a few days after his arrival in Havana. The foreign ministry building — MinRex, its bureaucratic acronym — was an imposing glass and steel building on a broad plaza which fronted on the Malecon, the beachfront boulevard and seawall beyond.

After running a gantlet of *milicianos* just to get into the building, Ed was confronted by a female guard in full camouflage uniform and boots, with a sidearm and a rifle beside her as she sat behind a high wooden pedestal in the lobby just inside the massive double doors.

The vast marble entryway was empty of furniture and people except for a number of other guards at several hallways and stairways leading off to offices and conference rooms, Ed supposed. The grim miliciana filled out a small card with Ed's name, age, citizenship, birthplace, who he was expected to see, and the day, month, year and time. She sent one of the other guards upstairs with the card.

Since there was nowhere to sit in the austere place, Ed stood and waited ten minutes before the telephone rang on the miliciana's desk, directing that he be escorted up the handsome, wide stairway into the offices of the regulators of Cuban information.

Waiting in an anteroom was a chunky, cleancut young man in his late twenties who introduced himself as Ernesto Lopez of the seccion de prensa. He was polite and pleasant, dressed casually with an open-necked sport shirt outside his trousers. He took Ed inside a small office, which connected with another set of rooms, where he met Antonio "Tony" Perez and said hello again to Paco Almeida, whom he had met at the airport upon arrival. The three comprised the leadership staff of the foreign press section of the department headed by Ramiro del Campo. Paco was the section jefe and Lopez and Tony worked for him, along with several others who functioned as chauffeurs and guides to visiting journalists. These were the "minders," who kept track of reporters and other visitors to ensure they didn't wander too far on their own or dig too deeply into the regime's operations and its people.

"I'm a bit nervous about this guy Ramirito," the correspondent had confided to his driver as they had approached MinRex that morning. "I've only been here a few days, but I've already been warned that he's got a well-earned reputation for being ruthless against Yankees and counterrevolutionaries during and after the Bay of Pigs."

Blake was a Jamaican-born Cuban who had been employed as a driver by The AP during that turbulent period. He turned, grinned broadly and half-nodded. But he said nothing encouraging to Ed as he drove up to the ministry building.

Lopez and Paco were friendly enough as they sat around Paco's desk and waited for Ramiro to receive Ed. They talked about Ed's trip from Mexico City, asked his ideas about the Cuban job and about his life in New York City.

It turned out both spoke English, Paco being much more fluent than Lopez. At that time, the use of the language in Cuba created suspicion, so it was used sparingly.

The flamboyant Paco, in his thirties, launched into stories about his time in the United States. He'd lived and worked in New York, New Jersey and Miami prior to the revolution. Castro was chasing out Batista while Paco was working as a bank clerk in New York. Paco said he immediately quit his job and flew to Havana to offer his services to *la revolucion.* Ed later found out Paco had left behind a wife he was unhappy with, plus a child. So there was more to his story about being a dedicated revolutionary than he let on.

In fact, Paco loved the good life, even in bleak, economically depressed Cuba.

Lopez was younger, much more reticent about his personal history. He was a hard-core believer in the Cuban style of socialism and was studying history, the Soviet language and foreign affairs at the University of Havana. When he opened up, he was a walking, talking exponent of the revolution's theories of a new world free of capitalism and "imperialism."

It was the duty of these two to keep tabs on the reporter for much of the time he was in Cuba.

Del Campo finally received Ed in his large, cool office, which looked out toward the blue-black Atlantic. He didn't deign to speak English. But Ed didn't expect it.

"*Como estás? Todo va bien?*" he said, pumping Ed's hand and clapping him on the shoulder. He sat the new correspondent down and began peppering him with questions. Diminutive and smiling, Ramiro reminded Ed of an oldtime movie villain, with slicked-back hair and shifty eyes. He was clean-shaven and neatly dressed in black slacks and starched, white guayabera shirt.

Ramiro started out by remarking on the "turmoil of Latin America" and asserted that many countries were lapsing into "imperialist dictatorships" beholden to the United States. After his effusive greeting, there was little subtlety to the man. He bored right in and demanded to know what Ed thought of the political situation in turbulent Chile, in Mexico, about the escalating war in Vietnam, about the student protests in the United States, about "the shameful oppression of blacks in your country."

He asked the writer's opinions about the invasion at the Bahia de Cochinos (the Bay of Pigs), the Crisis of October 1962, JFK, Nixon and news topics of the day. Ed took pretty much a middle-of-the-road view on everything, trying not to provoke any harsh feelings. They continued that way for about forty-five minutes. When the barrage of questions came to an end, Ramiro invited the reporter to lunch the following day.

It took place at a plush restaurant at the Focsa building, a forty-story towerlike spire covered in glass. Situated in Vedado, the newest section of Havana, it held many Soviet offices, along with those of Cuban officials,

military personnel and government bureaucrats. The two took the elevator
to the penthouse floor, which was given over to La Torre, meaning the
tower — a classy, private club and restaurant for Cuba's new ruling elite,
diplomats and visiting VIPs.

The place had a huge bar, a main dining room with large windows
overlooking the city and the ocean, and several smaller, more-private
dining areas. Waiters wore full dress, utensils were silver, glassware was
crystal, the booze imported and the view spectacular.

Ramiro was treated deferentially and by name. They were seated at
an elegantly set table in one of the smaller rooms. And after a scotch and
soda, a shrimp cocktail and some excellent steaks, Ramiro bored in with
more questions trying to determine Ed's politics, his prejudices and any
preconceived notions about la revolucion.

Then he hit Ed with the question he had been anticipating since his
arrival in Cuba: What about Ed's half-brother?

"What about him?" Ed replied. "I haven't seen Miguel since I was a
child. I visited him in the interior (of the country) with my mother. He was
about ten years old, and I was six. I haven't seen or heard from him since."

"Well," Ramiro half-smiled. "I can tell you he is serving a long
prison sentence at the Isle of Pines. He was caught spying for the CIA
around the time of the Bay of Pigs invasion. He's just another stupid
contrarevolucionario."

Ed felt like reaching across the table and punching Ramiro. But he
quickly realized that the man was trying to provoke him. He managed
to hold his temper and tried to mask the rush of emotions he felt: the
overwhelming sorrow and helplessness. Despite their estrangement, he
had a deep love and respect for his half-brother. He was aware of Miguel's
unbending moral character and somehow knew that he'd become deeply
involved in the underground struggle against the Castro regime.

But Ed shook his head and said nothing.

"*Bueno*, he's safely put away, and neither you nor I have to worry about
it," Ramiro said, implying heaven knew what. "Times are different now,
and we have allowed you into our country as a reporter for the international
press. So let's just see how we can get along. *Está* bien. *Nos vamos?*"

"Okay," Ed said slowly, still in a daze. "I'm here to do a job as a
reporter. Nothing else."

With that, del Campo signed the check with a flourish and the two left, riding down the elevator in silence. Del Campo waved once before he got into his chauffeured car and drove off. Ed preferred to walk back to his office, his brain a muddle, his stomach heavy from an unexpectedly big lunch.

He knew his half-brother had remained in Cuba all these years. He was happy being a farmer-rancher deep in Cuba's interior, far from the power struggles and machinations of the Castro regime in Havana. Even though Castro had expropriated the large family ranch, Ed had known that that Miguel was a man of the soil, a man who loved Cuba too much to leave it. He was a survivor, and he would do what it took to continue his life in the Cuban ranch-and-farm country.

But Ed felt slapped in the face by del Campo's disclosure as to the extent of his half-brother's counter-revolutionary activities. But a political prisoner? All these years in Castro's notorious concentration camps? That was hard for Ed to fathom just after his arrival in the 1960s.

A Cuban official wouldn't be lying about something like that. And, it began to dawn on him that del Campo thought he had a trump card against Ed. With Miguel Hidalgo in prison, Ed Brophy would surely watch his step as a correspondent. And —Ed could almost read del Campo's mind — there was less of a chance that the reporter would at any time cooperate with the hated CIA, if that was his intention.

Because of the CIA's involvement in assassination attempts against Castro, its direction and training of the Bay of Pigs invaders and its work in the missiles crisis of October 1962, members of the Castro government rightly or wrongly suspected that everything that went awry and everyone who opposed their policies was somehow connected to the clandestine American agency.

In fact, the Castro regime assumed that any American — reporter, businessman, visitor, even some of the commercial airplane hijackers that showed up in Havana asking for asylum — were CIA spies, or at least informants.

REVOLUTIONARY CUBA

In The 1960s

OUR MAN IN HAVANA

Ed's arrival in Havana was an entirely new experience although he had visited briefly with his mother as an adolescent. He had reported from Mexico, various Central American countries and Caribbean nations such as the Dominican Republic and Papa Doc's Haiti. But there had been little to prepare him for the experience of becoming an American correspondent in a Cuba fast becoming a communist stronghold in the Americas.

Waiting at the airport was the man he was replacing, a Colombian citizen named Hugo Artemisa. He was accompanied by Paco Almeida, a tall, good-looking fellow who seemed to Ed not at all the typical Cuban bureaucrat.

They greeted Ed enthusiastically. Artemisa said Paco was there to ease the way through funcionarios from Customs, Immigration, Security and whoever else waited to interrogate and pass judgment on a Western journalist entering Castro's Cuba. Rather than ease the way, the opposite turned out to be true. Paco and Artemisa were no help at all. There was to be no breezing-through the maze of military bureaucracy at the airport.

After a lengthy wait in the sweaty terminal amid dozens of rifle-bearing guards and airport officials, Paco returned from a whispered get-together with officials and strolled up to inform them that his efforts to avoid the bureaucratic mill at the airport had been nixed by superiors.

"I tried, but they give the orders here," shrugged Paco apologetically to the incoming AP man.

The tired Ed spent two hours filling out forms and undergoing interrogation by different batches of military and civilian authorities. His luggage underwent a meticulous search. The inspectors even squeezed toothpaste out of tubes and opened sealed cans of the British pipe tobacco he smoked, John Cotton's. Pill bottles and other personal items came under special scrutiny. Finally, Ed was cleared to enter the country. The trio drove off to a hotel near The AP office.

During the half-hour trip, the gregarious Paco regaled his compañeros with tales of his worldly experiences. Rumors abounded in Cuba at the time and Paco added his share. He joked heartily enroute about recent speculation of "secret tunnels" for Soviet missiles, camouflaged anti-aircraft emplacements, and "dozens of military arsenals" allegedly hidden in the countryside surrounding the city.

"Yeah, the Soviets have been good to us," Paco said with a sly grin that made it difficult to tell whether he was being sarcastic or jokingly boastful.

Strange, but that had become the new Cuba, a land of paradox. Ed was learning fast.

In Paco's other life in the United States, preceding the Castro takeover, he said he had worked aboard a cruise ship out of Miami in the 1950s and boasted of his amorous adventures with young ladies and rich widows aboard ship and in a number of foreign ports. He was employed at a New York bank before hurrying back to Cuba to join la revolucion. Of course this was after Batista's surprise departure, when there was no longer any fighting to be done.

It turned out that Paco, and his colleague Lopez were happy to get a new journalistic face that they could keep track of and thus justify a lot of their time away from their dreary office at the Foreign Ministry.

In effect, they became Ed's at-a-distance "minders," appointed by the ministry to loosely track his movements, activities and contacts — and perhaps confirm their theory that any *Yanqui* coming into the island under whatever guise was either a CIA agent or would eventually become one.

Paco, in particular, became a tour guide-friend-inquisitor to Ed Brophy in the first few weeks of his assignment, each feeling the other out about his intentions and opinions.

The Cubans knew, of course, that Ed's late mother, Marina Hidalgo, was a Cuban who had divorced her Cuban husband, Jose "Pepe" Hidalgo, and had gone to live in the United States in the 1930s. At that time,

Hidalgo was a well-to-do rancher from the island's interior. Marina's younger son, the Cuban-born Miguel, had grown up on the ranch with his father, Jose. Miguel was about four years older than Ed, whose father had married Marina in the United States.

They met when Ed and his mother traveled to Cuba for a visit. The Cubans hadn't objected to any of this personal history when they considered Ed's request for a resident visa as AP correspondent. It didn't seem to matter. In Ed's mind at least, it had been a sign of a lessening of the Cuban paranoia about state security.

A room had been reserved for the new American correspondent at the Hotel Riviera, a large, well-located hotel in Vedado. It had been built in the 1950s with American Mafia money and was still outwardly prosperous in the early Castro years, minus the casino operations.

The Colombian-born Artemisa was in the process of vacating the apartment leased to The Associated Press on the fifth floor of a six-story building near the office in Vedado. The AP digs had a small balcony that overlooked the venerable Hotel Nacional, which had a colorful history under Batista and the American mobsters. The austere early years of the revolution had resulted in neglect, and the grand, neocolonial establishment needed paint, repair and proper maintenance, as did most of the capital's buildings.

The AP office was just around the corner from the correspondent's apartment. It was part of an entrance wing on the ground floor of an unimposing, four-story residential building housing military officers, several families and the prominent Cuban surrealist painter René Portocarrero. The entrance was set off from the sidewalk by a walkway that led to wide double doors. To the left as one entered was The AP office and down the hallway were other rooms with frosted-over entrances, no doubt a spillover from the Cuban bureaucracy. A slow, creaking elevator carried tenants to their crowded apartments on the upstairs floors.

The AP occupied a small set of rooms that had once consisted of a medical suite. The office now had a small reception area, a smaller, narrower room to the side used for several teletype machines and supplies, and a separate office just off the reception area for the correspondent. It was all bright and neat, but it badly needed paint and a lot of maintenance work.

Surprisingly, Ed inherited two longtime AP employees: Blake, the driver, who personally owned a dilapidated 1950s Cadillac, and an office manager named Wilson. Both were Jamaica-born Cubans who had worked for The AP on-and-off since the early 1950s, when Havana was in its prime. They were both bilingual. Blake had ferried American tourists around in the capital's heydays of the 1950s.

Later, after becoming better acquainted with the new correspondent, Blake and Wilson spoke freely about the poor state of their second country and the miseries being endured by their families and other working people in Cuba.

They longed to return to Jamaica with their families — Wilson had an aged mother and Blake had a wife and daughter — but couldn't obtain government permission to leave. The two were of great assistance to Ed throughout his stay, often filling him in about what was happening on the street, or passing on the latest rumor.

Ed spent the first week meeting people and familiarizing himself with the city. He liked to go off on his own, when Paco did not insist on lunching with him or driving him in a ministry vehicle to the beach or a tourist site.

He wandered the streets, eating at small cafeterias, talking with affable Cubans of all stripes, including many in uniform of one sort or another.

Vedado was a busy section of Havana that was like a buffer between Habana Vieja, Old Havana — the original colonial settlement and its protective fortresses — and Miramar, the once-elegant residential area for the rich and well-to-do.

Vedado, where his apartment and office were situated, was a lively, newer part of town largely built up in the boom years of the 1950s under Batista. It included sprawling middle-class residential neighborhoods but also had most of the city's more modern hotels and office buildings, government ministries, several hospitals and some well-frequented restaurants.

Miramar was the elegant part of Havana, where many of the *palacetes* once owned by wealthy Batista government officials and prosperous businessmen were situated. The once-palatial, colonial style houses were now occupied by bureaucrats, and schools of indoctrination for young children, including the *Pioneros*, the communist equivalent of Boy Scouts, and *academias* for young girls, who all wore blue skirts and white blouses.

The Miramar neighborhoods also housed Soviet bureaucrats, milicianos, foreign embassies and occasional visiting VIPs. There was housing for diplomats and major government officials. Here and there were the more heavily guarded domains of the powerful Interior Ministry, a loose amalgam of security personnel, militia and professional military officers. Most importantly, Miramar was known to Cubans as the location for the all-powerful counter-intelligence service — the feared G2 (pronounced Heh-Dos in Cuban Spanish).

What every Cuban and visitor alike considered the true Havana — Habana Vieja — was one of the most architecturally outstanding cities in the world.

It was the old 16th century colonial section of the city, with its narrow streets built into a grid pattern and teeming with people. It was a busy port during Spain's heyday, serving as a major stopover for shipping traffic coming and going throughout the New World.

Now, a mere half dozen years into Castro's revolution, *Habana Vieja* seemed suspended in time: It was steeped in history and still beautiful in places, but the lack of upkeep and restoration had rendered many of the elegant buildings and mansions into crumbling, even dangerous, relics of a bygone era.

It was sad to see the faded splendor, and to know that because of the revolutionary government's immediate priorities — education and medical assistance, housing and, most of all, the fitful production of consumer goods — it could not, or would not, do anything to try to preserve one of the world's great heritage cities.

Ed walked for days, taking it all in, enjoying the liveliness of the Cuban, for regardless of his station in life, Cubans enjoyed life and each other. They laughed and joked in the grimmest of times. Everyone had a favorite story, and they all tried to outwit the authorities in one way or another. It was in their blood.

In Habana Vieja, the poor lived much of their lives on the street, or on their balconies, elbowing aside their wash to shout down at their neighbors. In the sidestreets off the Avenida Del Prado, they crowded into small, rundown housing, sometimes a family of ten in two or three rooms. Many occupied structurally unsound buildings, verandas, patios, arcades and nooks and crannies.

But they were always ready with a quip or a joke, or a helping hand for a neighbor, even sometimes a Yankee stranger.

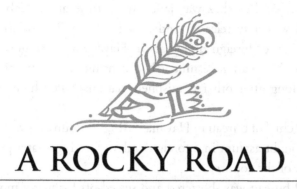

A ROCKY ROAD

Ed had begun his coveted reporting assignment in 1964. It was a posting long denied by the Cuban regime to most American journalists. After persistent efforts, however, Ed had received official approval Cubans for a visa.

It was a tentative venture for the Cuban government following its inward-looking turns after the Bay of Pigs Invasion in 1961 and the October 1962 Missile Crisis.

The Castro revolution's machinations since those two epic events had been under-reported by the American media, if they had been reported at all, because Cuba had closed in upon itself after Nikita Khrushchev had capitulated in a dangerous confrontation with American President John F. Kennedy in 1962.

Now, several years later, at the height of the Cold War, Cuba was assuming a significant new role in world affairs that made it necessary for The AP to try to expand its limited reporting out of Havana. Castro, Che Guevara and other top Cuban leaders had established close political and economic ties not only with Moscow, but with Peking and Hanoi and a host of Third World nations.

The Associated Press bureau in Havana was closed down when the Castro regime carried out a massive roundup of suspected "counterrevolutionaries" during the CIA-led invasion at the Bay of Pigs in April 1961.

Among those arrested was Associated Press newsman Robert Berrellez, a roving correspondent, who had been busily reporting the mobilization in Havana during the invasion by exiles.

The intrepid Berrellez was jailed for a time at La Cabaña prison fortress and was only released and expelled from the country through the intercession of foreign diplomats in Havana and the government of Mexico. The Mexican government had continued to maintain relations with Cuba long after other hemisphere nations called home their own diplomats.

The AP chief of bureau in Havana during the Cuban invasion, Herald K. Milks, sought asylum in a foreign embassy and was later granted safe conduct out of the country.

The AP bureau was shuttered and sealed-off for many months until Cuban authorities began permitting a series of temporary, non-American journalists to report for the international agency on a limited basis. The interim newspapermen ensured that the AP maintained a tenuous presence there by keeping a low profile. They reported primarily on Castro speeches, periodic government communiqués and other "official" news. They were restricted to Havana. Their contacts were limited, they were constantly watched, their reportage monitored and often censored since communications (telex and telephone) were controlled by the government.

Consequently, there was little reported to the outside world about what was really going on within that highly charged society. Newspaper readers, radio listeners and television viewers could glean little about government dissidents, political prisoners, and the daily life of the Cubans — what they believed, said and did.

That was the situation during Artemisa's tenure.

It soon became obvious to Brophy and other Cuban watchers, that judging from all the Cuban rhetoric — in Fidel Castro speeches, at United Nations proceedings, international conferences and in bilateral dealings with their Latin American neighbors and others — that the revolutionary government now hungered for respect and recognition among nations.

Ed believed the time was ripe for change, that the Cubans now wanted the world to know of their struggles and their victories. But he knew that the Castro regime would have to be gradually convinced that its standing and, perhaps, some of the respectability it sought, could only come about by being more open.

One way it could do this, Ed reasoned, was by allowing The AP to establish a permanent bureau and by permitting a resident correspondent to write about Cuba's day-to-day life firsthand, to let the ordinary people and some of the regime's leaders talk more openly.

Brophy began his efforts to obtain a Havana posting by obtaining permission from key AP brass in New York to initiate a campaign of gentle persuasion of the Cuban regime. Specifically, he sought to have the Cubans agree to have the international news agency assign an American as resident correspondent in Havana. AP General Manager Wes Gallagher and Personnel Director Keith Fuller agreed that the time was right for such a push.

"Go for it," Fuller said when he called Ed to his seventh-floor office at 50 Rock.

Ed wrote to the Czechoslovakian embassy in Washington D.C., which at that time was the intermediary for the Cubans in the United States. Because of the meltdown in Cuba-U.S. relations in the early 1960s, the Czechs represented Cuba in the United States. The Swiss Embassy in Havana handled American affairs in Cuba.

In his notes to the Cubans via the Czechs, Ed argued that Cuba had not been getting the attention it deserved in the world press because of the restrictions imposed by its own government on reporters. He suggested that Havana should credential a correspondent knowledgeable about Cuba's historic place in the world, and one who would be objective in his reporting about the Castro regime's expanding influence in the world affairs. That person would have no previous bias as a reporter about Cuban events. He would have an open mind about Cuba and its revolution.

This effort on Ed's part was like a shot in the dark.

After several weeks, a Mr. Hromodka, cultural attaché at the Czech embassy, replied. He wrote Brophy that he had forwarded Ed's letters to the Cuban embassy in Mexico for dispatch to officials in Havana. From Hromodka, Ed learned who in Mexico and Havana was responsible for getting such a request into the proper hands. He then sat down and wrote a lengthy letter in Spanish. He emphasized that since Cuba had been closed off to the world for so long it deserved to tell its side of the story along with what was being pieced together about Cuba in the foreign press.

Virtually everything written in the western world about the Castro regime was negative, Ed pointed out in his letter. And what better vehicle than The Associated Press for objective reporting about the revolution and its impact on the people and daily life. The AP, he stressed, had earned a worldwide reputation for trustworthy and objective reporting over more than a century.

The AP was respected for writing both sides of any story, Ed wrote. Surely, the Cuban government would benefit by casting a little light on the positive things the revolution was doing for its people, along with some of its problems.

Brophy argued that the reporter would have to live in Havana and be given some freedom to talk to its people and to some of the government leaders setting policy. That was the key issue at hand.

Several more weeks went by before Ed received a polite note from Hromodka asking for biographical information and a detailed history of his education, his travels and reporting career. After that was done, another polite note from Hromodka informed him that he was welcome to visit the Cuban embassy in Mexico City and apply there for credentials and a visa to report from Cuba.

Ed headed for Mexico. After a week or two of haggling with Cuban embassy officials in Mexico, and more waiting, a visa was finally issued: for ninety days. While there, he would have access to some of the key people he would need to convince about a longer stay. Fair enough.

Ed had had little first-hand knowledge about Cuba and its eight million people. In effect, he was "untainted" by any previous reporting about Cuba, as one official who had approved his entry into the country later told him. A number of American reporters over the years had been allowed brief visits and then gone home and written endlessly about the evils of the Castro empire, this official complained.

"What we want is the world to hear our story, to give a true picture," he said. It was then that Ed knew for sure that this had become the regime's new posture, which coincided exactly with what he had argued for.

Havana was viewed as an exotic outpost for reporters. It looked to be a rich source of news, but one that could also lead to endless frustration, all depending on how much freedom the Castro government was willing to allow. In other words, it was really a question mark.

Ed soon learned that a correspondent had to expect the unexpected and to function in a closed society that had few remaining trappings of its prior history. He was subject to off-and-on oversight by the Cubans, who always suspected him of working for the CIA. And, along with the rest of the Cuban population, he found himself enduring the steady brainwashing from the nonstop propaganda factory that Cuba had become. You couldn't turn on a radio or TV set or read a newspaper that didn't drip with fulsome praise for everything the new regime was now doing. When that didn't seem enough, the media endlessly recounted *la revolución's* glorious past.

Halfway knowing the circumstances involved, Ed flew into to Havana from Mexico City for the first time. The challenge and the adventure had begun.

TROPICAL TURBULENCE

According to historians, the 780-mile-long island of Cuba was inhabited by native Indians from about 3500 BC.

Since its "discovery" by Christopher Columbus in October, 1492, it has been the stuff of legend, a fascinating place so strategically located at the crossroads of the Old World and the new that it figured prominently in the history and development of Spain, England, France, Portugal and its next-door neighbors Mexico and the United States.

The Spaniards became the heavyweights in Cuba's development. Diego Velasquez established the first seven Cuban settlements in 1514 and Spanish colonialists soon took total control, eventually wiping out Cuba's native population and ruling with a heavy hand for almost four centuries.

Along with a Caribbean neighbor, the Dominican Republic, Cuba served as a strategic transit point for Spanish fleets carting the wealth of the New World to Spain in the 1500s and 1600s.

Cuba's history has been a turbulent one ever since. Ed vividly read and studied this history of the scenic, strategic island nation.

Cuba became a battleground for pirates, adventurers and colonialists, and the ensuing Spanish reign over the lush tropical land was a cruel, exploitive era. Cubans in the easternmost province of Oriente finally rebelled at Spain's reactionary policies in 1868 and conducted a series of uprisings in abortive struggles for independence.

Cuba's trade with the United States became of increasing importance to both countries in the mid-1800s, especially because of American investment in Cuban sugar production. Encouraged by their ties to the

U.S., Cuban patriots Jose Marti, Antonio Maceo and Maximo Gomez led separate, disorganized attempts to overthrow Spanish rule in what was called a second war of independence.

Assuming a growing interest in its Caribbean economic partner, the U.S. tried to force the Spaniards out through diplomacy and threats directed to the ruling aristocracy in Madrid. In January 1898, the U.S. battleship *Maine* was sent to Havana as a warning to the Spaniards. Three weeks later, the *Maine* mysteriously blew up in Havana Harbor.

It was never proved that the Spaniards had blown up the ship, which cost the lives of 266 American sailors. But President William McKinley declared war on Spain in April 1898, and Teddy Roosevelt became famous for leading his troops to victory at San Juan Hill.

The Americans occupied the island until a constitution was drafted, and Cuba officially achieved its independence in 1902.

But it was easy to see that Cuba's independence from Spain resulted in a dependence on the United States. A series of corrupt governments headed by homegrown power-grabbing individuals in Cuba repeatedly necessitated American military intervention to restore civil order and maintain its rich sugar and tobacco interests.

As a result, Cuba became, in effect, an independent American territory, much like Puerto Rico and The Philippines.

By 1920, Cuba's sugar and tobacco production were controlled by Americans. U.S. and foreign companies had by then built most of Cuba's infrastructure and were operating most of its essential services. What Cuba didn't have or what it couldn't produce or manufacture locally, it imported, mostly from the United States. And the U. S. was the island's best customer for its sugar, nickel, tobacco and other raw materials.

Tourism began to flourish in the 1920s and 1930s because of Cuba's liberal attitudes on drinking, gambling and prostitution.

Newly appointed correspondent Brophy was not too surprised to learn that in the decade when the rest of the world was preoccupied with World War II, Fulgencio Batista, followed by Presidents Ramon Grau San Martín and Carlos Prio Socarrás, headed corrupt governments in Havana.

Through a series of coups and rigged elections, Batista took over for a second time and assumed dictatorial powers through much of the 1950s.

A ruthless, repressive ruler, he nevertheless welcomed foreign investment, particularly in hotels and casinos, and pursued tourism aggressively.

After World War II, it became inevitable that the exotic Caribbean island would become an American playground. It was a time when America prospered and Havana became a boomtown and the tourist capital of the Caribbean.

Tourism transformed the capital into a thriving, busy metropolis in the 1950s. It was primarily driven by Cuban nightlife and gambling. Businessmen, Cubans and American expatriates thrived. It was a busy time of construction of modern office and residential buildings, roadways, government ministries and public structures.

Cuba's poor, and there were many, were ignored.

Havana's nightlife achieved worldwide notoriety. With a population of almost two million, Havana was the largest city in the Caribbean and, besides casinos and strip clubs, it featured fine restaurants, a nightly lottery, jai-alai, cockfights, horse racing and other forms of gambling to attract the well-heeled *turistas* seeking thrills.

By the late 1950s, the years immediately preceding the Castro revolution, the Cuban capital boasted five topscale hotels with thriving Las Vegas-style casino operations financed largely by Mafia mobsters. Havana's tallest building, the 40-story Focsa, was built at this time.

But the good times quit rolling on New Year's Day, 1959.

That's when Batista abruptly fled the country, frightened by his army's inability or ineptness in opposing what the rebels were accomplishing in the interior.

The dictator's corrupt rule had been slowly undermined for several years by increasing unrest in Havana and other large cities: by university students who had attempted to assassinate him, by striking workers and small merchants, and by frequent incidents of sabotage and terrorism by various underground groups.

Batista's large, well-equipped, but poorly paid army could never manage to control the small group of rebels in the mountains and along the coastline of the eastern part of the island. The army leaders and troops were reluctant to engage the guerrillas and managed to suffer one embarrassing defeat after another in skirmishes with units of Eloy Gutierrez Menoyo's rebels in the Escambray Mountains and Castro's *barbudos* in southeast

Cuba led by Che Guevara, Camilo Cienfuegos, Castro's brother, Raul, and others.

In the summer of 1958, Raul Castro came close to provoking an all-out military confrontation between the rebels and the United States which could have spelled disaster for the bearded ones in the mountains. Castro's younger brother ordered his troops to confiscate food, vehicles, medical equipment and other supplies from the American-owned Moa Bay Mining Company in Oriente. When they withdrew from the area, the ruthless Raul forced a dozen employees, including ten Americans, to accompany the rebels.

Soon after that, two dozen American sailors and marines were kidnapped from a bus transporting them from the town of Guantanamo to the Guantanamo Bay Naval Base, the sprawling American installation on Cuba's southeast coast.

After threats by American congressmen to invade the area and forcibly recover the hostages, Fidel Castro ordered that they be released, thus putting an end to the threat of another incursion by American Marines. That would have been a disaster for the rebellious Cubans. Another intervention by the American government into what was going on in Cuba would probably have brought a halt to any rebellious movements.

In fact, Batista had often asked for American military assistance but had been rebuffed by Washington.

The rebels continued to expand their operations and grow in strength, primarily by recruiting peasants from the areas in which they operated.

By the end of 1958, the beleaguered Batista was receiving alarming reports that his troops were being overwhelmed by guerrilla units. The speculation was that Fidel Castro's men numbered in the thousands when, in truth, they were a small, scraggly band of warriors.

The foreign news media had a principal role in creating Castro's larger-than-life iconic image. The story at that time was that he had thousands of battle-ready troops scattered throughout the mountains and valleys of southeast Cuba and was slowly moving toward the capital. That was fiction, but it sold newspapers.

In the early hours of January 1, 1959, after celebrating New Year's Eve with a formal-dress ball, Batista decided to take the money and go. He and his family and most of his government ministers and high-echelon supporters hopped aboard waiting aircraft and fled the island, never to return.

Fidel Castro was suddenly victorious. All he had to do now was to swoop down from the mountains and assume control. But, he didn't realize this at first. He was a bewildered man, hundreds of miles from Havana. Word was slow getting back. He didn't know what had happened. Confusion reigned for a day or two.

For the most part, Cubans weary of the excesses of the Batista government wildly celebrated its collapse. They took to the streets of the capital and a few other nearby communities, fighting with local police and vandalizing homes and properties of Batista officials and supporters.

In Havana, small groups of rioters attacked members of Batista's government and broke into casinos and destroyed roulette wheels, slot machines and other gambling equipment. They knocked the heads off parking meters with baseball bats and paraded up and down the streets for hours, drinking and dancing victoriously for most of that day. It was, after all, the First of January.

The only casino to escape the mob violence was the famous *Salon Rojo* at the Hotel Capri, where one of its owners, American movie actor George Raft, stood defiantly at the entrance and stared down a group of rioters. Mobster chieftain Meyer Lansky, who built the Capri and controlled much of Havana's gambling scene, was absent from the hotel that morning after celebrating New Year's Eve at the casino.

The little resistance put up by policemen and soldiers in Havana and elsewhere was quickly swept aside by members of underground organizations such as the July 26th Movement and the student-led Revolutionary Directorate. They were anxiously waiting for their absent leader, Fidel Castro.

They assumed control in the absence of civil authority, taking over radio and TV stations and warning the army and Batista supporters not to form a military junta. They didn't.

In Oriente Province, Fidel Castro was slowly beginning to comprehend what was happening in faraway Havana. He had had little direct communication in recent days with those Havana-based groups.

He had spent New Year's Eve at the rural home of a friend. Learning of Batista's sudden abdication from radio reports the following day, Fidel became extremely angry. He assumed that the Cuban Army had pulled a fast one, preempting him and pulling off a military coup. Either that or a rebel group in the Escambray Mountains led by Eloy Gutierrez Menoyo and an American adventurer named William Morgan had moved in on their own.

Batista had fled because of his fear of the rebels in the mountains. He didn't say which mountains. But Cuban Army leaders were known to have grown increasingly impatient about the whole thing, and there were rumors of a coup.

Fidel assumed the worst.

"Those son of a bitches (the army) have taken over the government; now we will have to fight them," Castro fulminated. Friends set out to discover what had taken place after Batista's abrupt departure.

After that initial confusion, word finally reached Fidel that many of Batista's army commanders also had gone into hiding. The army had not assumed control of anything. Batista had fled because of his fear of the rebels in the mountains. Period!

Only then did Castro issue orders for several of his top commanders to hurry to Havana. He discounted the idea that that Menoyo and Morgan in the Escambray Mountains had any direct role in forcing Batista into exile.

Fidel and some of his men then marched into Santiago, and the rebels were greeted as liberators by officials of Cuba's second-largest city.

Castro had dispatched Camilo Cienfuegos, Che Guevara and their guerrilla units to Havana, and he soon set out himself. As they marched toward the capital, the small band of rebels was quickly joined by hundreds of volunteers eager to join the victors.

Fidel and his ragtag band — traveling in an array of old army vehicles, pickups, citrus trucks and confiscated cars and taxis — wended their way clear across the large island and arrived in Havana on January 8, 1959, to a heroic welcome.

Habaneros, who had been without a dictator for all of a week, greeted this articulate *rebelde* enthusiastically. Here was a living legend! They liked his rhetoric, his beard and his macho fatigues and boots.

Some even believed he was The Savior, comparing him in appearance, age and promise to Jesus Christ, particularly when a white dove, or maybe it was a pigeon, landed on his shoulder during one lengthy speech.

He spoke forcefully to the crowds about a new society, free of Yankee imperialism and government corruption.

The masses believed him.

Many were soon to learn he had become the prime minister from hell.

RUMBLINGS OF DISCONTENT – 1961

Gale-force winds thundered throughout the agricultural valley near the border of Cienfuegos and Matanzas Provinces, southwest of Havana. The tops of towering royal palm trees sheared off and thick, leafy branches of cottonwoods, banyans and centuries-old oaks went tumbling crazily after overturned ranch carts, feed pails and wooden fences. Horses and cattle stomped nervously in the big barn and outlying lean-tos at the ranch.

Vaqueros, some of them on horseback, others afoot, rounded up calves in the wind-driven rain. Members of the ranchhouse staff scurried about, bringing out lanterns and candles from storage. Drinking water was drawn and put into big jugs, extra food supplies were wrapped and placed out of harm's way.

All of this in preparation for an out-of-season storm bearing down on Cuba's midsection from the Caribbean. Surely, not a hurricane in early Spring, but it paid to be prepared.

The cook and helpers who attended the members of three families living in the big house criss-crossed windows with tape and boards to keep them from shattering if the wind and rain gusts reached hurricane strength.

In the midst of all this came a pounding on the massive front door. Miguel Hidalgo hurried up and threw open the door to a soaked but grinning Jaime "Jimmy" Woods standing there in the quickly fading daylight.

"*Entra, hombre,*" Miguel called out to his friend, shouting to be heard above the roar of the howling wind and rain. "Come on in, Jimmy, I'll get you a dry shirt and jacket, amigo. What a time, eh?"

Although the timing of the visit was unexpected, Jimmy's intent was not. Miguel, Jimmy and the others had talked it all out before, and it hadn't taken much to convince Miguel to go along. They were to begin serious efforts to help overthrow Fidel Castro. And now was a time for action.

Their contribution would be small but significant in the overall picture, the stocky Jimmy had argued. Miguel was ready for anything that would damage the Castro regime in any way, particularly since he'd been arrested and kept incommunicado from his family for four days the previous month.

Suspicion of black market activities was the only explanation given by the G2 Security officers who had taken him away to Havana for interrogation. In the end, they had let him go, but with stern warning about the consequences for any such dealings in the future.

In the 1960s, when the government began instituting controls on food production and distribution, it held conferences throughout the agricultural areas, asking farmers and ranchers to adopt "a revolutionary conscience." This meant that they had to increase production but not sell their harvests on the open market, as they had been doing, or trade among themselves. The government was to set quotas and prices, and take most of their production.

Since their livelihoods depended on selling their commodities for profit, the farmers and ranchers quietly rebelled. A black market soon flourished. Many farmers and ranchers withheld some of their harvests to sell or trade. Government overseers were at first tolerant. They had a hard time keeping tabs on such activities, anyhow. But they began cracking down hard when the government instituted food rationing among the populace.

Miguel had been caught, and he and others were held out as examples to other farmers and ranchers.

For the serious, emotional Miguel, whose family had been in the farm and ranch business for generations, this was intolerable. He had a wife and a three-year-old daughter, and his brief detention convinced him to work against those "communist bastards who are now in control of our whole way of life."

Miguel's primary job was as a sugar mill engineer. As such, he was valuable to the Castro regime, which still relied on sugar as its number one export and foreign-exchange producer. But not valuable enough to be left alone by those *hijos de puta.*

Despite his relatively secure job, Miguel became a rebel whose blood boiled at the harsh conditions being imposed throughout Cuban society. He was a well-educated, idealistic young rancher who believed that Castro communists were setting the rules for everything, no matter how stupid they might be.

Along with their countrymen, the Hidalgo family suffered from the numerous new government restrictions and increasing threats to their daily lives. Miguel and his father, Francisco, had had their ranch confiscated but had been allowed to continue living and working there under the new rules for agricultural reform.

These conditions could be endured, perhaps, at least until the next government changeover. But the Cubans' most significant loss, Miguel believed, was their loss of freedom — freedom to come and go, to work their own land, to criticize, to get a fair hearing. No one else had previously denied them their personal rights during his lifetime. He viewed this as a sin, something that he could not tolerate, something that he had to fight to change.

He and several close friends organized a small number of farmers and ranchers into a *circulo* that met in secret to talk about their difficulties and what they could do to resolve some of the problems and help each other. The discussions soon became heated, and what started out as a small, rather benign fraternity, grew into a clandestine action group.

"Everything we're facing comes from the same source," the rural society's leader, Evaristo Melendez, had said at one of their last meetings.

"That source is our newest dictator in Havana, the one who everybody said was our savior, the one who was going to set us free from the corruption of Batista. Well, maybe he did, but he's bringing down on our heads a whole new set of problems. He wants to arbitrarily transform Cuban society into his own image, and he's going to trample over all of us in trying to do it."

With such sentiments, and with talk brewing about a possible invasion by the Yankees, it didn't take much to convince Miguel that now was a time for action.

Their efforts were puny and easily disregarded at first. But their numbers had grown in the past year. They had even organized small groups in other regions. Underground cells were already active in the capital. Rebellious students at the University of Havana were particularly active.

Now, Jimmy had made some contacts that would allow the ranchers and farmers to do something besides talk and complain about the circumstances. He informed Miguel he had become friendly with American expatriates who had asked him to supply information about Castro's military preparedness in the areas to the east and south of Havana, the sugarcane and citrus-growing country in the soft rolling hills where Jimmy's family had once farmed and raised livestock.

Jimmy, the son of an American father and Cuban mother, had dual citizenship, but he had lived in Cuba all his life. This was his home, and he didn't like what Fidel Castro and his people were doing to it. He had readily agreed to supply information to the Americans, and he found some willing help in Miguel and a half-dozen other of his longtime friends.

Miguel, too, was a Cuban patriot who loved his country, but his patriotism did not extend to the Castro regime, which began to break its promises to the people almost as soon as it took over from Batista.

Miguel and Jimmy were to report on new military installations, large troop movements and maneuvers, anything of a military or strategic nature taking place in the countryside around Havana. This was to be evaluated in the U.S., which was widely believed to be planning some kind of military operation against the Castro regime.

"*Vamos, chico,*" said Jimmy in his curious accent. Then, in English, "Let's take a drive."

Miguel kissed Joanna, his dark-haired wife who had come in from the kitchen to greet Jimmy.

"I've done all I can here for right now," Miguel told her, referring to precautions about the approaching storm. "The others are doing their job, and I'll be back before the night is over. Don't worry."

Joanna did worry, but she and Miguel had talked it all out, and she agreed that it was better to do something than just continue to accept the radical changes to their beloved Cuba being imposed by Castro, Che and the others.

"Cuidado, vayan con Dios," was all Joanna said.

Jimmy drove his battered Ford pickup carefully but at good speed through the rapidly darkening, hilly roads for about an hour before coming to one of the area's highest points. The rain had decreased to a heavy drizzle here.

Jimmy had brought binoculars, Miguel a battered but serviceable camera. It was their plan to survey the surrounding area as far as they could see and drive over it, both at night and during the daytime, observe and photograph anything out of the ordinary and then report any changes over the coming months.

"The next few months are critical for us," Jimmy told Miguel as they drove. "There will probably be all kinds of activity. There is a lot of talk about what Fidel is doing to reinforce the military installations and protect the coastlines. They say there are underwater caves with missiles, that Soviet troops are providing special training to set up antiaircraft guns and rockets."

"This is a hell of a night for seeing anything," Miguel replied, shaking his head slowly. "Why are we going out tonight? I thought we were going to your place to meet with your friends and plan things."

"That's out for now," said Jimmy with a grin. "When we start bringing in something, then we'll meet with my friends. . . and, it's better to start like this tonight," he added after a pause. "Nobody else is going to be out that doesn't have to be. You and me are looking for stray calves in a storm, *chico.* Call it a practice run. Once we get the layout of the area, the next few weeks will be easier."

FLIGHT TO FREEDOM

Miguel and Jimmy were busy over the next few weeks.

The exhilaration of taking positive steps against the Castro government, of participating in something he saw as meaningful in Cuba's turbulent history, was overpowering in Miguel. He was like a small boy carrying the burden of a big secret around with him. He felt liberated, somehow, from the tyranny of all those military jackals around him.

He and Jimmy had been successful beyond their expectations.

Over the past few weeks, they had reported to Jimmy's new friends both in person and by radio that there was a lot of military activity in Matanzas province, next door to Havana, and that anti-aircraft guns had been placed on the outskirts of the capital. Government patrol boats had increased surveillance around the fishing ports along Cuba's southern coast, and there was a large dredging operation taking place in the beautiful Bahía de Cienfuegos, which opens onto the Caribbean.

The two men were praised by Jimmy's "friends," and they were gratified they were seriously helping in a silent war which would one day see Fidel driven out of their beloved Cuba.

Then things started to go wrong.

On a cool night in mid-April 1961, Joanna was in the kitchen with Berta, the cook, after having put her daughter, to bed for the night. She and Miguel planned a get-together with two couples, who were neighbors from a nearby village, and several friends over from Havana. They would pool their resources and have a sumptuous *criollo* dinner: pork, black beans, white rice, yuca, salad and beer or rum. Afterward, there would be strong coffee.

Suddenly, the front door slammed, and before she could hurry out to greet her husband, Miguel was in the kitchen. He kissed her quickly and guided her by the arm back to the living room.

"Joanna, I don't have time to explain but I would like for you and Marina to go stay with your aunt and uncle in Fort Lauderdale. Get ready right away, please. I've already called your uncle Rodolfo and he knows you're coming."

"Wait, Miguel. Tell me what the problem is. What's happening?"

"They've arrested Jimmy. They may come after me. We've been helping the *contrarevolucionarios*, as you know," he told her in a single breath. "I don't want you here in case Jimmy and the others are forced to talk," Miguel explained. "I've made arrangements with Xavier, you know, Martinez. He's one of us. He'll fly his crop duster to Florida from Matanzas and take you two and his own wife and children. But it's got to be early in the morning, so we have to drive to the field near Matanzas pretty soon. He'll fly out at dawn. We can't afford to take a risk and wait to see what happens here. Xavier will make it. He'll get everybody to safety, I'm sure of that."

"But, Miguel," Joanna protested. "If you are arrested, I can help you better if I stay here."

"No, no. *Vamos*," he said gently, guiding her into the bedroom. "Let's pack and get ready to go. . . . I've been stupid, maybe, but I'd be even more so if I let you and Marina stay. These people are too eager to arrest anyone even suspected of working against them. We could all be charged with treason."

Then, taking her hands, he pulled her to him and said, "It may be that nothing will happen. I'll join you as soon as I can, or you can come back. Meanwhile, you will be safe in Florida with Rodolfo and Isabel. Let's hurry."

POLITICAL PRISONS

Two days later, as Miguel worked on a set of gears and other dismantled parts from the Buena Safra sugar mill, two men in civilian clothes drove up in an army vehicle.

"Miguel Hidalgo?"

"Yes."

"We want you to come with us."

"Where? Why?"

"We're going to Havana. We're from G2."

Those were almost the only words spoken on the trip into the capital.

That's the way things were being done now. Anyone suspected of "plotting against the state" would be approached at any hour and told that G2 wanted to question him or her. He or she was driven away, usually not to be seen or heard from until days, or weeks later, if ever.

Sometimes, when the suspect would simply disappear, persistent relatives or friends might find out months later that he or she had been tried, convicted and executed, or that detainee was serving twenty or thirty years at the dreaded Isle of Pines, at La Cabaña, or one of the other concentration camps for political prisoners sprouting up throughout the island.

Where, when, why was arbitrary — this was the new "justice" handed down by Fidel Castro's revolutionary government.

"Crimes against the state" . . . "Counterrevolutionary activities" . . . "Conspiring against the government" . . . These catchall charges meant the same thing, perhaps to different degrees. Broad enough phrases to encompass almost anything that might be suspected as opposition to *La Revolucion.*

Miguel and Jimmy were among many thousands of suspects being rounded up in a broad sweep across the island by Interior Ministry troops and G2 officials in mid-April 1961.

Signs of rebellion had increased throughout the island: a bombing here; the theft of military weapons and vehicles there; more men, women and children risking their lives by setting sail to Florida aboard leaky vessels. In Havana, a terrorist bomb exploded in the capital's largest department store, El Encanto, another near the PepsiCola factory. A few days later, another blast destroyed the seven-story building housing the department store along with other businesses.

In mid-April 1961, "mystery" planes strafed and bombed Cuban airfields at Ciudad Libertad in Havana, in San Antonio de los Baños and in Santiago.

Invasion jitters swept the island, fueled by Castro's long speeches against the Yankees and his growing list of Latin American "lackeys."

Fidel had launched the third year of his revolution in January, expressing deep anger about the trend toward a Latin American quarantine of Cuba and what he called anti-revolutionary fervor in the United States. He placed his military forces on full alert against what he called Washington-inspired aggression.

In his New Year's Day speech from Campo Libertad, the Army headquarters from which deposed dictator Fulgencio Batista fled on Jan. 1, 1959, the bearded Castro claimed that the United States was ready to carry out an armed invasion against the island. He dispatched Foreign Minister Raul Roa to New York to call for action against the U.S. by The United Nations Security Council.

The massive number of arrests in Cuba intensified in April when several old World War II American bombers hit several targets on the outskirts of Havana.

On April 17, 1961, Cuban exiles trained by the CIA mounted an invasion at the Bahia de Cochinos, the Bay of Pigs. Castro's military reacted quickly. It had been expecting something like this. As 1,400 troops invaded at the poorly chosen swampy beachhead on Cuba's southern coast,. The Cuban regime responded with thousands of troops and artillery.

Government supporters throughout the country went on a rampage against anyone suspected of cooperating with the exiles or participating in any rebellious activities. Thousands of men and women suspected of "crimes against the state" were rounded up and herded into the large Havana Sports Stadium, into auditoriums, moviehouses, jails and prisons. These "internal foes" of the revolution eventually included a number of Americans, businessmen and professional people who had been Cuban residents with their families for years.

Hundreds of summary executions were carried out under the direction of Che Guevara, who personally shot a number of suspected *rebeldes* at La Cabaña, where he originally made his headquarters.

Among those arrested were three Roman Catholic priests at a church where American currency and a small cache of weapons were found.

The day before the invasion, a B-26 aircraft flying from Nicaragua bombed San Antonio de Los Baños Air Base and strafed Havana as part of the invaders' attack. The plane was shot down by the Cubans. There were about a dozen sporadic sorties by B-26 aircraft over Cuba during that week.

The bombing missions failed to have much of an impact on the Cuban Air Force, which was considered a primary target. The Air Force actually was in a rebuilding process and had more planes than pilots. There weren't any defections by Cuban pilots, some of whom had been training in Soviet MIG jetfighters. CIA planners and invasion leaders also expected a substantial number of desertions by members of Castro's army, but they failed to take place.

Anti-aircraft fire brought down an airplane piloted by an American who had bombed infantry forces and a small airfield in the south-central region of the country. Official Cuban reports said a total of nine aircraft were shot down during the attack by "mercenaries." Several of the fliers were later identified as Americans.

The invasion of *Brigada 2506* turned out to be a disaster for the exiles, the American CIA and the new administration of John F. Kennedy. Officials at the CIA said, after the fact, that they had been unaware of Cuba's preparations for an invasion.

It was a major victory for Fidel Castro, but there were long-term consequences. Although the Cuban Army was victorious — killing or wounding some 200 of the invaders and capturing 1,200 within seventy-two hours — the reign of terror against the general populace to root out dissidents was to be a heavy chain around Castro's neck for many years.

Curiously, there are few accounts of Fidel Castro actually killing someone. His brother Raul and Che were more than willing to carry out individual punishments, including executions and mass slaughters before, during and after the Castro takeover of the government. Of course, Fidel sent many men to the *paredon* and had others killed on the spot on his order, but he did little of that personally. In his post-revolutionary days, in fact, Fidel tried hard to acquire a reputation of a benevolent dictator. But he later proved himself to be vengeful against suspected enemies. At that period, brother Raul was the shifty eyed menace in the background.

The whole issue of political prisoners weakened the Cuban leader's credibility in the world community, however, and it cast a large blot on claims that his was a popular revolution to transform Cuban society for the better.

The wave of arrests of those in any way suspected of assisting the enemy, directly or indirectly, led to the establishment of hundreds of prisons, concentration camps, work farms and similar facilities.

Among these prisoners were Miguel Hidalgo and Jaime "Jimmy" Woods.

Others faced an even grimmer fate. For example, two Americans and seven Cubans who had been arrested in early roundups and charged with transporting weapons were executed by firing squads in Havana on the day of the invasion.

The Americans were identified by the Cubans as Howard Anderson, father of four children, and Angus McNair Jr., both of Miami. Anderson had been arrested on his return to Cuba after taking his wife and children to the United States.

A number of hasty claims by Cuban exiles and CIA sources in the United States that Castro had been killed or incapacitated by the invaders were spurious. Castro and his military leaders proved to be ably prepared, and they reacted quickly and forcefully to the invasion. Later newsreels and photographs showed the "maximum leader" in battle dress at the Bay of Pigs, on foot and in army vehicles, directing the cleanup operations and the roundup of prisoners.

A communiqué signed by Castro and broadcast over Havana radio on April 20, three days after the invasion, said the exile attackers "suffered heavy casualties (while) dispersing in a swamp area from which no escape is possible . . . Large quantities of arms of American manufacture were captured."

The communiqué also disclosed that government forces experienced "a high toll of courageous lives" but no numbers were given. The invaders included "many sons of the rich" who had fled Cuba shortly after the Castro takeover.

Indeed, a son of counterrevolutionary leader Jose Miro Cardóna and the sons of exile rebel leaders Antonio de Varona and Dr. Antonio Maceo were among members of Brigada 2506, as were the sons of other prominent Cuban émigrés. Also among those captured were several sons and other relatives of officials who had been with the Batista regime.

"We thought the Cuban militia and the army would join with us," Cardóna's son, Jose Miro Torres, admitted on Cuban television three days after the invasion. Another prisoner said the troops were told by the CIA that there would be a general uprising of the Cuban population when they landed on the island.

There was no uprising.

The fighting lasted barely three days.

Miro Torres and other prisoners publicly questioned on Cuban TV said the invasion force had left Puerto Cabezas, Nicaragua, aboard five merchant ships escorted by a frigate and later joined by two destroyers.

The Cuban capital itself was somber during the invasion, jittery but relatively quiet. Trucks, buses, jeeps and private cars rolled through, transporting troops and artillery south toward the front. Army and militia troops reinforced security at government buildings.

The citizenry was bewildered, but many had expected some kind of an attack. Residents had heard sporadic gunfire or bomb blasts for days. Some went into hiding, fearing they would be picked up by authorities. Unless it was necessary to venture out into the streets, most Habaneros stayed at home, and even foreign diplomats were restricted from traveling. Radio and television listeners in Miami, Key West and other Florida coastal communities twirled their dials and tried to tune into Havana broadcasts for news about what was happening and what was ahead.

Cuba's military strength was evident everywhere; it had been seriously underestimated by the CIA and exile leaders. Firing squads in several of the major prisons were busy, and the roundup of foreign nationals and Cubans suspected of sympathizing with the rebels continued for months.

From Moscow, Soviet Premier Nikita Khrushchev boomed out his support for Castro. But he didn't repeat his earlier pledges to shower rockets on Americans who did battle against his Caribbean friends. President Kennedy warned the Soviet Union bluntly to stay out of the situation.

A PRISONER OF THE REVOLUTION

Virtually incommunicado, Miguel knew little about the exile invasion but suspected there had finally been some sort of uprising against Fidel, at least that was his hope as he was taken to Havana. Otherwise, he thought, all of this would be meaningless. He mulled his circumstances as he rode to G2 headquarters with the two grim-faced, nameless strangers.

He was guilty, he knew. He had violated laws. But he also knew that many others who were picked up and given long prison sentences, even executed, were guilty of nothing more serious than associating with suspected *contrarevolucionarios*. Or they just happened to be at the wrong place at the wrong time. He'd been lucky once, but he was doomed now, he believed.

Had Jimmy been forced to talk? Had the others? Perhaps they had arrested him for associating with "suspicious elements," another of the regime's vicious phrases.

The more he thought, the more tightly fear enveloped him. What would become of him, of his wife and child? What about his work as an engineer at the sugar mill and as supervisor on the state-confiscated ranch which his family had carved out of the wilderness? He had failed them all, he thought.

And what is to become of our country with people like this giving the orders?

The Revolution. It had started so well. Fidel Castro, who became so idolized, had triumphantly traveled the length of the island into Havana after Batista fled. Girls threw flowers in his path, old women cried and called him savior. He was the same age as Jesus at the time of the crucifixion, some said, and he looked like him. He, too, wore a beard. He promised social change, a new order, justice for the poor.

Fidel was welcomed by those who knew that their beloved island was in a grievous state and badly in need of change from Batista. In public, he was praised by politicians and the rank-and-file of government servants, by the local press and the clergy. Less friendly were the rich, the landholders and the big businessmen. But what could they do? They had to go along with it, to see what happened.

After all, this wasn't the first revolution in Cuba. And sooner or later, the ruling class always became like the previous one; give it time. Many Cubans believed this was just another power struggle, a changeover in names and faces in the palace. Everyone knew Batista was getting too big a crook for anybody's comfort. Even the Americans wanted him out.

Viva la Revolucion!

"Where is your family? Why did they leave the country?" the questions resounded over and over in Miguel's semiconscious brain as he lay groaning on the floor where he fell from his chair after blows to the head and shoulders. Suddenly, Miguel knew, he was at G2's infamous "interrogation center" in the ritzy suburb of Miramar, and there were no laws or human rights policies observed here, in this place of torture.

"If you are as innocent as you say, why are they gone?"

His inquisitors had been at it for two days. They had found out about his and Jimmy's information-gathering activities. He, Jimmy and the others would be tried as spies and executed, his jailers told him. He might as well confess, tell them everything about their collaboration with the American CIA and perhaps they would be allowed to live, maybe even return to their former lives eventually.

"*Dale en los cojones otra vez*," let him have it in the balls again, the jefe ordered. Two men held him down on a bench similar to a doctor's examining table. Another guard jammed the electric prod to Miguel's genitals.

The screams reverberated throughout the building until Miguel passed out again.

Much later, his own screams woke him. He'd been undergoing the merciless torture and interrogation in his nightmares after finally having been returned to his cramped cell and allowed to sleep. Miguel found himself lying on a stinking mattress on the floor. A narrow window about eight feet from the floor let in what appeared to be early morning light.

As close as he could tell, he'd been subjected to almost three days and nights of interrogation, interspersed with threats, fists and electric shocks.

He wasn't sure what he'd told them, but it couldn't have been much more than what they already knew. His only thoughts now were that if he was lucky, he had undergone the worst of it until his trial. After that, he might even welcome *el paredon.*

He considered his life finished, all because he was a Cuban caught up in a revolution.

In school and at the university, he'd dismissed the often-exaggerated historical tales of Cuba's violent, revolution-filled past. Exploits of the country's most-revered heroes — Jose Martí, Antonio Maceo and others — had barely stirred him.

He considered himself different, aloof from the country's political past, perhaps because most of the evils were centered in Havana, the capital, and he'd always considered himself a rancher, an educated one, for sure, but a totally apolitical rancher nevertheless.

Political, business and social intrigues and ambitions were for others, not for him. Even in his own time, the machinations which had brought Grau San Martin, Prio Socarrás and Batista in and out of power in Havana had had little personal meaning. His heart, his family and interests were in a world apart: the farm and ranch country of Matanzas and Cienfuegos.

But all that was before Fidel Castro. Slowly but surely, he had been caught up in the fervor and later devastated by the Castro regime's failures and the never-ending violence of the life around him. This became personal, for him and his family, as well as the whole of Cuba. He had then started to believe that this reign of terror could not be tolerated.

Now, he had become entangled in it and might lose his life, alone, anonymously, as so many others had.

PRISON HORRORS

One of Edward Brophy's priorities as Havana correspondent was to piece together information about Cuba's vast number of political prisoners, including Americans, serving long sentences at institutions scattered throughout the island and the Isle of Pines.

Horror stories about the treatment of these "enemies of the people," their often-brutal interrogations and tortures, had circulated for years both inside and outside of Cuba. On the whole, most of the accounts came from within the prison walls, from the inmates themselves in smuggled notes and detailed letters written in tiny manuscript on tissue paper. Relatives allowed to visit the inmates also provided some of the details.

Little by little, these accounts added up to a searing indictment of the inhumane treatment of those convicted — some on the flimsiest evidence — of counter-revolutionary activities. Many specific cases were documented and denounced by various international bodies, including the Human Rights Commission of the United Nations, the Organization of American States, the International Commission of Jurists, and Amnesty International.

Cuba's only response to the allegations was silence. It was unmoved by the critics and the lengthy reports, and the regime never responded to international inquiries about the conditions or the numbers of prisons and prisoners. The Castro regime ignored it all.

The number of political prisoners was estimated at 30,000 to 40,000 at its peak in the mid-1960s. Cuban exile leaders put the figure at upwards of 50,000, even 100,000. In 1965, Fidel admitted to a visiting journalist that there were 20,000 men and women serving sentences for "antirevolutionary crimes." There were reports of as many as 150 prison facilities, ranging from concentration camps to prison farms, scattered throughout the country.

Although Cuba is a big island, it was a tight society, especially so in the mid-1960s. One way or another, the miserable plight of the prisoners was an open secret among the general populace. But there could be little open protest in a police state.

It was almost impossible to find a family who had not had its life turned upside down by the revolution. If there were 50,000 political prisoners, or even half that, there were many times that number of relatives and close friends of these detainees.

Add to that the increasing numbers of people who had left, legally or illegally and who now called themselves political exiles in Miami, New York, Union City, even Denver, Salt Lake City and Albuquerque. Each person who fled left behind relatives, friends, associates, employees and acquaintances. Then, there were those who willingly stayed in Cuba and were undergoing a shockingly different, sometimes traumatic, daily existence. Many had lost businesses, homes, land.

Even the loyal Castro supporters, and there were many, were enduring privations.

In effect, Fidel Castro had had an overpowering, long-lasting effect on all of the Cuban population. It was easy to see, then, why Cuba had become a police state; Castro and his supporters had to make it so in order to retain control and stay in power.

No other change of government, legal or illegal, in Cuba's turbulent history had ever wrought such changes.

Under these conditions, there existed an "us and them" mentality on many issues, which were determined individually by each and every Cuban. A black market came into existence because of these conditions — a black market not just of material things such as food and the unlawful exchange of pesos for foreign currency, but a black market of information, of ideas, of plans and hopes.

And in this distrustful atmosphere, everyone was always looking over his shoulder, keeping an eye out for the regime's watchdogs. People often would turn and walk away from a trusted friend if he or she was accompanied by someone whom they didn't know, or if there was a suspicious person nearby. Ed encountered this more than once, and in the beginning was mystified by it. But he quickly came to understand.

One of Ed's dispatches pointed out that one out of every four Cubans was a government informant. The national director of the Committees for the Defense of the Revolution (CDR) disclosed in mid-1965 that the organization of neighborhood spies had more than two million members. Cuba's population was about eight million at the time.

Castro had established the CDR in 1960 as "a system of collective vigilance for every apartment building, every city block, every neighborhood . . . to protect ourselves from counter-revolutionaries and the imperialists."

The neighborhood informants had done their work well during the Bay of Pigs and its aftermath, as many of the political prisoners could now attest.

One way or another, those who had relatives and close friends as political prisoners often knew each other and exchanged information about the different institutions and camps and the conditions under which the prisoners lived, about who had been tortured and executed, about who had become leaders whose wills were still unbroken by their jailers.

In a sense, Ed was fortunate in his quietly persistent quest for information. Among those Cubans who had occasionally been employed by the AP office in Havana, in the pre-Castro 1950s, was an elderly gentleman who now became extremely helpful. Dr. Adan Rivero was a lawyer who in the 1950s had drawn up contracts for The AP's news services supplied to Cuban newspapers and radio stations. After Ed arrived, Dr. Rivero would drop into the office from time-to-time, cordially greet Blake outside and exchange a friendly word or two with Wilson, busy at his routine tasks, before knocking discreetly on the open door to the correspondent's office.

Despite crippling arthritis and other ailments which caused him to walk slowly, painfully, with the assistance of a cane, Dr. Rivero managed to get around and pick up the latest rumor on the street. He had influential friends who often provided small snippets of inside information about the regime. He and the reporter would chat amiably and at length. Ed found him a fountain of information about his native Cuba, its history, politics and current conditions.

The two became close friends.

During his second visit, Dr. Rivero confided that his only son, now in his mid-thirties, had been a political prisoner since 1961 and was now at the Isle of Pines. With his deep-set brown eyes blinking away tears, he described how he was allowed to visit his son once a month, and the dreadful conditions he found him in.

Ramon Rivero was one of the *plantados*, the recalcitrants who refused communist indoctrination in exchange for better treatment and the possibility of getting their sentences reduced.

Dr. Rivero was greatly worried about his son's worsening physical and mental state.

"I often find my son with fresh wounds and bruises on his face, on his shoulders and legs," he said quietly, almost whispering. "Most of the time, he's wearing only his undershorts. He has a long beard, he's got some kind of stomach or liver disease and he's thinner every time I see him. He says he will die before accepting indoctrination."

Ed then confided to Dr. Rivero the story of his half-brother, Miguel Hidalgo. He told the elderly man about how he had been informed of it by the Foreign Ministry official. Miguel had been imprisoned because he was a *contrarevolucionario*, but that was all Ed knew. He believed Miguel was hauled off during or shortly after the Bay of Pigs invasion, but that he couldn't determine his status now.

The reporter had managed to find out that Miguel's wife and daughter had left Cuba and now lived somewhere in California. He couldn't contact them. Miguel's father Francisco was dead, and Ed had been unable to find anyone in Cuba who could give him any information without disclosing his personal interest.

With the help of Dr. Rivero, Ed soon slowly tapped into the network of prisoner families. He was able to obtain disparate pieces of information about prison conditions and about some of the more widely known inmates.

Finally, he could begin tracing his brother through the vast prison system. What he might do after he found out where he was, Ed didn't know. Any contact, given their relationship and Ed's job, could be dangerous for both.

Among the Americans serving long prison sentences, he discovered, was Lawrence Kirby Lunt of Santa Fe, New Mexico. Lunt, who had a

Belgian wife and three children, had been the administrator of farm holdings in western Cuba's Pinar Del Rio Province since the mid-1950s. He was secretly tried by a revolutionary tribunal along with several Cubans.

The government charged that Lunt, then thirty-eight years old, had contacted the CIA in Washington on one of his frequent trips to the United States and arranged to furnish economic, political and military information from Cuba. He did this for several years, the Cubans alleged, along with recruiting Cubans to report on military movements.

Lunt, who was a former U.S. Army officer, denied it all. But he was serving a thirty-year sentence. His well-to-do Belgian father-in-law tried unsuccessfully for years to free him from prison.

Another prominent American in a Cuban prison at that time was Frank Emmick of Toledo, Ohio, who was bustling around the American Club in Havana in October, 1963, when G2 agents burst in and arrested him on charges of espionage.

Emmick, a short, red-haired look-alike to actor Mickey Rooney, was president of the American Club. He protested his innocence, but the government claimed he provided information to the CIA. Emmick suffered two heart attacks while serving a thirty-year prison sentence. He was forty-eight years old when arrested.

Rafael del Pino, born in Cuba and a naturalized U.S. citizen, had been a boyhood friend of Fidel Castro and later served in the U.S. Army in Korea. He was attempting to land a light plane on a highway near Havana in July 1960 when he was shot down. Legal efforts to free him by prominent American attorney James B. Donovan were rejected by the Cubans.

Donovan was later instrumental in gaining the release of all of the Bay of Pigs captives.

In mid-1965, CBS Corespondent Bert Quint was arrested in Havana upon his return after a short leave in Mexico City. He spent fourteen hours in a 9-by-6-foot cell before he was released and returned to Mexico. His crime was that he was "against the revolution," but there was no elaboration. Quint was the son of George Quint, a former staff member of The Associated Press.

There were other Americans and many once-prominent Cubans in Castro prisons.

Dr. Rivero was a well-educated, highly intelligent man and the soul of discretion, especially in matters concerning political prisoners because he knew that any repercussions would be suffered by his captive son. But he and others slowly opened up to Ed about the penal conditions and the sufferings of inmates, particularly of those who adamantly refused to admit to any wrongdoing in exchange for better treatment — *los plantados.*

These plantados were strong-willed men, along with a number of female prisoners, who held steadfast to their ideals and refused to change or bend their principles in any way. These prisoners usually could be found in the concentration camps and fortresses with the harshest conditions and most brutal guards.

Among the toughest institutions, which were carrying out "trials" and executions, were La Cabaña and Castillo del Principe, both in Havana; the infamous complex at the Isle of Pines, southeast of the Cuban mainland in the Caribbean; and Boniato in Oriente Province. The Isle of Pines is considered by many scholars to be Robert Louis Stevenson's fabled *Treasure Island.*

Many of the plantados were held in damp windowless cells. They were in poor health, subjected to biological and psychological experiments and often beaten and tortured. Many were in rags or in total nudity after having rejected the prison uniforms their captors demanded they wear. Some rebelled by going on hunger strikes that lasted for weeks.

Many other political prisoners confessed to "crimes against the people" and sometimes implicated others. In exchange, they were treated less harshly. They were submitted to various forms of "rehabilitation." Usually, they were "indoctrinated" in Marxism-Leninism and sometimes sent off to work on prison farms or sugarcane fields. Eventually, some could expect to have their long sentences reduced by a few years.

FROM BARBUDOS TO BUREAUCRATS

Juanita Castro's eyes flashed fire.

Fidel's sister was secretly preparing to leave her country, to become another political expatriate like so many of her compatriots who had managed to flee their homeland for reasons economic, political or familial.

"Fidel is a traitor to Cuba," she told a small group of friends gathered in a stuffy, crowded Havana apartment in 1964. "He will bleed our country dry to satisfy his megalomania . . . His arrogance, which was apparent from a very early age, has led him to communism. And, you know that communists seek total control over everything, especially your daily lives and dreams."

Miss Castro, several years younger than her brother, had assisted him and a small group of friends from their university days when they were still forming their ideas about a Cuba free of dictatorship and corruption. She continued her support after Fidel's forced exile and his return from Mexico as a rebel leader in the Sierra Maestra mountains of southeastern Cuba.

So she was shocked, she confided to her closest friends, when her brother's totalitarianism came to the fore shortly after he took power from Batista.

"We were greatly worried. He wouldn't listen to anybody. He won't even see me. Now, some of us can no longer take it."

Just before she left for Mexico City, she told Ed in an interview, "I have to choose between communism and my conscience. But I have to leave my country to prove where my allegiance lies. It's certainly not in Cuba with Fidel. . . I have to leave here to get my voice heard, to get the world to listen to what a monster he is."

The life of a Cuban was very much complicated by Fidel Castro, one way or another. Many who stayed put were active supporters of Fidel and the promising new world of what they then believed would be a combination of Socialism and old world Capitalism. After Batista, almost anything was worth a try.

Some who stayed — to borrow a phrase from the *New York Times* in a different context — "did not have the education or skills to leave, or were fiercely attached" to their families and their homeland.

Some, of course, were well-educated people of professional classes; some retirees who didn't want to get involved; and then, there were the fast-growing young who couldn't leave, although many may have wanted to.

A month or so later after her exit, Juanita Castro was in exile in Mexico. From there, she made her way to Miami. She became an outspoken critic of her brother's policies and an untiring advocate for exiles seeking the overthrow of the Castro regime — despite the earlier American-led fiasco at the Bay of Pigs.

Later in 1964, Castro surprisingly acknowledged some of Cuba's problems. He blamed them on "inexperience, incompetence, superficiality and irresponsibility" by some of his most-trusted associates, the leaders of his revolution. Fidel had the largest stake in the master plan to transform Cuba, of course, and he hated any incompetence or indifference to that credo.

It hadn't taken long for the astute Fidel to learn how to govern, but many of those closest to him never did, or did so after years of frustration in changing over from guerrillas to become civic and military leaders. Many of them assumed some of the most important positions of power in the new leadership structure. But the early years were as bewildering to some of them as they seemed to the outside world.

As a young rebel, Fidel had led an ill-conceived, badly carried-out attack on the Batista Army's well-fortified Moncada Barracks in Santiago on July 26, 1953. Eight of the motley band of attackers were killed and a dozen wounded. It was so poorly planned Fidel had never even seen the garrison beforehand and had only a hazy idea how it was laid out. For instance, the poorly led group was so incompetent it attacked the garrison's barbershop thinking that it was the weapons armory.

Fidel, in fact, led from behind; he was never actively involved in the action and didn't fire a shot. Most of the attackers were easily captured and jailed.

Fidel was tracked down several days later and imprisoned. Along with the other plotters, he was sentenced to fifteen years at La Cabaña. Instead, they went to the huge prison complex at the Isle of Pines, off Cuba's southern Cuban coast. There, Fidel spent much of the next two years in isolation, reading a lot, writing letters and polishing a grand manifesto on the order of Hitler's *Mein Kampf.*

Castro's manuscript was later published under the title *La Historia Me Absolvera,* "History Will Absolve Me." Much like Hitler's long work, it was to become the symbol of his rebellion.

Widespread word of the brazen attack on the Moncada Barracks did provide some impetus for others, however. It helped give rise to the July 26th Movement and similar organizations composed of young people, most of them students at the University of Havana who wanted the Batista government overthrown. After that, who knew?

Fidel was freed from prison by Batista under a general amnesty in May 1955.

He soon joined his brother Raul in exile in Mexico City, where they eventually recruited Che Guevara and a smattering of other disaffected Cuban exiles. Eighty-two men then "invaded" Cuba from the Mexican coast, on November 25, 1955, aboard a battered 21-meter yacht. The crossing nearly became a disaster and the landing on December 2, 1956, has been described as more of a shipwreck than an invasion. The yacht named Granma ran aground on Cuba's marshy southwestern coast.

These distant facts raced through Ed's mind as he sat listening to Fidel speechifying to a Havana conference of the Cuban Labor Confederation in 1964. He was talking about some of the regime's shortcoming and mistakes in the earlier period.

"We are not going to undervalue the importance of the imperialist blockade," Fidel told the labor group, speaking particularly about the tension-filled days in October, 1962.

But, he admonished, it was an overall lack of experience by his revolutionaries-turned-bureaucrats that led to some of the administrative and longterm problems in the first years of the revolution. He did not go into these details publicly. However, he boasted to heavy applause from the labor delegates that "the aggressions of our enemies have resulted in a great improvement in our armed forces."

Incidentally, that meeting was held in what later was named Cine Charles Chaplin, named for good ol' Charlie of Hollywood silent movie fame. The movie theater previously had been named Blanquita, the Cine Atlantic and the Cine Karl Marx. In the 1960s, it hosted the few open meetings of the Central Committee of the Cuban Communist Party. More recently it was the site of internationally famous performances ranging from Billy Joel's troupe to Moscow's Bolshoi Ballet.

As if to underscore the importance of better management and a greater sense of responsibility that he demanded, Castro fired three Cabinet members during the year for "administrative errors." Economic Minister Regino Boti and Foreign Trade Minister Alberto Mora were booted from their posts and sent off to the provinces.

The third official fired was Labor Minister Augusto Martinez Sanchez, who then attempted suicide. Martinez Sanchez, who fought alongside Fidel during their guerrilla days, shot himself in the head "after being relieved for serious administrative mistakes," an official communiqué announced. But, Castro and President Osvaldo Dorticós soon added that "these errors in no way affected his (Martinez Sanchez') personal, moral and revolutionary honor, and his unquestionable loyalty to our cause."

Those early years of the Castro regime also were beset by all manner of conspiracies, mostly from outside the island: political intrigues within the government, a CIA-led "Dirty Tricks Operation," half-assed assassination plots, exile incursions.

Overcoming them all, the Castro regime began shifting its foreign policy. After years of ignoring what went on around it, Cuba began focusing its attention on Third World nations.

Egged on by Communist Party hardliners such as Blas Roca and by the increasingly restless Che Guevara, Castro began courting African nations such as Angola, Guinea, Mozambique, Algeria, Mali and Morocco.

Cuba started out by establishing embassies and missions, seeking closer economic, political and cultural ties, starting with Africa and later in Latin America.

Primarily, it was providing assistance to insurrectionists. These efforts were directed by Guevara. No longer would the Castro regime just sit back and fight off the conspiracies at home. It would take its anti-imperialist fight around the world.

Guevara would spend weeks touring and meeting with leaders in these African countries, urging "a common front against imperialism" and declaring that Cuba should serve as an example to others as an anti-imperialist stronghold.

Much like what the Soviet Union was doing for Cuban students, the Cubans now began offering scholarships for African students in Havana. Cuba also began sending medical teams and teachers to some of the African areas and, later to a few Latin American countries. Some of these delegations often included government agents.

More clandestinely, Guevara began making overtures to dissidents in Latin America. He offered guerrilla training and arms to help overthrow oligarchies and what the Cubans called stooge governments propped up by American imperialism.

The CIA reported at that time that the Cuban leadership had created "a highly professional espionage and subversion agency" that was trying to overthrow the governments of Venezuela, Guatemala and Colombia.

Communism had suffered reverses in Brazil, Chile and British Guiana at the time, but "the export of revolution continues to be a key policy of the Castro regime," a CIA report said in mid-1965.

Meanwhile, Castro and company were continuing to play the Soviet Union against the United States, and both against Communist China, which was beginning to make its presence felt among Third World countries, including many in Latin America.

Ed kept trying to interview Castro, to pin down his personal political views. He attempted to determine whether Castro was trying to transform the Caribbean island into another satellite of the Soviet Union or as a fervent hotbed for revolutionaries of all stripes.

In the brief encounters with the prime minister at social and official functions, Ed would try to convince him that Castro's ideas should be

Isaac M. Flores

publicly spelled out for the benefit of newspaper readers around the world. This could best be done in an interview.

Castro would nod, smile and wave off such entreaties, saying "I will tell you what we are doing along with everybody else . . . We are constantly talking to the people."

While Castro proclaimed himself a socialist and later a communist, he was always a self-styled "Fidelista" rather than a dogmatic believer in Karl Marx, Lenin or the other theorists. He tailored socialism and communism to the tropics, to his own ideas and to whatever he believed were Cuba's needs. In time, he exasperated — and often outfoxed — Khrushchev, Yeltsin, Gorbachev and Brezhnev as well as China's Mao and U.S. Presidents Eisenhower, JFK, Johnson, Nixon, Ford, Carter, Reagan, Bush and Clinton.

In 1961, he told the Italian communist newspaper *Unita* that his revolution was "fighting for the final liquidation of the exploitation of man by man and for the construction of a quite new society, dominated by a new class."

Then, he went on, "The Americans and the priests say this is communism. We know full well that this is not so. And yet, we are not afraid of the word."

But at one time, he *had* been afraid of that word, and he imprisoned or executed close battlefield friends who discovered their revolutionary ideals had been betrayed by Fidel. They called him a communist, and he punished them. Matos, Menoyo, Camilo Cienfuegos and others are examples of his betrayals. Later, of course, he acknowledged publicly that he truly was: a socialist and then a self-styled communist.

Times change and lives are lost because of it, Ed Brophy wrote.

While he was creating his own world of Fidelismo, Castro continued to strengthen his ties to the Soviet Union although he was greatly disappointed by Khrushchev's abrupt turnabout during the October, 1962, missile crisis.

After keeping the world on the edge of war for two weeks, Khrushchev pulled back his intermediate range ballistic missiles and removed the Soviet Union's not-so-secret rocket emplacements on the Caribbean island ninety miles from the United States.

The Soviet pullback came, of course, after President John F. Kennedy began stopping Soviet shipping enroute to Cuba and threatening to bomb the missile sites. As part of the Soviet-American agreement, Kennedy promised not to invade Cuba.

Castro, however, suffered a major embarrassment over the missiles. He admitted in 1964 that it was his idea to put the IRBMs on the island. He certainly didn't want to give them up, and he thought the Soviet leader had capitulated too quickly. He wanted to threaten and talk about it endlessly.

This all took place, of course, shortly after Castro had achieved a major propaganda victory and instant world recognition by repelling the CIA-backed invasion of Cuban exiles in the marshes of the *Bahia de Cochinos,*

But all of that was now old business.

Now, in the mid-1960s, the Castro bureaucrats were hard at work trying to repair the damage they had wrought in Cuba's economy, in its trade relations and in the production of basic consumer goods. Rationing of everything from shoes to rice, even cigars, milk and rum, was playing havoc with the normally stoic Cubans. Blackouts were common, running water was an iffy thing, transportation and housing were strained to the limits.

The new leaders were, however, making progress in the fields of education and health care, which had received priority emphasis and were being extended to everyone throughout the island. The Agrarian Reform Act confiscated large landholdings and made hundreds of tenant farmers new land owners throughout the country.

While Soviet military and economic aid was flowing into the island, the Soviet military was then training the Cuban Army to take over control of their surface-to-air missiles, short-range tactical missiles, and anti-aircraft and coast guard defenses. The Soviets equipped the Cuban Army. It supplied MiG jetfighters and trained a squadron of Cuban pilots.

Soviet technicians and military troops numbered 12,000-15,000 in the 1960s, plus hundreds of embassy personnel. The Soviets had their own housing, schools and clubs in Havana and in several cities in the interior.

Along with the Soviets, other East-European countries increased their trade with Cuba, extending the island highly favorable, subsidized terms. The Soviet bloc aid and subsidies, including military equipment and supplies, were estimated to total some $3 billion a year at one point.

Ed found the Havana port crowded with freighters from the Soviet Union, East Germany, Czechoslovakia, Poland and Hungary, among others. Dockworkers and *milicianos* unloaded heavy equipment, trucks, road graders, buses, power generators, refrigerators and vehicles, along with numerous military supplies and boxes of weapons and ammunition.

In those days, Soviets and East Europeans filled the streets, hotels, bars and restaurants of Old Havana. Portraits of Khrushchev and Lenin hung alongside posters of Fidel and Che in some places. "*Tovarich*" and "*drushba*" were among the greetings mixed in with "*amigos*" and "*compañeros*."

Che Guevara was unusually sanguine about Soviet economic aid.

In a March, 1964, interview on ABC's "Issues and Answers" program, Guevara said Cuba and the Soviet Union both recognized the value of their trade partnership.

"The (American) blockade has taught us how to manage our economy in the future," Guevara said about efforts to expand agricultural production and negotiate bilateral trade agreements with other nations.

Asked what would happen if Soviet aid were to stop, Guevara pondered for a moment, then said, "If you refer to all our exchange, then I can answer that the life of the country would be paralyzed. For example, oil: All of our oil, almost four million tons, comes from the Soviet Union."

But, he said Cuba was paying for it with sugar and other products. Although this was essentially true, Cuba was receiving special prices and heavy subsidies in all of its trade contracts with the Soviet bloc.

Agricultural production in Cuba had received a sharp setback earlier in the year when Hurricane Isabel virtually wiped out the tobacco crop and ravaged fruit and vegetable crops in a sweep across the rich growing region of Pinar del Rio Province.

In December of 1964, while attending a session of the United Nations, Guevara appeared on CBS' "Face the Nation" television program in his camouflage fatigues, boots and beret.

Asked about the tensions between the two countries, Guevara said he would like to see better relations with the United States. But, "If we have to kneel for peace, they will have to kill us first."

Meanwhile, Cuba's neighbors were not at all happy with how Castro was stirring the political pot in the Caribbean. Daily newspaper reports detailed some of the intrigue. Some countries were extremely agitated by how Cubans were providing direct assistance and indirect support and inspiration to some of the dissidents in their own nations.

Meanwhile, Venezuela, the Dominican Republic and several Central American countries continued to support Cuban exile training sites, Ed wrote. Several of these were used as launching points for smallscale incursions by exile groups with high-sounding names, most of them headquartered in Miami.

These groups, often led by veterans of the Bay of Pigs invasion, stubbornly believed that taking a few boats containing men and weapons into isolated regions of the island would incite the general populace to rise up and join them in a rebel offensive against Havana, much as Fidel Castro himself had provoked years earlier.

None of these operations succeeded in their grand schemes. But the Florida-based exiles continued to try, and to coax other nations to join in.

Ed also talked to many people that had participated in one small action or another against Batista's government, leading to the totality of events that eventually came to be the Cuban Revolution. He delighted in the details. Some of the raw and unlinked accounts from former Batista soldiers — and even quiet rebels now homeless and still haunting the streets of the larger cities — often were supported with letters and old documents. Many of their still-vivid accounts were backed up by former enemies, many of them distant cousins and uncles who fought against them, all fighting in the name of a nebulous cause.

The American correspondent took it all in, sorted and sifted until it all funneled down into a crude history, an understanding of what it was all about. Through it all, he later realized, he began to have a sense of his own place in this, and even his own belonging. And so he wrote about those times in later years with empathy for most of those involved on one side or the other. They were Cubans, all believing they had the right answers to stabilize their homeland and to lead it to its potential.

One of the outstanding stories of the 1950s and early '60s he pieced together had to do with the strange adventures of Spanish-born Eloy Gutierrez Menoyo. Ed was convinced that Menoyo's part of this historic Cuban revolution was special, and crucial for its success.

This one man led many lives, going through repeated cycles of success and failure. He eventually became what Ed called a philosopher-pacifier, trying vainly to convince exiles and Castro followers they should all learn to live together. Fat chance, was the general consensus.

The Madrid-born Menoyo and his brother Carlos, who lived in Havana in the late 1950s, took part in an ill-fated assault on Batista's presidential palace in Havana in 1957. Carlos Menoyo, one of the leaders, was gunned down in the attack. So at the age of twenty-two, brother Eloy, whom everybody knew simply as Menoyo, became a vigorous avenger, a tireless hard-driving rebel against the Batista dictatorship.

After a brief trip to Miami and consultation with exiles, he sneaked back onto the island and assumed leadership of a new anti-Batista organization called the National Front, which was based in Banao in the Escambray Mountains of Central Cuba. This came to be known as the Segundo Frente del Escambray.

Menoyo's small army, supported by money from Miami exile groups and weapons from the Dominican Republic, did much of the early fighting against army troops while Fidel and his ill-supplied rebeldes were still floundering around in the mountains and countryside of southeast Cuba.

Along with an American adventurer named William Morgan, Menoyo attracted volunteers and formed the men into fighting units against the more-heavily armed Batista soldiers in open battles. This was a new warfront, a more aggressive one, bringing the battle much closer to the Batista military leadership in Havana.

Batista was alarmed at *la resistencia.* Fidel was a pesky opponent, but he was way off in the Sierra Maestra. Menoyo was close to home.

Over the years, Cuban history has been rewritten to give Fidel Castro and his band most of the credit for the early successes of the revolutionary movement. But, in the opinion of analysts of the time, much of the credit belongs to Menoyo and small unsung groups of frustrated rural people acting on their own. Menoyo's operations were doing more to enrage Batista than Fidel was, these historians contend.

However, once the the Fidel Castro story was born, it kept feeding on itself. Herb Matthews of the New York Times was at the forefront of foreign and national reporters creating the overall Fidel Castro myth.

The rebel movement fostered at the University of Havana and many other anti-Batista activists in the Cuban capital eventually came to believe that Fidel was their annointed leader — even if Menoyo was the one enthusiastically battling Batista troops.

A group called the Revolutionary Directorate based in Havana, originally created by Menoyo, now wanted to call the shots. They wanted Menoyo to shift his efforts to the towns and cities rather than continue fighting in the countryside. Fidel Castro wanted one of his comandantes to take over from Menoyo in Banao and in the rural area around the capital.

Menoyo would have none of that. He refused Castro's overtures to change his plans.

Along with some of the Havana-based politicians and business leaders, Menoyo wanted a constitutional form of government, but he always believed that the revolution belonged to all of Cuba, of the whole *pueblo*, not just for the benefit of those in Havana. He turned down Castro's "order" that he join his Escambray rebels to the Castro units in Oriente Province.

From then on, Menoyo was considered an outsider.

Eventually, the Havana-based Revolutionary Directorate came to consider Menoyo a traitor "to the ideals of the revolution" for refusing to do as it wanted, and it turned its back on him. Ostensibly, he wanted no role in the Castro movement. He had his own.

But it was important to realize, Ed learned, that Menoyo had expressed no personal ambition to take over the government in place of Batista. He was willing to let more experienced men assume the top spot as long as they followed the constitutional path.

Gradually, however, he went along, reluctantly, and accepted the popular belief that Fidel Castro was to be the head of a new revolutionary government.

By then, the Castro brothers and Che had recruited more volunteers and successfully carried out attacks in Santa Clara and elsewhere in the southeast. Fidel thus assumed the leadership mantle he had had always coveted.

He later became convinced that he would have to get rid of Menoyo because of his stubborn manner and independent thinking. Dr. Rivero and many others fueled Ed's curiosity about those times, and about the unsung hero Menoyo.

After Batista fled, Menoyo and William Morgan were among the first anti-Batista warriors to arrive in Havana. They patiently waited for Fidel, who trekked across the island from Oriente Province to the capital to become the president-prime minister-dictator a week later.

Soon after Fidel took over, however, Menoyo became one of the first to recognize Castro's leftist intentions. He was alarmed and said publicly that Fidel was following a road leading to socialism and communism. He threatened to reorganize his guerrilla group in the Escambray and return to rebellion — seeking a true constitutional government. Before he could try to bring this about, however, he was forced into exile.

It didn't take long for Menoyo to begin carrying out forays into Cuba with the newly formed Miami-based exile group Alfa 66. In late 1964, Menoyo and others launched an expedition from the Cay Sal Bank into Cuba, near Baracoa. But the group was captured just a few weeks later by Castro's army.

Menoyo was exhaustively interrogated for a week and finally was dragged before Fidel.

"Eloy, I knew you were coming, and I also knew I would capture you," Fidel said.

He was summarily sentenced to *el paredon* for execution, but his sentence was later reduced to life in prison. He spent time in five of Fidel's dungeons, including Isla de Pinos, La Cabaña and El Principe in Havana. Following his conscience, he became a *plantado*, refusing to accept "political rehabilitation" and underwent all of its rigors. He became temporarily crippled, lost sight in his left eye and suffered partial hearing loss.

Finally Spanish authorities intervened. Spain's President, Felipe Gonzalez, wrote a personal note to Fidel asking for Menoyo's freedom. Fidel's response: "We cannot free a terrorist so that he will soon be free to direct terrorist attacks into Cuba with Miami exiles."

But this brought international attention to the case, and Menoyo was finally freed after some twenty-two years in prison. After spending some time in Spain, he returned to Miami and received a grand reception by exiles.

His romance with the exiles did not last long, however. He abruptly announced he wanted a political reconciliation with the Fidel Castro regime. This was treason to the exiles.

Menoyo then returned to Havana and surprisingly reunited with Fidel.

The exiles retaliated, calling for his assassination, but Menoyo remained in Cuba, seeking a way to bring exiles and Castroites together into one country under a more democratic form of government. This was at the time that Fidel was admitting that yes, he was following a communist path.

So that was the story of a rebel called a traitor by both sides of a revolution, spending more than two decades in Cuban prisons and then returning from Florida exile to seek peace and democracy in Cuba. He was shunned by exiles, and Fidel Castro was not enthusiastic. Although the Cuban regime never legitimatized his efforts, it tolerated his presence.

Curiously, this Spanish-born enigma— this hero-traitor-pacifier — all this time remained a naturalized citizen of the United States and never became a Cuban.

"I am sandwiched between the extreme right in Miami and the extreme left in Cuba," Menoyo said in recent years. "That is the price one pays for being independent."

Eloy Gutierrez Menoyo died of a heart attack in Havana in October, 2012, without having achieved his latest mission, of bringing together the two societies — one based on communism and the other on democracy.

Menoyo and other exile leaders such as Manuel Artime and Manolo Ray failed in their anti-Castro missions because they had naively believed Cubans on the island would be inspired to carry out popular revolts, which were never forthcoming. Either nobody was interested, the word never got out, or those who were supposed to rise up and support exile invaders were too fearful of the consequences.

While there was not a general rising-up in revolt, there was considerable activity on the island itself by small groups unhappy about how things were turning out. In effect, some of these groups nurtured rebels against the so-called rebels of Fidel Castro, who were now trying to run the country.

The *contrarevolucionarios* were slowly coming into being.

Correspondent Brophy wrote that the Castro regime was extremely concerned about rebellion at home in the mid-1960s. Interior Ministry troops, G2 counter-intelligence agents and militia kept busy rounding up suspicious individuals and breaking up dissident cells.

The regime's police-state grip on the country grew ever tighter, even as it was reaching out to other countries for economic and political support and respectability. Everything seemed to be flying in different directions.

After chasing out a number of priests and closing Roman Catholic churches earlier in the decade, the government began cracking down on Protestant groups, especially foreign missionaries.

In an early-morning raid in Havana and several places in the interior, police arrested forty Baptist preachers and thirteen laymen of the Western Cuban Baptist Convention on charges of spying for the United States.

Among those hauled in were two Americans, the Rev. Herbert Caudill, who was sixty-one years old and head of the convention, and his son-in-law, the Rev. James David Fite, thirty-one. From disparate accounts from the missionaries and Cuban sympathizers, Ed determined that twenty other Baptist ministers and prominent laymen had been arrested throughout the island in previous days.

The regime alleged that Caudill, who had been in Cuba since 1929, and the other churchmen "working under the cloak of religion, organized a counter-revolutionary group for missions of espionage and subversion."

Caudill, who was from Waynesboro, Georgia, was sentenced to ten years in prison. Fite was given a six-year sentence on the same charges of espionage.

Court records made available later indicated that thirty of the other missionaries and laymen arrested at the same time received sentences ranging from two to thirty years in prison.

TREASURE ISLAND
& LA CABAÑA

Miguel roused himself from a tortured sleep as the guards banged on bars and began serving a lumpy, runny slop they called *avena,* a half-raw mixture of cooked, grainy flour that was his first meal in days. He was filthy, his skin crusty where it wasn't covered by the clothes he'd been wearing when he was taken from his ranch.

He'd lost track of time and only remembered that he and several other unfortunates had been transported a long distance in the back of a military truck, presumably from Havana to a prison in the interior. But he seemed to recall riding a ferry, too.

"*Por fin despierto,*" came a disembodied voice in a harsh whisper, jarring Miguel fully awake. "*Creia que estabas muerto,*" added the phlegmatic voice in what seemed to be an American accent. "You're finally awake. I thought you were dead," repeated the gaunt, hollow-eyed man standing over his mattress in the half-gloom of early morning.

"Where am I?" asked Miguel.

"You're at the national penitentiary complex at the Isla de Pinos," replied the voice. "You remember the Isle of Pines . . . Robert Louis Stevenson? They call this place *Presidio Modelo,* the model prison. I'm Richard. Do you remember who you are? Miguel briefly told him who he was and what he remembered about getting to this place.

It turned out Richard was an American, married to the widow of a prominent Cuban dissident. The dissident had been executed after he was discovered organizing a plot against Castro. Richard himself had been convicted of "crimes against the state" and had been at the Isla de Pinos for almost a year. His wife had managed to escape the clutches of G2 and was in exile.

Miguel remembered that Isla de Pinos was off Cuba's southern coast and as large as metropolitan London. It was a base for pirates plundering Spanish ships sailing the Caribbean in the 16th and 17th centuries and had first been used as a prison by the Spaniards, who exiled a number of Cuban independence leaders here.

Now, it was a notorious den for many thousands of prisoners rounded up and tortured by the Castro regime. There never was any treasure here.

Richard and Miguel were among scores of inmates crowded into a *circular*, one of a number of circular cellblocks or galleries built around a large enclosed courtyard occupied by guards and prison officials. Richard became Miguel's self-appointed "mentor" in his early days at Isla de Pinos and their paths, too, would keep crossing for years in the various prisons, camps and hospitals where they would be moved.

At the Isle of Pines, Richard had been interrogated and brutalized repeatedly because he refused to accept the prison system's rehabilitation plan. Richard thus became one of the plantados, his revolutionary ideals unchangeable.

Several weeks after his arrival, when prison officials demanded that Miguel accept the plan, he, too, refused and suffered the consequences.

Sometimes, relatives of some of those inmates were forced to witness their beatings. They, too, were threatened by guards in efforts to get them to convince the recalcitrants to submit to the so-called rehabilitation, which the guards and prisoners simply called the "The Plan."

Some of *plantados* were deprived of any prison clothing. They were reduced to wearing only their shorts. Others went naked. They were forced to remain in their cellblocks or placed in isolation and were given little medical treatment except in extreme cases. They were subjected to long periods of interrogation and torture. Guards frequently conducted painful body searches. The little food they received was barely edible and sometimes infested with insects or their droppings.

Miguel thought of it as a long nightmare, where days became weeks and then months and years. When they weren't in isolation or sleeping on the floor in the open cellblocks, they were doing forced labor for twelve to fourteen hours a day.

Richard told Miguel that except for the guards who enjoyed wielding their truncheons and nightsticks, the Isle of Pines was preferable to some places such as the dungeons in Boniato, where prisoners were kept in tiny windowless cells like animals in cages, sometimes for years at a time. The more rebellious ones could become fodder for the firing squads at La Cabaña.

Things were no better for female political prisoners at a lockup in Guanabacoa, where it was said only 37 of 277 of the women had accepted the rehabilitation plan. They, too, were treated as plantado*s*, in this case plantad*as*, the female equivalent.

In late 1961, the prisoners at the Isle of Pines were informed by the guards that dynamite had been embedded in the walls throughout the complex and that in case of any attack by the Americanos, the prison and all of its occupants would be blown up.

"We were threatened like this from time-to-time, to try to keep us in line, I suppose," said Richard after his release many years later. "But this threat turned out to be real," Richard continued. "I know because prisoners who were there in 1963 said they saw work crews removing the dynamite . . . Why? Maybe it had served its purpose. Who can guess what those arbitrary bastards will do."

Richard, Miguel and a number of other inmates considered potential troublemakers were eventually transferred to La Cabaña in Havana, where their ordeal continued in different ways.

They were put in *Galera Siete,* considered the worst section of the Colonial-era fortress. Miguel had been there before.

Che Guevara set up his headquarters at La Cabaña soon after the revolutionaries got to Havana in 1959, and he personally directed firing squad executions of many of the Batista loyalists and the counter-revolutionary "elements" who came later.

Fortaleza de San Carlos de La Cabaña — known simply as La Cabaña — originally was one of the Spaniards' largest fortresses in the Americas, possessing fixed upper-story battlements and cannons and a massive complex of tunnels, trenches, a parade ground, military barracks and open courtyards carved out of cliffs and rocky ledges ranging from eight to fourteen feet high.

Some of the *galeras* were more recently built into the cliffsides and had little or no natural light and clammy wet walls and floors. Groups of prisoners undergoing rehabilitation were often herded by guards on horseback into trenchlike open grounds, where for short periods they could stretch out, dry their clothes and get some warm sun.

"A *galera* was maybe meant to hold eighty prisoners, but most of the time there were 200 to 400 in there," Richard recalled later. "*Galera Siete* was the tough one. It was seldom that anybody there was let out to even see the sun."

Shortly after arriving at La Cabaña, a prisoners' rebellion against wearing the mandatory blue uniforms was put down by clubbings and bayonets, sending a number of the injured to a hospital while others suffered through their wounds without medical assistance.

The *plantados* equated the blue prison uniforms with the rehabilitation plan, and they wanted nothing that would identify them with that. They reasoned that their counterrevolutionary activities would have been for nothing if they gave up on their opposition to the regime while in prison. After prisoner-guard clashes, hunger strikes and other rebellious acts, the prisoners would usually win out, so-to-speak, by wearing only their shorts rather than donning the prison garb. Sometimes they were issued yellow garments, but prison officials stopped doing that when the yellow uniform began to be recognized by other prisoners as a proud sign of independence and rebellion.

The anti-communist, anti-Castro beliefs of these *plantados* were so strong that many served their twenty-or- thirty-year sentences and never relinquished those feelings.

Comandante Huber Matos, one of Fidel's earliest followers, became one of the heroes of the revolution that overthrew Batista. But, not even a year after Castro took over the government, Matos became disillusioned with the way things were going and wrote a letter of resignation from the army, alleging that the Castro government was infiltrated by communists.

Castro called this treason and had him arrested. Huber Matos was tried and convicted of counter-revolutionary activities by a military court and was a prisoner at La Cabaña when Miguel and Richard arrived there. Matos never surrendered his ideals and became an inspiration to others and a hero to those on the outside, particularly after smuggling long, philosophical letters out of prison. These detailed their tortuous day-to-day conditions.

In a letter Matos wrote to his wife and made available to *The New York Times*, he said, "There is something in my situation which gives me more pain than imprisonment itself: It is to be labeled and treated as an enemy of the People, knowing as I do that I am part of that People, and that their cause is my cause . . ."

Another longtime resident of La Cabaña was Antonio "Tony" Cuesta Valle, who was captured along the Cuban coast on one of many incursions that brought exiles and weapons into the country. After serving more than ten years of a thirty-year sentence, Cuesta smuggled a letter out of La Cabaña addressed to the Human Rights Commission of the United Nations.

Cuesta was then blind and had a crippled left arm as a result of blowing up his boat before his capture. Now, he wanted nothing more than to die.

The letter was an eloquent and emotional appeal calling for Cuba's release of its many female prisoners, plus the old and the sick, held throughout the country. In exchange, Cuesta offered to go before a firing squad. He called on the U.N. Commission to "carry out your duty" and demand that Castro free those less fortunate than himself.

Cuesta said he was getting no medical attention and that he was living like a rat, with barely enough room to lie down to sleep in a crowded *galera*. "When it rains, which is often," he wrote, "the rudimentary toilets are flooded, and human excrement covers everything. Food is scarce; we have never gotten bread, meat or vegetables."

The letter received extensive publicity worldwide, but as with other such missives from political prisoners, it brought no tangible results.

Ed learned that Miguel and Richard had also shared prison quarters with Menoyo, who was renowned among the rebels for his exploits in the Escambray and his controversial episodes with Fidel.

PIZZA WITH FIDEL

Jean-Paul Albrecht was trying to get some sleep after working virtually around-the-clock for several days when the telephone jangled at his bedside, jerking him to a sitting position in bed.

"Mr. Ambassador," said the voice in English. "This is Ramiro del Campo. The prime minister would like to meet with you. He hopes it is possible for you to do so now."

It was 1:30 a.m. on a Friday morning in October, 1965. Albrecht, the Swiss ambassador to Havana, grumbled a bit but he couldn't very well refuse. So he quickly consented to a meeting with Fidel Castro and listened some more to del Campo.

After hanging up, the ambassador called his secretary at her home and had her call a friend, who in turn was told to dial Ed Brophy's apartment. All the woman said when the reporter picked up his telephone was, "*Perdón, queria a Lola*" (Sorry, I wanted Lola). She than quickly hung up.

The signal had been arranged a week before.

The ambassador, who represented American interests in Cuba, had told Ed in confidence that he had held meetings with Castro at different all-night restaurants on the Malecon Boulevard in the past few weeks. And Ed had prevailed on Ambassador Albrecht to tip him off if it happened again. So . . . if the correspondent happened to be out for a late drive and happened to spot any "unusual activity," he would stop and investigate, naturally. And, if he just happened to see Castro and his entourage, he could try to try to talk to him there or arrange for a private interview.

Castro just might agree. One never knew. This was Cuba in the 1960s, after all.

Ed was anxious to question Castro not only on the mysteriously absent Che Guevara but on many other matters that had gone unanswered over the past few weeks.

For instance, it was known that the Cuban leader was increasingly exasperated by the large numbers of people risking their lives to flee from their island paradise. There also had been evidence of a growing impatience among the populace with the increasing amounts of bureaucratic paperwork and red tape connected with obtaining exit visas. Lengthy lines of Cubans daily jammed the street in front of the old American Embassy, which was now the U.S. Interests Section, operated by the Swiss.

After receiving the anonymous phone call that night, Ed rousted Blake from his house nearby, and the sleepy chauffeur and the correspondent set out in Blake's ancient Cadillac. The side streets were nearly deserted, but the Malecon was lit up brightly in spots, and there was a fair amount of traffic even at this hour.

Sure enough, parked haphazardly on a side street and around a restaurant called La Costa Azul were several military vehicles, two big vans, a couple of old Lincoln town cars and a big, black Mercedes.

La Costa Azul was a late-night beer bar and pizza place just before one crossed the Almendares River from Vedado into Miramar. It was set back from the coastal road among towering palm trees and consisted of a small thatched-roof bar and a concrete patio with umbrella tables open to the sea breezes. It served doughy pizzas of unidentifiable cheeses — no pepperoni, sausage, peppers or anything else in rationbook Cuba. Still, a pizza's enchanting blend of spiced-up tomato sauce and its ingredients — whatever they might be — made for a hearty meal.

Half a dozen *milicianos* shouldering automatic rifles patrolled the sidewalk and were stationed among the trees and bright -red bougainvillea on the winding pathway leading to the indoor part of the restaurant.

Ed had earlier directed Blake to drop him off at a park across the wide boulevard. He had walked across and as close as he could to the small knot of military personnel and guards dressed in civilian clothes. Just before he was challenged by a grimfaced guard, he spotted a friendly face.

"Hey, Luisito," he called. "I'm just passing by on my way home and noticed the crowd here. What's going on? Is Fidel here?"

Luis Almeida, a protocol officer, strolled up, shook his head in exasperation and held up both arms.

"Maybe he can spare me a few minutes," Ed persisted. "You remember I made a request to see him several weeks ago."

That's the way it was in the mid-1960s. Requests by reporters for personal interviews were generally ignored, but if you happened to be around when Fidel swooped in somewhere — a restaurant, a hotel lobby, a beach gathering, an experimental farm — he might clap you on the shoulder and engage you in conversation. Now, here he was at a pizza bar.

He was a well-known night owl, and some of his talks with foreign journalists in the past had taken place at impromptu sessions in the wee hours. The ebullient Castro enjoyed surprising people with his casual unannounced drop-ins, particularly in the middle of the night.

Luis, looking grim and a bit out of his element now, was uncharacteristically nervous. He shrugged at Ed's query about an interview. He rolled his eyes a bit and said Castro was dining with friends. Eyeing the guards, he gestured unobtrusively that Ed should wait, however, and made no attempt to send him away. Pushing his luck, the reporter joined the protocol official as he strolled to a concrete bench near the sidewalk. They sat, waiting to see what happened.

Some fifteen minutes later, Ambassador Albrecht and an aide came striding by. He nodded curtly at Ed Brophy, got into his chauffeured car and drove away into the night.

Luis jumped up and went quickly up the path to the restaurant. Ed waited some more. After another five minutes, Luis reappeared with a tight smile and said the prime minister would meet with Ed briefly. The two hurried up the winding pathway.

"*Bueno*, what are you doing up so late?" Castro greeted him, extending a cheese-smeared hand but remaining seated at an outdoor table before a large pizza.

"I heard they had good pizzas at this place," Ed replied, deciding that the occasion called for informality.

Then the reporter said, "*Primer Ministro,* I am pleased to see you. I couldn't resist the chance to stop by and maybe ask you a few questions."

"*Está bien, sientate.* But no more questions for now. Sit down over here." Fidel gestured to the concrete table next to him since his was full of Army officers in camouflage fatigues slurping beer and eating pizza along with him. A bottle of red wine sat half empty on a nearby table. Wind whipped the umbrellas over the tables.

Ed straddled the bench so that he could look at Castro directly.

"I thought, perhaps, that we could talk about some things that are of interest internationally — not necessarily here," Ed tried again awkwardly. "Maybe in your office sometime soon. It would give you a chance to explain your views on some things and maybe answer some of your critics."

"No, *hombre*, what critics? I told everyone what I wanted to say in my last speech. . . But I'm curious about what you want to know. En que piensas a esta hora? (What are you puzzling over at this hour?)

"Bueno, una cuestion es de las salidas al exilio," Ed managed to say. (one issue is the many departures for exile).

Meanwhile, Luisito had sat down next to Ed and ordered beer for both of them.

"*Mira, tu sabes, como gringo, que tenemos muchos enemigos en el gobierno Americano,*" he said. (You know we have a lot of enemies in the American government.) Then, again lapsing into a mixture of English and Spanish, he added, "Esos exiliados. They also cause many problems. But, you know, I think that . . . We will be better off when all the lumpen and gusanos leave. Que se vayan."

Ed was startled and began to ask whether he would get rid of all his opponents by throwing them out of the country. But Fidel put up a hand and stopped him. "No questions," he said emphatically. "I am thinking of making another speech very soon. You be there as usual, and you can write it all down."

Fidel then smiled good-naturedly and turned back to his food.

There was some small talk around the table about the Cuban baseball season. Fidel looked up and reminded everyone that the World Series was starting soon in Los Angeles. And he said he liked the Dodgers. (The Dodgers beat the Minnesota Twins 4 games to 3.)

After biting on another slice of pizza, shaking his head and muttering to himself that it was hot, Fidel seemed to remember something he wanted to say. He swiveled round on the concrete bench, took a swig of his beer and looked directly at Ed.

The Castro entourage was making ready to leave.

"It's a busy time," Castro announced, somewhat apologetically. He stood up and stretched."It's my pleasure seeing you again," he said, bending over and placing a hand on Ed's shoulder, keeping him seated. He shook he reporter's hand and walked away, trailed by his attendants.

"*Gracias, Primer Ministro*," was all Ed had had time to say.

Luis and Ed left their beers, followed the group out and down the shrub-bordered pathway to the street, where Castro and his party were pulling away in a blur of exhaust fumes.

The next day, Ed was called to the Foreign Ministry and questioned by Ramiro del Campo about how he had happened to come upon the Castro-Albrecht meeting. Ed had his story prepared about its being pure chance.

"*Está bien*," del Campo said, unconvinced. "But if you want to keep your visa, I would advise you not to write about this encounter with the prime minister. You save it for your memoirs. You understand, *que no*?

Not wanting to risk getting thrown out of the country, Ed took the advice.

He could inquire further and write about the situation without mentioning the late-night meeting. The pizza party, though, provided another glimpse into the perplexing persona that was Fidel Castro.

Several weeks prior to that chit-chat, Ed had traveled into the interior with a small party of government officials trailing after the Prime Minister in a car caravan as he visited a number of villages along the Camino Central, Cuba's central highway tortuously making its pot-holed passage through the country's ever changeable mid-section.

The correspondent had written a personality piece, describing Castro as "a forceful, articulate speaker, a great persuader and phrase maker, a methodical instructor to 'the masses.'"

The words were not farfetched. Everyone with whom Ed talked praised him for his concern for the poor and the illiterate, for those without proper shelter or medical care. A foreign diplomat known for his bluntness described Castro to the reporter as "a great pitchman, a preacher, a teacher, an actor and father figure all rolled up into one hell of a personality."

Whatever else his enemies thought about Fidel, as everyone in Cuba referred to him, he was the country's moving force.

Without his constant prodding, cajoling, lecturing, everything would bog down. Other officials around him always provided plenty of words but little action. Fidel followed his dialogues with action of some sort or another. As a motivational instructor, he had no equal in Cuba.

Wherever he went—— and he seemed to be in one place one day and at the opposite end of the large island the next— he "oriented the masses" (*orientar*, meaning to direct or teach—was a favorite word in the Cuban Communist lexicon).

Castro's interests and travels were diverse, Ed wrote. In these early days of his revolution, he was in his element whether making a lengthy speech to hundreds of thousands of people, or personally talking to dirt farmers, or artificially inseminating cattle with a syringe.

Despite his nocturnal habits, he was always up at an early hour in the countryside, bouncing over mountain roads in a jeep, carrying his campaign for greater production into the hills and valleys of the island's deep interior.

He'd climb a mountainside to tell coffee growers how far apart to plant their trees and what fertilizer to use; stroll through a tiny rural schoolhouse and hold campesinos and their children enthralled while reading a book or writing a sentence on their blackboard. He escorted medical personnel into remote villages, and issued orders that health care be more readily available. He told everyone he wanted school construction made a priority.

He sat and listened to what the people had to say, individually or in small groups, and they were not bashful about speaking up about their needs. He'd shake his head or nod in agreement, his fatigue cap pulled tightly down to his eyes and cigar clasped firmly in his mouth. He ate and slept among the peasants.

He was accused of many wrongs, but no one accused him of being an aloof, desk-bound bureaucrat in those years.

However, a former member of Castro's security team later turned out to be one of his fiercest critics. Juan Reinaldo Sanchez, who said he was fired by Castro after 17 years of helping to protect his life and privacy, wrote a book while in exile in Spain called *La Vida Oculta de Fidel Castro*

(The Secret Life of Fidel Castro) in which he said his former boss was indifferent to proverty while living a luxurious life.

Sanchez wrote that Castro maintained some 20 homes across the island, owned a yacht, employed a fulltime doctor and had a personal chef who prepared his meals.

Although Castro publicly denounced drug-trafficking and punished several highly placed military officers for engaging in such activities, Castro himself was responsible for huge illegal drug transactions, according to Sanchez, who died in 2015.

FREEDOM ON THE
HORIZON

Although the nocturnal encounter with Castro didn't result in an interview, it turned out to be highly significant for Ed, thanks to Ambassador Albrecht.

The Swiss diplomat had been the surrogate for American interests in the Cuban capital for four years and was a busy man, especially of late. Albrecht was a chunky, easy-going fellow who put his gregarious nature to good use as a diplomat. Castro often used him as a pipeline or as a guideline in trying to gauge Washington's attitude on different issues. And Washington kept the wires to Bern, the Swiss capital, busy with behind-the-scenes communications.

Most of this usually wound up in Albrecht's lap.

The correspondent had had a number of get-togethers with Ambassador Albrecht, from which both benefited. Albrecht sometimes requested Ed's personal views on current happenings in Cuba, or asked to be filled in on a trial, conference or other event that neither he nor his aides could have attended. The reporter, in turn, elicited whatever information he could about Albrecht's frequent meetings with Castro and other government officials.

He had often been a guest at diplomatic receptions at the small embassy and at the ambassador's residence. Ed also made it a point to get around to the other embassies that maintained relations with Cuba. Among the most

119

prominent were Canada, Mexico and Israel, but the list of representatives to Cuba seemed to be growing rapidly.

That diplomat-reporter relationship might have seemed unusual to those covering diplomacy in other foreign capitals, but this was Cuba in the 1960s — still a closed-off society in many ways — and things just worked differently here. Virtually everything was unorthodox. The government was operating on a learn-as-you-go basis. There were few protocols among diplomats and reporters, although they were always wary because of the mercurial nature of the times.

Ed made sure to visit the ambassador a couple of days after the encounter with Fidel. Albrecht surprised him by declaring frankly that his last several meetings with the prime minister involved "immigration issues." Although careful not to elaborate on specifics, he discussed some of the difficulties. And Albrecht strongly implied that something new was in the works.

As close observers were aware, one of the major problems perplexing the Castro regime at the time was the issue of Cubans — and many American expatriates — who now wanted desperately to leave the country.

The regime's authorities had been angered by the overwhelming numbers of men, women and children showing up day-after-day at the old American Embassy near the Malecon, now being used by the Swiss consular staff. They wanted exit visas to the United States. And while most applications were processed, the actual number of U.S. entry visas was restricted by the U.S.

Americans living in Cuba also had different obstacles to overcome if they wanted to return to the U.S.

On the rise, alarmingly, were the numbers of Cubans fleeing the island by any means they could use, braving the shark-infested sea in small boats and even rubber tubes in efforts to reach the Florida coast. Hundreds had already lost their lives in these dangerous crossings.

A case in point was that of Vladimir Santiaguez and his older brother Fabricio, a tall, well-muscled, gentle man. Vladimir, shorter and in his late 20s, had met Ed at a meeting in a coastal village near Havana. Santiaguez and his brother lived by themselves and made their living from the sea. They usually sold their good-sized catches to the local-area stores or to restaurants in Havana and made a pretty good living. One day, a bald, portly man who called himself an "inspector" showed up at their little house.

"*Bueno, y que?* Why do you think you are different? You've got to go through the system. You know you have to sell your catch to the cooperative, not go around and getting your own prices from whoever you favor."

The stranger had abruptly announced this to Vladimir as he answered the door one evening. Vladimir, a shy, bespectacled former university student, was taken aback.

"*Bueno, nosotros no sabíamos eso,*" he responded. "We didn't know about the new rules. We don't go out (to sea) every day, but when we do, we'll check in with the cooperative for sure."

"*Bueno. Ya saben,*" the hefty inspector said. "Now you know. I'm not going to arrest you today. But if you don't start selling your fish through the cooperative I'm going to send over a couple of agents from the G2 to see about it. Don't say I didn't warn you, *okah?*"

From then on, Vladmir and Fabricio knew they were in danger of being accused of counterrevolutionary activities and maybe thrown in a prison for a few years. They agreed they would keep some of their catch and turn most of it over to the cooperative. This way, they could continue to supply their favorite customers. They managed to get away with this for a few weeks.

Meanwhile, their lives were fast becoming intolerable.

"Why not get out. Others have done it," Fabricio said one day.

That's when they decided to leave their country. On the quiet, they outfitted their boat to sail across the straits to Florida. It took them three days and a lot of praying, but they made it while many didn't.

Ed later met Vladimir in Orlando, of all places, and Vladimir told him the story over lunch. He had changed his name to Max and ran a successful computer fix-it shop.

Similar stories now became a tremendous embarrassment for the Cuban government both at home and in Europe and Latin America, where Cuba was trying hard to rebuild good relations.

The unspoken, hot-potato issue having to do with immigration involved 600 Americans and their Cuban relatives, a total of about 3,000 people. They were also prohibited from leaving Cuba. Ed wrote about them extensively, and the articles received a lot of play in American newspapers and they even resulted in heated discussions in the U.S. Congress.

As a result of the tipoff by Albrecht, Ed stepped up his reporting on the immigration issues. He was sure something was about to take place since Fidel Castro was not one to dawdle once he got an idea about resolving any problem.

Sure enough, in a speech at the end of September 1965, Castro flung down a gauntlet for the administration of President Lyndon Johnson. He announced that no longer would Cubans with relatives in the United States be prohibited from leaving the island. They were welcome to leave anytime they wanted. The United States would have no choice but to accept those "worms" who wanted to go.

"Nobody who wants to go needs to go by stealth," Castro declared in a thundering voice. But he referred only to Cuban citizens, ignoring the American residents who also wanted to leave.

The small fishing port of Camarioca would be the exit point, he said, adding that his government could even provide ships for the departing Cubans. He would also allow exiles living in the U.S. to sail across to Camarioca without Cuban interference to pick up their outgoing relatives. This was an astounding offer, given past history. It demonstrated how anxious he was to get rid of the loudest critics of his regime.

"In all revolutions, the departure of privileged classes is an absolutely normal occurrence," Castro said later, glossing over the fact that most of those who wanted out were not the wealthy or well-to-do. Most of the well-connected had left the country in the first few years of the revolution. Most of those dissenters now in question had, for one reason or another, missed previous opportunities to leave and were now desperate, some destitute.

Castro's seemingly impromptu announcement did cause immediate problems — in the United States.

Evidently caught by surprise, President Johnson publicly replied that if Castro was serious, he could negotiate for the Cubans' safe conduct with the Swiss embassy in Havana. And he suggested that the International Red Cross take part in arranging such a transfer.

Castro quickly followed up with another speech in early October. He declared he was ready to negotiate but rejected President Johnson's suggestion that the Red Cross take part in such efforts.

"We have won a battle for liberty," he told a cheering audience in Havana's Charles Chaplain Theatre. "They (the Americans) have no alternative and no other way out" other than to accept his open-door policy and receive the many thousands expected to take advantage of the offer.

No one had any idea how many were anxious to go.

Pressing his advantage, Castro shouted to the audience, "And let the United States permit any (American) citizen to come freely to Cuba. Let them permit representatives of Negro organizations to visit Cuba so they can see how racial discrimination has disappeared in our country."

As a result of the Cuban embargo imposed by the U.S. in 1961, it was unlawful for most American citizens to travel to Cuba, and this was what Castro was now flouting. The Castro-controlled electronic media also featured radio reports and television newsfilms showing the brutal treatment of American blacks during the civil rights movement in the 1960s. The Communist Party newspaper Granma was filled with such accounts and photographs.

Oddly, Castro used this same speech to announce that Ernesto "El Che" Guevara had given up his revolutionary and military positions, and his Cuban citizenship, to fight imperialism on "other battlefronts." Fidel provided no other details on El Che, but he a lot more to say on that topic later.

After some more give-and-take on the immigration issue, the U.S. State Department told reporters in Washington it had proposed to Cuba that the U.S. government set up a transportation system for the refugees.

"It would be an orderly system of reliable transportation provided at no cost to the refugees," said John H. Crimmins, the State Department's coordinator of Cuban affairs. "It would be either by sea or by air."

Castro pre-empted this by setting October 10, 1965, as the date Cubans would be free to leave from Camarioca, the village in Matanzas Province, about 75 miles east of Havana. As a result, anxious Cuban exiles living in Florida were soon breaking U.S. law by sailing every imaginable kind of vessel across the Florida Straits to get to Camarioca to pick up relatives and friends.

An orderly system went out the window, at least in the beginning. The little-known port of Camarioca soon became a bedlam of activity, with Cuban exiles arriving from Florida and other U.S. coastal points and those eager to leave Cuba scrambling to get from their homes throughout the island to the Camarioca port.

Since the exile boaters took off without U.S. government authorization, they expected to be punished on their return to the U.S., but they said they were ready to accept any penalties imposed. Ironically, Cuban officials in Camarioca were so helpful that they wouldn't let the arriving exiles pay for food, lodging or gasoline needed for their return trips.

You could almost see most Americans shake their heads and hear them say, "Ah, those Cubans; they are just being Cubans."

While the boatlift was under way, Ambassador Albrecht and the Castro regime worked out a plan for an airlift of American aircraft to ferry the Cubans out in a more orderly fashion. The "Freedom Flights" began in November, 1965, and went on for years. By the time they eventually ended in 1973, the Freedom Flights had transported 260,000 Cubans to the U.S. in the largest airborne refugee operation in history.

By mid-1965, the United States had already taken in almost 300,000 Cubans who had left the island since the triumph of the Castro revolution in 1959. Cuban exile sources in Miami had originally estimated that upwards of 50,000 more would leave as a result of Castro's new open-door policy in 1965.

As events later showed, they were far off in those early estimates.

Camarioca proved to be a precursor of a much more extensive boatlift of Cubans out of the port of Mariel in 1980. At that time, Castro again threw open the doors to Cubans who wanted to leave the island. Out came an assortment of refugees ranging from the unemployed poor, to families, to rough common criminals purposely set free so that they, too, could embark.

As a consequence, from mid-April, 1980, to September 26, 1982, another 125,000 refugees made their way to U.S. shores aboard some 1,400 vessels taking part in the Mariel boatlift. At least 27 people died, 14 on one overloaded boat. Most of those arriving in Key West were placed in refugee camps in Florida and in several other states for processing.

Many who were identified as hard criminals were locked up in federal prisons for eventual return to Cuba, but others escaped the American dragnet and returned to their criminal activities in their new homeland.

Camarioca, Mariel and the Freedom Flights were considered major victories by Castro in his continuous jousting with Washington.

For the rest of the western world they became a further embarrassment for the Cuban regime. The troubling question was, was the dictatorship really that bad? The old saying is that you vote with your feet, and those refugees were certainly doing that.

Cuba gained enormously from the mass departures by siphoning off most of the disgruntled and those whom Castro called the "the *lumpen* who only benefit from the work and production of the faithful."

In many cases, those who left were potential troublemakers for the revolution. For the Mariel boatlift, for instance, Cuba had emptied many of its jails to rid itself of thousands of common criminals, a few of whom were returned by the U.S. None of Cuba's political prisoners were freed, however.

Finally benefiting from the Freedom Flights in the 1960s were the American citizens who had spouses, children or other relatives whom they refused to leave behind in Cuba. They had persistently complained — to the Swiss ambassador, to other foreign diplomats, to foreign reporters and anyone else who would listen — that they were being forgotten in the negotiations that sent hundreds of thousands of Cubans to American shores.

An example of those in the American group that Ed Brophy wrote about had to do with a woman born in Chicago and married to a Cuban. The husband had served in the diplomatic service overseas under several Cuban presidents, including Batista. They had a young son who had been born in Havana between his assignments.

After Batista's hasty departure, they returned to Havana. Now, under the Castro regime, they sought a way out.

The wife was told several times by authorities in Havana that she could seek an exit visa and be repatriated to the U.S. But she would have to leave behind her husband and son. As a Cuban, the husband would have to qualify under the regime's immigration policies, which were a time-consuming process that could take years. But the real hangup was the Cuban-born son.

Cuba imposed a strict ban, preventing young men between the ages of fourteen and twenty-seven from leaving the country before serving in the military. Since the boy would soon be fourteen, he couldn't leave without completing his military duty, Cuban authorities ruled.

Another case involved an American who had owned a small business and lived in Havana at the time the Castro regime took over. He had a Cuban wife and four young children. Under current rules, the Swiss Embassy advised the husband to have other American relatives who lived in the U.S. "reclaim" him and leave his family temporarily behind in Cuba. He was told that once in the U.S., he could than "reclaim" his wife and children, and they could then leave on the refugee airlift.

"Outrageous. I won't do it. We cannot be separated. I have no assurances of anything. What if they (the Cubans) change their mind," the American told Ed.

Mexican President Gustavo Diaz Ordaz made a special plea to Castro for the release of the American group. Finally, under pressure from Mexico, from American public opinion and some members of Congress, Ambassador Albrecht and Washington succeeded in getting Cuba to permit safe-conduct to Mexico for the group of about 3,000. Special charter flights transported them to Mexico City, from where they traveled to the U.S.

Ed came in for praise from some of the departing Americans for the newspaper accounts he had written of their plight. Several men and women sought him out at the airport for a big Cuban abrazo as they were about to leave the communist island.

In contrast to all of this, what came later was even stranger. The regime suddenly re-imposed strict emigration restrictions, and many Cubans were forbidden from leaving their own country. Period.

When things finally settled down from the hectic comings and goings of the 1960s, there came into prominence what became known over the years as the "white card." Anyone could apply for a white card, meaning that that person was asking the government for permission to emigrate. This was a bureaucratic arrangement which proved to have its dangers as well as its ultimate reward. Permission to eventually leave your homeland was the reward, losing your livelihood in the meantime was quite likely.

The person wishing to depart had to fill out a series of forms and pay the government $200, which to the average Cuban could be a year's salary.

If you eventually received a white card, you were placed on a lengthy list of those who wanted to leave, usually to the United States, Puerto Rico or Spain. But it exposed you to your employer, friends, neighbors, the neighborhood watch committee and militia. You would certainly lose your government job, if you had one, and you had better watch your back at all times, even among your friends. You became an outlier, with your name on a so-called blacklist.

The blacklist was long. It marked you as a dissident. Later, author Yoani Sanchez called it "our own Berlin Wall without the concrete or land mines." She was on the blacklist.

Much later, she was given a white card and traveled widely. Because her writings were widely known, she was enthusiastically received in the United States, Mexico and everywhere else she traveled. There were many such stories about individuals and families who eventually earned their "freedom" from their own homeland.

CHE GUEVARA'S
MISADVENTURES

All of a sudden, Che Guevara was everywhere . . . and nowhere.

Giant-sized images, lifelike posters, portraits, leaflets tacked up on walls — all showed the scraggly bearded, beret-wearing Argentine doctor who became a hero of the Cuban revolution. They began popping up throughout Havana and smaller cities and country roads in the interior in mid-1965.

His image was everywhere, but el Che himself was nowhere to be seen in all of Cuba.

True, the government had acknowledged early in 1965 that el Che was visiting in Europe and Africa in his capacity as minister of industries, but months went by and there were no details about this very public man. He seemingly had started off his long journey In New York in late 1964 and then visited China. After that, he was gone from public view.

Any questions about the whereabouts of Fidel's executioner and jack-of-all trades in 1965 were ignored by Castro and his underlings. Che had literally dropped from sight.

Until the sudden appearance of his likenesses, and a flood of copies of his book *Guerrilla Warfare* into Havana bookstores, there had even been rumors that Guevara and Castro had had a serious falling out, and that Guevara might have met the fate of other revolutionary heroes who had crossed the "maximum leader."

Adding fuel to the stories was the fact that Guevara's Cuban-born wife, Aleida March, moved out of their home in Havana and returned to live with her parents in Santa Clara, in the interior of the country.

Meanwhile, the public adulation was whipping into full force by the time of the July 26, 1965, celebration of the beginning of the Castro revolution. It was widely believed among Cubans on the street that either Che Guevara had died, or that he was carrying out a secret assignment overseas, or . . . whatever their imaginations could conjure.

The speculation was endless.

More curious was the fact that during previous July 26 celebrations, the only posters carried aloft and plastered on walls were those of Fidel Castro and his onetime deputy, the Cowboy-hat-wearing Camilo Cienfuegos. There now was a mystery surrounding Cienfuegos, too. The official story was that he was killed in a plane crash in the first few months of the revolution.

But few believed that.

The site of the airplane crash was never found. And there was widespread speculation then that Cienfuegos had become even more popular than Fidel among the masses of revolutionary followers, and that this couldn't be tolerated. His postersize images disappeared from public view. But Cienfuego's name, his reputation and and his revolutionary achievements were never forgotten by el pueblo, who generally referred to him by his first name.

Meanwhile, Ed, along with other journalists in and out of Cuba, tried to unearth some trace of Che Guevara. The stories about him became so ubiquitous that an American magazine ran a cartoon showing then-President Lyndon Johnson issuing orders to Superman, Dick Tracy, The Phantom and Tarzan to find Guevara.

Castro even declared in a speech that the rumors about conflicts between him and Guevara were groundless, as were those about him and Camilo Cienfuegos.

But Castro refused to say where Che was, except that "wherever he is or whatever he does, we may be sure that he will always achieve revolutionary goals." As for the gossip in the United States, Castro joked that if American officials were so anxious about Che Guevara, the U. S. should order one of its secret U2 spy planes to find him and photograph him.

Outside reports soon began circulating that Guevara had been spotted in a number of Latin American countries. Officials in these countries complained that Castro was trying to spread his brand of revolution by sending Guevara to stir up the dissidents and disaffected throughout the hemisphere.

Venezuela and Bolivia protested formally to the Organization of American States that the Castro regime was trying to foment revolution in their countries. The Dominican Republic had long considered itself a target.

Ed wrote of reports by dissidents that the Castro regime was operating training camps for recruits from various South American countries. A special target, according to these reports, was Chile, but they also involved Caribbean neighbors Colombia and Venezuela among others.

Castro continued his coyness about his revolutionary confederate until a September 28, 1965, speech before a national meeting of the Committees for the Defense of the Revolution (CDR) when he abruptly announced that he would issue a statement on Guevara in a few days. His attention up until then had been focused on immigration issues, especially the Camarioca exodus.

In early October, the Cuban government abruptly announced major changes in the makeup of the governing party's leadership. From now on, the organization would officially be known as the Cuban Communist Party and its National Directorate was to be its Central Committee.

Castro became the party's secretary-general, succeeding oldtime Communist Party leader Blas Roca. The big surprise, however, was that Ernesto Guevara's name was missing from the list of those on the party's Central Committee. Che was no longer listed among the Cuban revolutionary elite.

In a later speech that October, Castro broke his silence about his onetime sidekick. Guevara, Castro declared, had resigned his government positions and his commission as comandante in the Cuban Armed Forces.

Castro further declared that Guevara believed he had completed his duties in Cuba and that he would carry on his "battle against imperialism" elsewhere. Fidel then produced an undated, handwritten letter from el Che announcing his new course of action.

"Other countries of the world demand my modest efforts," the Guevara letter read by Castro said.

Holding the letter high before the crowd, Fidel Castro read other parts that praised him (Castro) highly, calling him a "shining statesman" who was at his best and most decisive during the October 1962 missile crisis.

"I can do what you are denied from doing because of your responsibilities as Cuban leader," Castro quoted from Guevara's personal letter. "In the new fields of battle, I shall carry the faith that you instilled in me, the revolutionary spirit of my country . . . the obligation to fight against imperialism wherever it may be."

Mocking his enemies, Castro then said the imperialists had been kept busy speculating whether Guevara was ill or had died, whether he'd been purged of his leadership posts in the Cuban government or whether he and Guevara had come to a parting of the ways.

"We feel this explains everything," the prime minister declared waving the document around. "As for the rest of it, let our enemies worry."

He told the cheering crowd he'd received Guevara's letter in April of that year, meaning presumably that Guevara had by then been busy in his new endeavors for most of that year. Castro didn't explain why he was only releasing it in October.

Castro was full of surprises this day, Ed noted in his reportage.

The speech and the letter served to fuel even more speculation: that Castro had written the effusive note himself, that all of this proved that el Che had renounced the Cuban revolution, or that he'd been killed as a result of his guerrilla activities in Africa and that Castro was keeping the news from the people. Or . . . that one could endlessly speculate.

Guevara's absence, the earlier disappearance of Camilo Cienfuegos, and the conviction and imprisonment of the popular Huber Matos as a counter-revolutionary left Fidel and his brother Raul as the major survivors of the small group of rebels who had made it into the mountains of southeast Cuba to begin the rebellion against dictator Fulgencio Batista in 1956.

Guevara was graduated with a medical degree from Buenos Aires University and came from an old, aristocratic Argentine family.

He met the Castro brothers in Mexico, where they began planning their revolution against Batista. Guevara was considered an expert on guerrilla warfare, having reached Mexico after spending time with rebel groups in several Latin countries.

After the overthrow of Batista, Guevara turned to economic planning. He became head of Cuba's national bank in the first year of the Cuban revolution and in 1961 became minister of industries, a post he held until his mysterious departure.

Journalists and academicians piecing together the Guevara story years later discovered that he had traveled to Czechoslovakia, East Germany and several African countries in disguise in 1966

Che eventually reached Brazil and made his way slowly into Bolivia. Throughout 1966 and into 1967, half a dozen countries in Central and South America reported sightings of Guevara and evidence that he and a small company of Cubans had been in contact with dissident groups in their rural areas.

Bolivia seemed to be a specific target, especially in the rugged, southeastern mountain region that contained the center of its budding petroleum industry. That Andean nation called on the Organization of American States (OAS) and the United States for assistance against the foreign intruders.

President Lyndon Johnson and Secretary of State Dean Rusk once again spoke out forcefully against Cuba. Johnson urged Latin American nations to unite against such outside terrorism. Bolivian President Rene Barrientos offered a reward for the capture or death of Guevara.

The OAS formally sanctioned Cuba for the fifth time and urged Africa and Asia to join with Latin America in condemning such activities. Cuban Foreign Minister Raul Roa refuted the allegations, saying the United States was using the occasion to mask plans for renewed military aggression against Cuba.

Meanwhile, Che was busy training the few recruits he could muster among the Bolivian peasants, many of whom were hardscrabble farmers and Indians. He also attempted to win over some of the country's tin miners, with little success although the miners were often at odds with the government and mining companies over poor working conditions.

Many of the Bolivians, especially the non-Spanish-speaking Indians, were indifferent to the talk about rebellion by the strange foreigners. "You talk to them, and in the depths of their eyes you can see they don't believe," Guevara wrote in his diary, referring to the Bolivian miners.

An attempt to associate his small group with Bolivia's Communist Party was unsuccessful when party leader Mario Monge rejected Guevara's efforts to declare himself the military leader in the country.

Guevara reportedly maintained sporadic contact with Havana over shortwave radio. But there was little assistance coming from Cuba despite letters to the Cuban leader from Che outlining the rebels' difficulties under extremely trying conditions. From all appearances, Guevara was on his own. Castro could have supplied help in various ways but did not.

The Barrientos government maintained pressure by keeping its Army Ranger patrols busy scouring the mountain hideouts. The guerrillas were meeting increasing hostility from peasants and farmers in the countryside, and the Ranger patrols were often guided by reports from rural informants. Steady rains, the Andean-mountain country and the guerrilla band's inability to maintain a consistent food- and weapons supply soon began to take its toll.

Guevara's diaries, found after his death, said that some of the Cubans, as well as the few Bolivian recruits, began coming down with incapacitating ailments. Morale kept sliding downhill. Government troops kept finding the guerrilla camps, often tracking them with small airplanes.

Guevara realized he badly needed outside help. But all he got were visitors such as French philosopher Regis Debray, Argentine leftist Ciro Bustos and the German-born communist Haydee Tamara Bunke, who had taken on the guerrilla name of Tania.

Debray, Bustos and Tania, all of whom had unsuccessfully tried to provide some sort of liaison between foreign sympathizers and the guerrillas, traveled with Guevara and his dwindling band for a brief period in mid-1967.

The hardships got to the point that Guevara decided to split his group in two. He took Debray and Bustos with him, leaving Tania and the other unit at a base camp. Debray and Bustos soon wanted to return to La Paz, and Guevara reluctantly sent a trusted Bolivian lieutenant to escort them out to one of the villages, where they gave themselves up to government troops. Along with them was a freelance photographer from Chile who had managed to find the guerrillas on his own.

Debray and Bustos were jailed in La Paz, but the photographer, George Roth, was released after the Bolivian military decided he had valid press credentials. Word that the internationally known Debray was in a Bolivian prison brought an outcry from communists, leftist intellectuals and others around the world. The French government protested to Bolivia.

But to no avail. Debray and Bustos were held for trial, convicted and given thirty-year sentences. Debray was freed after three years largely due to the intervention of French President Charles de Gaulle and a number of prominent writers and philosophers, including Jean-Paul Sartre and Andre Malraux.

Guevara and his few remaining guerrillas wandered aimlessly during the Bolivian winter. Their main goal by then was to keep from starving to death.

A government patrol tipped off by peasants soon ambushed the second group and killed off its members, including Tania. It was only a question of time now before Guevara could be tracked down, too.

And on October 8, 1967, the rangers surprised the desperate guerrillas at dawn. Guevara, suffering badly from asthma attacks, was wounded in the ensuing firefight. He was placed on a stretcher and taken to the nearby village of La Higuera for questioning.

Ernesto Che Guevara was shot to death the following day, reportedly on orders from the government in La Paz. But there are conflicting accounts of his end.

"Guevara chose the wrong country, the wrong terrain and the wrong friends," declared President Barrientos.

Prompted by a massive propaganda campaign started personally by Fidel Castro, Che Guevara soon became a martyred icon, a worldwide symbol of guerrilla resistance. He was praised from many quarters, often by those who had no idea how resoundingly he had failed as "an artist in guerrilla warfare," as Castro eulogized him.

Guevara also had failed miserably as an economic planner in Cuba as he, Castro and the other rebels floundered, trying to find their way, through the first few years of their revolution.

In those days, Fidel believed in the Soviet concept that industrialization could come about at the same time as his selfstyled improvement of agricultural reform. He put in place a program called collectivization, whose result was the takeover by the regime of large privately held ranch and farm properties. Along with that, he tasked Guevara with the industrialization of the new society. While Fidel arduously pursued collectivization and began modest improvements in the production of foodstuff, coffee, tobacco, citrus and husbandry, Guevara tried to modernize the existing industrial base and to maintain and continue to operate the American and European companies that had been confiscated.

About this time, Guevara also became head of Cuba's Central Bank, and he used those two positions to become a virtual spokesman for his adopted country, especially on American and European television programs. He glowingly outlined "la revolucion's" history and its purpose, along with appeals for funding necessary day-to-day operations. Politics and the island's longterm agenda seemed to be glossed over in these conversations with TV personalities.

Guevara was popular among the regime's general supporters, especially among the rural people, but he was often ignored by Castro's inner circle in Havana in those early years. He seemed now to be out of his element as an implementer of those ideas he had fought for, on a lonely course all his own.

Castro never liked to share the stage with anybody. But for his own purposes, the Cuban leader now was grandly singing the dead Guevara's praises. He now was linking Che Guevara's name with Cuba's greatest heroes of the past like Jose Martí . . . and Camilo Cienfuegos.

A Castro-manufactured legend was born, on very shaky premises.

Since then, the Cuban regime has persistently promoted Che's name and plastered his bearded face on those giant, jaunty posters as a shining example of a successful revolutionary leader. Cubans young and old were urged to "emulate" (a favorite phrase among them) the leadership and heroism of this larger-than-life warrior.

He has been a worldwide hero to casual rebels — with or without a cause.

But an objective assessment of Guevara's guerrilla adventure in Latin America would have to conclude that it had been an embarrassing failure for Che himself and for the Castro regime.

HARD TIMES

Prisoners at Isla de Pinos and other penal institutions were often forced into long hours of hard labor on farms, in road construction, sugar harvesting, building army barracks, chopping down trees — with very little nourishment and poor medical attention.

The exhausting work, horrible nutrition, unsanitary living conditions and the mosquitoes, rats, lice and other vermin combined to breed disease of all kinds in the galeras. Medical care was rudimentary and only provided in the most serious cases of illness or injury.

Some prisoners at Isla de Pinos went to extremes to escape the punishing labor conditions and the brutality of the guards.

They chopped off fingers or toes. Some injected themselves with motor oil, causing their legs or arms to swell hugely. This would get them some time off, but they often suffered grave consequences, including amputation.

Another method that would gain them a temporary reprieve was to lay out some of their precious stash of sugar or a piece of candy on the barred windows that were sometimes open to the outside. This would attract bees. They would catch as many as they could and cup them over an arm or a leg so the bees would sting, resulting in a large swelling.

Many, of course, didn't have to fake anything.

Miguel's condition kept getting steadily worse. In addition to painful joints and festering sores on his legs and back, he began vomiting green and yellow bile and couldn't eat anything. Finally, after about four days of this, he was taken to the medical dispensary, where a Czech doctor diagnosed his condition as "Malta Fever." He was placed in a corner of the dispensary, curtained off from the staff and several other patients and started on antibiotics and intravenuous feeding.

After ten days of this, he was deemed well enough to be released, and the Czech medic recommended that he be transferred to a farm camp, where he could do light work while he regained strength. "The country air and sunshine will do you some good," the doctor said dismissively, virtually pushing Miguel's pale, wasted body out of the dispensary in the care of guards

Miguel was transported to Matanzas, the province where he had once lived and worked, in the back of a canvas-topped military truck carrying three side-armed soldiers and five other prison-pale patients.

He knew that as soon as he recovered, he'd be moved again, probably back to La Cabaña or the Isle of Pines. But when he reached the rehabilitation farm called "La Luisa," he learned that the Isle of Pines prison complex had been closed down and the thousands of prisoners transferred all over the country.

Fidel had had a bright idea to transform the Isle of Pines into *Isla de la Juventud*, the Isle of Youth, and use it as a large training and indoctrination area where students lived a disciplined life, studied, worked and learned to be good communists. The notorious complex, which had housed many thousands of prisoners since early in the century, was turned into a massive boarding school, taking in special students from throughout Cuba and other nations.

It was at La Luisa agricultural camp that Miguel learned that his friend Jimmy had been killed at the Isle of Pines during a short-lived prisoners' mutiny. Miguel could obtain few details. He mourned for Jimmy, and for his own future.

At the camp, Miguel was put to work in a newly built citrus plant deep in Cuba's orange and grapefruit groves. Concentrating citrus fruit into juices was one of the revolution's emerging industries. Fortunately, the job wasn't overly strenuous since it consisted of sorting oranges, some to go into juice and the rest shipped overseas. He did this for eleven hours a day, with a one-hour break at mid-day.

He and his co-workers were housed in tents. They used a common latrine and showered out in the open. But his body began to recover. His fever and chills slowly dissipated and he began gaining weight and getting some of his strength back. A robust man before his arrest, his weight had dropped to 125 pounds at the worst of his illness. He was now up to 140 and gaining slowly.

He knew, however, that the sooner he got better, the sooner his easy life would end because he still adamantly refused to accept the regime's "plan," even though this might mean a reduction in prison time and more lenient treatment. His jailers wouldn't tolerate someone like him among those undergoing indoctrination and rehabilitation.

His orange-sorting job came to an end after five weeks and he was assigned to a crew that harvested the oranges. They'd get up before daybreak, eat a sparse breakfast and jump on flatbed trucks that drove them to the groves, where they spent most of the daylight hours climbing up and down ladders with heavy sacks of oranges on their backs.

Although Miguel found it tough at first, his body gained strength and within a few weeks he was holding his own with the other harvesters.

"*Oye, muchacho*, there's nothing wrong with you. Go back to La Cabaña," one of his new friends joked about his abilities as a picker.

"You can always join the plan and maybe stay here until the end of your sentence," mocked another.

Miguel smiled but paid no attention. Although he was grateful for all the time he could spend away from harsh prison conditions, he wouldn't even consider going back on his beliefs to accept the regime's style of "rehabilitation."

His whole world changed again, however, on a stormy day close to the end of the citrus harvest. The day started out rainy and got worse until the crew chiefs decided at midafternoon that conditions were so bad they couldn't pick any more fruit. "*Vamonos de aquí.* Things aren't going to get better," one of the jefes shouted out.

They were ordered back to the camp site. Miguel and three or four others climbed in back of a pickup, which was partially loaded with crates of oranges, for the mile-long trip back to the barracks and tents of La Luisa.

For some reason — their speed, the dark storm, the rutty clay road — the pickup failed to negotiate a sharp curve and went flying down an embankment, rolling over several times with its fruit and human cargo.

The driver and one of the passengers in back were killed. Miguel and two others survived but were badly injured.

When he regained consciousness three days later, Miguel was in a hospital bed at El Principe prison in Havana. His left arm was broken in two places and was in a cast, he had a severe scalp wound that had been closed with numerous stitches, both his legs had tendon and ligament damage that would require a long period of rehabilitation, and he needed surgery for two crushed vertebrae.

"You were lucky, but maybe not, depending on how the spinal surgery goes," one of the doctors at the prison hospital told him in brutal honesty. "The vertebrae were badly crushed. The rest, you'll recover from eventually. But we don't do such surgery here so you'll have to wait your turn to be transferred somewhere else."

Miguel said nothing, but he asked God silently why he'd chosen to spare his life if he might be a cripple forever.

PAINFUL FREEDOM

"Well, the first part of the operation was a success," said the surgeon as Miguel groggily opened his eyes to see the long-bearded doctor in a yellow gown towering over him. Miguel lay on a hospital bed in the surgical ward at Calixto Garcia Hospital in Havana.

"We managed to clean out the area in your lower spine pretty well, but the fusion is only temporary. We may have to operate again in a few months to make a more permanent bridge between the vertebrae."

With that announcement, the doctor was gone. Miguel was left to put his questions to the orderlies and prim nurses who moved in and out among the beds occupied by patients. He was told he would probably have a metal plate to hold his vertebrae together in the lumbar region of his spine.

The large ward was clean and orderly. Bright sunshine flooded in through open windows that lined one wall.

Eventually, he was returned to the medical unit at El Principe prison. The pain from the surgery gradually subsided and he was able to walk on crutches. One night, however, the stab of pain became so intense, he began screaming. The guards ignored pleas from other prisoners for a doctor. They reluctantly came up with a half dozen aspirin tablets. Finally, at midmorning, an intern appeared, asked a few questions and said he would submit a report.

Late in the afternoon, the medic was back with some pain medication. Two agonizing days later, Miguel was transferred again to the same hospital, where he was probed and X-rayed for hours. He was then operated on for a second time.

When he came to, a Soviet doctor was there, looking on somewhat anxiously. He smiled.

"Okay," the amiable surgeon told him. "We fixed you up now. No more lingering pain since the nerves aren't exposed. Eventually, you might be able to walk to the *paredon* on your own."

In his drugged state, Miguel hoped the doctor was making a grim joke and wasn't expecting the patient to be put to death after they had performed two critical operations on his back. He smiled through his pain at what he hoped was dark humor.

In his halting Spanish, the Soviet surgeon explained the six-hour operation in detail.

He had inserted a two-inch metal "cage" around the fused vertebrae and placed titanium screws to hold everything together. Living tissue and muscle would eventually enclose the metal device and it would become part of Miguel's spine for the rest of his life. Meantime, there would be painful therapy sessions and then a return to his prison life.

He was lucky la revolución was generous and took good care of the injured, the doctor said pointedly.

After three days, Miguel was relieved to be able to stand and take a few steps with assistance, clanging around with an assortment of tubes and hoses sticking out of his lower belly and backside. A few more days and his tubes and monitors were removed, but it was painful for him to walk and could manage only a few steps on his own.

This careful treatment in the hospital was followed by long weeks of recuperation and shuttling between the hospital and prison, during which he again contracted the mysterious fever and chills that the Czech medic at La Cabaña had diagnosed as "Malta Fever."

His condition then worsened to the point where he was spending weeks in a hospital bed, unable to stand and walk on his own because of the pain in his bowels, and the alternating fevers and chills that left him drained and delirious. The muscles in his broken arm and his legs ached all the time. But his lower back appeared to be healing well.

He was so bad off, however, he was moved from the open ward into a small room with only two other male patients. Again, he was connected to machines and tubes and fed intravenously. He feared several times that he was close to death, and he was ready to welcome it. The occasional doctor who came by seemed unable to control his disease, although the spinal surgery appeared to have been successful. The white-uniformed nurses, who wore white socks and brown or black shoes, were attentive but chary about medications.

But then his fever began diminishing and things looked hopeful again. After another week, he was able to walk and eat almost normally. With little pain and only a slight fever. He was returned to the main prison, where the miserable housing conditions eventually led to a recurrence of the mysterious fevers, chills and pain.

Back to the medical unit for several weeks.

One day, as he was walking around the ward unaided, word filtered down to him from the nurses that he would be released.

"Released? You mean from the hospital?" asked Miguel of a male nurse who had been attentive and friendly throughout his darkest periods.

"No, *compañero*," said the black nurse in a hushed voice. "It looks like no more prison for you. They think you are too much trouble and don't want to put up with you anymore. From what I hear, once you leave here, you are on your own."

Freedom, thought Miguel bitterly. They break you down and then they get rid of you. He'd been in prison seven years. It seemed a lifetime. He was a physical wreck, and his mental state was close to the breaking point as a result of the accident, his injuries, the surgeries, his lingering disease, and from coming so close to death several times.

Now, he wasn't sure he really wanted to go anywhere.

He had nowhere to go! His family was gone, his father dead, their ranch confiscated by the government. He was afraid of freedom. Strangely, he'd gotten used to the hospital routine, even though much of it was a feverish blur.

He had reached such a state of mind that the hospital and El Principe prison were tolerable to him despite his ailments. The poor food, constant searches, even the beatings of those suspected of malingering, were constants in his life. His newest illness had nearly conquered him, and he'd found a certain comfort in the hospital.

These were the only things in his life that were real since he wasn't sure anymore about anything.

He had feared that the doctors would give up on him and order him back to the dank, cold floors and walls of La Cabaña, where a man could die without an apparent reason except that he'd simply given up. Not that he feared death. He'd often wished he'd died in the truck accident or during any of the numerous crises since then. But now he knew that he wouldn't, and that scared him more than anything. He had to face up to reality again.

There was no longer an escape in death.

He now realized that death, as an alternative to imprisonment and serious injury and disease, ironically had had a great deal to do in keeping him alive. The fact that he could have died and therefore escaped his reality had sustained him in a macabre way. The real possibility of death had made life bearable and therefore had kept him alive!

Trying to sort this out taxed his brain and exhausted his whole being. But he knew he had to come out of it. He was to be returned to the real world precisely because he was too sick for them to deal with him. He was once more to be responsible for himself. He could no longer take refuge in being an invalid.

They were letting him go. He might die there and they didn't want that. Now, he was to be responsible for his own destiny. And he had never been more afraid.

"*Maricon, hijo de puta* (queer, son of a whore)," yelled one of the prisoners in a group milling around the courtyard of El Principe as he retrieved his few belongings. "You're going home and we will rot in here," screamed the prisoner.

Miguel said nothing, moving on quickly.

The day finally arrived. He was given a number of papers to sign, was presented with some well-washed pants and a shirt, shoes, a jacket and a small toilet kit. And he was shown out the door.

This was Freedom Day for Miguel Hidalgo.

Outside the hospital, he was met by an old family friend who had unearthed the story of his imprisonment, his injuries and now his release. The searing sun made him squint. The early morning humidity enveloped him, and the effort of walking more than a few steps was already taking its toll. Beads of sweat dripped from his forehead into his eyes and from his nose onto his lips and chin.

At the same time, he felt clammy cold and realized that his fever had returned. He almost turned back. But he knew he would never forgive himself. Besides, they wouldn't take him back. This was his rebirth. Hadn't he dreamed of it often enough?

This was the beginning of his new life.

HAVANA LIFE

Carmen was widening her dark eyes, coquettishly giggling and gesturing while telling her story. The guests in her house were laughing uproariously and shaking their heads in wonder at Carmen's account of her black market experiences.

"So we brought this live baby pig home and immediately put him in the bathtub," she was saying as she moved in and out of the kitchen to see how the dinner was coming. "You finish telling it, Carlos," she told her husband as she set the table.

Carlos, serving daquirís and grinning broadly, took up the tale from the beginning for their guests — two other couples and Ed and his companion, a vivacious woman named Lydia. "Well, we had to drive way out there to the countryside of Pinar del Rio," said Carlos in a slow, methodical fashion befitting a former diplomat, which he had been. "After many wrong turns, we finally came to this farm which had a small tilted sign identifying itself as La Escondida. We parked and walked, following a winding trail through the brush and trees until we came to the farmhouse, where we met Maria and Juanito, who had been told we were coming.

"They were glad to see us. Since we were so late, they thought we were lost. And we were, but we didn't tell them that. Anyhow, it was getting late, and we had a long drive back to el Vedado so we hurried up the chit-chat."

The reason for their trip was to acquire a live piglet. It squealed at them a couple of times but otherwise didn't seem offended when they bargained over its worth above its pinkish head. An agreement was quickly reached.

"I paid Juanito thirty-five pesos and took possession of the rope holding its neck," Carlos continued "We led the obedient little animal to the back seat of the car, where Carmen had prepared a little rug and blankets. The farmer tugged the docile little animal up in there. We then turned down an offer of a glass of wine, said goodbye and drove off."

Sipping his daiquiri on that early evening in their comfortable living room, the tall, slim Carlos fidgeted with the collar of his guayabera and looked like a guilty little child. But he continued the tale after a sigh.

"So far so good on the black market transaction. Even the porker cooperated," he said with a half smile, his moustache bristling a little.

"The piggy curled up into a ball in the back seat, his wide eyes looking around and his snout poking. He found nothing interesting but some old newspapers. Then, I swear, he kind of half-yawned, closed his eyes and went to sleep. He woke up once when we went over a bad bump. El animalito seemed a big agitated, you know, and we were afraid it might soil the borrowed car. But we stopped, led him out by his rope and waited patiently while he did some business in a bush. Apparently that's all the pig needed."

It was late in the day when Carmen and Carlos got back to their house in Vedado, and they had no problem sneaking the piglet around the side of the house and up the back stairs into their kitchen without being seen.

They thought.

The nosy next-door-neighbor-friend of Carmen's rang their phone the minute they stepped in the door. She informed Carmen that there had been some government people hanging around the neighborhood and to be careful. She had evidently seen the little pig but didn't mention him.

The excitable Carmen went into a small panic, whispering to Carlos that they would be arrested and wind up in La Cabaña. Christmas, two days away, would be ruined, along with the rest of their lives, Carmen wailed in their kitchen.

Then, hearing noises at the front of the house, she ran to the window overlooking the street and spied a jeep and two militiamen talking to a couple passing by on the sidewalk.

"Quick," she said to Carlos, running back to the kitchen. "We have to hide the pig."

Showing amazing strength, Carlos said, she grabbed the struggling porker and ran off down a hallway into a bathroom. She pulled back the shower curtain and deposited the now whining pig into the bathtub along with some towels. She ran back to the kitchen while Carlos was still walking up and down trying to figure out what to do. Carmen reached into the icebox, picked up a bunch of lettuce leaves and an orange and rushed back to the bathroom.

By this time, the pig was squealing as loud as it could, with its little claws trying to find enough purchase to climb out of the old-fashioned tub. The more it tried, the more noise it made. Finally, Carmen managed to quiet it down by stuffing some lettuce in its mouth.

"And then she started singing, Carmen, not the pig," said Carlos laconically, as his guests held their sides, laughing loudly.

"She sang in Spanish, she sang in English, she sang in French. And you know what? That little animal stopped scrambling to get out and became quiet. Its little ears were sticking straight up and twitching, listening to Carmen singing softly."

"And you won't believe this," Carmen interrupted as she came back from the kitchen to her laughing guests. "But as God and Carlitos are my witnesses, that piglet laid down and went to sleep — in the bathtub. I made him comfortable with a blanket."

Carlos, the epitome of seriousness and dignity, nodded solemnly, causing Ed and the others to laugh even harder.

Carmen and Carlos took turns all that night getting up and quieting the pig, usually by feeding it. Carlos claimed he didn't sing to it. The following day, a friend of theirs showed up early by prior arrangement. They threw a blanket around the pig, and their friend hustled him out to his truck and sped away.

A day later, most of the piglet was back in Carmen's kitchen, ready for the oven. Carmen was a little sad, but not sad enough to not cook the savory parts of the little piggy for their Christmas dinner with friends.

Merry Christmas.

"We didn't even get to name it," said Carmen, her dark eyes dancing, as they all enjoyed roasted piglet, black beans, white rice and plantains, the traditional Cuban Christmas holiday dinner.

The hilarious story was just a bit more than unusual in the ebullient Carmen's day-to-day "adventures" in communist Cuba.

She was an American of Spanish-descent, born in Chicago and possessing college degrees in fine arts and medieval history. A short, beautiful woman, with flowing dark hair, she had married the tall, quiet Carlos Casanueva when he was a consul general for Cuba, posted in New York by a previous administration in the 1940s.

Carlos was recalled to Havana after the Castro regime took over from Batista in 1959. At first, the Casanuevas were pleased to return to the city they loved. But things quickly soured. Since he was not considered enough of a revolutionary, Carlos lost any further opportunities for overseas postings and was given a meaningless job in the Foreign Ministry until he was forcibly retired at the age of 55.

Now, they couldn't leave Cuba because they had a young son who would soon be of draft age for the Cuban military. Their easy life became a downhill struggle like everyone else's.

So Carmen coped, like all Cuban housewives, figuring out ingenious ways to circumvent *la libreta*, the rationbook which was becoming more restrictive every day.

A lengthy list of items — rice, beans, shoes, lightbulbs, toilet paper, rum, even cigars — were rationed. Sugar, long the nation's No. 1 product, also was placed on the ration list later. The kicker was that many of these everyday products weren't to be had even when the rationbook said you were overdue. And when some of the items showed up in the bodegas, they were in such short supply that only those waiting in long lines for hours would get them.

Queues or long lines —*colas* to the Cubans — became a fact of daily life in front of bodegas or retail stores of any kind.

So Carmen and others had to *inventar*, a favorite term literally meaning to invent but used in the sense of outwitting the authorities. This often meant resorting to a black market. Carmen's Christmas piglet became an *invento*. Cubans loved to share their stories, or invento*s*, just for the laughs or the edification of their friends and neighbors — hopefully out of the hearing of the informants of the CDR.

"You live and learn, and the streets are the best teachers," said an elderly neighbor of Ed's one day. "You learn or you don't eat."

Carmen hadn't forgotten the easy, fun days of 1950s Cuba, when she and Carlos had come for extended stays from his overseas assignments. Her son was born in Havana. She had loved the country and its capital then and, despite everything, tried even now wherever possible to keep those good times alive for themselves and their guests.

The Casanuevas had invited Ed to their home the first time they'd visited the AP office to talk about possible repatriation of Americans and their families living in Cuba. They'd become fast friends, and Ed had met a lot of interesting people — Cubans and Americans, the once-prosperous and the always poor — through Carmen and Carlos.

It was through them that Ed learned early-on that there were 600 to 700 Americans, plus their relatives, who were prevented from leaving Cuba for one reason or another. Ironically, many of the native-born Cubans now had better opportunities to go to the United States than the Cuban-Americans did. After repeated news articles on the issue, however, the American group was finally permitted to leave years later.

It was through Carmen that Ed met Lydia, a graceful green-eyed Cuban who was a frequent visitor in the Casanueva home.

Lydia, born in the picturesque colonial city of Trinidad, had been married at a young age to a youth who played at being a university student and couldn't keep a job when he was forced to get out into the work world. They lived in Havana and didn't have any children, so Lydia went to work for a pharmacy so they could afford an apartment and some of the necessities.

Finally, Lydia got tired of it, divorced her no-good husband and moved into the home of a brother and sister-in-law in *Habana Vieja*.

In the 1950s and into the early 1960s, Havana's *farmácias* were extremely competitive and would send young women out to the homes of well-to-do matrons in Vedado and Miramar to demonstrate and sell a variety of beauty products. These saleswomen even fixed hair and did manicures for the ladies in their homes.

The personable, hard-working Lydia became one of the best in the business. And the talkative Carmen found a ready listener when Lydia came to call. They became fast friends.

When Carmen and Carlos met Ed in his office, Carmen decided he should meet Lydia. She invited them to a Saturday afternoon get-together for drinks and card games. And Carmen was right, they were immediately attracted to each other.

"This is the most beautiful Cuban woman behind the sugarcane curtain," Carlos told Ed, playing off the Cold War's "Iron Curtain" description of the Soviet Union and its allies. Lydia was olive-skinned and shapely, with a classic oval face set off by shoulder-length black hair and those lovely almond-shaped green eyes.

Their relationship quickly blossomed. She was witty and intelligent, knowledgeable about Cuba's turbulent history, and she had a "street-smart" toughness about her as a result of making her own way since leaving the small town of Trinidad for the big city at a young age.

They were soon spending most of their free time together, at Ed's apartment, at the beach, visiting friends or sometimes at the few restaurants they could afford and still served decent food.

For Ed, Lydia was a godsend. He had been in Cuba almost six months and he wasn't just lonely, he was feeling truly alone in a crowd. He was on the verge of depression and was feeling isolated, uniquely apart in the police-state atmosphere of this strange communist society in the middle of the Americas.

There were few people he could really talk to even though he came in contact with many individuals and was busy throughout the day. He'd made friends easily with a number of Habaneros, most of whom were warm and gregarious by nature, and he was on easy terms with the foreign diplomats he had met at receptions and conferences.

Still, until Lydia came into his life, there was no one with whom he could share some of his experiences, his small triumphs and concerns. Except for rare and strictly business phone calls with his office in New York over shaky connections, there was no direct contact with his American colleagues.

In Lydia, he found a common spirit, someone he could relax with and talk to quietly in private. In public, they conversed in general, guarded terms, never forgetting that everyone around them was a potential informant. She made no demands on his time and attention, but they spent most of their free time together.

She shared his feelings.

"I no longer feel lost and lonely," she told him one night, snuggling close. "I was like a stranger in my own country. Now, you fill my thoughts."

They had similar beliefs about what was happening around them. Despite their different backgrounds, they developed a strong affection for each other.

They were now languishing on his apartment's small balcony overlooking the Hotel Nacional and the ocean. They luxuriated in the cool breeze, sitting in twilight, the blue hour when the moon was already gleaming on the sea. Through thin clouds, the fireball of the westering sun was still beaming its dying rays on what they could see of El Morro, the castlelike fortress looming over the winding Malecon boulevard in Habana Vieja.

They had returned from the beach at Santa Maria del Mar on that late Saturday afternoon, tired and sunburned. There was nothing but cold water coming out of the taps then, so they had taken quick, ice-old showers, fixed drinks and moved out to the balcony.

"You must have the soul of your Cuban mother," Lydia told him, reaching out to take one of his warm hands.

"You look a lot like her," she said, pointing back to a small framed photograph on a table in the living room. "What was half-brother Miguel like then? Did your mother regret leaving her native country and her son? Was she happy?"

Ed laughed at the rapid-fire questions.

"Yes, she was happy. She always seemed to be . . . except for one period of time." But he didn't explain.

"I would say Miguel resembles his father more than he did my . . . our mother," Ed added, thinking back. "I don't know much about my brother's young life. You must realize I haven't seen him since we were children. But I seem to remember that he was much like our mother emotionally. You know, with a big heart, always wanting to please."

They were interrupted by the suddenly loud plumbing in the bathroom.

The open faucet over the bathtub was spurting out lukewarm water, so they rushed to take quick showers. You never knew when to expect such luxury from the Havana waterworks, so you had to take advantage of good luck. Gratified by their unexpected good fortune, they slipped into bed.

Both looked forward all week to their private times together. They talked quietly as he lost himself in those green eyes, their sparkle only slightly dimmed by the fading light through the bedroom window curtain.

Later, they again went out on the balcony with their drinks refreshed.

It was purple dusk, as Steinbeck had once described it, that time when the palms and buildings became shadowy outlines but the moon and setting sun dueled brightly in the purple skies. Moonbeams glistened on the smooth gray-blue of the ocean and everything was quiet around them. Even the busy traffic on the streets below seemed muffled as the sultry day turned into a cool night.

Lydia again took up the topic of Edward's mother.

"Why did she leave her husband and her young son? It seems to me that's one of the most difficult decisions a mother can make in life."

"I don't know all the details," Ed replied. "She told me her husband Francisco, was a slave to the ranch and rural Cuba." Ed was remembering a conversation he and his mother had when he was about thirteen.

Francisco Hidalgo was born on that rich farm and ranch area of Cuba, and he and his father kept acquiring land over the years.

"When his father died, Francisco believed he had to bring up his own young son Miguel in the same way he was reared, in the same place, doing the same things that he'd always done," Ed said. "Remember, I wasn't even born then."

He remembered his mother telling him Francisco "was always . . . gone from dawn to dark."

When their son Miguel began to grow up, Francisco would take him along to do the same things every day. "But I always wanted something better for him," his mother told Ed. "I sometimes wouldn't see my husband and young son for days."

His mother and Francisco began to argue about young Miguel's lack of education and what she saw as a very limited future for him. As Francisco became more adamant, Marina refused to have any more children. But Francisco wouldn't change. "The ranch was all he knew and all he wanted to know, and he insisted on bringing up Miguel in the same way," Ed said.

Finally, Marina and Francisco separated. She went to live with a childhood friend in Havana while a spinster sister of Francisco's moved in with him to run the house. When Marina asked for a divorce and custody of Miguel, Francisco Hidalgo agreed to the divorce but wouldn't concede custody of their son.

"When my mother saw that Francisco's sister and the boy's grandmother had become attached to Miguel, she wrenched herself away and left the country. She went to live with a sister in Florida. There, she met my dad, the boisterous Irishman. I was born about a year after their marriage."

Ed remembered that conversation with his mother as if it were only yesterday.

His mother wasn't bitter about her past, Ed said. But she always yearned for her young son to understand why she had left him, why Miguel grew up in Cuba and why Ed had been born in the United States and was a bilingual American. Outwardly, she was comfortable with her decision and with her life in the United States. She was happy with her American husband, Patrick Brophy.

Staring off toward the sea, Ed wound up his tale.

"She and I came to Cuba for a visit when I was about six. Miguel was maybe ten or eleven. And my mother was gratified to learn that Francisco had been sending Miguel to a small private boarding school and that her son was happy dividing his time between the school and the ranch. Later, Miguel went to the University of Havana and became an educated rancher. And . . . you know what's happened since."

CUBAN BEISBOL, CHINESE RICE

"Strike one," called out the courageous umpire, holding up a big fat forefinger. The batter, Fidel Castro in military fatigues, boots and black horn-rimmed glasses, turned around and glared. The crowd roared with laughter. Fidel dug in at the plate.

The left-handed pitcher on the mound wound up and threw a roundhouse curve that seemed to be way inside until it suddenly dropped and curled into the catcher's glove, splitting the plate.

"Strike two!"

The fans filling the Havana baseball stadium to the rafters that hot Sunday afternoon loudly hooted, applauded and whistled. The Cuban dictator stepped away from the plate, grumbling and whacking his boots with his bat.

"Fidel. Fidel. Fidel" came a chant from the crowd. "*Pégale, pégale.*" Hit it, hit it, some were shouting. "Let's see a homerun, Fidel. Show that lefty you can still hit."

His armpits wet with sweat now in the beaming sun, Fidel gathered himself, waggled his bat across the plate a few times, leaned forward and squinted at the pitcher. The lefty wound up and let fly.

This time the pitch was a fastball right down the middle and Castro made contact, bouncing it hard to second. The second baseman had the ball to first base so quickly that Castro didn't make it halfway up the baseline.

Laughing and waving his fatigue cap, he acknowledged the applause and ambled over to the dugout, mocking the pitcher with a fist.

It was all in good fun. Fidel Castro, who had pitched for his Jesuit high school team and fancied himself of major league caliber, surprised the crowd this day by showing up at a playoff game of Cuba's professional baseball league series.

He threw some batting practice balls and joked with the players and managers before the game. Then he went to the batter's box as the visiting team's leadoff batter and hit the sharp ground ball for the first out.

He didn't take the field but he stayed to watch the game.

Ed and Lydia were enjoying the sunny, hot afternoon as much as the rest of the crowd. They weren't surprised to see the gregarious prime minister mixing it up with the proletariat. He often appeared unannounced at public events and joined right in with what everyone else was doing. Around the fourth inning, Ed spied Castro and half a dozen army officers and other members of his entourage eating friend chicken, drinking beer and smoking cigars in a specially roped-off section of stands along the third base side.

Until he left in the sixth inning, Castro was the star attraction this afternoon, with the action on the diamond coming in second best.

That's the way it was in Cuban-style Communism. Things might be tough, but you could still take in a *beisbol* game at Estadio Latinoamericano and jeer or applaud whoever you liked, even the *maximo lider*. Of course, you shouldn't jeer him too loudly. No matter how grim life became, Cubans enjoyed the simple things like baseball, dancing, singing, eating, and joking or poking fun at themselves and each other.

A favorite saying was that under socialism/communism, a Cuban now only had two problems after waking up every morning: lunch and dinner. That, of course, assumed that he or she could get a cup of coffee and a chunk of bread for breakfast.

One of the apocryphal anti-Castro jokes quietly making the rounds went something like this (warning to the religious reader):

Fidel is talking to hundreds of thousands of people at the Plaza de la Revolucion when suddenly a clean-shaven Jesus Christ appears beside him in flowing robes on the elevated platform. He whispers in Castro's ear.

Fidel listens attentively, nods and tells the crowd: "Attention, attention, people. Comrade Jesus has something to say to you."

Jesus takes the microphone and says, "People of Cuba, I want to talk to you about this bearded man standing here beside me: Hasn't he given you bread to slake your hunger — as I once did?"

"Si, Si, Si," came the reply from the Castro faithful.

"Isn't it true that by inventing the ration book, this man multiplied the fish and the loaves of bread so that everyone could get something to eat?"

"Si, Si, Si-i-i-i," came the crowd's drawn-out reply.

"Isn't it true that this man has built hospitals and clinics to cure your illnesses, the same as I cured people?" Jesus continued, wagging a finger at the crowd.

"Si-i-i-, Si-i-i."

"And isn't it true that this man has been betrayed by all those exiles who are now in Miami — as I was betrayed by Judas?"

"Si-i-i-i-i-i," sang the increasingly enthusiastic crowd.

"Well, then, why haven't you bastards crucified him yet?"

One of the sayings on the street was that the only way to get the buses running, the water and electricity flowing and Havana's streets and parks cleaned up was for the Castro government to sponsor an international conference. Habaneros had recently seen evidence of this when platoons of workers and militia spent weeks sprucing up the city for the approaching Tri-Continental Conference. Havana was the host city for many such international gatherings once the Castro dictatorship decided to raise its political profile overseas and among its neighbors, particularly among Latin and African nations.

Prior to those international events, government workers got to work, cosmetically refurbishing popular restaurants and putting up new beer and refreshment stands, rebuilding parts of the airport terminal and shining up the city's top hotels.

The immediate beneficiaries of the clean-up, the good food and improved services at this time, however, were the rabidly anti-American delegates to the January 1966 gathering from Latin America, Africa and Asia. Representatives from leftist groups in some 70 countries gathered at the plush Habana Libre Hotel, formerly the Havana Hilton, to excoriate imperialism and praise socialism.

The official goals of the conference were to achieve "the solidarity of the peoples of Asia, Africa and Latin America in the struggle against imperialism, colonialism and neocolonialism" and to coordinate efforts for "true independence" for the people in those continents.

Of course, Castro was later blamed by the leaders of many of the countries from which those delegates came of cooking up revolutions against them.

A conference organizer told Ed and several foreign reporters that Cuba sponsored the gathering as "a way of demonstrating to imperialism that our country is not as isolated as they think it is."

Ironically, at the time of the nine-day solidarity conference, Castro was having some heavy-duty problems with China over rice, one of the main food staples for both countries.

The island's eight million people first heard about it when the prime minister announced that they would have to go on half rations of rice because the larder was virtually empty. Ration rice again? This was horrendous.

No other single foodstuff was consumed more than rice in Cuba. It was an everyday, fundamental component of virtually every meal. It was a belly-filling staple in good times and bad, often in combination with meat, chicken, beans and . . . whatever was available.

Castro blamed his Chinese allies for reneging on an agreement that would have traded Chinese rice for 800,000 tons of Cuban sugar. Believing they had a long-term barter deal, the Cubans "did not grow more rice ourselves because we were concentrating on other agricultural products," Castro said bitterly.

China explained it had a short rice crop and had to stockpile some of the harvest as a reserve "in case of attack," presumably by the Soviet Union, with which it was carrying on its own Cold War. China also was shipping large quantities of rice to North Vietnam, to support that country's war against the United States.

The angry Cuban leader, celebrating the seventh anniversary of his revolution, added in that somber speech that China also was unwilling to continue to extend foreign trade credits as in the past.

The feud between the communist partners grew more intense when a Chinese Commerce Ministry official replied to Castro's speech with a long statement alleging that the Cuban prime minister had lied when he said that China had broken the sugar-for-rice agreement.

The Chinese statement also strongly implied that Cuba was a small Soviet satellite state. This blew away any hope for a quick solution because Castro always had the last word in an argument. He quickly launched a second blistering attack against China.

In another long, rambling speech and in later talks with Ed and other journalists, the Cuban leader accused Peking of using extortion methods. China had, in effect, joined "the Yankee imperialist economic blockade" of Cuba by drastically reducing trade with Havana, he asserted.

And to top it all off, he charged that the communist Chinese were trying to subvert Cuba's armed forces through "a massive distribution of propaganda." There were a lot of leaflets floating around in Chinese, Russian and a peculiar version of Spanish.

Castro ordered the Chinese charge d'affaires in Havana to put a stop to it. But the campaign continued.

"The number of Chinese propaganda bulletins coming into Cuba totaled 58,041 despite direct and personal warnings of the president of the republic and the prime minister," Castro thundered in his speech.

He later told Ed during a chance encounter that he compared the Chinese campaign to one "continually employed by the United States by meddling in our internal affairs and attempting to impose their will over Cuba."

Months later, the dust finally settled with a renewed China-Cuba trade agreement. And no more was said publicly about attempted subversion.

The theme of many of Castro's speeches at this time dealt with the necessity for every Cuban to make sacrifices, for them to tighten their belts even more in the face of continuing shortages of consumer goods.

Another joke making the rounds during this period of austerity reflected the proud, nationalistic attitude of most Cubans despite the bad times:

A Frenchman, an Englishman and a Cuban are standing in front of a large painting of Adam and Eve at the Louvre Museum in Paris. They are speculating on the country of origin of the subjects of the masterpiece.

"He is so masculine. And she is a perfect feminine specimen," says the moustachioed French gentleman in his beret. "The scene is so erotic, so filled with temptation. They have to be French."

Shaking his head vigorously, the Englishman says, "No, no. You have ignored the serenity evident in their faces, the delicacy of their posture, the seriousness of their look and attitude. They must be English."

But the Cuban laughs. "You gentlemen are certainly unable to recognize the most obvious aspects of this painting. Look closely: They have no clothing or shoes. They have no home. They only have a measly apple to eat — and they still think they're in Paradise. They can only be Cubans."

A SURPRISE VISITOR

Ed was surprised one morning by a lanky stranger, casually dressed in a short-sleeve shirt and dark slacks, striding into his office.

"Hello, Ed," he said almost shyly, extending his hand for a quick shake. "I'm Herb Matthews."

Here was a journalistic legend in his own time.

Herbert Matthews, foreign correspondent for the *New York Times*, had achieved notoriety by interviewing and writing about Fidel Castro and his anti-Batista rebels while they were still a small, largely unknown group in the Sierra Maestra in 1957.

Matthews' articles praised Castro extravagantly, calling him "a man of ideals, of courage and remarkable qualities of leadership." The rural peasants worshiped Fidel, he wrote, and the feeling is "that he is invincible." At another point, he said that Castro's movement was a "flaming symbol" of the opposition to Batista and brought together "hundreds of highly respected citizens."

The *Times'* articles played a major role in bringing Castro's name before American newspaper readers and shaping the rebel leader's image at a critical time — a time when the few surviving rebels were in reality having little impact against Fulgencio Batista's army and were increasingly discouraged by the hard life in the mountains in southeast Cuba.

Ed recalled that the publicity bonanza brought many other foreign journalists to Cuba in the late 1950s in pursuit of interviews with this fearless, charismatic rebel leader. They wrote glowingly about the bearded guerrillas who had "invaded" from Mexico in late 1956.

What must have alarmed Batista was that Matthews seemed impressed by the number of rebel fighters under Castro's command. The truth was that the Castro group was composed of only eighteen survivors from the Granma landing and a few peasants they had managed to recruit from the rural countryside. They were woefully short of weapons and supplies and at the time of the first Matthews interview had fought in just one battle in the Sierra Maestra.

Castro and his brother, Raul, were said to have talked vaguely to Matthews about a second rebel unit and then paraded the few men available past the newspaperman a number of times to deceive him about the rebel strength.

Over the years, Matthews' tactics and his reporting on the Castro rebels were roundly criticized. Nevertheless, he'd continued his personal involvement with Castro and had been in and out of Cuba many times since. He seemed to have *carte blanche* with Fidel and the regime's top echelon in the 1960s.

And, now here he was on another visit to Havana.

"How about lunch with my wife and me?" Matthews asked Ed after the two chatted in the AP office for half an hour.

Herb and his wife, Nancy, were personable and easy to talk with over a leisurely lunch at the Focsa building's La Torre restaurant, where, as a VIP, Matthews had easy entrée. Although he offered few insights into his close relationship with Castro, he and Nancy talked generally about current-day Cuba. He continued to report for the *Times* and to enjoy Castro's friendship and write a number of books on the revolution long after the *Times* had disavowed his early reporting from the Sierra Maestra.

Surprisingly, Matthews had never visited the Bay of Pigs invasion site, and since Ed was planning a familiarization trip there, Matthews asked to join him.

The two Americans swapped stories along the tortuous road from Havana. They ate and drank well and were given a good tour of the invasion area and a museum being built at the battleground. They photographed each other at the *Bahia de Cochinos* on the last day of the trip before Herb and Nancy Matthews returned to the states.

The following year, Matthews retired from the *Times* and he and Nancy went to live in Australia. He wrote Ed a postcard, saying that they had found the perfect place, "without too many people, no noise whatsoever . . . and a lovely peace."

Castro was always wary of foreign journalists, particularly Americans. But he always showed a partiality to *The New York Times* even after Matthews left.

In his last year in office, Batista had begun censoring all Cuban and foreign newspapers entering the country as well as some of the local media. If government censors saw something they didn't like, they literally cut it out of whatever foreign periodical was involved, or they just held up distribution of the offending newspaper or magazine.

The Castro regime wasn't as obvious in the beginning. Instead, it controlled much of the news by issuing official communiqués and denying visas to those foreign reporters it didn't like.

Things rapidly worsened during and after the Bay of Pigs invasion, of course. A number of foreign journalists were chased out of the country and their offices closed down. Cuba's communication with the outside world went sliding downhill precipitously after that.

Its telephone, telegraph, telex and cable services were mainly run by foreign companies, all of which Castro was now "expropriating." Cuban technicians tried to keep everything working, but equipment was poorly maintained and replacement parts unavailable. Some of the equipment soon became unusable or obsolete and the whole system became a precarious mess.

Reporting from the Cuban capital became a chancy thing. Even government communications with other nations were difficult. Cuba would not pay the international corporations that controlled the overseas traffic. The island came close to complete isolation in the early 1960s.

Internally, the regime closed Havana's independent newspapers and radio and television stations, or just took over their operations. By the mid-1960s, the government had consolidated print outlets into two official newspapers: *Granma,* named after the boat the rebel group had used to reach Cuba from Mexico, and *Juventud Rebelde,* meaning Rebel Youth.

Things slowly began to improve when the Soviet Union and other Communist-bloc nations began trading with Cuba after the Bay of Pigs fiasco. Along with that, the Soviet bloc provided generous subsidies and technical help.

The communications situation hadn't improved much by mid-decade for reporters and the ordinary residents who wanted to reach relatives and friends overseas, however. The fact that the government operated or manipulated the island's communications system made it easy for censors in the Foreign and Interior ministries to monitor what every correspondent, a visiting reporter or ordinary citizen was sending out of the country.

In his case, of course, Ed had to find a way to communicate with his offices other than by the monitored telephone and cable lines. In a word, he had to *resolver*, to borrow a phrase from the Cubanos' street lexicon. He had to resolve his own problem. This meant circumventing the rules and finding other routes out of the country for his more descriptive reports.

Ed and the correspondents for Agence France-Presse, Reuters and United Press International knew that their reports going through the cable companies were routinely monitored. Ed personally confirmed this on a number of occasions when he was called into the Foreign Ministry to explain his interpretations of Cuban communiqués or Castro speeches and press conferences in his cabled reports to The Associated Press in New York.

His own resolution of the problem was through his good diplomatic contacts.

He arranged with friends at two different foreign embassies in Havana to include his lengthier, interpretive pieces in one or the other of the embassies' outgoing mail pouches several times a week. He would write out his articles on the typewriter, put them in sealed envelopes addressed to AP's New York headquarters in Rockefeller Plaza and slip the envelope to one of his accommodating diplomatic friends.

The diplomatic pouches and dispatches went from Havana to San Juan, Puerto Rico, or Nassau, in the Bahamas, and from there onward.

Several of the Western embassies had pooled their resources and engaged a charter flight service, which then flew a twin-engine plane into Havana once a week to bring in supplies. The embassy employees in Havana looked forward to the supply plane because they received personal mail and newspapers, good whiskey, medicine and other necessary items from the outside world.

The return flights carried out the sealed diplomatic pouches.

Embassy employees on the receiving end would send the contents onward to their destinations and post the AP envelopes to New York . That's how much of Ed's in-depth reporting and feature articles on the Cuban experience left the island — thanks to his friends and the embassies involved.

Ironically, throughout the decades of belligerence between the Castro regime and the United States, Cuba never lost its important connection to The AP's Latin American news service, called *La Prensa Asociada*. This service was transmitted in Spanish by radio signals from AP transmitters in New Jersey that were linked to AP's editorial offices at 50 Rockefeller Plaza.

The AP Latin American service was sold to major newspapers and government offices throughout the hemisphere. La Prensa Asociada had had clients in Cuba during the Batista era. But after the Bay of Pigs invasion, when the Castro government completed a takeover of all incoming and outgoing communication outlets, La Prensa Asociada was closed down to these Havana outlets.

Before long, however, the Cuban regime's technicians began intercepting the AP radio-teletype signals beamed to subscribers in Mexico, the Caribbean and Latin America. Cuban officials and the editors at the communist newspaper *Granma* thus kept right on reading and utilizing the top news of the day even after Cuba had kicked out American reporters and closed down all foreign news bureaus. This didn't mean they published or broadcast it directly. But some of those officials would sometimes use it for propaganda purposes.

In its takeover, the Castro's Cuba had kept all of the radio-teletype equipment The AP had installed in the 1950s when it sold and distributed its Latin American wire service to Havana subscribers — newspapers, radio and TV stations, embassies and some government offices.

The AP didn't learn until later that the government had continued to operate the equipment and print out the incoming Latin American newswire in a number of its own offices just as it had in the 1950s. Among those government entities who kept on tapping into The AP's wire were the Foreign Ministry and a suite of offices used by Castro at the Plaza de la Revolucion.

And, surprisingly, the Castro people obligingly continued to pay the monthly AP assessments for the news service. Since there was no AP representative left in Cuba after the shutdown, they deposited the funds into a special account in a Havana bank in the name of The Associated Press.

The catch was that the money was deposited in Cuban pesos, which were not convertible into U.S. currency. Aha!

But when The AP office was allowed to reopen in Havana, the AP correspondent began writing checks on the account and using the Cuban funds for daily operations and to pay the salaries of its two local employees.

A PLOT, A PURGE
AND PARTY TIME

In 1965, the seventh year of the Castro revolution, a bright young medical doctor and Army *comandante* named Rolando Cubelas decided he would never become the famous man he aspired to be unless he did something dramatic.

The popular Cubelas was one of Castro's commanders in the mountains during the struggle against Batista, and he had now become the director of Havana's large Manuel Fajardo Hospital.

But Cubelas was ambitious and restless, as were a number of other young military officers who had now become faceless bureaucrats. He'd talked quietly with friends about there being "no end to this life in which we are constantly at war with each other and the Yankees."

Comandante Cubelas decided to do something to change his, and his country's present course. He decided to kill Fidel Castro. This was in 1965.

On the pretext of obtaining medical equipment and training materials, he had arranged a trip to Paris in November of the previous year. There, he'd met with two former Cuban Army officers who were now in exile in Miami. They, in turn, introduced him to an official with the American Central Intelligence Agency.

In December, Cubelas flew to Madrid, where he secretly met with another old friend, Manuel Artime, now a prominent Cuban exile in Florida who had been a leader of the Cuban exile brigade that invaded at the Bay of Pigs. Along with most of the other invaders, Artime had been captured but eventually freed by the Cuban government. Now, he was still plotting against Fidel Castro.

At a Christmas Day meeting in Madrid in 1964, Artime talked Cubelas into joining an assassination plot against the Cuban prime minister. It took another trip to Spain in February before Cubelas agreed to be the assassin, and they worked out specific details of the plan. Later, Artime presented him with a telescopic sight and silencer for his rifle.

Cubelas confessed to all this at his trial, which Ed had managed to attend.

Also part of the assassination plot were two former Cuban Embassy officials in Madrid, identified by Cubelas as Odon Alvarez de la Campa and Jose Gonzalez Gallarreta. The two previously had arranged a meeting with a CIA official in Spain, who reportedly gave them $100,000 for their help in carrying out the plan.

On his return to Cuba, Cubelas brought in Roman Guin Diaz, who had also been a rebel *comandante* under Fidel. Guin had previously told Cubelas he had in the past furnished Cuban military information to the CIA.

Cubelas' trips to Europe didn't go unnoticed by Cuba's G2 intelligence service, however.

A report went to Fidel, who later called in his friend Cubelas for "counseling." At this point, the prime minister didn't know about the assassination plot, but he told his fellow officer he knew he had become disinterested in the revolution. And he advised Cubelas "fraternally" to change his ways and avoid becoming "an instrument of the enemies of the revolution."

In the face-to-face meeting, Cubelas vehemently denied any dissatisfaction with Castro or the revolution. Nevertheless, Castro ordered an investigation, which eventually uncovered the assassination plot. Cubelas and Guin were soon arrested, along with five other Cuban conspirators.

The imprisonment of the well-known Cubelas — who as an undergraduate had held the prestigious post of president of the Federation of University Students at the University of Havana — spurred widespread speculation in Cuba and overseas that the conspiracy had deep roots in the military, the medical community and possibly among university students.

Isaac M. Flores

Other arrests were expected.

In Miami, Artime denied any participation in the assassination plan. The CIA had no official comment.

Apparently because of the ongoing publicity, the Castro government decided to hold a military show trial at La Cabaña. This was a highly unusual step since most political trials took place behind closed doors in unannounced locations. The regime obviously wanted to publicly demonstrate its vigilance in such matters, and to show those who plotted against the revolution what they could expect when they were exposed.

There had been other schemes against Castro's life over the years, including several fanciful efforts by organized crime leaders in the United States working under the direction of the CIA. American mobsters wanted revenge after losing their casinos in Havana. Most of those exile plots never got beyond the talking stage, much like that of Cubelas.

The opening session of the trial had an audience of some 500, mainly military personnel, government officials and security agents. Much to Ed Brophy's surprise, he was allowed to attend after pestering the people at MinRex. Also in the large, badly lit courtroom were Cuban journalists and the correspondents for Reuters and Agence France Presse.

Another first was that the trial was taped for broadcast on Cuban television. Castro was not present.

The prosecutor quickly introduced a surprise witness who claimed he was a double agent. Juan Pelaez Canan, who described himself as a loyal Cuban, admitted he had been employed by the CIA until the previous month. Pelaez testified he was really in the service of Cuban intelligence during the three years he was in the pay of the CIA in Miami and Cuba.

Pelaez said he learned of the assassination plan against Castro from his brother in Miami. He identified his brother as chief of intelligence for an anti-Castro Cuban exile organization, the Movement of Revolutionary Reconstruction.

Cubelas then took the witness stand and readily admitted his role in the plot. He said he was to shoot the prime minister with the telescopic rifle provided by Artime. He told the tribunal of the secret meetings with Artime and CIA officials in Madrid.

In a loud, dramatic voice, the highly emotional Cubelas then asserted, "This was (to be) a cowardly act, to hide behind a window and shoot the prime minister . . . In this way, I fell into the hands of the enemy."

Bursting into tears, he cried out, "To the wall. To be executed, that is what I want. It is justified. . ."

The prosecutor, Jorge Serguera, urged an attentive jury composed of five military officers to impose the death penalty on Cubelas, Guin, Gonzalez Gallarreta and Alberto Blanco Romariz. He asked thirty-year prison sentences for Juan Alsina Navarro, Guillermo Cunill Alvarez and Angel Herrerro Veliz.

The curious trial took still another dramatic turn when Castro indirectly intervened. In a letter to the military court, he asked that the lives of Cubelas and the three others be spared. In the letter read in open court, Castro declared that the revolution was strong enough to be merciful even though the conspiracy was "one of the most cowardly and repugnant acts" to take place during the past seven years.

Death sentences would be "natural and severe penalties" for such a conspiracy, he wrote the prosecutor, "But I ask that you not appeal for the death penalty for any of those accused. The revolution is strong."

Castro evidently wanted to project a new image to el pueblo and international public opinion.

After reading Castro's letter to the court, followed by a short recess, the prosecutor called for thirty years of imprisonment for Cubelas, Guin and the two others, and lesser terms for the remaining defendants.

Dutifully, the jurors agreed.

The trial performance reminded Ed of another military proceeding which had taken place in 1959, the first year of the revolution. The accused was Comandante Huber Matos, a 40-year-old former teacher in the rural Cuban countryside.

Matos, who held a doctorate degree from the University of Havana, was charged with treason after writing Castro a resignation letter declaring that the revolution's leadership was falling into the hands of communists. He criticized the prime minister, an old friend, for allowing this to take place and for restricting his freedom of expression.

The star witness in that trial was Fidel Castro himself. He spoke for a total of seven hours. He told the court that Matos, who was then the head of military forces in Camaguey Province, had been conspiring with other officers against him lately and planned to lead a barracks revolt. Wearing a microphone on a cord around his neck, Castro had paced about and pointed a long finger, accusing Matos and his friends of supporting the interests of the United States and large landowners and supporters of Batista.

The dark-bearded Matos spoke briefly and denied all charges.

"I differed from Fidel Castro because the original objective of OUR revolution was 'Freedom or Death,' Matos said in an interview with Worldview magazine in 1980. "Once Castro had power, he began to kill freedom."

The handpicked military court quickly convicted Matos and was expected to sentence him to a firing squad, but Castro intervened then, as he did later in the Cubelas trial. Not wanting to turn Matos into an anti-revolutionary martyr, he asked the court to sentence him to prison.

Matos received a twenty-year sentence and was sent to the Isle of Pines. Twenty-one other defendants were sentenced to two to seven years.

Matos was subjected to beatings and other torture for much of his time in prison. He was finally freed in 1979 and flown to Costa Rica, where he rejoined his family. He later made his way to the exile hotbed of Miami, where he became an outspoken voice against Castro. He died there in March, 2014, at the age of 95.

Incidentally, Jorge Serguera was the government prosecutor at both the Cubelas and Matos show trials.

As for Cubelas, he achieved notoriety, but no glory. And his activities appeared only to have strengthened Fidel Castro's rule.

A few days after the Cubelas trial, dozens of high-ranking officials were purged from their jobs for a wide range of offenses, including some who were close friends of Cubelas. Among them was Comandante Efigenio Ameijeiras, who was a deputy minister of the armed forces. Ameijeiras was stripped of his rank and discharged from the army and from the Communist Party's Central Committee. Others were arrested and accused of irresponsible conduct, high living or "illegal, vice-ridden activities."

Ed Brophy later questioned Fidel about this during a chance encounter. Castro replied there were still forty or fifty "vice-ridden, parasitic" officials in the government. He didn't go into detail but repeated the assertion in an angry speech later. And he added that some Cuban officials were even ignoring counterrevolutionary talk by foreign diplomats.

The prime minister harshly criticized diplomatic functions where "bourgeois capitalist diplomats with evident corruptive spirit" tell dirty stories in the presence of Cuban government officials. Such activity is intolerable, Castro said, both on the part of the Cubans and the diplomats involved.

He mentioned two specific instances of "evident attempts to corrupt, bribe and soften" Cuban officials in the mid-1960s. One of the incidents took place in Spain, where members of a Cuban trade mission attended a party with "immoral women" and got drunk. The other incident took place in Havana at a reception given by a French diplomat, he said. No details were given and the diplomat was never publicly identified.

The purge of high-living officials exposed some of the dirty linen of the regime's leadership ranks. Many of the difficulties came about when military officers and civilians were converting the government from its old capitalist ways to a socialist-communist system, whatever Fidel chose to call it at the time. They were guerrilla fighters one day and government managers the next.

They had become directors, administrators, supervisors, bosses and lesser bureaucrats. And, as Castro pointed out, there were now increased contacts with foreigners and all manner of temptations for Cuban officials, who nevertheless were expected to set examples for the proletariat.

None of this is to say that fun-loving Cubans, at all levels, didn't have their small pleasures. The Cuban capital in the 1960s was not, by any means, the swinging, wide-open tourist lure it was in the 1950s, but Cubans always managed to have a good time despite the police-state control on virtually every activity.

Nightclubs, restaurants and bars were beginning to thrive again, frequented by those who could afford them. Movie houses, which were more affordable, showed Soviet and East European films when they weren't running Hollywood movies of the 1930s and '40s. There was an increasing number of concerts, ballet performances and sporting events as part of the communist emphasis on sports and culture — policies now being adopted by Cuba.

Many Cubans enjoyed street parties and lazy weekends at the beach.

Havana's famous Tropicana nightclub barely missed a beat from the Batista era into the revolutionary period. In unstoppable fashion, its glittering indoor-outdoor stage extravaganzas featured nearly nude women dancers in Las Vegas-style musical shows. "A bit seedy, but nice," a visiting French diplomat commented to Ed after seeing a show.

The cabarets at the large hotels — the Habana Libre, Habana Riviera, the Capri and the Nacional — also featured musical reviews with lots of healthy young women, risqué jokes and dining and dancing. In prerevolutionary days, much of the hotels' main attractions also had been casino gambling, but that quickly became a no-no when Castro got to Havana.

Local beer, and rum cocktails such as mojitos and daiquiris, were the drinks of choice since there was little whiskey to be had. Most cities had annual street carnivals with bands, floats, dance groups, and girls in elaborate costumes.

Ballet, both classical and modern, had always been popular in Cuba and remained a source of pride for the nation under Castro. Cuba's internationally famous prima ballerina Alicia Alonso was past her prime but was still performing and teaching ballet to young people.

The Soviet Union had a continuous shuttle of show business talent into the island, including the Bolshoi Ballet. It also sent a number of athletes and sports teams to compete against the Cubans.

Films from Czechoslovakia, Poland, Hungary and Communist China were shown throughout the island. Touring groups of performers from other countries were popular in the countryside.

The diplomatic colony kept busy with its own functions, but there was a dip in the number of government people attending these dinners and parties as a result of Castro's purge.

Some members of the diplomatic colony and a few Cubans even played a round of golf now and then . . . or half a round. There was one golf course left in Havana, a nine-hole layout open to everyone who still had some clubs and walked up to play.

How this one one course remained open puzzled Ed. So he inquired about it. He learned that the revolutionary regime had taken over all the golf, tennis and country clubs and turned most of the real estate into army bases, military drill fields, heavy armor storage depots and other government uses.

Ed heard several versions of how this one golf layout was spared. It seems that several golf enthusiasts from the Canadian and British legations had spoken to Cuban officials about leaving at least one course open for morale purposes for their personnel. The Cubans eventually relented, but only halfway. The government took half of a fairly short, flat course in Vedado and turned it into a cow pasture. The golfers playing the remaining nine holes stayed away from the barbed wire fences and mooing cows on the other side.

Ed put in some playing time with diplomats and a young Cuban who had been a caddy for the well-to-do during Batista's time.

Someone in the government also had relented to similar appeals from tennis players and kept hands off four clay courts at the former Vedado Tennis Club, a once-exclusive family center that had now been turned into a hodgepodge of classrooms and military training facilities.

Ed wandered over to the tennis courts one Sunday morning, looked the place over and stayed for awhile to watch an intense doubles match between some middle-aged men. It turned out they were former members of the club while it was in its heyday. One of them had gone to the University of Miami and had been a standout on the tennis team when it was ranked among the best in the country.

His doubles partner was an ambidextrous switch hitter who *always* hit forehands. He switched his racket from hand to hand, depending on where the ball was hit to him. He was equally good with either hand. Their doubles play was excellent.

The players, two of whom wore patched-up tennis shoes, were hitting with wooden rackets and old Dupont tennis balls that must have been hit thousands of times. There was no woolly fuzz and very little bounce left on them. There was no place to buy new balls even if they could have afforded them. But these players were happy, shouting and arguing line calls as they probably had always done.

"I live for weekends. This takes me away from reality," one of the men said to Ed when he found out he was an American journalist. "I used to own a small chain of stores that sold American kitchen appliances," he said. "Fidel took it along with everything else. Now I'm a desk clerk at the Habana Libre ."

"Why don't you go back to Ohio?

"I can't leave Cuba because I have a Cuban wife and Cuban-born children. You know how it is."

NEW LIFE FOR A REBEL

Miguel came awake slowly to the chatter of birds, the whispered rustle of tree leaves and the muted sounds of playing children. He was in a soft bed. An early morning breeze drifted in through an open window. The strange sounds, the bed, the window, all combined to befuddle him into thinking he was dreaming, or already in another world.

He dozed for another five minutes before sitting up with a start thinking he might be dead.

A soft rap on the door brought him to his senses. He was in Tano's house. His friend, Antonio "Tano" Castillo, and his pretty wife, Adelia, had met him at the prison hospital and brought him to their home in Almendares, a section of Havana adjacent to Miramar.

He'd been in bed for almost two days, sleeping fitfully, alternately drenched in sweat and shivering with cold, now rousing only to sip soup and take some aspirin and antibiotics that Adelia had acquired from her doctor.

Tano and Miguel had grown up together in Cuba's ranch and farm country. They had gone to the University of Havana together. It was there they met Adelia. She and Tano had married after the Castro revolution began. Tano had left school and gone to work for a company of engineers that designed and inspected maritime shipping containers for the government.

He was now an administrative official at the Port of Havana, and since his work was considered essential to the revolution, he and Adelia managed

175

to live comfortably. He had somehow stayed out of Castro's sphere and hadn't been required to join the Communist Party.

How his hospitality for a newly released political prisoner would affect Tano's position he didn't know. But he told Miguel he couldn't have done otherwise. That was earlier in the morning before going off to work.

"Are you better today, Miguel? asked Adelia, walking quietly into the room. "Teresita is bringing coffee and breakfast things. You should try to eat something. Tano will be back at noon."

"Delia" had also grown up in ranch country but came to live in Havana with an aunt and uncle when she began attending the university. She'd studied medicine but hadn't completed her courses before marrying Tano and moving into this house a year after Batista's downfall. They had two small children. Her parents had been killed in an auto accident on a visit to St. Louis, Missouri, when she was a young girl. Her American-born father, Julian Mendez, had been a physician there before coming to Cuba.

Adelia and Tano had tracked Miguel's grim odyssey through Castro's prison system, knowing that his wife and child were gone from Cuba and that he had no close relatives that could help him. Now they had brought Miguel into their home.

Teresita poured him hot tea and offered toast and a softboiled egg. She was a family friend and helped Adelia with the kids and with work around the house.

"As soon as Tano gets here we'll go see our doctor," Adelia said. "He's one of my former professors. He'll tell us what's wrong with you for sure, not like those butchers at the prison hospitals."

"Ay, 'Delia, I don't know whether all your trouble is worth it," replied Miguel, sitting up in bed and shaking his head slowly. "Those bastards have left me crippled and they say my disease, whatever it is, will kill me. You and Tano and the children are at risk just for putting me up here."

"We will see. We'll see what the doctor says," said 'Delia. "Meanwhile, you eat. Food and rest are very important. You need your strength."

Miguel took a hot shower for the second time in years and was soon feeling like he might not die after all, not right away anyhow. Returning for lunch, Tano helped him into the kitchen.

"No *tengas pena*, Miguel. Don't worry about 'Delia and me. Nothing is going to happen, you'll see. You'll stay with us until you get better."

After a hurried lunch, Tano took his patched-up 1957 Chevrolet out of the garage and they drove Miguel to a clinic in Vedado run by Dr. Alberto Baca. After examining him for a half hour and questioning him for another twenty minutes, Dr. Baca would only say that any specific diagnosis would have to wait on the results of blood tests and other exams he would conduct over the next few days.

"Even then, it may be difficult to pin down any specifics," the aged doctor said. "From your condition and what you tell me, you appear to have yellow fever, or a variant of it, which is about the same as malaria. But it could be a combination of diseases. *Tu sabes*, we don't have all the facilities we need to conduct thorough testing."

Dr. Baca gave him a box of antibiotic capsules and a small supply of painkillers, plus a list of foods he should and shouldn't eat. He sent him home with the Castillos until he could see him again in three days. A second visit to Dr. Baca brought the news that blood tests showed he did have Yellow Fever, that he was severely anemic and his metabolism low. This resulted in more medication and a hefty supply of different vitamins.

"There's not much we can do to treat Yellow Fever beyond what we're doing now," the doctor said. "It is potentially fatal. Many cases clear up by themselves but only after a long recovery period. With you, there's a strong possibility of kidney and liver damage because it was neglected for so long. We will conduct such periodic testing as we can. You must rest and avoid any stressful activity. I want to see you once a week for the next few weeks."

Tano and Adelia urged him to stay with them until he recovered. All three realized that he couldn't get along on his own in his weakened condition. There would be slow improvement, the doctor said optimistically.

His other injuries appeared to heal well with time. His lower back became less painful with the use of a cane. He no longer had a recurring problem with his vision and his blinding headaches were of shorter duration. He now slept soundly for several hours at a time, although he still awoke drenched in sweat.

Miguel slowly acclimated himself to his new world. The heat and humidity of summer began to dissipate, becoming more comfortable. The days were sunny and warm and the nights cooler. He began to walk slowly, first around the house and then longer walks through the pleasant neighborhood and into a park filled with uniformed children from the government-run schools.

With help from another friend of the Castillos, Miguel managed to complete a telephone call to his wife's uncle, Rodolfo, in Florida's Palm Beach County.

Rodolfo, the manager of a sugar mill in the Florida Everglades muckland around Lake Okeechobee, was surprised and happy to hear Miguel had been released from prison. But he said Joanna and daughter Linda had left Florida and were now living with her sister Andrea in Sonoma in northern California.

It took another week to complete a call there through Cuba's fitful telephone system, and finally the family was reunited over long distance.

Joanna wept at length when she heard his voice and had to turn the telephone over to their daughter until she composed herself. Linda was ten years old now and in fourth grade. Schoolwork involved "a lot of reading and writing — in English, of course — although I speak Spanish at home." She told him she liked math and history "because they cause me to think a lot. . . I think a lot about you, papa, all the time."

Joanna was overjoyed after their seven long years apart but was sobered by the news that he couldn't leave Cuba right away. Miguel didn't tell her the full extent of his physical problems, but he said he was in good hands with Tano and Adelia.

"Please do everything you can to leave that country," Joanna pleaded, urging him not to get involved in anything that might land him back in prison. "We can make a good life right here in California, or in Florida," said Joanna, who was working as a nurse's aide in a hospital.

He told her he was anxious to rejoin them and that he'd try to do so as soon as he could. Weeks went by, with Miguel doing little but eating and sleeping. He did small chores around the house or helped Adelia and Teresita, the next-door friend and cook who showed up at the Castillo house every morning and had breakfast ready by the time everyone was up.

The doctor told him on one of his visits that his fevers, chills and paralyzing headaches would eventually disappear, but that they could recur at any time and could become critical because of his weakened liver and kidneys. He was taken off some medication, however.

As Miguel's body slowly strengthened, his depression worsened. He knew he was of little use in Cuba, even if he were to recover from his disease and injuries. And he had many doubts about starting over a new life in the United States, if he were allowed to leave his country.

He tried to be optimistic in his brief telephone conversations with his wife and daughter, but this didn't come easy to him when he felt so useless.

He took long walks as part of his therapy and to get away from the house as much as possible. He wandered aimlessly through the beautiful, but now-neglected, residential streets of Almendares and Miramar.

Many of the elegant homes abandoned by their owners and confiscated by the Castro regime had been turned into schools, military training centers and bureaucratic offices. Schoolchildren of all ages —including the sons and daughters of dirt-poor campesinos from the interior and those from city-bred parents who lived in cramped, cold-water apartments — seemed happy enough as they ran and played outdoors.

One day, as he sat on a concrete bench in a neighborhood park, he heard someone approach from behind.

"*Oye, chico,* a hushed voice said as Miguel turned to see a bearded man in dark glasses and baseball cap come walking up to him. "Don't you remember me from Camaguey? *Soy yo,* Roberto Madera."

"Roberto, of course, what a surprise. What are you doing here?" asked Miguel as the visitor slid onto the bench alongside him.

Madera had been one of the farmers jailed along with Miguel in a militia sweep of "black market profiteers" back in 1960. They had spent three days in a jail in that sprawling interior city and had stayed in contact for several months after that, until Miguel was arrested with Jimmy on the anti-revolutionary charges.

Madera had spotted Miguel in the park several days earlier and had waited to make sure he had the right man, he said.

"When I saw you this morning, I followed you." Then, with a look of concern, he said, "You don't look well, Miguel. I heard about your imprisonment. *Que tragédia.*"

"You should have seen me a few weeks ago," Miguel said quietly, emotional now about meeting someone he knew from the past.

It turned out that Madera lived in Havana now, with his sister and brother-in-law and their family. After trading stories about the past few years, Madera confided that he was helping some anti-Castro exiles smuggle weapons into the country from Florida, Puerto Rico and the Dominican Republic.

"You're crazy, Roberto. They'll get you the way they got me and Jimmy," Miguel blurted out.

"No, amigo, things are cooking now. I think we can get something going against this *hijo de puta,* (meaning Fidel Castro). The military is unhappy, the Pope's calling on him to release political prisoners, the U.N. and the Latino countries know he's 'exporting revolution,' as they call it. But . . . most of all, the people are very restless and hungry, hungry for a change as well as for decent food."

"But," argued Miguel in a quieter voice now, "what good will it do if you can get a few people in here with some weapons? Those exiles, they talk big but when it comes to action, there is very little of it that is meaningful."

Miguel continued his criticism of the Miami-based exile organizations he had heard and read about. "Alfa 66, RECE, el Frente, MIRR, none of them has carried out successful operations in Cuba. And yet, they all talk as if they're in a fullscale war with Fidel."

"Look, let's get away from here," Madera said placatingly. "We'll go to this little bar I know on the beach and we can get a beer."

Roberto Madera led the way a few blocks into Miramar and to an outdoor bar, where they sat among the palms and mango trees facing the ocean. Madera nursed a beer while Miguel had a bittersweet soft drink.

"*Mira, chico,*" Madera said as they sipped. "We're going to do something big soon. We've already had two small boat landings with weapons and explosives, and we're planning several major operations. Soon"

Where did these boats come from, Miguel wanted to know.

"We have friends from Cayo Hueso (Key West) who come and go along the coast in Camaguey."

"Well," said Miguel, "shooting at *milicianos* or trying to infiltrate a few exiles and weapons in here isn't going to do much to overthrow Fidel, Roberto. "Look at what happened with the so-called resistance after the Bay of Pigs. There was *no* resistance . . . And, recently, they've arrested most of those *guajiro* fighters still hiding out in the Escambray."

"We've got to continue. Every act, no matter how small, against these *cabrones* will help inspire others," insisted Madera, interrupting his friend, fearing that he was winding up for a lecture.

Ignoring his protests, Madera said, "Our next plan is to get a couple of big speedboats to come right into the Havana coast and blow up the house of President Dorticós with rockets. You know where that is, not too far from here right on the coast."

"Who is 'we,'" Miguel asked.

"Well, our own group here is made up of Havana people, mainly university students, and some unhappy rural people, farmers, sugarcane growers and fishermen from the interior who are crazy to get Fidel and his crowd. We communicate back and forth with the exiles. It may not sound like much, but these are dedicated men, believe me."

"Why Dorticós if you want to get Fidel?" Miguel asked, sitting back, willing to hear out Madera and his crazy plan.

"Well, you know that Fidel moves around all the time, so he's hard for us to track right now. But . . . We want to show that we mean business. So . . . we do what we can."

Madera went on, "Along with the shelling of the president's house — who knows, we may be able to kill the bastard in his bed — we plan to blow up a couple of police stations here and in Camaguey. If we do that, we can get more people, maybe even some of the army units, to support us. And we'll get more help from the outside, too, you'll see. It may turn out to be more than symbolic."

Miguel sipped his drink, shaking his head slowly but not saying anything.

"Look, we've got to get Fidel little by little," Madera persisted. "That's the only way the army and the people will come alive and do something, if they know someone is fighting. You say the Yankees and exiles looked ridiculous with the Bay of Pigs. Well, look what Kennedy did to those bastards Khrushchev and Castro over the missiles in October, 1962.

"You were in prison then, but it was through the efforts of people like you that the CIA first knew about the missiles. And before that, you did something, Miguel. You helped to open the eyes of the world to this *cabrón*. Why stop now?" Madera added, looking directly into his friend's tired eyes.

"*Porque estoy jodido.* I'm all fucked up," replied Miguel slowly, his eyes tearing. "Look at me, what they did to me."

He couldn't stop the tears running down his face. He didn't know why he should be overcome like this. He didn't feel disheartened enough to cry in prison. Why now? Was it for himself? His ruined life? His country?

"I'm going away if I can," Miguel whispered to his friend. "And I won't be back ever again no matter what happens. There's no more Cuba for me. Nobody is ever going to be able to throw these bastards out. Don't you see, Roberto," he continued, his voice rising. "This isn't just another revolution like Cuba has had throughout its past. The Fidelistas are transforming everything. Everybody knew that changes were necessary when Batista got out, of course. But Fidel, he's turning Cuba and Cubans into something we're not.

"From what I can see, we're nothing but servants — stupid, obedient, communist servants. We're not proud Cubans like we used to be in the past, no matter who the strongman boss was. We've always carried out wars and revolutions in this country. But I don't think anyone knew what those words really meant until Fidel took over. *Nothing* will ever be the same again. He gets stronger every day, and it will take a fullscale war to get rid of him, not guerrillas or *gusano* exiles with hit-and-run attacks . . . or sabotage."

Madera looked at him sadly, slowly shaking his head.

"Give it up, Roberto. Go to Miami with me," Miguel persisted. "We'll become *gusanos* (worms), too. Find some jobs, make a new life."

Madera stared at the ocean waves breaking over the Malecon. He sipped his beer and nodded thoughtfully, not saying anything for a minute or two.

"No, amigo, I'm staying right here and doing what I can. We'll get rid of these communist bastards one way or another. There are too many who hate him for him to escape much longer. You are sick and depressed, Miguel. Maybe you *should* go join the exiles in Florida. There are plenty of us here and on the outside who will keep trying. I'm not going to become a goddamned waiter or bellboy in a Miami Beach hotel, like a lot of those who left here. Fuck that. I'll die here first."

They parted amicably, promising to see each other at the same spot in a couple of days, after Miguel's doctor visit.

That night, Miguel couldn't sleep for thinking about Roberto Madera and his friends. At least they were doing something. But, then, he reminded himself, he was now a broken man because he believed like Madera a few years ago and had tried to do something about it.

This morning, when he blurted out that he was leaving his beloved Cuba to become another faceless, jobless exile in Miami, he was convinced of his sudden choice. But now . . . Madera had given him something to think about. Maybe he was right. Maybe . . .

EXILES ATTACK

The explosions could be heard all along the Havana waterfront from Miramar to Habana Vieja. Bright orange flames streaked into the dark, moonless skies above a heavily guarded military compound near the Almendares River Bridge. White smoke billowed for blocks around, smothering trees, shrubbery, houses, all along the wide boulevard.

Residents along the neatly landscaped area facing Miramar's Fifth Avenue, with its tall Royal Palm trees, were jolted awake by the blasts. They ventured out into the streets warily, peering out at the Atlantic. Gunfire could be heard in the distance, apparently resounding off the placid, white-capped sea where several vessels were dimly visible several miles offshore.

"I can see a fast-moving boat exchanging gunfire with two slower-moving boats from the *Guardia Costál*," said one onlooker with binoculars.

For a full half hour, the three vessels could be dimly seen weaving back and forth, the red-and-white blasts of gunfire reflecting off the ocean sporadically. A Cuban gunboat arrived on the scene and "boom!" "boom!" It didn't take the large white boat long to score a direct hit on the much smaller, darker intruder, catapulting several of its crewmembers overboard and creating a smoky fire aboard. The whole scene was lit up by the flames, quickly turning into spirals of black smoke.

The coast guard vessel closed in and several sailors could be seen boarding the smoking boat, which had the name "LIBERTAD" brightly painted in yellow on its bow.

Meanwhile, onshore, firefighters and members of the Cuban militia fought to limit the damage to the smoking military compound, which included the sprawling two-story house occupied by President Osvaldo Dorticós. One of the rocket blasts from the exile vessel had scored a direct hit on a large fuel tank on the property and several army vehicles parked nearby, creating thick smoke and tall, red-and-yellow plumes of fire. One wing of the house was also ablaze, onlookers could see.

Ed and his driver, Blake, managed to get to the scene as a coast guard vessel towed the scorched and bullet-scarred exile boat to shore. Reports circulated that two of the attackers had been killed and two seriously wounded and captured. Two others were missing and presumably drowned.

The incursion into Cuban waters and the attack on the Dorticós compound was more "successful" than most, but this was just one of hundreds of raids by Florida-based exiles against their homeland in the 1960s. Ed and other reporters couldn't immediately find out whether Dorticós was home at the time.

But the stocky president, in a suit, white shirt and tie, appeared on television the next day and, adjusting his horn-rimmed glasses, assured an off-screen interviewer that he was all right and that the attackers would soon be dealt "with the extreme justice they deserve."

The daring attack on Havana especially provoked the ire of Fidel Castro, who accused the CIA of supporting it. The Cubans charged that the exile launch sailed from the Florida Keys despite an agreement between the two countries to try to prevent such activities.

U.S. officials denied all allegations and said they had long sought to discourage such exile raids. They pointed out that a number of similar expeditions had been prevented from leaving Florida waters in the recent past.

"Hit-and-run raids have no value, and on the contrary they are harmful to the interests of both countries," State Department official Georges Michaels said on American television.

But to Roberto Madera and his small band of counter-revolutionaries in Havana, the raid was a success because it had been carried out with coordinated planning. It had gone virtually as planned, except for the exile losses.

Dorticós himself would have been no big prize; he was just a figurehead for the Castro government. The attack, though, was seen as more than symbolic. It was another call to arms for the scattered counter-revolutionaries within Cuba who refused to give up their dreams of overthrowing Castro.

The attackers couldn't target the maximum leader himself because he was becoming increasingly conscious of his personal security, cutting down on impromptu appearances and never spending the night in the same place twice. He now moved about in secrecy. Castro's enemies were never able to pin down his whereabouts very successfully.

The mild-mannered Dorticós was named president in 1959, shortly after the Castristas chased out Batista. The president provided legal and administrative leadership in the early days of the revolution, when Fidel's bearded rebels began taking over the government. With a scholarly, meek look accentuated by his glasses, Dorticós was instrumental in arguing Cuba's case in international bodies such as the United Nations. He worked alongside Foreign Minister Raul Roa and U.N. representative Carlos Lechuga during the 1962 missile crisis talks.

His injury or death would have been a notable victory for Communist Cuba's enemies. But, such as it was, the anti-Castro rebels could finally claim they had carried out a successful attack, however minor it might have been seen in the rest of the world.

To Ed and objective foreign observers, however, the terrorist foray served to strengthen the Cuban propaganda mill against the CIA and Florida-based exiles. It gave Castro more fodder for his never-ending campaign against the Yankees.

As if taking their cue from the attack on the Dorticós compound, however, numerous small acts of sabotage and hit-and-run incidents took place over the next few weeks in Havana and other Cuban areas inland, but mainly in the larger towns. What little resistance there was to the Cuban regime was suddenly energized into action. All at once, these small rebel groups wanted to make their own statements, however small.

The attacks included the sabotaging of a runway at a military airfield near Santiago, the takeover of a Cuban patrol boat by a band of defectors in a fishing village in Matanzas Province and the hijacking to Miami of a commercial flight from Cienfuegos to Havana. Several men raided a construction site and made off with a large supply of dynamite.

The anti-Castro exile groups also became more creative in their actions. Besides stepping up the number of seaborne incursions and depositing small quantities of men and weapons along secluded coastal areas, they began to attack Cuban missions in some foreign countries. They experimented with airborne incursions onto the island. An old B-26 airplane dropped bombs in the countryside, one partially destroying the home of peasant Domingo Baños near Consolacion del Norte, nine miles from the Niagara Sugar Mill.

In addition, the regime was bedeviled by a number of defections of Cuban embassy personnel overseas, including the important legations in London and Tokyo.

There was little publicity within Cuba of such activities, but there was a lot of buzz among the people on the street. Rumors abounded:The military would turn against Fidel, his top lieutenants could not be trusted, the Yankees would soon invade again and this time they would complete a takeover. Such speculation was fueled by these sporadic attacks from outside the country.

Ed was busy on two fronts, reporting on this renewed spate of anti-government attacks and making secret efforts to track down his brother. After numerous quiet inquiries among his Cuban sources, he learned that Miguel had been near death in the prison system and had been released, presumably to die on his own.

Finally, from Dr. Rivero and his friends, Ed received word that his brother was alive and recuperating quietly somewhere in the Havana area. He redoubled his efforts to seek him out and help him in any way he could.

Miguel, not knowing anything about the activities of his half-brother, had reached an agonizing decision.

Convinced that he wouldn't be allowed to leave the country, and equally certain that his deep hatred for the Castro regime would never allow him to rest, the recuperating ex-political prisoner had quietly joined the resistance. After long discussions with his friend Madera and others, Miguel convinced himself that to die in the struggle against Castro was better than to live in exile like a whipped dog.

All of this was taking place at a time when the Cuban government was taking stock of itself, casting off in disgrace some of those leaders who had lost their revolutionary fervor, reorganizing some of its hidebound, nonproductive activities, and cutting back on some of the extreme bureaucracy.

The armed forces, too, were undergoing a transformation. Ed talked to some officers who were restless and sought changes in operations. Some were being abruptly transferred away from their families, sent to Africa or the Soviet Union, or forced out of service with nowhere to go and nothing to do. A few defected to other countries.

Toward the latter part of the 1960s, critics within the country became bolder and suddenly appeared to be more numerous, perhaps because they came to believe there was safety in numbers or because the once-feared CDR neighborhood informants were not as quick to denounce suspects as they used to be.

These *lumpen,* or *gusanos* — Castro's favorite words for what he deemed to be traitors to the revolution — would secretly gather at someone's house and commiserate over the hard times and recount experiences in beating the system. They talked more openly about not having enough rice, meat, milk, shoes and other necessities for themselves and their families, about their struggles to leave the country, their fears that their sons, brothers and friends would be drafted and sent to die in Africa. Some even wrote and recited counter-revolutionary poems and songs.

There was usually a grim humor to these tales because of the Cubans' propensity to laugh at the situation or themselves, even in the roughest of times.

There was a widely told story about a middleaged lady sitting quietly on a bus looking out a window. Suddenly, she stood up and shouted, "Oh, Cuba, my Cuba, what have they done to you?"

A plainclothes G2 agent sitting nearby jumped up, grabbed the woman by an arm and said, "Come with me, fat one, and we will explain it all to you."

She got three months on a work farm.

REUNION AND RESOLVE

The brothers finally met in a small, darkened second-floor apartment in the busy port area of Habana Vieja. Ed had been driven to the site by two friends who had painstakingly arranged the late-night reunion.

He and his friends waited in a tiny, stuffy room for about thirty minutes before hearing muffled noises on the stairway and then seeing the door burst open. Two men stepped inside. The thin, bearded Miguel walked quickly across and stopped directly in front of his taller, dark-haired sibling as if to satisfy himself that this was the half-brother he hadn't seen since childhood.

After a wordless few seconds staring into each other's eyes, their arms went around each other in a tight *abrazo,* and suddenly they were both trying to talk as their eyes filled with tears. The more-emotional Miguel sobbed audibly.

"*Que milagro, por fin,*" said Ed quietly, as both struggled for words. "It's a miracle that you're even alive, Miguel. We've got a lot to talk about. I've been trying to find you to try to help you. Tell me how can I help?"

"Getting together like this is enough right now," the rebel said in a whisper, wiping his eyes and trying to smile. "I thought I'd never see you again. My friends informed me of my . . . our . . . mother's death about five years ago, but that's all I know."

"Yes, she worried about you until the end. Neither she nor I could get any information after your aunt died in Camaguey. We only knew you had been imprisoned in 1961. Let's sit and talk. I know this must be dangerous for you. I know you're deeply involved in *la lucha* again.

"*Si, hermano* . . . I can't stay long. We are deeply involved in this. I must take precautions, for my men as well as myself."

Miguel motioned to his partner to cover the door while he moved warily around the room and looked out of the window. Ed only now noticed that his brother had a sidearm. The other man had an automatic rifle at his hip.

"We are part of the resistance, such as it is," said Miguel matter-of-factly. "We've got to be careful. You've got to be careful," he told his brother. "You are taking a huge risk meeting with me. It could mean your life or imprisonment if they connect you to us — to me."

"Miguel, tell me why you are involved in this now. I thought you were done after nearly dying in prison. I thought you might go back to the ranch or maybe get out of the country. I had no idea you would return to a life so . . . full of danger . . . with so little chance of success."

"We have our small successes. They do not come easy, true," replied Miguel quietly, shaking his head. "But I'm doing the only thing my brain and my heart ask me to do. Beyond that, I don't care for anything else. As long as I have strength, I'll keep on fighting against these *hijos de puta.*"

They spent what was left of the night sitting together, sipping from a rum bottle and talking quietly — the rebel leader and his reporter brother from the states.

Ed told his Miguel he appeared to be coming to the end of his tenure with the Castro regime. Government people had begun closing doors to him, shelving his requests for interviews and for travel into the interior. He told his brother he'd been called into Ramiro del Campo's office several times in the past month to explain news reports written by him that had been picked up in European newspapers by Cuba's diplomats overseas.

Miguel reluctantly recounted some of his prison experiences. He told of his recovery and described his recuperation at the home of friends, of the careful attention of the doctor who had seemingly arrested the life-draining symptoms of Yellow Fever.

"When I regained some of my strength, I thought of escaping to Florida. But, in the end, I knew I wouldn't be happy," he said. "I would never rest, in my soul, unless I did everything I could to help those who are risking their lives to eradicate this madman from our country. That's the only thing that's worthwhile to me now."

When they parted, they vowed to get together again as soon as it could be arranged, knowing the risks involved for both. Ed promised, to himself as much as to Miguel, that he would help in some way, that he would do all in his power to help his brother when the opportunity arose.

After more than four busy, tension-filled years of covering the Fidel Castro reign, Ed's tenure was, indeed, approaching its end. The signs were all there. The government minders apparently were tired of dealing with him, weary of trying to convince The Associated Press correspondent to write only the good things about the Cuban revolution.

At a time when Cuba was attempting to leverage its friendships with the Soviet Union and Third World nations into a broader role on the international stage, its many flaws also were being exposed for the world to see. The Castro regime was more in the public eye than ever. It was constantly being called upon to explain itself on human rights, prisoner abuses, its covert activities in Africa and Latin America and the hardships and subjugation of its own people.

Officials didn't want these things pointed out in detail by foreign reporters.

Ed, along with visiting journalists and the growing popularity of radio and television reporting out of Cuba, were becoming very difficult for the Castro regime to deal with. The only way they knew to control this was to try to control the reporters.

As a resident correspondent with a worldwide readership, Ed came under greater scrutiny than most because he was there day-to-day and was extremely active, talking to people at all levels, checking on as many government activities as he could.

The Foreign Ministry was now turning down many of his requests for travel and access to various agencies and officials. The situation evolved slowly for months, his complaints met with a shrug. It became evident that he would soon be asked to leave Cuba, or to be forced out.

So Ed Brophy entered a new phase of activity, one in which everything took on a greater urgency. He worked longer and harder on his list of must-do stories.

And in the back of his mind, always, was now the thought that he must somehow help Miguel — his newfound brother. In what way, he still didn't know, but he felt extremely heavyhearted and guilty that they had been reunited only now, at a critical time in both of their extremely different lives.

Time had speeded up for Miguel, too. The heavily bearded rebel, still in frail health but tireless in devoting himself to the anti-Castro movement, was increasingly regarded as a strong, experienced leader in the renewed cause.

He had some time ago left the sanctuary of his friends' house and the frequent visits to the doctor after convincing himself that rebellion was all that was left for him to accomplish in life.

His negative view of the anti-Castro movement, as he had once expressed to his friend Madera, had undergone a complete transformation. He now firmly believed it was the only path to follow.

He was moving about now between the city and the countryside, planning and participating in small acts of sabotage, any clandestine activities that would keep alive the spirit of rebellion. These activities would hopefully attract more recruits to the movement. They needed a wider awareness among the populace, Miguel could see.

Ironically, he now had a nervous energy that wouldn't tolerate any doubts by his fellow rebels that these minor acts of rebellion were insignificant and that they had little meaning in the overall struggle. He became their leader.

"It is now or never," was his constant refrain. "Either we do something now or it will never be done," he argued. "We've got to keep up our actions and increase our numbers until we again draw the kind of international attention that can pressure this madman to get out."

As for his own well-being, Miguel had convinced himself that he did not die as a prisoner for one reason. And that reason was so that he could give his life in pursuit of a free Cuba. He knew that his wasted body would soon fail him, and that he could die at any time.

But before that happened, he would help take down the tyrant.

SUMMONS

Ed and the quiet, intelligent Blake, who had become a good friend as well as his driver, were having a drink in Ed's apartment and were deep in conversation about the Cold War and other topics of the day when a heavy knock on his apartment door startled them.

"Who the hell could that be at this hour," grumbled Ed, who had gotten in late that evening from covering the Cubelas military trial at La Cabaña.

At the door stood Ernesto Lopez from the Foreign Ministry and a heavyset man whom Ed did not recognize. "Ramiro requests the pleasure of your company in his office," Lopez said, smirking.

"Now? It's almost midnight," Ed said, eyeing the sidearm strapped to the stranger's ample waistline. He was in civilian clothes but nonetheless menacing.

"*Ahora mismo.* I can drive you," responded Lopez.

"No, Blake is here and he can take me and wait," Ed said pointedly, suspicious now because of Ramiro's recent criticism of his reporting."*Okah*," Lopez replied, deliberately bastardizing the Yankee "okay," which he had been doing since his visit to the Soviet Union that summer. "But don't keep him waiting, amigo."

Lopez turned and stepped into the waiting elevator along with his stocky, grimfaced friend.

Ed expected his meeting with Ramiro to be another harangue by the MinRex officer about how the correspondent was distorting Cuba's position in the foreign press. Usually, Ramiro would refer to one or two recent AP articles published in European newspapers, and he would claim Ed had ignored more-positive facts. His reporting had even been criticized in the Communist Party newspaper *Granma* recently. He had been called a "tool of the CIA," signaling a new, tougher government attitude toward him.

The correspondent's usual defense to these arguments was to request specifics about where he had supposedly erred. Then, he'd offer to write another article on the subject if given access to further information and to government officials he could quote. Ramiro's bluster usually degenerated into more generalities at that point.

But this meeting didn't go according to form.

Ramiro was calm. He didn't shuffle or wave any papers at him. He began by asking Ed how long he'd been in Cuba, as if he did not know, and asked how he'd been treated during his stay. It was as if he were reviewing the record, summarizing the reporter's tenure.

Ed reminded him he had been on the job, with some time out, for almost four years.

"I think we have treated you well, Eduardo," Ramiro said. "I also think you've been here too long, doing the same things. It may be time for a change for you. We should give you an opportunity to go to Vietnam or Moscow or someplace like that. What do you think?"

Ed, who was tired and needed sleep, was slow to react. But the message was unmistakable. And he wasn't going to let Ramiro get by with glib generalities.

"Ramiro, tell me frankly what you mean. Are you asking me to leave Cuba? Are you threatening me about something I've written that you don't agree with? What is it that's brought me here? I'm in no mood for doubletalk."

"Okay," the short Foreign Ministry official said, standing up from his high-perched seat behind his desk. "We've decided we can no longer tolerate some foreigners, particularly those who may have ties to the CIA, who go around our country doing whatever they want, seeing whoever they want and writing whatever they want."

That was certainly clear enough. He stopped, grinned and squinted his eyes a little. Ramiro let that statement hang there for awhile before continuing.

"I could point to several things you've done, and stories you have written, which are damaging to this administration. The latest situation is your meeting with people who are working against our government. We could have you expelled tomorrow. Instead, I'm giving you two weeks to arrange with your organization for a replacement. After that, you will become *persona non grata*. Ernesto will help you arrange your departure."

Ed was stunned by this reference of his meeting with "people working against our government."

Fearing he might have placed Miguel in jeopardy, he kept his mouth shut, preferring not to explore the subject further in hopes that the Cubans lacked more specific information. He shook his head, slowly stood and took Ramiro's extended hand.

"It's been good while it lasted," Edward said lightly. "I'll talk to my bosses tomorrow and start things moving. I don't want to argue about anything."

Ramiro escorted him to the door, and that was that. His time in Cuba was virtually ended. He had come to expect this in recent weeks. But now that it had happened, he was surprised that he was saddened by the whole thing.

It was time to go, to leave Cuba. Ed believed he had done his best over the years to report as objectively as he could, the good along with the bad. But, now, Ed admitted to himself that it had become increasingly difficult to discover and report the positive things about the Castro regime.

In the grinding, day-to-day life in Cuba, Ed had come to empathize with the ordinary, often-bewildered Cubans who didn't quite comprehend what their government was doing. On the other hand, he saw and reported on the fanaticism that drove many others to support the Castro regime.

Everyone was desperately waiting for the promised new society.

Now, Ed worried about his brother. He had hoped to help him, somehow. He believed that his previous reunion with Miguel would lead to further meetings. He wanted to try somehow to smooth the troubled road that his rebellious relative was on. But he was about to lose any chance of that.

Two weeks.

He had a lot to do in that time. His priority, though, would be to meet with his brother and persuade him to leave the country. The reporter knew, however, that there was little chance of that, judging from Miguel's strong feelings — his obsession — about his duty to remain and fight.

But he would try.

The next day Ed cabled his foreign editor, Ben Bassett, telling him to seek a Havana replacement and asking Bassett to place a call in to him at the apartment.

FAREWELL

Meanwhile, Cuban exiles became increasingly bolder in their incursions to their island homeland.

Another vessel sailing from the Florida Keys was captured by Cuban coastal defenders as it tried to slip undetected into Havana. The boat was loaded with plastic explosives, hand grenades, machine guns and other weapons, supposedly to be used in another assassination attempt against Castro.

There was also a large quantity of propaganda leaflets demanding LIBERTY FOR CUBA and declaring WAR UNTIL DEATH. The boat never made it onshore. Two exiles aboard were killed, two drowned in trying to escape and two others were wounded and captured.

Their leader was Antonio "Tony" de la Cuesta, a commando chieftain with a record of more than a dozen smaller attacks against Cuba. Cuesta was gravely wounded and imprisoned, and years later made an impassioned plea for political prisoners. An emotional and widely publicized letter he smuggled out from La Cabaña provoked international condemnation of the Castro regime, but it brought no immediate changes in their treatment.

Shortly after the latest attack, the Cuban Interior Ministry issued an unusual communiqué that listed the names of the invaders, the specific type and dimensions of the vessel and the intended mission. The objective, according to the prisoners' confessions as reported by the daily *Granma*, was "to carry out an attempt to assassinate the prime minister of the revolutionary government in order to create conditions favorable for an imperialist aggression against the Cuban revolution."

The government accused Cuesta of being a CIA agent and said the launch had departed from a site in the Florida Keys that was a base of operations for an anti-Castro exile organization known as "Comandos L." This was a new group, unknown to Ed.

The U.S. State Department denied the allegations and again said it was doing all it could to discourage exile attacks on Cuba from American soil.

Another well-publicized incident was the arrest in Key West of Rolando Masferrer, a prominent refugee who had been a lawyer and newspaper publisher in Cuba during the Batista era. He had once headed a private army in rural Cuba known as *Los Tigeres*.

He was now accused by American authorities of attempting to launch an invasion of Haiti in hopes of fostering a rebellion that would spread to Cuba, as unlikely as that seemed.

Masferrer had a colorful, if checkered, history in Cuba, achieving much of his power under Batista. He was then a congressman and a senator and published *El Tiempo,* a daily newspaper in Havana, before forming his private army in his native Oriente Province. The Tigeres, who were said to have numbered several thousand, were organized to fight Castro and the rebels who landed there from Mexico to try to depose Batista in the 1950s. But the self-styled civilian army was used for any strongarm purposes Masferrer fancied in that part of the island, according to knowledgeable officials in the province.

Correspondent Brophy hurried his preparations to close out several news stories, contact his sources and attend to personal matters before his enforced departure. He managed to get word to friends of Miguel, but he didn't want to press for another meeting if his brother considered it too dangerous. He also realized they might never see each other again.

Ten days went by before one of his valued contacts with ties to various underground groups got word to Ed that Miguel would be waiting for him the following night at a house in the industrial working-class neighborhood of San Miguel del Padron, on the south side of Havana Bay.

As instructed, the reporter drove to a little dead-end street called Acequia about 1 a.m. He parked his borrowed car on the *cul-de-sac* and rendezvoused with two elderly residents of the area who were to escort him to the meeting place.

After a three-block walk in the dark, quiet neighborhood, the trio came to a small, neat house set well back from a plastered-block fence. Its gate opened into a winding, stone pathway that led to an overgrown patio surrounded by mango trees. One of the men knocked on the heavy wooden door at the house's entrance to the left of the patio. They walked in without waiting for a response.

The dark-bearded Miguel sat with Roberto Madera and a burly man at a table in the large living room, drinking beer and looking at Texaco road maps spread out and overhanging the table edges. Miguel jumped up and embraced his brother. They were speechless as they broke the abrazo.

Ed and Madera shook hands warmly, and in an emotion-filled voice Miguel turned and introduced the owner of the house, Luis Acevedo. The stocky, balding Acevedo led the brothers across the room to a couch and easy chair, and he and Madera walked out.

The brothers spent a half hour in quiet conversation, with Ed telling the rebel leader he was being expelled from Cuba.

It's probably for the best," said Miguel. "You don't want to hang around here too long. There could come a time when you want to leave and they may have other ideas. I'm surprised they allowed you to stay this long. Never before, with journalists . . . maybe never again."

Ed then expressed his concern for his brother. And he told him so, urging him to leave the country. After five minutes of spirited debate, Ed finally began to understand the depth of Miguel's feelings against Castro and his devastating hold on the country.

"There may come a day, *hermano*, when you can help," the sad-eyed Miguel said soothingly. "We will need all the help we can get from the outside . . . I think we all have to be patient. It's just a question of time. Not if, but when."

But Ed wouldn't leave it at that.

"I promise you that when the time comes, I'll join your cause and help you accomplish your mission," Ed told him in a choking voice that was now barely a whisper.

Miguel nodded then turned away. He found it difficult to express his strong feelings of kinship with his brother.

Madera and Acevedo walked back into the room at this time. "Time to go, *jefe*," said the tousled Madera. He and Acevedo walked out into the patio through a side door, leaving it partially open.

The brothers embraced, perhaps for the last time. The Cuban guerrilla leader turned and quickly walked out. The Yankee journalist was met at the door by the two men who had escorted him, and the three walked back to Ed's car.

His last night as a correspondent in Castro's Cuba was spent with Lydia, the woman who loved him and helped him sustain his sanity in this crazy world. She cried. He cried. There was no putting it off any longer. They were finally facing the fact that they were separating, perhaps for years, perhaps forever.

He was being forced out. She was being forced to stay. She had repeatedly applied for exit permits from the Cubans and entry permits from the Americans through the Swiss. There were delays, always delays. Too many applicants, too many Cubans wanting refuge in the United States.

There was nothing she could do but wait. Maybe a few more weeks, a few months. There was no way of knowing. And, meanwhile, she would continue to make her own way in her troubled country.

Their future together was clouded, too, because Ed had not yet been reassigned by The AP. He was going into New York headquarters for an indefinite time before being assigned to another overseas post. He had several options, but any discussions with his bosses would take place in New York.

Their doubts were suppressed. They tried to be hopeful.

"I will call you from New York," Ed promised, knowing the uncertainties of telephone calls between the two countries. "I'll call you as often as I can. I'll try to find a way to help."

She was the stronger of the two, the more practical.

"I will always love you, even if it takes years for us to get together. When I get out, I'll find you, wherever in the world you are."

He wouldn't allow her to come to the airport with him the next morning. The only one that saw him off on his flight to Mexico City was his stolid friend Blake.

REVOLUTIONARY CUBA

In Modern Times

SECRETS AND A
FATEFUL DECISION

Ed's current tourist visit to Cuba was turning out to be an invigorating experience, when he could overcome his feelings of concern for his brother and his helplessness in witnessing a country spiraling into a deeply clouded future.

It seemed to him, in 1998, to be a more open, more-relaxed society than what he remembered, although still a rigidly controlled police state — a puzzling paradox.

Except for his nagging thoughts of unfinished business, he was now enjoying the opportunity to explore the island virtually unfettered, unlike during his previous residency and a few quick reporting trips in-between. He hadn't had the time in those working days to relish Cuba's natural beauty or to fully appreciate its history and historic locales.

While he played the role of tourist, Ed made discreet inquiries among a few trusted friends about Miguel Hidalgo, who in the intervening years had achieved notoriety among Cuban dissidents for his daring guerrilla operations against the regime. There had been no way in the intervening years to communicate with each other.

"*El Halcon*," the Falcon, was what the Cuban military and counter-revolutionary agents of the Interior Ministry called him as they tried to hunt him down. They used the term interchangeably for the guerilla chieftain himself and his rebel unit.

Ed was informed that the Falcon rebels had for years eluded their pursuers, carrying out smallscale but destructive attacks on military installations, weapons depots and even a short-range missile facility on the southern coast near the Guantanamo Bay Naval Base, which was in American-held Cuban territory.

Ed had managed to contact several of his old trusted sources, including one who was now an underground liaison between the public dissidents who formed a disorganized opposition to Castro and the guerrilla groups. Yes, the old man believed he could eventually get word to Miguel. It would take some time.

It had been more than twenty-five years now, Ed mused. Miguel was in his sixties and still very active. He had obviously recovered well-enough from the different political prisons, the horrible beatings, the injuries, disabilities and the life-threatening disease he had acquired.

While he waited for word from his source, Ed walked throughout the city, drove into the interior on short trips, met with old friends and acquaintances when he could find them, and with his journalistic outlook took the pulse of the people on this tropical island nation ruled by a dictator who had outfoxed nine U.S. presidents.

The government-controlled tourist office in Vedado routinely approved his application for extension of his visitor's visa for another three weeks. All that was required by the government these days was a return-trip ticket out of Cuba, proof of a hotel room and his word that he had enough American currency for his visit.

Seeking a new ambience away from the bustling Nacional and its free-spending clientele, he moved into the Hotel Inglaterra in the colonial part of Habana Vieja.

The newly restored, British-style Inglaterra was popular with Europeans who often spent several weeks on holiday or business in Cuba in the 1990s. It was just off the busy, tree-lined Paseo del Prado and across the Parque Central, giving it a quiet, sedate atmosphere in the midst of a bustling area of Old Havana. It was within a short walk of a number of tourist sites, restaurants and bars. The old Capitolio, the former home of the Cuban Congress and government, patterned after the U.S. Capitol, sat grandly nearby amidst a swarm of taxis, buses, 1950s American automobiles and pedestrian traffic.

He had just finished breakfast a couple of days after checking in at the Inglaterra and had returned to his room to retrieve a light jacket when the phone rang. It must be the front desk, he thought. Nobody knows I'm here. He knew it was highly unlikely that Madera or any of Miguel's people would be contacting him by phone.

"*Eduardo, como estás,*" said the vaguely familiar voice on the phone. "It's Diego Sierra. You may remember me from the MinRex. I used to be in the protocol office for foreign visitors."

"Oh, sure, Diego," Ed said, puzzled. "What's going on?"

"Listen, Eduardo, I'm in the lobby. I'd like to come up and see you for a few minutes. Okay? Room 415, *que no?*"

"Yes, okay," said Ed warily. "Why not?"

He didn't like this at all. The Foreign Ministry must have dispatched Diego Sierra to throw him out of the country as a result of his past experience in Cuba. And how did they know he was here. The hotel people must have kept tabs on him at the Nacional and now here.

He didn't have much time to ponder over what Sierra might want before a discreet knock on the door announced his presence.

"*Hola, compañero,*" said Sierra, walking into the room, shaking his hand and slapping him on the shoulder.

He remembered Sierra as an ebullient young man anxious to please the VIPs and other foreigners he used to escort around the country for MinRex, the Foreign Ministry. A quarter century later, he was a self-assured, well-dressed middle-aged man with a serious, no-nonsense look about him despite the bouncy greeting.

"What are you doing here, Diego? I'm just a *turista* now. Nothing for you guys to worry about."

"*Mira, chico,* don't be alarmed. I'm just paying a friendly call on an old friend. But . . . I know you won't stand for a lot of bullshit for very long. So if we can sit down for a few minutes, I'll tell you why I'm here."

When they were settled into comfortable armchairs near the big windows overlooking the park across the boulevard, Sierra launched into an explanation for his visit.

"First, let me tell you, I'm now with the Ministerio del Interior, the infamous MinInt, with its G2 and its secret police and all that," he said with a nervous laugh. "Let me quickly add that there's no surveillance on you, if that's what you're thinking.

"I'm with the Counter-Intelligence Division, but that's not why I'm here. I am not on official business. I just happen to know of your half-brother Miguel. In fact, the Falcon is quite famous here, or should I say infamous? The reason I know of your relationship is I had access to your file in Ramiro del Campo's office at the MinRex all that many years ago. We also have a big fat file on your brother at G2, but there is nothing in it about you. Only a few of us at MinInt know about your relationship now. That's why I'm taking a chance like this."

Ramiro del Campo was long gone from the scene, Ed knew.

He now gritted his teeth, surprised and puzzled. But he said nothing.

"Believe me, I am putting *my* neck on the line by being here," Sierra continued. "If word of this meeting gets out to my bosses at Interior, I'm dead. But, as for you, I don't think anyone else in present-day Cuba gives a damn what you're doing here, as long as you behave yourself and spend a lot of money, which you appear to be doing."

Sierra then bluntly informed Ed in so many words that he was part of a very small group of individuals in his division at Interior that had begun to empathize with *contrarevolucionarios* like his brother. These few individuals at the Interior Ministry had been slow in convincing themselves that perhaps the anti-Castro rebels were not totally wrong.

They were Cubans, after all. They all had a different view of how to run the country.

Not only that, Sierra said, but this small group of agents — who were supposed to be among the most diehard Castro supporters — in reality wanted the dissidents to succeed. But they realized how inadequate the rebel actions were.

"Total crap in the long run," Sierra said. "Although in themselves these small attacks are well carried out. Your brother knows the ins and outs; but they are a, how do you say it, a drop in the bucket, no? So . . . We've been thinking it over, my friends and I, and we thought maybe we could help el Halcon a little, you know."

The dissidents at MinRex were too small in number, but they might be able to work out a plan "with the help of somebody who knows the action."

Ed was becoming more confused by the minute.

Sierra then plainly told Ed that he and his small group of friends had decided to help the rebel cause. That was the message he came to deliver. Yes, they realized the dangers involved. But they were totally exasperated with the way things were going with Castro, and they were determined to quietly help the Falcon and his rebels. Sierra had been dispatched by his friends to enlist Ed's assistance.

"*En total*, we want you to pass the word on to your brother, to tell him that we are willing to, quietly, but very secretly, help his rebels in any way we can — by furnishing critical information, facilitating his group's movements, helping them obtain some of their weapons and supplies. Certain things like that. But in return, we want something, too."

Sierra paused, letting his information sink in.

Seeing the quizzical look in Ed's eyes, Sierra continued. "I'll tell you something else: My friends and I also have the support of a few officers at MinFar, the Ministry of the Armed Forces who feel the same way. *En total*, some of them are also fed up with things as they are, amigo."

Ed was taken aback by this strange information, the sudden burst of "candor" from someone he'd barely known more than twenty-five years ago.

He decided to be frank.

"Look, Diego, I don't know what the hell you're up to, but I suspect that you and your buddies think you can use me to entrap my brother and become instant heroes. You're correct that I won't take much bullshit, but that's all I'm hearing from you right now."

Sierra threw up his hands and began shaking his head the second that Ed rose from his chair and began talking.

"I know, I know, I know. You don't believe me now, and I don't blame you. But I wanted to get right to the point. I'm giving it to you straight. I want to prove to you that we are sick and tired of this fucking mess made by Fidel and his people. I don't want to go into all the obvious reasons, but let me give you a few facts.

"The most important is that my colleagues and I know where Miguel Hidalgo is right now. We know how many men he has, who many of his above-ground contacts are, and we know about some of his most recent activities. I am also putting my ass on the line here by telling you now that we're withholding this critical information from our big boss . . . You remember old redbeard, the notorious *Barba Roja*, no?

Sierra scratched his head, rubbed his eyes and then lobbed another bombshell at the dumbfounded Ed.

"Barba Roja doesn't yet know what we have recently found out: that you are waiting to meet with your brother for a happy reunion after so many years. Does it surprise you that we know?

"Publicly, officially, we have a widespread manhunt out for the Falcon," Sierra continued without pause. "But my small crew and I know just where he is at any given time, and we can arrest him and execute him and the others anytime we want . . . If we want. Believe me, Eduardo, we don't want to do that. We want him to succeed and somehow overthrow this bastard Fidel. Meanwhile, as I said, our asses are hanging out on the line."

Although apprehensive, Ed decided he wanted to hear more about this in-house revolt, if that's what it was. He nodded encouragingly while his brain tried to make sense of what Diego Sierra was saying.

As if unburdening himself, Sierra went on to say that the small group of disloyal officials in the two ministries did not yet constitute a strong enough base for a *coup d'etat*, but that their numbers were slowly growing.

Now he and his friends were trying to hurry the action along by trying to help the Falcon.

"We can't wait around. We feel the time is right, right now. So our best chance is to throw in with the underground *contras*. Your brother heads the most active and most successful unit. They don't fuck up too much. They use their wits, along with their *cojones*, otherwise they wouldn't have lasted this long. We finally infiltrated them about six months ago, and we now know everything they've been doing since then."

But, Sierra said slowly, for emphasis, the people he was speaking for now, this dissident group in the counter-intelligence section, decided to leave the Falcon guerrillas alone in hopes they could do enough damage to encourage more of the key people in the two ministries to finally move against Fidel.

Given the general degree of dissatisfaction he said existed among the officers of the two ministries, he believed that any specific action against Castro would result in a major uprising by the discontents in the Cuban Armed Forces and the powerful Interior Ministry in general.

But that might not be enough against Castro's army.

"We can do it. But we need a trigger," Sierra said, once again raising his thick eyebrows and nodding his head. "We've got to start something soon in order to cause a big uprising. Otherwise the time will pass us by, again," he paused, assessing the speechless Eduardo with his bright dark eyes.

"We've had opportunities before," Sierra added. "But never like this."

Ed finally reacted. He was not convinced. He shook his head and gripped his chair.

"I cannot control what my brother does. I haven't even seen him in more than twenty-five years. I don't know where he is or what he does. Since you seem to know of a reunion, maybe you can tell me about it," Ed told his visitor sarcastically.

Sierra grinned and nodded. He was silent for awhile.

"I once had a brother, too," he said in a softer tone.

"He was a common soldier in the Cuban Army, killed in Angola in 1979. They didn't even have the decency to ship his body back to Cuba for burial. My mother was devastated. I know a lot of people who fought in Angola and Ethiopia who are out on the streets right now, living from day-to-day. All of this while the *hijos de puta* like Castro and the generals of MinInt and MinFar live like kings in Miramar or Siboney.

"This shit will never end by itself," he continued at a slower more reflective pace. "My friends and I are not yet in a position to end it by ourselves. If the opportunity comes, sure, we'll grab it and come out in the open and do whatever is necessary. But for right now, we want to help those who are actively fighting this son of a bitch. This we can do quietly, without compromising ourselves until we're ready."

"What do you want from me, to put my brother on the line? In even more danger than he is now?" Ed asked. "I need proof that what you're saying is true. I just can't go on your word. And my brother isn't going to swallow any of this on *my* word, if I do get to see him."

"I knew you would feel that way, and that's okay. I'll prove to you, and to Miguel, that we know where he and his men are at any given time," Sierra said.

"We will do this . . ." Sierra paused and slowly continued, lowering his voice another notch, "Two of my men and I will go wherever and whenever your brother says. We will be alone and unarmed. And we'll discuss our plans with him then and there. But here's the key thing — He doesn't even need to tell us *where* to meet him.

"How's that? Just give us a date and time, and we'll be there, because we know where he is, where he goes, what he does. "That should prove something to you and him, *que no*?

"Now," he said, standing up, "I thank you for listening to me, Eduardo. It's good to see you again. I think we can work together. If you agree to this, call this number and leave word for me to call my cousin. I will come to you as soon as I can.

"But if you decide that it's too risky," Sierra added. "If you just want to forget about this conversation, that's up to you. We won't bother Miguel. We know what he's up to, and we want him to succeed. My regards. *Hasta luego, amigo.*"

With that, before Ed could say another word, Diego Sierra walked out of the room.

Ed sat and thought for awhile, shaking his head slowly in wonder. "This is bizarre," he said, the thoughts escaping from his mouth in a low whisper. In a way, he thought, it's typically Cuban, especially in a society that has hardly known anything else but revolutionary intrigue.

He decided to lay it all out for Miguel when they met and let him decide what to do. Maybe Sierra was on the level. Perhaps he was providing a breakthrough that Castro's enemies needed. This guy seemed sure of his ground.

Ed himself had come to a significant decision during his short time back in Cuba. He had convinced himself to join in the effort to overthrow Castro. How, he wasn't sure yet, maybe actively join his brother in the underground movement. If his brother would let him.

Yes, he would be glad to cast aside everything else in his life if they could work to accomplish that goal. It might seem unthinkable for a no-nonsense American to turn his back on a comfortable existence to do something as radical as this. But he felt as if he'd been waiting all his life for such an opportunity: to help bring about a change in the course of history by overthrowing a despot like Fidel.

On thinking it over, the whole thing seemed overly dramatic. Almost like a movie plot. But that's the way he felt.

He had vowed to help Miguel, and now he could fulfill that promise.

In his own way, Ed was as stubborn as his half-brother once he made up his mind to act. Damn the consequences and his easy life. It was time to do something meaningful.

The only sure thing in his thinking right now was that there would be no change in Cuba without eliminating Castro. The last few weeks had convinced him that a determined opposition, with the proper support from the unhappy populace, could bring this about. Now, if Sierra was being straight . . .

Of course, Ed knew that many heads had rolled after ill-fated efforts to assassinate *el maximo lider* during his more than four decades in power. But his experience and study of the record showed that most of the attempts had been poorly planned and just plain amateurish, including the bizarre plans by the CIA and organized crime mobsters in the 1950s and '60s that featured exploding cigars and attempted poisoning of Castro's food and drink.

A thoughtful, meticulous plan carried out by a small group of underground guerrillas who had the knowledge and experience gained from years of clandestine activity could successfully carry out the deed, Ed believed. If Diego Sierra's story checked out, they would now have assistance from a small but significant quarter of the regime, a group of insiders.

Ed hated to admit it, but Diego Sierra was convincing.

To add to the picture, the whole panorama of Cuban society was more open than it ever had been during the Castro era. With an emphasis on tourism, which had become the country's biggest moneymaker, there was less of a police-state atmosphere.

This could work to their advantage. He already found himself thinking along those lines.

Despite the regime's continued efforts to keep everyone in line, there was much activity beyond its control. Foreigners came and went, commercial activity of all kinds was now the name of the game. People weren't getting arrested just for hanging around street corners. Even prostitution was out of the dark corners. Openly expressed opposition to government policies by a few was tolerated, within limits, but it was as flexible as a rubber band that stretched until it suddenly snapped back with a hurtful sting.

Ed Brophy was anxious to meet and discuss all this with his now-notorious brother.

THE NEW CUBA AND AN OLD FRIEND

The most significant change Ed encountered in 1990s Cuba was that its economy now revolved around the American dollar, the almightly greenback that was outlawed in the intoxicating days after the Castro rebels chased out dictator Fulgencio Batista.

The dollar again was made legal tender and began circulating when the regime woke up to the fact that tourism and capitalist-style commerce would help compensate for the crushing loss of financial aid and trade from the old Soviet Union. The government maintained the peso as its national currency, however, and most of the Cuban population still were dependent on it — except for the few who received American currency from overseas.

In Ed Brophy's view, the new dollar-based tourist economy appeared to be succeeding beyond Castro's dreams. Cuba once again had become one of the most desired vacation playgrounds in the world. Free-spending tourists, especially Europeans, provided much of Cuba's desperately needed foreign exchange.

Ironically, while Cuba began its return to American currency, the United States maintained its embargo of the island and permitted no general tourism of Americans except for specially licensed groups and individuals. Europeans, Asians, Latin Americans came and went at will, enjoying Cuba's beautiful beaches and easy-to-take prices. But few

Americans booked into the luxury hotels or checked out the magnificent beaches.

Cuba's free-swinging ways during the Soviet era were shocked into reality in the late 1980s.

Castro had not-too-secretly derided Premier Mikhail Gorbachev's wide-ranging reforms throughout the Soviet Union. His concerns turned into a nightmare when Gorbachev began taking a long, critical look at the Soviet Union's highly subsidized trade and outright gifts of military and civilian goods to Cuba.

After Perestroika and the Soviet leader's downfall, Boris Yeltsin and his incoming crowd of hard-line communists took an even tougher attitude about the economic assistance to their Caribbean partner. The belt-tightening reforms and new demands made on Cuba and some of the other Soviet partners brought about the collapse of most of their bilateral trade agreements.

Finally, overall Soviet economic support to Cuba, which by some estimates amounted to some $3 billion a year, died out almost completely.

What Castro had always feared had come to pass. Instead of continuing to build communism, the Soviets were now resorting to capitalism and democracy, whatever that was. Now, in the 1990s, Castro was slowly doing the same thing, out of the same necessity.

Ed returned to his hotel one day after lunch with an elderly couple he had looked up for a Miami friend, and he was handed a note along with his key. The note read: "Eddie, call me at the Mirasol Beach Resort in Varadero at (5) 69-7090." It was signed Gregorio Yzaguirre. Ed was astonished to learn that Gregorio was in Cuba. Strange things go on in this world, he thought.

He had known Yzaguirre in Barcelona, way back in . . . what was it? About 1960-61, when Ed had visited that beautiful city frequently. Young Gregorio had been part of a rabble-rousing group of students who had adopted the separatist cause of the Basques as their own during Gregorio's final year at the Universidad de Barcelona, or Universitat Barcelona, as it was known in the Basque language.

The students held rallies, protest demonstrations and petition drives to help publicize the small but growing Basque movement for independence from Spain. By then, the Basques' hated enemy, Fascist dictator Francisco

Franco, was in his third decade of iron rule. The rebellious students in that region used the separatist movement as their own way of protesting Franco's overall policies in Spain.

Inevitably, Gregorio was arrested. His father, a prominent businessman, spent a week contacting and pleading with government officials to release him.

When he was freed, Gregorio spent a year in Paris before returning to the university. He eventually earned his degree and went to work at an architectural firm before deciding he had a better future by running his father's hotels.

Gregorio remained a rebel at heart, although a compassionate one. As a manager, he was always eager to help his struggling employees get ahead. He became deeply involved in Barcelona civic causes during the waning years of Franco's power, and he generally came down on the side of the lower classes.

He and Ed enjoyed each other's company during the times when the reporter was on assignment, and they had kept in touch over the years. Later, they had occasionally run into each other in one European capital or another. To hear that he was now in Cuba warmed Ed's heart. Here, at last, was another soul with whom he could talk openly.

He called Varadero right away. Gregorio's secretary informed him that he was in Trinidad for the day but that she'd been instructed to invite him to the Varadero Beach resort. She asked if Mr. Brophy could meet Mr. Yzaguirre for lunch at the hotel the following day.

Ed drove to Varadero in a rental car the next morning.

Gregorio was a stocky, sparse-haired man with the look of a bustling, European businessman, which he was. But he was still the same goodhearted soul, ready to laugh, and to linger for a lengthy discussion on a variety of issues over a seafood paella and Spanish wine.

He was a globetrotting executive, the multilingual, worldwide marketing director of Hoteles Mirador S.A., a Barcelona-based company which built and managed hotels with the financial participation of the two dozen countries in which they were situated. The company had its basis in the two Barcelona hotels built in the 1950s by his now-deceased father.

Lunch was in the Circulo Español restaurant at the elegant Varadero Mirador, a sprawling beachside establishment opened just the previous

215

year. The company also planned to build and operate a new five-star hotel in Havana and several smaller Mirador hotels elsewhere in Cuba.

After pleasantries and talk of families, the topic became Cuba and Castro.

"*Mira, amigo,*" the outspoken Gregorio said, "what the communists are doing with this country is not only a disaster, it is very weird and hard to understand. Knowingly or not, Fidel is creating two societies, the rich and the poor, just like the old days under previous dictators."

Ed nodded encouragingly, eager to learn what his worldly friend thought about this particular government.

"It is amazing to me how a whole society can become inured to a dictatorship over the years. We Spaniards tolerated Franco for forty years, and many of my friends lived under Salazar's brutal repression in neighboring Portugal just as long.

"Now," Gregorio continued, "they've got one of the longest-lived strongmen in the world right here. What Cuba needs is a radical change. The Cubans have a history of palace coups and revolutions; what's keeping them from another?"

"Well," said Ed more quietly, looking around warily even though they were in a small private dining room in the large restaurant, "it may be that this regime is probably even more repressive than those of Franco and Salazar."

Ed sipped his wine while his friend mulled that awful thought over.

And, without thinking things through, Ed continued, "Your company is busy dealing with the dictator and his gang here, just like so many other corporations from Europe and Latin America are doing, even from Japan."

Ed stopped, realizing he was being unfair to his friend. He started to apologize but Gregorio put up a hand and shrugged it off. "Yes, we are, maybe part of the problem along with the others," he agreed. "It's business," Gregorio said, looking chagrined. "In today's business world you deal with everybody or you get left out. You don't have to like them, necessarily. We're dealing with the Chinese, the Indonesians, the Vietnamese, the Turks, the Filipinos — and if Russia ever decides to talk, we'll see what we can do there."

While Ed was mulling this over, Gregorio told him he'd met Castro at a reception for foreign businessmen when he first visited Cuba in 1993.

They had exchanged pleasantries and small talk on a number of other occasions since then. Although Castro was known as a micromanager, the contract negotiations, financing, construction and other matters were handled by "quite competent young people specializing in their various fields."

"I guess he's learned over the years that he doesn't quite know everything," Ed said with a smirk. "The country *is* producing some fine technicians."

Gregorio said a number of the Cubans he dealt with had received economic and financial training in Moscow, France, Spain, even England.

"More often than not, they are young, knowledgeable and deadly serious. Some are friendly, but their manners need work. They cover up what they don't know pretty well. They concentrate on business. They don't know good wine and don't handle anything other than rum very well. Fidel is personally very pleasant, and very intelligent. I've never seen him drink at these occasions."

"But he's the greatest propagandist since Goebbels," the Spaniard continued. "What he and his cronies have done here is abominable. There is no other word for it. Castro and his gang are the world's biggest liars and hypocrites, especially to their own people. Maybe all dictators have to be master hypocrites to remain in power. And I agree that the Cubans are probably worse off than the people in my country were under Franco."

The deaths of Franco and Salazar meant the end of fascism in Europe, Ed observed. "When will communism end in the Americas?"

Neither friend was willing to guess.

When their meal was over and they were having Spanish cognac and Cuban cigars, Ed frankly told his old friend that he had decided to join his brother's rebel cause, and why, trying to explain his conscience and motivation.

Gregorio was astounded by this.

"You and your conscience are crazy," he blurted, smiling tightly, uncertain whether Ed was serious.

Ed assured him he was deadly serious.

"I feel my whole life has been leading to this," he said. "Like my brother, I want to give my life some meaning by helping to change this country's fate. . . . I realize this sounds corny, but I can't help that."

Gregorio thought this over for awhile.

"Damn. That's a big step, Eddie. I wish I could be with you," Gregorio said slowly, reflectively. "*Coño!* That's the ultimate challenge, I should think. But a man needs to fulfill his life, as you say. I wish I was capable of something like that. But . . . too many responsibilities. I want to help, though," he added after a while. "Tell me what you need. Let me help, Eduardo."

Ed told him the only way right now was to keep his eyes and ears open about Cuban politics and the military. He told Gregorio about Miguel's activities but didn't mention the visit from Diego Sierra and his talk of a brewing *coup d'etat* — or at least the possibility of one.

"Everything right now is in a state of flux, though. I'm waiting for word from my brother. I hope we can get together and talk things over and see what develops. He may not see it my way."

The two old friends decided to meet again as soon as Ed and Miguel had reunited. Ed asked how long Gregorio's stay in Cuba would be. Almost two months, Gregorio replied, with short trips to Miami and Nassau in-between.

With that, lunch was over. Gregorio had to travel to Holguin and Santiago to look over some possible hotel sites. But he'd be reachable through his secretary. He told his friend to stay at the Mirador as long as he wanted, but Ed said he should get back to Havana so he wouldn't miss any word from Miguel.

"*Un abrazo, mi heroé,*" said Gregorio emotionally, pulling Ed up from the table and wrapping him up in a big bear hug. "Let me know what happens. I'll help you however I can."

Ed was left alone to ponder their talk. Perhaps his friend would realize the incongruity of his offer to help overthrow the dictator who was making it possible for him and his company to add to their profits. Perhaps it wouldn't matter to such a man as Gregorio, a former rebel himself. Of one thing Ed was sure, he was a true friend with a big heart and a trustworthy soul. And . . . maybe he *could* help.

SOCIAL PHILOSOPHY
AND A NOTE

Ed drove back to Havana and the Inglaterra later that afternoon after spending a couple of hours on the beautiful beach fronting the Mirador resort. He saw some lovely, shapely women, but they were all attached.

That evening, leaving the Inglaterra and walking to a nearby restaurant, Ed was stopped by a young man selling cigars in the park across the street. Smiling and thrusting a box of Cohibas in front of him, the youth slipped him a note. Ed nodded and tucked the slip of paper in his pants pocket as he brought out some bills. He picked up one of the cigars, gave the man some money and walked off jauntily lighting the cigar.

He was sure the note had to do with Miguel. But he would wait to read it. He continued through the small park and walked the four short blocks to the restaurant. He was meeting an old Cuban friend whom he'd managed to contact through the University of Havana.

Rufino Boza was a retired professor who still taught a few classes at the law college. He was a gregarious, talkative man who liked Americans. More of a philosopher than a lawyer, he'd been a trusted source for Ed in the 1960s. The professor was surprised to hear from the correspondent again and gladly accepted the invitation for dinner.

This short round man liked to discuss politics, economics, philosophy, whatever his companions were willing to engage in over good food.

Ed was delighted to see that his now gray-and-grizzled friend hadn't changed in manner over the years. Over a beer after both ordered roast chicken and *moros*, a combination of black beans and rice, Boza peppered Ed with questions. After grunting over the American's short answers, Boza started answering some of Ed's own questions.

With slight encouragement, he began talking about Cuba's two societies, one made up of the fortunate ones who had access to American dollars and the other composed of those whose lives depended solely on the Cuban peso.

Life had become somewhat easier in the past few years for some of his fellow Cubans, particularly those functioning in the tourist industry or those who received dollars from exile relatives or friends, Boza said.

"Still, poverty has weighed down many, many Cubans and some of them exist marginally, I tell you. Every day, the gap widens between those who have and those who don't, in either currency. For some, daily life is like treading water — you forget about going anywhere and only hope you can stay in place, and you'd better not bitch about it too loudly."

Boza spoke from experience, that of himself and his many close friends who didn't have to be prompted to tell their stories.

What about Cuba's reputation for having no unemployment, for its rapidly-improved health care, its education policy that supposedly encompassed everyone, Ed asked his professor-friend.

"One has to give Castro his due for helping many *guajiros* who had nothing and no expectations of ever having anything. But making education and health care available does not really resolve the many problems for the vast majority, amigo, especially those in the cities who were either middle class or working to get there before the Castro revolution came along."

"As for unemployment," Boza continued, "the regime tries to keep workers satisfied, and it provides a lot of make-work jobs at very low salaries. Often, several people will share one job. They cut the hours each person works, and *voila*! You can have two people doing one eight- or ten-hour job, sometimes even three people.

"An example I know about personally," he added, "is a position of hotel clerk at the Habana Libre. It's divided up into six shifts over twenty-four hours. So you've got six people, each working four hours a day. Technically, they're all employed. But can they make a decent living that way? No. So if you don't have anything supplementing that, you're in trouble. Or, you look for an additional job. And so it goes."

The regime uses employment as a way of keeping everybody tied to the system, he added.

"The government provides for you so you will, in turn, remain loyal to the regime. Some people are given what we call zombie jobs. They get very little work to do and are paid a few pesos. They support Fidel because he gave them a job."

Ed said he'd found that foreign observers were bewildered by the circumstances. They didn't see how the Castro regime could continue to exist under a dual economy: one based on tourist dollars and the other on Cuban pesos.

Boza agreed, throwing up his hands. "We'll just have to wait and see how that works out," he said, shaking his head.

The country is getting needed foreign exchange but at the expense of the old, the poor, the needy, he said. All that foreign money eventually winds up in the hands of the government. And don't forget the young. Most Cubans, themselves, are bewildered, but especially the young people, Boza said.

The young constituted the majority of the population of the country.

"There is an increasing number of young men and women who are unhappy and restless, and becoming more-so every day," he said. "You've got to remember that many of them were born after Fidel came to power. They have no firsthand knowledge of the revolution and may have no historical or political allegiance to Castro. Plus, they are very aware of their peers in the rest of the world. So they know they are being left out. For them, *no hay salida*, there is no exit, no way out."

Ed had found that young, well-educated people who should be looking forward to bright futures were instead scrambling for jobs in the tourist sector — as waiters, hotel employees, bartenders, beach attendants, taxi drivers — so they could get access to dollars. Many of the young no longer believed in the promises of their leaders. Whether they had been to state schools or not, they were completely alienated from government because they were only living the reality of the streets.

"If they don't have any *recursos* from the outside, their universe is the stuff of dreams," was the way the old professor put it.

He spread his arms and hands out in an all-inclusive gesture and said, "Look around you. This used to be a country of morals, no matter how poor you were. Now, since the Soviets left and Fidel declared 'the special period' of austerity, there has been a breakdown in society as well. The economic system went to hell, but so did we, as a people. We steal from each other and treat each other as strangers or, worse, as enemies. I could go on and on, but, meanwhile, I am ignoring this good food before us."

The peso, which was worthless overseas, was valued significantly lower than the dollar in Cuba. So much so that a cabdriver for tourists often made more money (forty or fifty American dollars) in a day than a doctor or engineer could make in a month (300-350 pesos).

A favorite joke in Havana was that Cuba had the world's most-intelligent taxi drivers. The college professors and the architects and engineers were now driving the cabs. Where else could a *turista* sit back and discuss philosophy, art or history with his taxi driver?

Ed pointed out that in contrast to the 1960s, when Castro and his followers "expropriated" foreign businesses and property worth billions, Cuba was now again open to foreign investment and private enterprise. Corporate investors and government officials from Spain, England, France, Brazil, Argentina, Mexico and other countries now scouted out new opportunities and negotiated partnerships with Cuba's newest generation of economic controllers.

"There are many similarities in Cuba today with what happened during Batista's time," Boza said. "Many things are coming around full circle — from capitalism to socialism and communism and back to capitalism. But there is the same top-down control by the government. Those in control get most of the benefits; the common people get left out."

Ed noted that although the Castro government tolerated prostitution, it hadn't returned to the days of the 1950s when Batista permitted mobsters like Meyer Lansky, Santos Trafficante and others to build and operate casino hotels at will.

"Yes, the mob paid off Batista and became a real power in Cuba," Boza said. "But that was then." When Batista fled, the mob had to pack up and leave, too. The casinos remained a thing of the past. But, with the resurgence of tourism, the expectation was that they would eventually return.

As interesting as his friend was, Ed's thoughts kept straying to his brother and the note in his pocket. Finally, he excused himself to go to the men's room. The note said Miguel was eager for a reunion, and it set out detailed directions on where Ed should go for a meeting that coming Sunday.

When Ed went back to the table, Boza expressed his appreciation for an excellent meal and good conversation.

"It isn't often I get to have either," he said.

He left him with a final word.

"It will be a madhouse when the end finally comes for this dictatorship, Eduardo. When Fidel goes, Raul Castro and his generals think they can retain control, and maybe they will for awhile. The exiles think they can flock back in and bring the Yankee style of doing things to 'their homeland.' That is highly unlikely. They are mostly happy where they are, and they are extremely fortunate to have been accepted, as they were, wherever they ended up. It will be many years before some degree of sanity is restored to this island. However . . . there's no such thing as 'normal' for Cuba. Never has been."

They embraced and promised to get together again soon.

The youth with the cigars was nowhere in sight as Ed walked back to his hotel.

CONSPIRACY BREWS

This time, the half-brothers met in a small house in Boyeros, a few miles from the international airport. About thirty years had gone by since they had seen each other. Ed drove from Habana Vieja to a late-night bodega called Tecolote on a small street between Parque Lenin and the National Zoo. There, he was picked up in a beat-up, rusty Chevrolet by Miguel's guerrilla sidekick, Roberto Madera, and another man who didn't identify himself.

They drove for about ten minutes, arriving at a small house in a heavily wooded area of dirt roads. Two rifle-bearing men opened a gate, and the car drove up the overgrown pathway to the house.

The gray-haired, bearded Miguel sat by himself in the dark patio at the back of the house smoking a days-old cigar that smelled of old shoes. He wore a pressed white shirt and had been pacing back and forth from kitchen to living room as he waited like a nervous cat.

When Eduardo appeared, the half-brothers embraced, then stood back and looked at each other wordlessly, appraising the changes the years had made. The American had gotten stockier. He still had most of his hair, now streaked with gray. The guerrilla leader had fleshed out, too. He looked weary but appeared much healthier than the last time they saw each other.

"It's the lifestyle and the good food, *hermano*," Miguel joked when Ed noted the change for the better. "For a long time, I couldn't eat . . . and now maybe too much. The medications and the constant activity are what keep me going. They're good for the heart . . . and the soul."

"I've heard about your active lifestyle, Miguel," said Ed through teary eyes. "You have quite a reputation. But I'm gratified by your good health, although each day must be a helluva danger to you."

"We live for one thing only and God has been good to provide me with time so that we can try to get that done," said Miguel softly, gesturing for his brother to sit down and join him in a glass of red wine from an open bottle on the little table in the patio. "When dictatorship is a fact, revolution is a duty," he said, quoting Pascal Mercier.

"This self-denominated *revolucion* has always had its *resistencia* but never before like this," Miguel fervently believed, speaking slowly and softly, almost to himself.

Ed was seeing a moodier, more serious side to Miguel.

"*La verdad* is, I am here to offer my help," Eduardo said, raising his glass. "I want to join your resistencia"

When Miguel started to object, Ed interrupted and carefully explained the reasons why he felt so strongly about doing something meaningful for himself, for Cuba and its people, for the memory of their mother, for his green-eyed Lydia and for so many others who had suffered. He laid out his strong feelings. It was good to talk about it, finally.

Ed then his told his brother about the visit from the Ministry of Interior's Diego Sierra and his claim that government intelligence agents had infiltrated the Falcon guerrilla movement. Either that, or they appeared to Ed have very good informants.

The guerrilla was grimfaced. He said nothing. This was serious business.

Ed went on, "The shocking thing to me, Miguel, was his claim that they claim to know where you and your men are and what you're doing at all times," Ed said. "But Sierra contends that this information is closely held by only a few people in his unit and that they won't act against you because they actually want to help you overthrow Fidel Castro. . . how about that?"

"That's pretty hard to believe," Miguel said, shaking his head in wonder. "I don't know who this guy is."

Ed had been skeptical from the beginning, but he carefully laid out everything Sierra told him in great detail.

"He says his group in MinInt is too small right now for them to initiate and carry out a successful attempt against Castro. But he says their number is slowly growing and that they have supporters in the armed services and other government ministries. I find it hard to believe, too. But, maybe."

Ed recited Sierra's offer to convince Miguel and his *guerrilleros* of their intentions.

"He says he can prove to you that they know where you are at any given time. All you have to do is give Sierra a time and date — without mentioning the location — and he will show up at that time wherever you happen to be."

"It looks like we don't have much choice," the guerrilla chief said, shaking his head slowly. "This guy, whoever he is, says they won't act on their information if we refuse, but how long can we rely on that? Unless this is a very elaborate trap, I'm inclined to believe that there *is* a conspiracy against Fidel within the Interior Ministry. I've heard rumors."

He reminded Eduardo that just a couple of years ago, the Castro brothers had virtually dismantled the MinInt as a result of a drug-smuggling operation that had gone bad.

When Cuba's involvement in Colombian drug-running into Florida was about to be exposed, Castro quickly denounced the key participants, who were all Interior Ministry officers, plus Army Division General Arnaldo Ochoa. Fidel put them all out to dry. They underwent a very public trial for conspiracy and other charges.

But there was no mention of drugs by anyone, Miguel recalled. They didn't want the world to know Cuba was in any way involved in drug-smuggling,

"On the eve of their trial, Castro promised Ochoa and a MinInt colonel named Tony de la Guardia that their lives would be spared if they did not publicly implicate him and Cuba in the drug-smuggling plot. The two men agreed. They didn't talk. But the day after the trial, the colonel and the general were tied to a stake and shot to death anyway. That's a good way to permanently shut you up. *Que no?*"

What happened then, Ed wanted to know.

"After that, the Interior Minister, General Jose Abrantes, was fired from his job, which incidentally included being the personal security chief for Castro. He's still in prison. So . . . you see, there's a lot of bad blood there."

After much discussion over Sierra's proposal, Miguel said he would explain the situation to his most trusted men to decide what to do. He would get word to Eduardo in a few days, and he could pass it on to Sierra.

For the present, however, the Falcon unit would concentrate on their business and put everything else aside.

Ed said he agreed with something Sierra had emphasized, that the only foreseeable way open to a major change in government was to eliminate Fidel. And right now appeared to be the best time they could hope for.

"If there's ever going to be a time when this son of a bitch falls, it's got to be now. He's getting old, the military is restless and the people are divided," Ed said.

"He's also getting very little help from his old friends, *los Sovieticos*," Miguel added, drawing his patio chair closer to his brother. Then, in a hoarse whisper, he said, "We are working on a plan right now to kill Fidel."

Ed was stirred. It seemed that everyone was thinking the same thing, the time is now. He sat quietly in the dark, trying to contain his excitement. "Tell me," he urged.

"If things work out," Miguel said, "we plan to do this the next time he visits Santa Clara, where he goes every few weeks. We know he has a special lady in that area. I won't give you the details. As you know, his movements are secretive, and he never stays in the same place more than one night. We have a couple of informants in good positions, but their information usually leaves us little time to act."

The guerrillas needed good advance information on Fidel Castro's movements in the next few weeks, the rebel leader stressed. "We need good intelligence. We're trying to reach someone close to the inner circle now. We think there may be enough dissatisfaction there to get someone to tip us off when the bastard goes into the interior. We need to know ahead of time."

Ed then thought of his Basque friend, Gregorio, and his close contacts with the government people around Fidel. Maybe he could help.

He told Miguel about Gregorio Yzaguirre, about his background, about his his strong feelings about fascism, communism and dictators such as Fidel and Franco. With Miguel's permission, Ed said he would determine if Gregorio could subtly feel out some of his Cuban contacts with ties to Fidel's inner circle.

"I trust him completely," Ed told his brother. "I think he'd be in the trenches here, if he could. Maybe he can come up with something we can use."

"Okay, but make no direct mention of our project," Miguel consented. "And, of course, nothing of this should be said to your MinInt friend Sierra, either. I trust you to use the utmost discretion. The wrong word to the wrong person can mean our necks."

Meantime, he told Ed, the guerrillas would continue to fine-tune their plans. "We'll soon be in position to take some action."

"As for me," Ed said. "I've renewed my visa. I'll be staying in Havana for awhile and continuing to play tourist. I've been meeting with old friends, and I'll see Gregorio again as soon as possible. With meticulous planning, we can help make your plan work and kill the bastard, finally. Not like the poorly prepared *desgraciados* of the past."

Miguel nodded. The two embraced and said goodbye after setting up a system for communicating with each other.

PLAN OF ATTACK

Ed's unexpected fervor reminded Miguel of his own enthusiasm for the fight when he decided he wasn't going to crawl off somewhere and die, or even to leave his beloved land. The passion has to be there for all of us or else we would be crazy to be doing this year after year, he thought.

Maybe fatalism went hand-in-hand with fanaticism, Miguel pondered.

But the time had now come to end it, one way or another. He and his small group of *guerrilleros* would put an end to Cuba's misery if their plan worked out. If it didn't . . . well, it could be the end of them.

The guerrilleros were not heroes of any kind to each other, to their families or those few who knew of their extracurricular activities. They were ordinary Cubans who, like Miguel and Roberto Madera, simply decided they had had enough of the dictator.

Some were mechanics of some sort, taxi drivers, bus drivers, stevedores. One had taught mathematics to teenagers in a small, quietly operated school. Another worked in a hotel and one operated a blackmarket bodega. But when the time came to drop everything and go out on a mission, they became, in a word, *terroristas*. That was the word used by Castro and his people about the small opposition to the communist regime.

The old veteran Madera was typical of many in the small group of volunteers. Diehards. They remembered what it was to be poor, but free.

They never celebrated their small victories or publicly lamented their losses. They didn't talk to anybody about what they did. They were always ready to go, most of the time with a little advance planning but sometimes momentarily, when the occasion presented itself. They knew they were right in what they believed. Nothing could change that.

After Miguel talked it over with Madera and several others, it was decided to go ahead with their own plans despite what might take place with Diego Sierra of the Interior Ministry's Counter-Intelligence Section. If Sierra was trying to trap them, or if he was playing some kind of macabre game, they'd have to deal with it when they met with him, if they decided that's what they wanted to do.

The cattle and sugarcane country around Santa Clara was the place where they planned it would happen. That was their best chance. And it was fitting, since Fidel annually commemorated the town's liberation from the Batista government.

Santa Clara, in Central Cuba about 200 miles from Havana, was the first major city taken over by the rebels. Che Guevara and his small group of guerrillas trooped in on Dec. 28, 1958, a mere three days before Batista fled the country. They celebrated that victory ever since.

Several elements of the plan Miguel had devised gave the Falcon guerrillas increasing confidence in its outcome. The first was that after years of trying, they had now succeeded in reaching someone within Castro's security detail to help them. A trusted assistant to the operational head of security for Castro had agreed to help out the dissidents with information on Castro's movements.

Army Lt. Ciro Betancourt, who often served as an "advance man" for the trips taken by the Castro entourage outside the capital, had first been approached by a cousin. The cousin's father had been tortured to death in one of the G2 interrogation centers, and he believed Betancourt would help the anti-Castro rebels. There was a link there because the G2's victim also had been Lt. Betancourt's uncle, Arcelio Lopez.

Lopez had been arrested and imprisoned by G2 after he failed in an attempt to hijack a small Cuban Coast Guard vessel, which he planned to load with relatives and friends and sail to Miami.

Before any of this took place back in 1958, a young Ciro Betancourt and several of his teenage friends had led a protest march in Havana in which gunshots were exchanged. Army troops shot and wounded four of the demonstrators. Uncle Arcelio had hidden Ciro and another youth in his rural house for six months during a manhunt by Batista's troops. Arcelio Lopez saved their lives.

Although there had been no communication for years between Betancourt and his family members, the Army officer recalled the old man fondly and had felt indebted to him all these years. The time had come to pay his debt to his uncle. Now an Army lieutenant, Ciro Betancourt was becoming increasingly disenchanted with the Castro regime and its duplicity. So when his cousin approached him, Betancourt decided this was a good opportunity to strike back at the G2.

He agreed to become an informant for the underground rebels, to tip them off about Castro's comings and goings when he could safely do so.

Another confidence-booster for Miguel's plan was that the manager of the Hotel Santa Clara, who had quietly been trying to help out the dissidents for years, had finally come up with some information that could prove valuable.

During Castro's last two visits to Santa Clara, the chief assistant to Cuba's Interior Minister had stayed at the hotel, the innkeeper had reported to Miguel. Both times, this government official had arranged for the chef at the hotel restaurant to cook large amounts of his renowned Spanish dishes. Two army officers would then collect the specially ordered dishes and drive off somewhere into the countryside.

By now, the hotel manager had figured out that the food was being picked up for some of the top brass forming the official Castro group, perhaps for Fidel himself. The hotel cook had told the manager they would probably do the same thing during this visit to Santa Clara.

Miguel had also discovered who Fidel was visiting on his trips to Santa Clara. Miguel's operatives were now watching the woman closely. A widow in her forties, Susana Abelardo, lived with her two brothers on a ranch near town.

Meanwhile, the anxious Ed contacted his friend at the Mirador resort in Varadero the next day. Gregorio asked him to drive over. Without going into great detail, Ed told him that it would be of great benefit to his guerrilla friends if Gregorio could try to get information from his Cuban business contacts about Castro's travels in the coming week-or-so.

"Good, I'm having some of the commerce and industry people and their wives over on Saturday for a dinner party here at the hotel," Gregorio said. "As I told you, there are a couple of these guys who are pretty chatty. Another has made veiled inquiries about job opportunities outside Cuba. You've given me a nice challenge, amigo, I'll see what I can find out."

"Thanks, Gregorio. Maybe you can come up with something useful, but take care of yourself. Don't be too obvious about it. If nothing comes out of it, forget it."

Ed stayed for dinner. The two friends talked over old times over good wine and cigars. He stayed overnight and drove back to Havana the next morning. He spent the next few days in his tourist routine after he and Gregorio agreed to meet again on Sunday.

Gregorio had by then zeroed in on a self-important commercial adviser, who had been educated in Paris, and was in almost daily contact with Fidel's closest aides.

In fact, this guy was friendly with the family of Nati Revuelta, a wealthy Havana socialite who had been married to a prominent doctor when she gave birth to Fidel's only daughter. His chatty friend informed Gregorio that Fidel's five sons by another woman, Delia del Valle, had been schooled in the Soviet Union. But the illegitimate daughter, Alina, had refused to go and turned out to be an outspoken thorn in Castro's side for years — in exile, of course.

Gregorio's target among Fidel's young advisers was Yael Pereira, who was part Portuguese and had been brought up near the Spanish border not far from Barcelona. Pereira had received part of his training in Moscow. He and two of his friends invited Gregorio to join them at the Tropicana Nightclub the next night. The Spaniard was only too happy to accept.

On Monday, Ed got a call at his hotel from Gregorio, suggesting a late lunch at Havana's Centro Vasco, an elegant Spanish-themed restaurant serving Basque food. Gregorio had spent the night at the Melia Cohiba, a gleaming new tourist hotel in Vedado. He'd stayed out until 2 a.m. with his three new Cuban friends.

"We had a lot to drink and got real chummy before the night was over," Gregorio recounted. "They invited some of the Tropicana dancers to sit with us between shows, and one of the girls was very interested in coming back to the hotel with me afterward. But I managed to resist."

Ed grinned and waited, noting that his friend looked a bit frayed, nonetheless, from the night of partying. Gregorio told his friend what had happened.

"Pereira and a guy named Yspiricueta — two of the three Cubans — collared me privately during the evening and asked me outright if I thought they could get a 'position' with my company if they stayed in Madrid at the next opportunity. What kind of revolutionaries are these?"

"What did you tell them?" Ed asked.

"I strung them along. Anyway, what you want to know is whether I got any info for you. The answer is maybe a little."

His new friend Pereira told him he was accompanying Fidel on a trip to the southeast and other potential tourism sites in the rural areas of the island. He thought the trip would take place within two next couple of weeks. The Castro retinue would fly to Santiago and then drive to Camaguey through Holguin, Sancti Spiritus and Santa Clara over several days, he said.

Castro and the others would be talking to local officials and visiting the possible hotel sites that Gregorio and representatives of a French company had inspected over the past few weeks.

"*Que fortuna!*" said Ed. "You would make a good spy, Gregorio."

"I think it was stupid luck to hook up with those guys who were just trying to impress me," Gregorio said, beaming.

Miguel was equally impressed by Gregorio's news when the half-brothers met again that Saturday in the same general area as before but at a different house. Miguel said he'd see if he could confirm the information through his own sources.

"Your Spanish friend has suddenly become valuable to us, Eduardo. We are fortunate that you and he are in Cuba at the same time, and that he's so well-placed. I think we've got a good plan. To make it work, we need reliable information, and this looks good if it checks out."

Miguel then told him the Falcon guerrillas had decided Miguel should meet again with Diego Sierra. Ed was to tell Sierra only that the Falcon rebeldes expected to meet with Sierra on that coming Sunday at six o'clock in the evening.

"Let's see how good his counterintelligence is," said Miguel grimly. "Let's see if he can determine where we will be. If he can, we'll be ready for him. If he plans a trap, I'm pretty sure we can smell it out and disappear. I'm not even telling *you* where we are going to be."

Ed didn't raise any questions or objections. The guerrillas knew what they were doing.

"Good luck, Miguel," said Ed as they parted with a lengthy *abrazo*.

BIZARRE SETUP

The Falcon guerrilla unit was composed of eighteen men equipped with automatic rifles and small arms which they acquired through foreign sources or which they had confiscated in raids on military storage depots. They also maintained a secret storage site near Havana where they kept explosives, other weapons, tents and ammunition.

Their attacks were carried out against military installations, supply warehouses and properties of Castro supporters and government officials. In nighttime raids, they dynamited government construction projects. And, lately, they had been supporting seaborne incursions by exiles sailing from Florida.

There had been changes in their personnel over the years owing to arrests, casualty losses and dropouts for various reasons. But their ranks had stabilized at a time coinciding with the step-up in their activities. Young and old, they were now dedicated to guerrilla warfare.

Miguel and Madera roamed throughout the island, scouting out targets and relying on a clandestine network of volunteers for their subsistence. They sometimes received money and weapons from old friends, the funds allowing them to acquire more supplies and ammunition, plus fuel and spare parts for three trucks and a couple of old but serviceable cars they kept in the Havana area.

The loose network of supporters included informants in many parts of the country.

Acting on Gregorio Yzaguirre's information, Miguel and Madera passed the word to those in Santiago and the other cities to monitor their sources closely in the next few weeks and to quickly relay any information on VIP movements.

In Santa Clara, Miguel and his deputy surreptitiously scouted out the ranch where Fidel's lady friend lived, along with the surrounding area. The widow Abelardo and her older brothers, Raul and Julian Pino, operated the ranch that had belonged to their father and was confiscated by the Castro government in the 1960s.

They bred beef cattle using artificial insemination methods developed by government veterinarians with the assistance of foreign experts. The word was that Fidel had become acquainted with Mrs. Abelardo during his frequent visits when the cattle-breeding program was getting started. It was his project. Fidel stayed overnight at the ranch on three previous occasions, twice in the past two months and both times when the brothers Pino were away.

She was the widow of Army Capt. Juan Jose Abelardo, who was killed in Angola during Cuba's African campaigns. Cubans trained and assisted rebel groups in several African nations at that time.

Miguel and Madera knew the extent of the heavy security surrounding Castro. They had run into it before. However, they received some help here.

"Some people I know from the early days have passed on some good info," said Madera, who had lived in the area in his youth. The Santa Clara informants told them that once Fidel was in the ranchhouse for the night on the two latest occasions, the armed patrol was reduced to five guards while the remainder of the security detail stayed in an outlying bunkhouse used by ranch employees. The ranch cowboys were sent away for a couple of days except for one or two who stayed behind.

This scenario provided an excellent opportunity to carry out their plan, Miguel believed. There would be casualties, but every one of his soldiers was anxious and determined to finish it, to eliminate the one man that made it necessary for them to live like this.

Ed expected Sierra to contact him again soon. If Sierra was telling the truth, his people must know that the brothers had met, and where — a circumstance which made Ed feel very vulnerable. He was no longer just an innocent tourist, coming and going with few people noticing or caring.

A call to Gregorio's hotel office in Varadero brought the information that he was still on the road and would call him when he returned.

The evening of the following day, as he was walking across the park to his favorite restaurant, he was approached by a man who asked for a light for his cigar and then quietly identified himself as a friend of Sierra's. Sierra would meet Ed the following morning in his room, the nondescript follow told him, quickly walking away smoking his cigar.

Sierra was sitting in one of the armchairs when Ed returned from the hotel's coffee shop the next morning.

"Well, make yourself at home," Ed said, perturbed at seeing Sierra in his room.

"*Hola*, Eduardo. I see you met with your brother," Sierra said with a grin and a quick handshake. "Forgive this intrusion. It won't happen again. What news have you got for me?"

"Well," Ed said slowly, still wary, "at least we know part of your story is true, about the surveillance."

After a lengthy pause during which the two men locked eyes, Ed said, "The Falcon guerrillas have decided to meet with you and your two friends. But, they too, have pretty good surveillance, and if they detect anyone else in the area that shouldn't be there, you might get hurt. Understood?"

"Understood," Sierra replied quickly. "Of course Miguel would want it that way. We know they're cautious, otherwise they wouldn't have survived this long. They have my respect. Everything I told you is true, Eduardo. We will prove it to the Falcon."

Ed told Sierra about Miguel's requirement that only three people show up in one truck and that to show their good intent, the vehicle should hold a sealed crate containing at least two AK-47s, four other assault rifles and a good supply of ammunition for those weapons. Ed was surprised by Sierra's quick acceptance of that idea.

"We can call it a gift of faith," Sierra said.

The meeting was set for Sunday, three days from now, at 6 p.m., Ed informed him. "As you claim, you know where they are all the time, so if you show up, unarmed, the meeting will take place. Even I don't know where that will be."

"*Bueno*. That's good Eduardo. Believe me. We're anxious to help and for Miguel to be effective against the regime. You'll see, after Sunday we will be working together. Tell your brother we'll see him then, just the three of us, unarmed, ready to talk. You're helping to make history by arranging this, Eduardo."

They shook hands and Sierra walked out.

Ed then used one of Miguel's trusted contacts in the hotel to get word to him that everything was set for Sunday. Next, he set off for Varadero, telling the Inglaterra's contact where he could be reached. At the Mirador, during a late dinner after his return, Gregorio recounted details of his trip into the interior and his business encounters with some of the Cuban officials.

"They are opening up more and more. We're getting real friendly," Gregorio said. "I've got my eyes and ears wide open. We've got high-level meetings here and in Havana over the next few days, so maybe I can shake something else loose from the Cubans soon."

Gregorio wanted Edward to stay at the resort a few days, but Ed only remained overnight and hurried back to Havana in case there was a change of plan by Miguel.

CONFRONTATION

It turned out that the Sunday tête-a-tête was set up in a swampy area overgrown with mangroves and underbrush deep in the Zapata Peninsula on Cuba's southern coast, southeast of Havana. The area was definitely not on the list of tourist sites. In fact, it was difficult to find and maneuver into unless one had previous experience and a four-wheeled vehicle, or a sturdy wide-bodied truck, and a good compass.

Miguel had purposely set the meeting time for 6 p.m. so that their "guests" could get there in daylight and allow about two hours before sunset for the talks, if necessary.

He staked out his men around the perimeter and on the dirt roads and trails. Several guerrillas were posted as scouts along the main road from Havana, and they communicated with Miguel and Madera with hand-held radios.

"If that *cabrón* can find us, they have pretty damn good intelligence. And maybe we should start worrying about that," Madera muttered.

"Maybe it won't matter, if everything goes well here," Miguel said. "We'll find out one way or another. One thing's for sure, he can't surprise us, and he can't bring an army in here without us spotting it long beforehand. They sure as hell can't see us from the air, either."

They waited, along with a third guerrillero named Vasquez, near two parked trucks in a clearing surrounded by, swamp oaks, cabbage palms and a stand of mahogany trees. The vehicles were well stocked with weapons, ammunition, water and other supplies. The three wore their sidearms and carried rifles.

Miguel's radio squawked at 5:40 p.m. The scout posted about ten miles away near the only good road leading to their section of the swamp informed him that a heavy truck carrying three men had just passed him. Apparently, they were going to get visitors after all.

Ten minutes later, another of the scouts called in and told Miguel the vehicle with three men was in the area. Miguel instructed his man to have four of the guerrilleros stop the truck, disarm the driver and passengers, if necessary, and escort them to the meeting site. Everyone was on high alert for any possible trap.

A few minutes later, they heard the truck rumble to a stop behind the mangroves. Then the three Interior Ministry counter-intelligence agents, escorted by the four armed guerrillas, walked into the clearing.

Sierra and his friends, identified as Yosmani Cruz and Eusebio Portillo, were smiling and affable as they walked up to the Falcon guerrillas. Sierra extended his hand and Miguel and Madera shook it.

"Thank you for receiving us. We are pleased to be in your company," Sierra said. "I've always admired your planning and persistence even in all of the years we were trying to capture you and your men."

Miguel nodded but said nothing as he and Madera led the three men through a small pathway into a secluded area where a military camp table and chairs had been set up. A cooler next to the table held water, soft drinks and beer.

"As you can see, we're not much on amenities. But we're extremely mobile," Madera said, only half joking.

"Mobility has always been one of your strongest assets," Sierra commented, taking a canvas chair and accepting a half-liter bottle of mineral water. His two companions and Madera and Vasquez dragged chairs about five feet away, leaving Sierra and Miguel at the table.

"What do you want exactly?" Miguel asked, getting right to the matter. "Why the sudden change of heart on your part, if that's what it is? Why are your spies changing sides, and what does that have to do with us?"

"Let me start by repeating to you what I told your brother," Sierra replied calmly. "First, I think we have just now proved that we have you under constant surveillance. How we've managed to do that, I'm not going to explain. We could have captured you anytime in the last six months, and we can trap you and take you in anytime we want in the future.

"But, in fact, we are *protecting* you now," Sierra continued, drawing out his words. "I know that must be hard for you to believe. But we are protecting you from our own kind and from the Army, which wants you even more than our Interior Ministry jefes do."

Sierra stretched and rubbed his left leg, which had developed a cramp. This caused a quick stir among the rebeldes, but everybody quickly calmed down and Sierra continued with a grin.

"What we want now is to convince you that you have friends who will work with you, cooperate with you and help you — however you want to put it. My small group within the Counter-Intelligence Section, plus another dozen or so officers whom I know in the Army, have convinced ourselves over the years that the Fidel Castro era must be ended. I won't bore you with when or how or why we have come to this decision, but we have."

"How could you help us? With information? How can we trust whatever information you may pass on?" Miguel interjected.

"How you confirm whatever we give you is up to you, of course, but there are other ways, too, that we can help," Sierra responded. "For instance, weapons and ammo. We've just brought you what you wanted. In addition, we can supply vehicles, maybe some explosives. There are various ways we can assist your operations. But what we want more than anything is to kill Fidel Castro. We'd like to help you do that."

Miguel nodded thoughtfully. Then after a pause, he continued to question and probe. Sierra sat through it patiently and made his argument that their efforts against the regime, and ultimately against Castro himself, should be combined for greater impact.

After much dialogue and argument, Sierra suddenly said, "Look, I've laid myself and my colleagues bare. I've exposed our activities and intentions to you. My people and I have become traitors to the revolution. You can expose me and the rest of us, if you want. But I don't think you will. That's why I'm here."

With only slight pause, the relaxed Sierra continued.

"If you decide not to work with us, nothing will happen to you as a result. I can promise you that. We will protect you as long as it doesn't expose us. But how long that will be I cannot say. It may be a short time.

But if we work together, I'll keep you constantly informed of our status and any possible danger to you."

Miguel remained skeptical. He hoped that Sierra wasn't just fishing for as much information as he could get before closing a trap. But he wanted to believe, and he could see the instant benefits. He called a break and took Madera aside.

"This is leading us nowhere unless we either decide to trust him or cut his throat," Miguel told his friend quietly. "He makes a very persuasive argument," he said thoughtfully. "But I don't want to be blinded by words . . . What do you think, Roberto?"

"I'm inclined to believe him. I don't think we have much choice anyway, since they seem to be able to track us so precisely. I think if they were laying a trap, they would've moved on us before now."

"Okay. I think you're right. We really have little choice. And if he's right, we have a lot to gain from this."

Miguel went back and quietly informed Sierra of their decision. Sierra nodded, then asked the other men to fall back, saying he wanted a private word with the Falcon. Madera interrupted, saying he and the others would inspect the MinInt truck's cargo. And they walked back to where the vehicle was parked.

After another ten minutes, Miguel and Sierra joined the others. A wooden crate sat next to the truck with its top pried open. Inside were the weapons and ammunition Miguel had asked for. The guerrilla chieftain nodded and, for the first time that afternoon, lost the grim look on his weathered face.

Miguel and Sierra shook hands silently. After a round of quick handshakes among the others, the visitors climbed into the truck. Before it pulled away, Sierra told the grizzled anti-Castro rebels, "We will soon see the benefits of this partnership."

Miguel resumed his grimfaced visage. He said nothing, but he waved back at the departing government agents.

Miguel then disclosed that Sierra had told him about Castro's forthcoming trip to the interior of the island, outlining his proposed itinerary starting in Santiago de Cuba. The approximate dates and stopovers tallied closely with what the rebels had been able to piece together on their own and from Eduardo's Spanish friend Gregorio.

"I didn't tell him about our plans, but I'm pretty sure he has an idea we plan to attack Castro somewhere on this trip," Miguel told Madera. "He said his group of dissidents was prepared to support us all-out on any assassination attempt because they believe anything else is just prolonging the evil."

"Are we going to ask for their assistance with our plan?" Madera inquired. "We can get word to him through Ed and our contacts in Havana if we decide to do so."

There they let matters rest.

CASTRO'S JOURNEY

Gregorio was spending quite a bit of time with the Cubans, but a week went by without any further information of any kind. At the start of the second week, however, his night-clubbing friend Pereira skipped a briefing session with Gregorio and his engineers about their construction plans in Varadero. Pereira left a message saying he would contact Gregorio the following week.

The day after that, Gregorio was told that a military officer who was supposed to meet with him about future projects would be traveling and unavailable for consultation for about a week.

He informed Ed of these developments, and Ed got word to Miguel, but there was as yet no word from their inside informant, Lt. Ciro Bustamante, who would travel with the Castro contingent. This probably meant he was finding it difficult to communicate with a contact in Havana.

"This looks like the time," Miguel told Madera. "If Fidel shows up in Santiago, we'll know that's the start of the 'inspection' trip that eventually gets him to Santa Clara. We'll be waiting for him there, amigo." The word went out to their close contacts in and around all those areas.

In the midst of these preparations, Miguel received word that his brother wanted an urgent meeting. Miguel sent word for him to drive to a little town south of Varadero named for Independence War hero Maximo Gomez. Miguel met him at the rural home of a guerrilla sympathizer.

"Sierra knows you are setting up in Santa Clara, and he has evidently surmised your intentions," Ed told his brother. "He insists on joining you with a half-dozen of his compañeros."

"I should have guessed."

"They'll be well-equipped, and he said they will travel in two trucks that will carry weapons and other supplies. They want to meet you at the Oscar Rodriguez farm on Wednesday afternoon."

"That guy. I knew it would come to something like this," Miguel muttered, walking back and forth nervously. "I don't know whether we want them on this. They could mess up our plans."

Then, calming down, he shrugged and appeared resigned to having the Interior Ministry agents along on his raid. "He doesn't leave us any choice, does he? Now we have no alternative but to trust him . . . Well, I hope he can take orders from me as well as he gives them."

"He did say he and his men would be at your disposal," Ed said placatingly.

"We'll make sure of that," Miguel said.

Ed remained seated and looked closely at his brother. "I hope you are prepared to tolerate one more last-minute addition to your group, Miguel. I've done all I can on the outside. Now I want to join you for the final strike."

"Look, Eduardo, I think you should go home. Go back to Florida and lead a good long life. This is no place for you. You could get killed."

"I assure you, I've debated all of the possibilities, the good and the bad, and my mind is made up. I can shoot. I can handle myself, and I can take whatever comes."

"Well . . . I'm not going to argue. I know you are as stubborn as I am, after all, you're half Cuban, *hermano.* So I'll have to accept whatever decision you make. But I hope you carefully consider the possible consequences for you."

"I don't need to 'consider' anymore, Miguel. My mind and my heart tell me this is the right thing to do. I will see you at the Rodriguez farm on Wednesday afternoon, too."

"All right. Until then," the frowning guerrilla leader said. He then threw an arm around Ed as they walked to his car.

Three days later, Fidel Castro met publicly with provincial, city and Communist Party officials in Santiago de Cuba.

On the evening of Fidel's second day in that city, Lt. Betancourt finally contacted a Falcon supporter. He hurriedlty told her that the Castro party planned to fly rather than drive out of Santiago. Another informant a little later reported that a twin-engine Cubana Airlines plane carrying the Castro entourage had departed the Antonio Maceo International Airport in Santiago at 9 p.m. Its destination was unknown.

This took Miguel by surprise. All their previous information indicated the government group planned to motorcade, stopping over at the various towns along the route. Had something gone wrong? Had the guerrillas been found out and Castro's trip cancelled?

No one on the outside knew of the Falcoln rebels' plans except Ed . . . and, of course, the G2's Sierra. Ed's Basque friend, Gregorio, had no specific knowledge of any of this, Miguel believed.

He and the ever-constant Madera were in a quandary.

The next day, Madera went to a pre-arranged spot near Santa Clara to pick up Sierra and Ed, who now became part of their group. Sierra's five men and the two vehicles were temporarily left behind while Ed, Sierra and Madera joined Miguel at the ranch.

Sierra suggested that Castro might have merely changed his plans, which he did frequently when traveling. There was nothing to do but wait and see what happened. Their qualms were put to rest later that day, however, after a contact in Holguin reported that Castro was in that city and scheduled meetings with Communist Party officials in that province.

"Evidently, they decided to cut out the overland part of the trip from Santiago to Holguin," Madera said thoughtfully. "Some of that is hard driving at night, I know. I'm willing to bet they will motorcade out from Holguin in a day or so and take their time getting to Camaguey, and then to Sancti Spiritus and Trinidad.

"Fidel likes to scuba dive at Playa Ancon, on the Caribbean near Trinidad," Madera added. "They may even stay in that area for several days before heading back up to Santa Clara."

"Sounds logical. Let's get word to the men to disperse quietly to Santa Clara," Miguel told him. "You know what to do."

Two days later, all the men had arrived at the Rodriguez ranch site, which they had designated as the operations center. The ranch was close enough to their target and only about five miles from Santa Clara. It was operated by a onetime employee of Miguel's father, an elderly rancher and sugarcane grower named Emilio Lazo. He had a large field of sugarcane on the property. The ranch got its name from its original owner.

The group consisting of Miguel, Madera, Sierra and Ed joined Lazo in the ranchhouse A dozen other men moved into a barnlike building that was used by sugarcane workers during the cutting season. The remaining guerrillas dispersed around the area.

Over the next few days, the rebels and their contacts plotted the Castro party's westward course through Holguin, Camaguey and, finally, into Sancti Spiritus and then to Trinidad. The group spent a day in the small Caribbean beach villages around Trinidad. On the seventh day of the excursion, the Falcon informants reported that the motorcade was headed back north to Sancti Spiritus.

From there, it was a relatively short trip into Santa Clara before returning to Havana.

The caravan's arrival at the Santa Clara cattle ranch run by the Pino brothers and their sister, Susana, came in late afternoon close to nightfall.

Miguel and his group were hidden across the overgrown road in the canefields several hundred yards away. Through binoculars, Miguel had a close look at the Castro party driving into the Pino ranch. Two SUV-type military vehicles painted in camouflage-green and two large gray vans, one obviously a mobile communications unit, parked in the patio driveway in front of the entrance to the large ranchhouse.

Three other military vehicles were driven to the barracks-like bunkhouse building about forty yards to the side from the main house.

Fidel, in military garb, and three other men in civilian clothes were seen going into the house.

Miguel and his men stayed well away from the ranchhouse at that point, but they were kept informed of some of the activities by a ranch employee whose regular job was to ferry supplies, men and equipment back and forth between the Pino ranch and town in a pickup.

The rebels' plan was simple.

Around 1 a.m., they would move into the woods and canefields to the rear and sides of the Pino property. At 3 a.m., a first unit of ten men would move quickly and quietly from their positions and surround the house, capturing or killing the guards posted outside.

Miguel and Sierra would make their way to the back door, break that down and enter the house through a small hallway leading to the kitchen. The stocky Madera, a sharpshooter nicknamed Guajiro and a third man wielding a sledgehammer and crowbar would assault the front door and a side window to gain entry.

The remaining men, about fifteen including Ed, would deploy quickly behind the first unit and open fire on the army and security troops expected to spill out from the barn and bunkhouse. The guerrillas would fall back around the house, making sure it was secure while holding off retaliatory fire from the soldiers and security personnel.

After their primary target was eliminated, the guerrillas planned to escape into the surrounding woods, reach the various vehicles that had been hidden near two rural roadways and escape to several designated sites miles away.

RAID

At 10:30 p.m. Miguel, Madera and Sierra moved into position in the canefield adjacent to the dirt road, some 200 yards from the ranchhouse.

Through binoculars, they could see the activity around the brightly lighted house. The army troops and security personnel were moving around the outlying barn and bunkhouse buildings. Two or three soldiers were working in the communications van in the patio driveway. The second smaller van, which had earlier in the evening made two trips into town and back, was again observed moving out slowly, with only the uniformed driver, heading toward Santa Clara.

He must be taking back the dinnerware that had been come with the food that had been picked up earlier at the hotel's Spanish kitchen, Madera smirked, recalling the hotel manager's tip about the specially prepared Spanish dishes.

The van came back shortly before midnight. By then, the lights in the house had been turned off except for the kitchen and along a hallway. There was no activity in and around the bunkhouse. One soldier still worked in the communications van near the house, and four armed guards had been posted, one at the back of the structure, one on each side and one in front.

The Falcon guerrillas spread out quietly, hunkered down and waited. Miguel and Ed had moved behind a lean-to that must have once been a wooden storage shed for cane and farm implements.

When Miguel went back toward his men, Ed was joined by Sierra. The American looked away and stared into space. He wasn't sure he wanted Sierra for company just then. The G2 agent sat down, and in his blunt manner asked, "Why are you doing this, Eduardo? It can't be pure altruism."

"I belong here," Ed replied tersely.

"I'm sure you're sincere about helping your brother and the Cuban people, but there must be something more than that," Sierra persisted. "You could be throwing away your life, amigo. This is *our* life. But you, you don't have to do this."

Silence.

Finally, Ed took a deep breath and said, "It's a long story, Diego."

"You can talk to me frankly, amigo. We're going into battle together. Tell me what you think."

"Let's just say I remember too much. I know too much about the inhumanities that take place in this country."

"Is it about Lydia?" Sierra pressed. "I know she was arrested and interrogated by G2 a few days after your departure in the 1960s."

"Lydia is part of it," Ed conceded reluctantly.

"I wasn't with G2 then," Sierra told him. "But I can assure you she wasn't mistreated," he said. "I secretly checked everything about the case later. I don't know why, exactly, but she was treated differently than most of the others brought in. I'm sure the agents who brought her in suspected something, but they also knew she had been treated for a heart ailment," he went on. "She was being interrogated when she became very sick. She was taken to a nearby hospital. She was treated there and went home a few days later. That's it. That was the end of it, as far as G2 was concerned."

"Unfortunately, that wasn't the end of it," Ed said, drawing out the words painfully.

Lydia was traumatized by the experience at the hands of G2, Ed said.

"Her old problems resurfaced, and her condition quickly worsened. When her exit visa was finally authorized she was too sick to travel so she had to wait another eighteen months for another visa. I talked to her whenever I could get a telephone call through — from New York, Lisbon, Madrid.

"She became despondent, which didn't help her heart. When doctors finally decided to operate to replace a valve and make other repairs, it was too late. She died in the hospital."

"I'm sorry. I didn't know she died that way," Sierra said.

"One of her brothers told me later in New York that if they'd recognized the problem and treated her correctly from the beginning, she could have lived a normal life."

"I'm sorry to hear that, Eduardo. That's a tragedy. Another tragedy in a long list of tragedies in this country."

They sat silently for a few minutes.

Ed then looked up and shrugged as if to shake off a bad dream.

"You want to know another reason why I belong here? My mother, our mother, Miguel's and mine."

Sierra nodded and offered him a cigarette, which Ed refused.

"As you know, my mother was Cuban. She divorced her husband and left her young son with him. She later emigrated to Florida. Her son is Miguel, who much later became the guerrilla leader you know. When young Miguel was first imprisoned, my mother began blaming herself, for not being there mostly. The more she thought about it and talked about it, the more she felt she had abandoned Miguel as a child; that she could somehow have prevented this. She would fall into long periods of depression. What she perceived as her failings, those unshakeable feelings of guilt, eventually grew into a monstrous demon within her.

"She visited psychiatrists at various places," Ed went on. "They would help her overcome those thoughts for awhile, but only for short periods of time. Over the years, she became incurably depressed. She died in the 1960s before her firstborn son, Miguel, was released from prison in Havana."

Ed said he believed it was fortunate that she never knew specifically about Miguel's horrible experiences or that he had turned to rebellion against his own country. "She wouldn't have understood, but . . . maybe she would have."

Sierra nodded, grimfaced.

After few minutes, he said, "I apologize for misjudging you, Eduardo. You *do* belong here. You are truly one of us."

About 12:30 a.m., Madera observed two men armed with rifles and sidearms, one in uniform the other in civilian clothes, being ushered into the ranchhouse through a back door. They presumably moved into the kitchen since no additional lights were turned on.

The Falcon unit began its deployment at 1:30 a.m., surrounding the property as much as it was possible to do from the adjacent canefields and the trembling trees and dense shrubbery. Two men were assigned specifically to move in with the first group and take over the communications van and the lone guard on duty there. That was a significant part of the plan.

The moon shone brightly at intervals through thin clouds moving in from the South. There was a soft, caressing wind and the scenario reminded Ed of the Florida Keys, where one moment the sky was bright and star-filled and the next a heavy rainstorm could signal a hurricane.

He was an experienced outdoorsman so he was used to Nature's vagaries. He was also prepared to kill, although he had never done so. He hefted an automatic assault rifle and silently followed orders from those around him on where to go and what to do. He felt alone but at peace with himself. He was doing the right thing.

He thought of the ironies of life.

At a time when satellites in space could photograph images on earth the size of a basketball . . . at a time of atomic and hydrogen bombs and the likelihood of biological weapons, men armed only with rifles and handguns still hid in the hills and tried to bring down governments — a sad but age-old necessity throughout Cuban history.

Ed told himself he was prepared to die, if necessary. Every single one of these men around him was ready to give up his life to overthrow the tyrant. He knew that, over the centuries, Cubans had tendencies toward grandiose acts when it came to their politics. And their time for that had certainly come to these men, he mused.

At 2:00 a.m., the Falcon unit attacked the house as soon as the communications van was secured.

Miguel had chosen Diego Sierra to lead the way with him toward the back door.

They moved quickly and surprised the lone sentry there. Sierra stabbed the man to death with a long knife he had unstrapped from his belt. They made little noise. At the same time, Roberto Madera and the rest of the advance unit quick-stepped to take out the guards at the front and sides of the ranchhouse.

Crashing through the back door, Miguel and his Sierra gained quick entry into a little foyer opening into a short hallway. The kitchen was to their left. Two astonished guards there jumped up, spilling their coffee cups on the white tablecloth. But the two attackers gave them little chance to use their weapons. One was shot in the neck with a silenced handgun as he approached the hallway. The other was knifed in the belly and slumped slowly against the kitchen wall, his bright blood flowing freely onto the tile floor.

The two leaders then heard Madera and his crew smashing through the front door and a side window. Heavy gunfire broke out outside. Miguel and Sierra then moved rapidly into the large living room. At the same time, Madera and his men were spilling into the house. They quickly spread out to cover all exits.

"We're controlling the house. Nobody can get out now," Madera reported tersely as Miguel appeared beside him.

"Be sure some men are posted outside, too, both at the front and the back," Miguel ordered in a hoarse whisper while hurrying toward the rear bedrooms. "Roberto, you follow us and check the side rooms along this hallway."

Miguel, armed with an AK-47 and his sidearm, ran down the hallway toward the big bedroom at the back, followed closely by Sierra. The door was closed but unlocked, and the two men burst in, prepared to fire. They believed they might find Fidel Castro and his lady either in bed or hiding in a corner or closet. But, the primer ministro must have heard the noise and gunfire by now and was probably armed and waiting, Miguel thought.

They would shoot Fidel Castro dead in either case.

However . . . the large bedroom was found to be dark and eerily quiet, given the mounting bedlam outside. Something wasn't right. Even before flipping on a light switch, the heavy-breathing attackers could see that the bed, the closet, and the room itself, were undisturbed. Empty.

Disconcertedly, the bed was neatly made up. A small window on the opposite wall was closed and the curtains drawn around it.

"The son of a bitch is gone, he and the woman," Miguel said through clenched teeth.

"Looks like they were never here," added Madera, who had joined them. "They may be hiding somewhere. Maybe the others . . . will find him."

Suddenly, the room brightened momentarily as if huge strobe lights had flashed. This was rapidly followed by a deafening explosion. Throwing open the window curtains, Miguel could see streaks in the dark sky and then, astonished, he heard the whining roar of jetfighter aircraft and booming, fiery explosions all around the house.

"How did this happen? They're attacking with jets," shouted Miguel over the explosions. "Outside, outside, quick," he yelled.

The three rebel leaders tried to round up their men and direct them into the woods in back of the house, but the swooping aircraft — two or maybe three MiG-23s — had circled back and were once more rocketing the area. Ear-splitting convulsions and swirling black-and-white clouds of smoke enveloped their world as the guerrillas scattered into the heavy woods.

The soldiers in Castro's security detail were now also abandoning their positions in the outlying buildings and running desperately into the brush and canefields.

As he ran, Miguel looked back.

The barn and several vehicles roared with wind-whipped orange flames. Horses screamed their high-pitched sounds of pain. Two of the military SUVs were moving slowly, weaving through the wreckage trying to get to safety. Dead and wounded warriors lay near the bunkhouse and around the ranchhouse, hit either from the rocketry or the prior exchange of gunfire.

Suddenly, as the guerrilla leaders struggled to regroup, the back part of the house exploded from a direct rocket blast, sending timbers, roofing, plaster and other debris flying in all directions. This was followed by waves of machinegun fire belching from the low-sweeping MiGs.

The last thing Miguel heard was Madera's voice, screaming in his ear, "Come on, come on, *jefe*, you can make it."

Then it all went black for the rebel leader.

As suddenly as they had come, the jetfighters were gone from the scene, leaving a torn, bloody, burning battlefield.

Ed was shot and badly wounded in the chest in the exchange of gunfire shortly before the jets had appeared. He was down onto his knees when he saw the fleeing men and the house erupting. As the planes moved away, he crawled toward the overturned communications van. He now lay on his back behind several bodies, unable to stop the blood oozing freely from the large, gaping wound below his breastbone.

He was thoroughly bewildered by the attack from the sky, but he knew that no one inside the house could have survived. Fidel Castro must be dead, along with many others. However it was done, that's what they had come for. He was comforted by that.

Wiping his eyes with a bloody sleeve, he stared at the moon, still scudding in and out of the clouds. The night seemed to have gotten brighter. Then he felt the cool breeze on his face suddenly become a wintry chill. He quieted, feeling a serene calm envelop him. And he thought of his brother . . . and Lydia . . . and his mother.

As he closed his tear-filled eyes for the last time, he heard the chopping, whirring noise of a single helicopter.

Then everything went quiet. He died peacefully.

GOVERNMENT COMMUNIQUÉ

Four days after the events at the ranch near Santa Clara, the Castro regime published a one-page communiqué in the official Communist Party newspaper *Granma*.

DECLARATION OF THE REVOLUTIONARY GOVERNMENT OF CUBA:

- Last Tuesday night, counter-revolutionary elements attacked a cattle-breeding ranch near Santa Clara, where President Fidel Castro had visited earlier in the day. The assault was carried out by a band of armed men against the ranchhouse and a military security detail which had been temporarily quartered in a dormitory building on the property.

- Fifteen of the attackers were killed by our revolutionary forces, including the person identified as their leader, Miguel "Falcon" Hidalgo. Four others who were captured were executed this morning after being convicted of counter-revolutionary charges by a military tribunal. Several others are being hunted throughout the homeland.

- Our patriotic forces suffered the loss of Tourism Minister Jorge Bravo, Gen. Aaron Salamone, the commander of Cuba's Eastern Army, and presidential security chief Nestor Alvarez.

- The revolutionary government is conducting an investigation and will submit to swift military justice anyone known to have participated in or assisted in this cowardly attack.

**Council of Ministers
Revolutionary Government
of Cuba**

QUESTIONS

As with all Cuban government communiqués, this one was confusing, woefully short on facts and misleading. It didn't begin to tell the story. But it was correct in one important detail, which one had to read carefully to deduce: There had been a near-successful effort to assassinate Fidel Castro.

What the statement covered up completely was that the plot carried out by Miguel Hidalgo and his Falcon *guerrilleros* had only failed because of *another*, unrelated, coup attempt against the Castro regime. This one was led by pilots of Raul Castro's own Air Force, the Fuerza Aerea Revolucionaria. Raul Castro, personally, was totally unaware of the situation.

Ironically, one group of plotters had unknowingly destroyed the other. This had the effect of leaving their mutual target unscathed. The Santa Clara ranchhouse had made an attractive target for both sets of plotters. They had both seen it as an unusual opportunity.

It was later determined, however, that Castro escaped even before Miguel's men attacked the house. By the time the Falcon unit closed in and the outlaw jetfighters attacked, Fidel was gone. Castro's security people had got wind of the pilots' suspicious activities and warned Fidel. The couple was then clandestinely evacuated from the ranchhouse.

At the time the Falcon guerrilleros and the two jets attacked, "el lider maximo" was secretly speeding back to Havana.

Completely unknown to the Falcon rebels or anyone else, the disgruntled pilots had planned the attempt on Castro's life for weeks. The

MiGs had simply swarmed over the ranchhouse and bombed and strafed everything in sight. It became an unfortunate circumstance for both sides.

The air attack destroyed the ranchhouse and outbuildings, and it killed and wounded many of the Falcon rebels and government troops at the site.

Castro's bizarre escape only came about because word leaked out from the Air Force base at San Antonio de los Baños that some pilots had been overheard planning something besides the nighttime flying exercises in which they were supposed to be participating.

When word of the rumors reached the Castro retinue at the ranch early that evening, the security chief was concerned enough to suggest precautions because those air maneuvers were taking place in their vicinity. He suspected some kind of plot, or even a coup attempt. Fidel was doubtful but quickly decided he was too exposed to take any unnecessary chances. He took precautionary actions.

He and his lady surreptitiously left the ranchhouse, and those left behind acted as if everything was normal.

It later became known that the couple had exited the house under cover and hidden in the back of the van used to ferry food and supplies to and from Santa Clara. The rebels led by Miguel Hidalgo had assumed the vehicle was on one of its regular runs to town. They had only seen the driver as the van pulled away.

Castro and his companion were dropped off at the house of family friends of Mrs. Abelardo, and she remained there while Fidel commandeered a small escort convoy from the town's military detachment to drive him to the Army's Camp Columbia near Havana.

Arriving there, he received word of the dual attacks on the ranch — the first by the rebels who penetrated the Castro defenses and the second, more deadly one, by the jetfighter planes and helicopters.

By making his secret exit, the Cuban leader had, of course, sacrificed several high government officials, his personal security detail and other top military men accompanying the group. The government officials mentioned in the communiqué were only three of a larger number of casualties in the Castro entourage. Most of the contingent left behind at the house had been oblivious to the rumors of a plot and of Castro's decision to leave surreptitiously.

Much of this information came about in the days and weeks following the occurrence.

A purge of military officers began immediately.

The only other public disclosure came when Raul Castro, commander of all the armed forces including the Fuerza Aerea Revolucionaria, went on television to announce that the Air Force chief, Gen. Jose Trigo, had been fired and was facing undisclosed charges. Sweeping changes were soon under way within the Air Force, the Army and the Interior Ministry.

Raul Castro told his TV audience, "The government is determined to strengthen our defenses against those who work against our revolutionary goals." He added his assurances of "the loyalty and integrity of our Armed Forces to our people and our revolutionary society."

Underground sources later reported the executions of the two jetfighter pilots leading the Santa Clara attack.

Except for rebel leader Miguel Hidalgo, none of the guerrilla casualties was publicly identified.

And the communiqué was either deliberately misleading or the Castro government was misinformed. Miguel had been seriously wounded, not killed, and he had been taken to safety. His friends had once again had come to his assistance and provided for excellent medical attention. He endured another long, arduous rehabilitation process. Unlikely though it seemed, he returned to fight for the only objective remaining to him — to kill Fidel Castro — Cuba would never be truly free without that.

Officials of the U.S. Interests Section in Havana were informed by Ed Brophy's friends in the United States that he had never returned home from his Cuban vacation. The American consular chief, now officially representing the United States in Havana, made inquiries. The Cubans professed to know nothing about the missing American tourist. The Americans began an investigation but, without Cuban cooperation, it led nowhere.

Eventually, Miguel and the few surviving rebels of the Falcon unit set about recruiting new members. The guerrilla squad reorganized and persisted in its quest to overthrow the Fidel Castro dictatorship.

Life continued as before on the troubled island.

CASTRO'S FINAL DAYS

CHANGES, CHANGES

There were many changes in Cuban society during the following years. But the self-denominated Cuban Revolution endured. Cuba was no stranger to revolutions, dictators and radical transitions in government, but never anything as smothering, and as long-lasting as this.

The Castro brothers and government planners gradually relaxed their tight controls on the economy, though, allowing small private businesses and enterprises to sprout up; private property could now more easily be bought and sold; dollars and exiles flowed in and out of the country much more freely despite U.S. laws; tourism spiraled, generating the necessary foreign exchange that afforded slow-paced industrialization and better production of household goods.

Food, medical attention and education had become more widely available, with strict limitations.

These were all changes for the general betterment of society, but *el pueblo* had been carrying out many of the prohibited practices on an underground-or-blackmarket basis for some time in any case. The regime had forced many functionaries off its payroll, and many had become smalltime entrepreneurs, setting up retail shops and expanding some of the activities they had been engaged in illegally for years.

New markets opened up for some once-restricted housing. Imported vehicles joined the hundreds of mid-century relics on the streets, even in some of the country's smaller towns. Many of the new merchandisers and consumers were receiving funding largely from family and friends in exile.

Many of the poor. however, continued as before, crowding into tenements and living from day-to-day.

Housing, transportation and unemployment, or underemployment, remained the same burden on the population that had existed from the beginning. While the economy eased somewhat, the poor didn't have any more money in their pockets than what they received from their friends and relatives overseas, who lived in relative luxury compared to them.

The Castro regime said most of the political prisoners had been released. Only several hundred remained in lockups, according to the Castro brothers, although the numbers were widely disputed and impossible to confirm. The government claim was that most of them had served their sentences or had been "indoctrinated" into the new society. Only the prisoners themselves, their relatives and close friends knew the truth. Small street protests concerning those still behind bars were tolerated by police, but they were largely ignored. Hunger strikes were still common in prisons.

Cuban dissidents on the outside smuggled in cellphones, and prisoners risked their lives taking photos and videos of prison conditions. Electronic media kept bringing the world closer to Cuban reality.

Testifying vividly to wretched conditions for political and criminal inmates throughout the system were videos, photos, audiotapes, letters smuggled out of prisons. Cuba remained the only country in the world to deny entry to its prisons for representatives of the International Red Cross.

One graphic video from an institution named Combinado del Este showed prisoners living in filthy conditions — raw sewage flowing in cells, mold growing on walls, sealed-off solitary punishment enclosures, food crawling with roaches and insects. Combinado had separate wings for foreign prisoners, which included Latinos, Europeans and several Americans.

Along with political prisoners, many current inmates were serving lengthy sentences for drug offenses or were mentally ill. One inmate identifying himself as an American named Douglas Moore said in a video smuggled out of Combinado that he had been singled out for abuse. He was sentenced in 2003 on a drug conviction.

"There is no justice in Cuba under the regime of Fidel and Raul Castro," he said in the video. "The Marxist brothers are not funny."

The overall changes being made in Cuban society, however, allowed Fidel Castro's brand of governing to become more open and accessible to foreign influence from every quarter but one — that of the imperialist nation to the north, as Fidel always described the United States.

Quite a paradox — the country that had adopted all those Cuban exiles was the one nation most shut out of participation in Cuba's rehabilitation; whether it even wanted to take part would be a controversial question for a long time across the United States.

Entire generations of Cubans remained uneasy. Their country remained a police state in many ways. Many who were born long after Fidel Castro came to power owed no allegiance to the revolution, as it was continually referred to. Some risked their freedom by protesting in the exile press or on digital social networks.

The young were fully aware of foreign cultures and societies, many of which enjoyed the freedoms they dreamed of. Some had access to cellphones, clandestine videos, foreign magazines — all of which caused them to realize what they were missing. But they were, in effect, locked in to the system in their homeland.

The Castro brothers tried to keep everyone in line with frequent warnings about a possible attack and attempted takeover of the island by the United States, but these threats were getting thin with age. Still, the Castro regime had its many enthusiastic supporters. Many still believed.

The rabidly anti-Castro rebels just wouldn't fade away, however.

Many knew that Miguel Hidalgo's half-brother, whom he had called Eduardo, had been killed in the 1990s, along with Diego Sierra and other dissident leaders, during the attack on the Santa Clara ranchhouse. But they also knew that Miguel had become became intensely involved again and still remained the leader of the Falcon unit. He had been badly wounded but, again, the doctors had worked wonders over the years.

What remained of the Falcon membership had regrouped and strengthened by younger men and women. The rebels stubbornly continued to watch and wait for another opportunity. Roberto Madera, also a survivor of the unfortunate jet attack on that dark night, had suffered superficial wounds and had again became Miguel's second-in-command.

Now, early in the new century, there came a time of relative quiet during a dictatorship of almost half a century. This period was about to come to an abrupt end, however.

El maximo lider, Fidel Castro, became seriously ill. Rumors began to circulate early in 2006 that he had cancer and was on his deathbed. The speculation became so rampant and so wildly creative that the government reluctantly declared that, yes, Castro was hospitalized, but no, he did not have cancer.

This did nothing to quell the hopes, the whispers, the jokes and maybes.

In his more lucid moments during this emergency period, Fidel gave up some of his duties to his close brother, installing Raul Castro as acting president. Fidel, of course, remained the supreme leader as head of the Communist Party and the National Assembly, Cuba's so-called parliament. And he was clearly still issuing the orders.

Miguel, now a thin, gray-haired, thick-bearded senior citizen, and his small band of diehard revolutionaries again believed they saw an opening.

"He will soon die, but we can't wait around for that son of a bitch to do anything. He's danced around things for too long," Miguel said one day, pacing about and puffing on a cigar in one of their rural hideaways.

The grizzled, ever-patient Madera finally said, "We've got to find a way to speed things along, jefe."

Madera, bald and clean-shaven, suggested they could infiltrate the security ring around Fidel in or out of the hospital. We've done it before, we can do it again, he said. "*Ha tenido suerte,*" Madera said. Fidel had been lucky before. "He can't always be lucky," he said quietly as he shuffled out onto a small balcony.

Miguel agreed.

Lt. Ciro Betancourt had been one of Fidel's few aides to escape the Santa Clara coup attempt; he had been away from the ranch arranging for the return trip to Havana. And he hadn't been part of the purge that took place after the twin attacks. Over the years, Betancourt was still considered a loyal member of Fidel's staff and had now achieved the rank of captain. He maintained contact with the contrarevolucionarios through intermediaries.

Once the rebels' plans were reactivated, they again sought Betancourt's help.

Fidel's circle was ever tighter around him. For months during this period, diplomatic officials, government ministers and foreign investors, including the Spaniard Gregorio Yzaguirre, kept their distance or were not received into audience. The once-enthusiastic Spanish businessman recruited by Ed was now out of the picture.

Meantime, the rebels had persuaded a hospital official to keep them periodically informed on what was taking place. Other hospital attendants dropped a word here and there.

This little network of informants was able to confirm that Fidel Castro had been operated on only after objecting vehemently to surgery. Castro had at first considered it life-threatening, and he would not allow it. The debate became such a lengthy one that his prognosis deteriorated and soon became dire. This abruptly resulted in emergency surgery and drawn-out complications.

"But so what," Miguel declared to his friends after finding out. "Isn't that what we all want, for him to die? But . . . no," he said after reflection. "Not like that."

"That would be too easy," said Madera.

"To die in a clean bed, in a neatly kept hospital room," Madera finished his thought. "No," he exclaimed. "I'm glad he didn't die. We've been working almost all our lives to kill him. And that's what we have to do because that's what he deserves."

"Of course," Miguel said quietly. "We have to make a bold statement to the world. Bring total change to our Cuban society. Finally bring peace to *el pueblo*. Call it revenge, call it stupid, call it whatever you want. But assassination is the only way. Raul and his people won't know what to do if Fidel is killed after surviving this business in the hospital."

That's the way they encouraged themselves, these rebels — ringing out these old phrases of patriotism and pueblo. They had a self-imposed duty. Once again, they believed Cubans were ready now, ready to leave their own miseries behind them. Why wait any longer?

"Almost anything else will be better," Miguel muttered.

To outsiders, the Cuban regime appeared to be drifting while Raul Castro began exercising his new authority. Raul tightened the reins on the armed forces but began relaxing the rigid nationwide security system which relied primarily on informants, for instance. Some of the constant propaganda lessened. There seemed to be a loosening of top-down policy. At the same time, he caused widespread perplexity over a series of new governmental reforms which were slowly being put into place to help "democratize" the economy, as Raul phrased it.

While some of these sometimes confusing changes were taking place, Raul Castro eased the way for a few more comforts. Cubans were now permitted to stay in the hotels where they had only been allowed to enter if they were employees. Ordinary Cubans could legally acquire cellphones and laptops. Restaurants, bars and nightclubs began to operate more freely. Once again, it was becoming respectable for families to have fun at the beach.

Despite the revolution's self-vaunted medical acumen, several of the attending physicians were dismissed after Fidel's emergency surgery. A specialist was flown in from Madrid during the Christmas holiday period in 2006. El pueblo asked why but got no answers. Speculation became the order of the day on the street.

Dr. Jose Luis Garcia Sabrido, was sixty-one, a handsome, moustachioed man. He was chief surgeon at Madrid's Gregorio Marañon Hospital. His specialty was surgery on the digestive system and in transplants. He had been educated in the United States, Canada and The Netherlands.

On the 26th of December, he told The Associated Press in Havana that Castro did not then have cancer. The Spanish surgeon disclosed, for the first time in public, that the Cuban leader was recovering from a delicate operation. He would not elaborate.

Sabrido told reporters he had flown in on a personal visit to see Castro and consult with the patient's medical team. "While respecting confidentiality, I can tell you that President Castro is not suffering from any malignant sickness. It is a benign process in which there have been a series of complications."

Venezuelan President Hugo Chavez visited his "friend and mentor" numerous times in the hospital. The two were often shown on TV, chatting and laughing.

Several years later, in the summer of 2011, Chavez was diagnosed with similar medical problems as those of Fidel. And after months of consultation and tests, he, too, underwent surgery in Havana. He, too, recovered, although many of the details were never publicly disclosed.

The Venezuelan leader's malady recurred a year later, and Cuban doctors once again operated. From then on, Chavez went back and forth between Caracas and Havana, receiving chemotherapy and radiation treatments even while going through an election brought on by a strong opposition to his 13-year-old socialist "transformation" of government and society.

Chavez was narrowly reelected and only then was it disclosed he suffered from pelvic cancer and that there had been a recurrence. He eventually died in a Cuban military hospital. His death and a subsequent election to choose a legal successor brought on a dangerous period of turmoil for that important South American nation — and for Cuba.

That country was shipping some $4 billion of oil every year to Cuba, and the Castro brothers had been greatly concerned over threats by Venezuela's political opposition to cut that supply chain. Fidel Castro had for years been repaying Chavez' largesse by supplying thousands of medical personnel, teachers and military trainers to the nearby country. As a result of the threat to his lifeline, Castro sent additional hundreds of intelligence agents into Venezuela just prior to the 2013 special election.

"The Cuban people considered him an accomplished son," the regime's official newspaper, *Granma*, said of Chavez after his death. "They have admired him, followed him and loved him like their own." The Castro government declared two days of mourning and flew its flags at half staff. At the same time, it worried about its economic future.

The Iranian government also declared its admiration for Chavez and sadness about his death. President Ahmoud Ahmadinejad declared that Chavez had died of a "suspicious illness."

The man who had been handpicked by Chavez as his successor, Nicolás Maduro, won a special election for president by a mere 2 percentage points in April 2013. Venezuela's future became cloudier.

As the political and economic turbulence increased there, the Castro brothers worried even more. After all, Fidel once proclaimed that Cubans and Venezuelans were "Venecubans." Venezuela exerted a strong force in other South America nations because of his country's vast oil resources and Chavez' political outspokenness against the U.S.

Fidel's pupil obsequiously followed his mentor's teachings in constantly vilifying the United States for everything that went wrong in their world, Miguel and Madera believed as they following the unfolding events closely.

Americans officials publicly remained silent but watchful over events in Venezuela, both during and after the Chavez reign, because Venezuela also supplied much-needed oil to the U.S. At various times, the United States was accused of interference in Venezuelan politics in one form or another. At one point, Chavez claimed American agents planned to assassinate him, and his successor continued that bellicose rhetoric.

Meanwhile, Fidel slowly recuperated, as much to his own amazement as well as everyone else's.

Another factor for the rebels to consider was the leadership of the Roman Catholic Church. As the "more democratic economy" began in Cuba, Pope Benedict XVI visited the country to help celebrate the 400th anniversary of the nation's patron saint, Our Lady of Charity.

On an earlier trip to Cuba, another pontiff, the late Pope John Paul II, had lectured Fidel on the importance of freedom of expression. Before John Paul stopped over in Havana, he had spent several days in Miami, where he was wildly received by huge crowds and spoke in Spanish to Cuban exiles. But his visit to Cuba disappointed many of those enthusiastic exiles and the U.S. Government when he indirectly criticized the American economic embargo of the island.

"In our day, no nation can live in isolation," Pope John Paul had said after a Mass at Havana's massive Plaza de la Revolucion.

He continued, "The Cuban people, therefore, cannot be denied the contacts with other peoples necessary to economic, social and cultural development, especially when the imposed isolation strikes the population indiscriminately. . . (this makes it) ever more difficult for the weakest to enjoy the bare essentials of decent living — things such as food, health and education."

This went over very well in Havana, but not so well in Washington.

Exiles had expected John Paul's trip to Cuba to result in big changes in their homeland. But this was not to be, even on a small scale. Fidel released a small number of political prisoners, and there was some relaxation of the tight reins on the Catholic Church in Cuba. But there was little else.

Miguel and Madera watched the events closely, and they thought an opportunity might present itself while the regime's security and military machine was focused on the pope. But, if anything, security was tightened even further and the rebels continued to wait, anxious for action.

John Paul's successor, Benedict began his 48-hour trip to Cuba in March, 2012, again following a sojourn to Miami. That visit also produced nothing tangible, although it did provoke some give-and-take with Cuban authorities.

In his speeches, always ringed by the towering images of the Cuban revolutionary leaders, Pope Benedict brought up the topics of "authentic freedom" in Cuba and the church's longstanding opposition to the American economic embargo of the island. He met with both Fidel and Raul Castro and told them they should use the strength of God to "build a society of broad vision, renewed and reconciled."

He repeated Pope John Paul's s words that they ought not to be burdened by "restrictive economic measures, imposed from outside the country."

Pope Benedict, strongly anti-Marxist, was said to have portrayed the Cuban political system as unworkable. But there were no details about that. In what appeared to be a rebuttal, Marino Murillo, vice president of the Cuban Council of Ministers, told reporters, "We are updating our economic model but we are not talking about political reform."

The Vatican said Fidel and the Pope joked about old age: Fidel was eighty-five, and the pope was approaching his eighty-fifth birthday.

On the whole, the prepared pope-speak seemed more directed at the historical record than at any hope for change in policy, either in Cuba or the U.S.

During all of this, Miguel and Madera impatiently plotted, at times seething with anger at the goings on. First, the interferences in routine activities brought on by the Venezuelan president. Now the comings and goings of the two popes led to increased government security measures, and this caused the rebels some headaches in keeping up with Fidel Castro's daily activities.

Precious little information was made public. But when the occasion presented itself to propagandize a little, the Cuban regime seemed to stage everything from the hospital, with Fidel usually in his red-and-white track suit smiling weakly and waving. At other times, Fidel wrote and issued long philosophical essays on many topics.

He was taking this time, a spokesman said, for reinventing himself as "a senior statesman." He was "revisiting history and revisiting his own history."

He was also rewriting some of his own history.

"Matters of war, peace and international security are a central focus," of Fidel Castro's thoughts and writings at this time, according to official spokespersons.

Time brought many changes, of course, but Fidel never lost that look and attitude of a know-it-all warrior who stepped-in-and-out of a longtime role as a teacher of recalcitrant students. He would point his finger at you, or at the world, and tell you how it was done in no uncertain terms.

REBELS ON THE MOVE

A year after Fidel's operation and a touch-and-go recovery period, Raul told reporters that his older brother has "a healthier mentality, full use of his mental faculties with some small physical limitations. . . We consult him on principal matters."

In a rare newspaper interview years later, Fidel said he was "at death's door. But I came back."

He described lying in his hospital room. "I couldn't aspire to live any longer, much less anything else," he told the Mexican newspaper *La Jornada*. "I asked myself several times if (the doctors) would let me live under these conditions or whether they would allow me to die."

Meanwhile, brother Raul had fully assumed his new title of Presidente de la Republica de Cuba. He remained comandante of the country's armed forces, keeping total control of the security apparatus throughout the island, along with everything else.

Normally a frowning, taciturn individual, Raul now joked with reporters that although they were five years apart in age and looked differently, there was absolutely no difference between him and his brother on political matters. But the one-party system allowed for differences of opinion, he asserted. And the Communist government had sometimes had its flaws. But then, he again emphasized, "Our system must become more democratized." He gave no details or explanations.

Later, he said the government changes would take place over a prolonged period, again giving no reason or timetable. Foreign observers believed he wanted to avoid many of the mistakes made during and after the fragmentation of the Soviet Union.

These changes would proceed "without hurry or improvisation, working to overcome the old dogmatic mindset," Raul Castro said in one speech. There was much grumbling among the populace over that. The people wanted major transitions now.

An American congressional delegation traveled to Cuba on a factfinding mission early in 2012 and met with President Castro, Foreign Minister Bruno Rodriguez and National Assembly President Ricardo Alarcón. There were no resounding agreements announced on anything, and very little factfinding.

It was during the changeover in leadership that Miguel, Madera and the others began to see real opportunity once again for decisive action. As the years went by, they had grown even more passionate in their singleminded cause to scrub the nation of its evil.

As any casual student of Cuban politics knew, Fidel Castro, and only Fidel, was still in charge. He would continue to be the one person with total control until he died. Fidel Castro *was* the Cuban Revolution, and it would always be thus no matter what changes in title might take place.

These contrarevolucionarios, however, weren't interested in a *coup d'etat*. They believed the Cuban people would do what they had to once they eliminated the one man they knew was responsible for their troubles. That was their unchangeable course over the decades.

Tracking his movements through their spies, the rebeldes allowed their plans to slowly unfold according to whatever was taking place in Fidel's daily activities. It was a long frustrating time for them.

Fidel had regained some of his weight but remained weak and under medical supervision. And while he was the recipient of all this attention and security, what do you suppose he must be thinking? Miguel mulled this question over and over in his mind. Castro had plenty of reasons, certainly, to suspect treachery, treason or assassination during this time of enforced physical disability.

Maybe, the Falcon thought, Fidel was like one of Shakespeare's godforsaken kings, believing that royalty is its own protection. But he doubted this.

The rebeldes knew his penchant for hopping around from place-to-place, fearful of his whereabouts becoming known to his enemies. When he moved out of the hospital to an isolated house of a friend in the fishing village of Cojímar. he abruptly moved out again after a couple of days. He evidently decided it might be too exposed, or maybe he just didn't want to stray too far from his doctors. In any case, he and his little retinue left there in the middle of one rainy night.

Madera then discovered Fidel was in a G2 compound in a Havana neighborhood not far from the hospital.

The rambling safehouse was once one of the stately mansions of the rich, cozying up to the coastline. The palatial house was set in a residential area that included offices of several embassies, apartments and buildings that had been converted into boarding academies for young Communist *pioneros,* boys too young for the military.

The safehouse, known as the Villa Reyes, had a long approach from the street, along with a sentry gate. It was surrounded by palms and bougainvillea. A sloping green lawn and well-trimmed shrubbery bordered a walkway leading to the front entrance. A side yard and pool were equally spacious and looked out onto the gray, flat horizon hemmed in by the impossibly blue ocean. Lazy, white-capped rollers lapped onto a rocky shore and up to a short stone wall.

Madera had once stayed in a more modest neighborhood nearby and knew the area well.

Two veteran nurses had been designated by the hospital director to oversee Fidel's round-the-clock care at his new abode. One of them, Rosamaria, had been persuaded by her husband to help out the rebeldes whenever an occasion presented itself. She had been quite reluctant at first.

"I'm not sure about that," Rosamaria told her husband Rafael Franco one night. "I don't think I should risk my life. Fidel is a kind-enough man. He argues with the doctors, but he's never had anything but praise for us, his nurses. . . I carry out my profession as honorably as I can, Rafael. You must respect that."

Rafael said he was worried about their future.

After a standoff over several days, Rosamaria said, "If I decide to help you and your friends, a lot will depend on the circumstances at the time.

Only I can decide that, Rafael." She closed off the conversation with that nebulous idea.

One day, the food she brought Fidel caused him a violent episode of vomiting and diarrhea. A visiting physician and the other nurse in the house rushed in to help. Panicky, the second nurse called the hospital for an ambulance, which showed up within minutes. Rosamaria had reluctantly carried out her part of the rebeldes' plan.

The patient was loaded into the vehicle under heavy guard and driven away.

But in the ensuing commotion, the residence was left unguarded except for the sentry at the gate and two guards patrolling the grounds. The guerrillas easily penetrated those defenses and went to work in the dark. Over many months, they had acquired dozens of sticks of military dynamite kept in special storage depots by the army, two of which the rebels had quietly raided.

They now carefully interconnected these devices and planted them throughout the storage basement. They seeded the outside of the house with similar explosives. They were ready. They waited for Fidel's return.

They were so sure that Fidel would come back here that they holed out in a house being rebuilt nearby. Miguel found it hard to relax while the patient was kept under hospital supervision for two days. On the third day, Capt. Betancourt managed to get word out. Fidel was leaving the hospital that night with a security detail.

"The time has arrived my brothers," Miguel passed the word to the six men handpicked for the job. The contrarevolucionarios moved out quietly, unobtrusively.

Sure enough, Fidel and his attendants moved back into the coastal Villa Reyes.

The last remaining obstacle, which Miguel and his crew had to resolve in real time, was how to get two men close enough to the main structure of the house to hook up their dug-in maze of electronic wires into a main cable. This would then connected to an 18-inch-square, battery-operated control box, just like those seen in the movies. The controller was to be manually activated to blow the special dynamite. The whole thing was a bit old-fashioned, perhaps, but the system had worked well on a small scale when tested.

The vehicles driving in and out of the gate, and the changeover of the patrol guards and security people that night, created just enough of a diversion to allow Miguel, Madera and their men to sneak into the compound and close to the house itself. One man had volunteered to find his way into the basement to ensure their wiring was secure. They all knew theirs was a suicide mission.

After those inside appeared to be settled in, shortly before midnight, the rebeldes' small unit moved into action quietly and efficiently.

All went according to plan until one of Fidel's security guards decided to poke around at the basement storage area, which was reachable from the outside through a crusty, vine-covered half-window with a hinge that opened upward. Prying it open and peering in, the guard thought he saw movement in the dark recesses of the basement, but his cry of alert was muffled by one of the rebels who quickly slit his throat.

The brief outcry did not go unheeded, however, sending two other inquisitive guards hurrying up to that side of the house, which was enclosed in dark shadows created by moonglow peeking through heavy foliage.

Miguel and two of his men followed and crept up behind the guards. But they were seen and gunfire broke the quiet of the night. That drew wild fire from others. Suddenly, everything went out of control.

Lights went on in the house, shouts rang out. Heavy weapons spurted fire from the windows.

The shooting continued until the guards managed to overcome the attackers. Miguel was hit several times by the scatterfire of an AK-47. He was then mortally wounded when a shotgun blast tore him in two as he twisted about trying to set off the dynamite. But his dying body sprawled heavily onto the old-fashioned detonator and this set off a horrific explosion.

The house and everything around it blasted outward and upward. Its flaming pieces, along with parts of human bodies, came splattering down with heavy force over a wide area. Even the trees and dense foliage were enveloped.

The huge explosion created a white-hot fire and sent orange-and-gray funnels of smoke spiraling upward through the dark night into the thin high clouds. The spectacle could be seen along the coastline all the way into downtown Havana as the ocean breeze gently wafted colored smoke over the neighborhood and all the way into the old town.

Hundreds of Habaneros rushed to have a look at the conflagration. Cars, buses and trucks hurriedly began arriving and parking helter-skelter along the Malecon. Rifle-bearing Army troops and militia began moving in.

"Pa'lante. Pa'lante," (move forward, away from here) the troops ordered.

Searchlights began piercing the shadows around the trees, but beyond the fire and smoke only the white ripples of the ocean could be seen through the dark leafage. Black-clad security troops moved through the crowds of onlookers and into the sidestreets, searching for they knew not what.

Emergency personnel, firefighters and investigators from every government department eventually arrived and got as close as they dared to the villa. They paced and poked about in the wet darkness until daylight. But there was nothing they could do except pick up and cart away parts of human remains and an assortment of scorched items.

In the lingering smoke of the sun-splashed dawn, all that could be seen was a large cavity in the ground as big as the parking lot of the baseball stadium. Everything was still smoldering. Everyone in and around the rambling house had been blasted to pieces. Two neighboring structures were spewing gray smoke and yellow flame.

The blast area was finally pacified and fully secured a day later. It was roped off and impossible to reach by the curious.

A widespread investigation was immediately ordered by Raul Castro. An official communiqué was issued that morning over radio and television making public what was already known. The published version in the following day's official newspaper *Granma* ambiguously reminded *el pueblo* that a transition of government had been previously arranged and that Raul Castro remained head of the government and military.

The ever-curious Habaneros went home and stayed there, not knowing what to expect.

There was no effort made to explain further, leaving it to the world to furnish its own version of the sequence and consequence of events that night. Nothing was said about Fidel Castro.

There were only a few things that were known for sure — the bodies of Miguel and Madera were among the dead. Government doctors confirmed their identifications after piecing together their remains. Fidel Castro's revolution had had taken many lives with it. What came next, only time would tell.

A legend eventually developed about the valiant rebels, their courage and perseverance against heavy odds. In one fable, Miguel's dying thoughts were said to be that *la revolucion contra la revolucion* was over and that he and the others had achieved their objective.

El Pueblo was overwhelmed by the events of that night. Tension was heavy in the air. What to do next was the question on everyone's mind. But the quandary was soon resolved since, once again, Fidel had outfoxed the foxes.

Minutes before the house exploded into ashes blowing in the light breeze, Fidel scaled the seaside wall with a bodyguard and waded into the water. Wheezing badly, with water lapping to his scraggly beard, he and his personal aide splashed through dense reeds and were finally pulled into a small boat. They eventually reached a bigger, motorized vessel with the barely visible name — *Granma Dos* — sloppily painted on the side.

Once the passengers were aboard, it sped away from the ghostly scene that night.

EPILOGUE

At the time of this writing, Fidel Castro was still alive, still nominally in charge of his revolution, philosophizing about the world in general and his place in history. The Cuban people continued to endure whatever fate had in store. More than half a century had gone by in Cuba's long history, and Fidel was still in the middle of it — bigger than life.

In a revolution that was seemingly never ending.

##

ACKNOWLEGEMENTS

The book is based on thorough research, personal experience and extensive interviews with most of the subjects involved.

I offer my most sincere gratitude to all of the Cubans and Americans who made this work possible — those who were there or who were in exile at the time. For obvious reasons, I cannot specifically acknowledge those who helped. But if you are reading this, ustedes saben quienes son. Un abrazo.

##

Isaac M. Flores
September, 2015

Printed in the United States
By Bookmasters